Emile Zola

DOCTOR PASCAL

ÉMILE ZOLA

DOCTOR PASCAL

Translated by Ernest A. Vizetelly

SUTTON PUBLISHING

First published as *Le Docteur Pascal* in 1893

First published in this edition in 1989 by Alan Sutton Publishing Ltd,
an imprint of Sutton Publishing Limited
Phoenix Mill · Thrupp · Stroud · Gloucestershire

Reprinted 1995, 2000

British Library Cataloguing-in-Publication Data

A catalogue record for this book is available from the British Library.

ISBN 0-86299-698-8

Cover picture: detail from portrait of Émile Zola *by Edouard Manet
(photograph: Bridgeman Art Library, London)*

Typeset in 10/11 Bembo.
Typesetting and origination by
Sutton Publishing Limited.
Printed in Great Britain by
The Guernsey Press,
Guernsey, Channel Islands.

CONTENTS

Chapter I
Simple Faith and Sturdy Science   1

Chapter II
The New Elixir of Life   26

Chapter III
Some Family Skeletons   58

Chapter IV
The New Holy Alliance   82

Chapter V
The Genealogical-tree   108

Chapter VI
Dark Days   136

Chapter VII
Love   159

Chapter VIII
Through Golden Hours   177

Chapter IX
The Scythe of Death   199

Chapter X
Ruin!   223

Chapter XI
Farewell!   249

Chapter XII
Doom   278

Chapter XIII
Life's Labour Lost 310

Chapter XIV
Mother and Child 335

BIOGRAPHICAL NOTE

ÉMILE ZOLA (1840–1902) was twenty-nine when he wrote *La Fortune des Rougon*, and he had already gained considerable experience of life. He was born in Paris on 2 April 1840, but in 1843 the family moved to Aix-en-Provence where his father, an enterprising engineer from Venice, had finally gained permission to build a canal system to provide the town with regular fresh water. Unfortunately, François Zola died in 1847, before his project was complete, leaving his wife and child with very little money. Madame Zola, with her parents, was forced to live among the poor of Aix, so Émile would have early become accustomed to the rough life of the poverty-stricken. However, money was found to send him to school, where he did well at first, but soon found his own creative writing more entertaining than schoolwork, and he enjoyed playing truant with his great friend, Paul Cézanne (the painter-to-be).

In 1858, he was very distressed by his family's move to Paris. He missed Cézanne and the country life. Although he attended school, he failed his *baccalauréat*, partly through nerves and partly through ignorance. At the end of 1859 he accepted employment, found by a friend of his father, in the Excise Office. After two months of clerical drudgery he 'dropped out' and lived precariously in the poor Latin Quarter of Paris. He tried to write, but spent much of his time daydreaming and observing life in a frenetically busy Paris, a city in the throes of an architectural rebirth, which was doing nothing to improve the lot of the poor. At this time he met and befriended the artists who were to be the leaders of the new Impressionist School, and he was in regular communication with Cézanne. He was finally rescued in 1862 when he was hungry, cold and ill, and living in a filthy lodging house frequented by thieves and prostitutes: some poems were accepted for publication in a provincial newspaper, and yet another friend of his father found him a post with the publishing company Hachette.

During the next eight years Zola gained a reputation as a controversial journalist and writer. His defence of the scorned painter, Manet, particularly marked him as a rebel, while his novel *Thérèse Raquin* (1867) was described as 'putrid literature . . . a mass of blood and mud'. Such an extreme reaction, of course, was good publicity and Zola was not afraid of such criticism. In the meantime he had left Hachette and was working as a freelance writer for various journals and provincial papers. He met Alexandrine Meley, a seamstress, whom he eventually married, and moved into a small house near Montmartre. All this time he had been reading widely: philosophy, history and physiology, and he became acquainted with the Goncourt brothers, who helped him to form his own literary philosophy.

At last he was ready to plan what was to become the major work of his life: *Les Rougon-Macquart: histoire naturelle et sociale d'une famille sous le Second Empire*, which begins with *La Fortune des Rougon*; includes *Nana* (1880), *Germinal* (1885), *La Terre* (1887), and concludes with *Le Docteur Pascal* (1893). As Zola explains in his preface to *La Fortune*, his aim is to explore a fictional family in a scientific way, showing what he believed to be the inevitable effects of heredity and environment on this extended family and on the societies in which they lived, throughout the time of the Second Empire (1852–70). With his own concept of 'naturalism', founded on his scientific reading, Zola was developing the realist tradition of Flaubert and Turgenev, using the same infinite variety of character and circumstance as Balzac whom he admired and sought to emulate. But, unlike Balzac who worked from intuition and imagination, Zola did an enormous amount of research and planning for his novels, experiencing, wherever possible, the places and activities that he described. And, of course, he developed themes and variations based on personal experiences. Plassans, for example, is the Aix of Zola's childhood; many of the Rougons are based on families he knew there. Miette, the heroine of *La Fortune*, was probably inspired by Louise Solari, for whom Zola is believed to have cherished a romantic and undeclared love, while Silvère personifies his own romantic nature. When considering the plot of *La Fortune*, it is worth noting that Louise had died in 1865, and with her many of Zola's romantic dreams. The position of *La Fortune* as the first of the *Rougon-Macquart* series explains why the development of the plot is frequently interrupted with detailed character description and historical explanation.

Unfortunately, the original serial publication of the novel was interrupted by the Paris siege and civil strife of 1870–1. During this time Zola moved out of Paris, but in 1871 he returned, to become immersed in the Rougon-Macquart world for the next twenty years. In 1872 he changed his publisher and laid the foundation for a lasting friendly relationship with Charpentier, who was attracted by Zola and his plan for the series. But it was not until the publication of *L'Assommoir*, the seventh of the series, first published in book form in 1877, that Zola's work started to sell really well and he achieved his ambition of establishing himself as a powerful controversial literary figure in France. He was also becoming wealthy, and by 1878 he was able to buy a second house in Médan, outside Paris, which grew bigger as his work progressed, and where he regularly entertained a group of young admirers, including Guy de Maupassant and Paul Alexis, his first biographer.

In Russia, on the other hand, Zola had been accepted as a popular writer for some time and his link with St Petersberg had been further strengthened by his friendship with Ivan Turgenev, then living in Paris. The kind-hearted Russian had introduced Zola to the publisher Stassyulevitch, who agreed to pay Zola for the proofs of his novel and to commission a series of essays for his magazine, *The Messenger*.

In spite of his success, the 1880s were difficult years for Zola. In 1880, first his friend, the writer Duranty, died, then Gustave Flaubert, who had been an admired and close friend for eight or nine years, and finally his mother; in 1883, Turgenev and Manet died. Zola had always been of a nervous disposition, which manifested itself in psychosomatic disorders, and these were exacerbated by the bereavements, as Zola succumbed to depression. He was also, as usual, working under considerable pressure, producing a novel almost every year, as well as other literary work for the stage and the press. In 1885, after painstaking research, *Germinal* was published. It was a resounding success. In it is the character of Souvarine, a Russian political emigré in the unlikely situation of working in a French mining community. It is believed that this character was suggested by Turgenev, who, when he died, had been planning a novel on the Russian revolutionary movement. Zola was thus expressing some of the ideas and theories of his dead friend. A year later, *L'Oeuvre* appeared, a study reflecting Zola's disillusionment with the Impressionist movement. After supporting them in their early ventures, he had lost interest in his former friends when they became more preoccupied with light and technique than with subject matter, and he felt that Cézanne and the rest were artistic failures. This negative outlook, expressed in the novel, finally severed Zola's relationship with Cézanne and the movement generally. In 1887, just as he was concluding *La Terre*, Zola was the victim of a cruelly personal attack from a group of writers who, presumably resenting his success, accused him of obscenity in his novels and a repressed private life. The erotic elements of his novels and his childless marriage were probably conducive to the form of the attack. Although he maintained his usual rather bluff exterior in the face of these insults, it is difficult to believe that the dark, bearded figure with deep brooding eyes, as portrayed by Manet, did not hide a sensitive and vulnerable interior, and it is possible that the attack led to a serious self-appraisal, and his subsequent positive action.

During the years of tension, Zola had put on weight, and he became aware that, because of his involvement in his work, he was no longer experiencing life at first hand – he was becoming removed from reality. So, in 1888, he took himself in hand. He lost weight, and his personality brightened; he began to practise photography, for which he showed considerable talent. Then he fell in love with Jeanne, who had been employed by Madame Zola to help with the household sewing. He secretly provided for Jeanne to move into an apartment in Paris, courted her and she had two children before Madame Zola found out. After the initial shock, Madame Zola decided to remain with her husband, and consequently he maintained both households until his death.

The *Rougon-Macquart* series was finished in 1893, but Zola went straight on to produce a trilogy concerned with religious and social problems, *Les Trois Villes*, and then started his final series, *Les Quatre Evangiles*, novels which were to be both moralistic and optimistic about the future. The fourth of this series was never written.

On the whole, Zola's work was not well received in England at the end of the nineteenth century, but he was respected in some quarters, and in 1893 he was invited to visit London by the Institute of Journalists. He stayed for five weeks, spending time with the writer George Moore, and the Vizetelly Company, who were the first translators of his books into English. His second and final visit to England, in 1898, was under very different circumstances, as a result of the notorious Dreyfus Affair.

In order to point out the anti-semitic prejudice of the French military courts in failing to recognize the innocence of a French-Jewish army officer, who had been wrongly accused of passing information to the Germans, in order to provoke further action, Zola wrote a letter to the press, entitled *J'accuse*. This famous diatribe successfully led to a resumption of the case, and Zola was forced to flee to England to avoid a prison sentence, as the court persisted in asserting the innocence of the likely suspect and the guilt of Dreyfus. He stayed in Surrey and Upper Norwood for nearly a year, until finally the Appeals Court agreed to grant a petition for a retrial, and Zola decided to return home, whatever the consequences. No action was taken against him, and he was eventually absolved in the general amnesty which followed Dreyfus' pardon in September 1899.

His involvement with the Dreyfus Affair aged Zola and slowed him down in his writing, but he completed *Vérité*, the third of *Les Evangiles*, and he was planning the fourth when the accident happened which caused his death on the night of 28 September 1902. He died of carbon monoxide poisoning, the result of a blocked chimney in his Paris apartment. There is a theory, and a distinct possibility, in the light of the emotional reaction to the Dreyfus case, that the chimney had been purposely blocked, but there is no evidence. Émile Zola was buried in Montmartre, but his ashes were transferred to the Panthéon in 1908.

Between 1871 and 1902, Zola had produced twenty-six full-length novels, eight volumes of essays, three volumes of short stories and a collection of plays. The *Rougon-Macquart* series demonstrates a mammoth literary feat, an artistic construction of immense variety and vitality. Zola was, according to Professor F.W.J. Hemmings, 'the first of those who raised sociology to the dignity of art, he was the prophet of a new age of mass psychology, mass education and mass entertainment, an age in which the part is never greater than the whole.'

SHEILA MICHELL

CHAPTER I

THE room, with its shutters carefully closed, was full of a great peacefulness amid the heat of that sultry July afternoon. Only some slender sunbeams penetrated by the three windows, darting arrow-like through the slits in the old woodwork; and a very soft light prevailed in the shady spot, bathing everything in a delicate, diffusive glow. It was also cool in there, compared with the torrid, overpowering heat felt out-of-doors under the blazing sun, which was setting the house-front afire.

Standing in front of the press facing the windows, Dr. Pascal was searching for a memorandum which he had come to take from it. With its doors wide open, this huge eighteenth-century clothes-press—of carved oak, with strong and elegantly-wrought iron hinges—displayed upon its shelves an extraordinary accumulation of papers, reaching to the farthest depths of its roomy flanks. Manuscripts and portfolios of documents were here piled up and up to overflowing, in higgledy-piggledy fashion. For more than thirty years the Doctor had flung into this press every page of writing that had come from his pen—from the briefest memoranda to the complete manuscripts of his great works of research on Heredity. And so it was not always easy for him to find what he sought there. Nevertheless, full of patience, he continued rummaging, and when he at last laid his hand upon what he wanted, he smiled.

For a moment longer he lingered beside the press, reading the memorandum in the light of a golden sunbeam, which reached him by the central window. Although he was nigh his sixtieth year, and his hair and beard were white as snow, he looked, in this early-morning radiance, still sound and vigorous, with his face so fresh in colour, his features so delicately marked, and his eyes still so limpid and child-like that, as he stood there in his tight-fitting, brown velvet jacket, he might have been taken for a young man with powdered locks.

'Here! Clotilde,' he said at last, 'you must copy out this memorandum. Ramond would never be able to decipher my abominable writing.'

Thereupon he came and laid the paper beside the girl, who stood working at a high desk in the embrasure of the right-hand window.

'Very well, master,' she replied.[1]

She had not even turned towards him, all her attention being concentrated on the pastel drawing at which she was slashing away with broad, fast-repeated strokes of her crayon. A branch of hollyhock, with flowers of a strange violet tint, streaked with yellow, was blooming near her in a vase. But, although she did not turn, one could plainly see the profile of her little round head with fair and short-cut hair—an exquisite profile, serious in expression, with a straight forehead, contracted by her application to her work, a sky-blue eye, a small delicate nose, and a firm chin. There was something delightfully youthful about the nape of her bent neck, of a fresh milky whiteness under the little golden curls which strayed here and there. Clad in a long black blouse, she was

---

[1] From the girl calling the Doctor 'master' it must not be inferred that she is his servant. She is, in fact, his niece, and simply calls him *maître*, or master, because she looks up to him as being such by reason of his great attainments; in the same way, indeed, as M. Zola himself is thus addressed by his literary disciples. As the expression will frequently occur in the story, it is as well that the reader should understand its exact sense at the outset.—*Trans.*

very tall, slim-waisted, small-breasted, and supple—with that elongated, sinuous suppleness which the divine figures of the Renaissance display. In spite of her five-and-twenty years, she had remained so youthful in appearance that she looked barely eighteen.

'And you must put the things in this press to rights a bit,' the Doctor added. 'It is no longer possible to find anything.'

'Very well, master,' she repeated without raising her head. 'By-and-by.'

Pascal had gone to seat himself at his writing-table at the other end of the room, in front of the left-hand window. It was merely a table of blackened wood, littered like the shelves of the press with all sorts of papers and pamphlets. Then silence again fell ; profound peacefulness once more prevailed in the soft half-light, amid all the overwhelming outdoor heat. Besides the old oak-press, the spacious room, some thirty feet in length, and a score in breadth, contained two bookcases filled to overflowing ; and antique chairs and arm-chairs stood here and there, in a disorderly fashion, whilst the only ornaments, and these barely distinguishable, were some pastel drawings of strange-coloured flowers, nailed to the walls, upon which was a rose-work-patterned, drawing-room paper of First Empire style. The three folding doors, the one communicating with the landing, the one leading into the Doctor's room, and the one giving admission to the girl's— these latter at either end of the apartment—dated from the time of Louis XV., like the cornice which ran round the smoky ceiling.

An hour went by without a sound, even of breathing, being heard. Then as Pascal, by way of relaxation from his work, tore off the wrapper of a newspaper forgotten on his table—a copy of the Paris *Temps*—he raised a slight excla-mation : 'Ah ! so your father is appointed director of the *Époque*, that successful Republican journal which is publishing the papers found at the Tuileries.'

This intelligence must have been unexpected by him, for he laughed in a good-hearted way, with a commingling of satisfaction and sadness. And then, in an undertone, he resumed : 'Upon my word! Invent what one might, things would never be so wonderful. Life is really extraordinary. There's a very interesting article here.'

Clotilde had made no reply; it seemed as though she was a hundred leagues away from what her uncle was talking about. He himself spoke no further; but taking up a pair of scissors when he had read the article, he cut it out, pasted it on a sheet of paper, and annotated it in his big sprawling handwriting. Then he again approached the press, that he might put this fresh note away in it. But to do so he had to take a chair, for the topmost shelf was so high up, that, tall though he was, he could not reach it.

Numerous collections of documents, methodically classified, were ranged in an orderly manner upon this lofty shelf. These documents were of all descriptions—manuscript notes, legal instruments engrossed on stamped paper, and articles cut out of newspapers, collected together in batches, and enclosed in stout blue wrappers, upon each of which was a name in bold handwriting. It could be divined that these papers were lovingly kept in order, constantly taken out and examined, and carefully put back in place again ; indeed, this was the only tidy shelf in the whole press.

When Pascal had climbed upon the chair and found the set of papers he wanted, one of the fullest of the blue paper cases, on which was inscribed the name of ' Saccard,' [1] he added the new document to it, and forthwith put the portfolio into place again in its proper alphabetical order. Then, lingering there abstractedly for another moment, he complacently straightened a pile of papers which was well nigh toppling over. ' You hear, Clotilde,' he added, as he at last jumped down from the chair, ' when you set things to rights here, you are not to touch the papers on the top shelf.'

' Very well, master,' she answered for the third time, with her wonted docility.

[1] Pascal's younger brother, Aristide Rougon, *alias* Saccard, who figures so prominently in M. Zola's novels *L'Argent* and *La Curée* (' The Rush for the Spoil '). Clotilde is Saccard's daughter by his first wife, Angèle Sicardot.—*Trans.*

He had begun laughing again, with an expression of inbred gaiety. 'It is forbidden,' said he.

'I know it is, master.'

With a vigorous turn of the wrist he locked the press, and then flung the key into a drawer of his writing-table. The girl was sufficiently acquainted with his researches to put his manuscripts in order, and he also readily utilised her services as secretary, giving her his notes to copy out, whenever a *confrère* and a friend like Dr. Ramond requested communication of some document. But she was not a learned young woman, and he simply forbade her to read whatever he considered useless for her to know.

However, the profound attention in which he felt she was wrapt ended by surprising him. 'What is the matter with you that you no longer open your mouth?' he asked. 'Is it the copying of those flowers which so absorbs you?'

This, again, was one of the tasks that he often confided to her, the execution of pencil, water-colour, and pastel drawings, which served for the illustrative plates that he added to his works. Thus he had for five years past been making some very curious experiments with a collection of hollyhocks, obtaining many fresh varieties of colour by means of artificial fecundation. And in copying such flowers as these the girl brought to her task such painstaking minuteness, such extraordinary exactitude in respect both to drawing and colour, that he was for ever admiring her scrupulous care, and saying that she had a nice little round pate, clear and sound.

This time, however, as he drew near to glance over her shoulder, he raised a cry of comical fury. 'Ah! just put a stop to that! There you are—off to dreamland again! Just oblige me by tearing that up at once!

She had drawn herself erect, with her blood rushing to her cheeks, her eyes gleaming with all the passion inspired by her work, her slender fingers soiled with the red and blue pastel that she had been crushing.

'O master!' she cried; and in that word 'master,' so soft, so caressingly submissive, that name significant of so much self-surrender, by which she called him to avoid using either the term of uncle or that of godfather, which she considered stupid, there now for the first time passed a flash of rebellion, the revendication of a being who takes back what she has given, and asserts herself.

Nearly a couple of hours previously she had pushed the faithful, sober copy of the hollyhocks upon one side, and had strewn upon another sheet of paper a large cluster of imaginary flowers, the flowers of dreamland, alike extravagant and superb. 'Twas thus with her at times : a sudden bounding away from reality, a need to escape from it amid wild fantasies, and this even whilst engaged upon the most precise reproductive work. And forthwith she would satisfy her longing, reverting ever to that extraordinary florescence, but with such spirit and fancy that she never repeated herself, but, in turn, created roses with bleeding hearts, shedding tears of sulphur, lilies similar to crystal urns, and even flowers of no known form, that radiated afar like stars and scattered wafting corollets like tiny clouds. That day, upon a black ground, dashed off with hasty, impetuous strokes of her crayon, she had depicted a shower of pale stars, a streaming cascade of petals touched in with wondrous softness, whilst in a corner a chastely-veiled bud was opening—an expansion for which there was no name.

'Another one that you will be nailing up over there,' resumed the Doctor, pointing to the wall, where there was already a row of pastels equally as strange. 'But what, I pray, can it possibly represent ? '

She remained very grave, and stepped back that she might have a better view of her work. 'I'm sure I don't know,' she answered; 'but it's beautiful.'

At this moment Martine came in—Martine, the only servant, and now, after nearly thirty years of service with the Doctor, the real mistress of the house. Active and sparing of words, she also, although more than sixty, retained a young look as she went about in her everlasting black gown and white coif, which—coupled with her little pale, restful face, from which all the light of her ash-grey eyes seemed to have departed—lent her somewhat the appearance of a nun. She did not speak, but went and seated herself upon the floor in front of an armchair, the horsehair stuffing of which was protruding through a rent in the old tapestry covering. Taking a needle and a skein of wool from her pocket, she began darning the hole. For three days past she had been waiting for a spare hour in which she might repair this rent, the thought of which had haunted her.

' While you are about it, Martine,' Pascal exclaimed, gaily, as he took Clotilde's rebellious head between both hands, ' you had better sew up this little noddle here; there's a crack in it.'

Martine raised her light, faded eyes, and gazed at her master with her wonted expression of adoration. ' Why do you tell me that, monsieur ? '

' Because, my good woman, I very much fancy that it's you, with all your piety, that have been cramming extravagant, unearthly ideas into this nice little round noddle, so clear and sound.'

The glances which the two women exchanged showed that they understood one another. ' O monsieur ! ' said Martine, ' religion has never done any harm to anybody. And when folks don't share the same ideas, the best thing is not to talk of the matter.'

Silence fell, full of embarrassment. This was the only difference of views which brought an occasional falling-out between these three beings, otherwise so united and leading so confined a life. Martine had been but nine-and-twenty, just one year older than the Doctor, when she had entered his service at the time he was starting in his profession at Plassans, in a light, airy little house in the new town. And thirteen years later, when Saccard—one of Pascal's brothers, who had lost his wife and was on the point of marrying again —had sent his daughter Clotilde, then a girl of seven, to the Doctor, it was Martine who undertook to bring up the child, who conducted her to church and imparted to her some of the pious fire with which she herself had always burnt. Like the man of broad views that he was, the Doctor had let them indulge the joy of believing without restraint, for he did not consider that he had a right to forbid anyone the happiness of Faith. He contented himself later on with watching over the young girl's education, and giving her precise and healthy ideas on all things. During the sixteen years that they had been thus residing, all three together, in retirement at La Souleiade, a little *propriété* in a suburb of the town, at a quarter of an hour's walk from St. Saturnin, the cathedral, life occupied in great unrevealed labour had glided along happily—slightly disturbed, however, by a growing discomfort, the clashing ever more and more violent of their several beliefs.

Pascal walked up and down for a moment with a gloomy look. Then, like a man who is not accustomed to mince his words : 'You see, my dear,' said he, ' your nice little brain has been affected by all the phantasmagoria of the supernatural—your Providence had no need of you; I ought to have kept you all to myself; your health would have been much better had I done so.'

Clotilde, however, made a stand, her figure quivering, and her clear eyes boldly fixed upon his own : ' It is you, master, who would fare better if you did not obstinately confine yourself to your fleshly eyes. There are things beyond ; why will you not look and see ? '

Then Martine, in her fashion, came to Clotilde's help. ' It's surely true, monsieur, that you—a saint, as I tell everyone—ought to come to church with us. God will surely save you. But I tremble all over at the thought that you won't go straight to Heaven with us.'

He had paused in his walk, and beheld them both standing there in full rebellion ; they as a rule so docile, on their knees, as it were, before him, with the loving submissiveness of women conquered by his geniality and kindness. He was already opening his mouth, on the point of answering them roughly, when he bethought himself of the futility of a discussion : ' There, be quiet, do ! It is best I should go to work. And be careful that you don't disturb me ! '

Stepping briskly into his room, where he had installed a kind of laboratory, he shut himself inside it. He had expressly forbidden either of them to enter this chamber, where he occupied himself with certain medicinal preparations which he never spoke of to anyone. Within a few moments the women could hear the slow, regular taps of a pestle in a mortar.

'Ah! well,' exclaimed Clotilde, smiling; 'there he is, up to his devil's cookery again, as grandmother says.'

Thereupon she staidly set herself to finish copying the stalk of hollyhocks. She was careful that her drawing should be minutely accurate, and skilfully matched the tones of the yellow-striped, violet petals, even to the most delicate shades of decoloration.

Martine was again on the floor mending the rent in the armchair. 'Ah!' she muttered, after a pause, 'what a pity that so good a man should take pleasure in wrecking his soul! For, it can't be denied, I've known him now for thirty years, and he has never given pain to anyone. His is a real good heart; he would deprive himself to help others. And so pleasant he is, too, and always so well, and always merry. It's a crime on his part not to make his peace with our good God. Isn't it so, mademoiselle? We must compel him.'

Surprised to hear Martine talk at such unwonted length, Clotilde gravely assented. 'Certainly, Martine, it is sworn,' she said; 'we will compel him.'

Silence was again falling when the tinkling was heard of the bell fixed to the front door downstairs. The house being over-large for the three people that dwelt in it, this bell had been placed there that it might serve to warn them of the arrival of strangers. The servant seemed surprised by the tinkling, and grumbled indistinctly. Who could have come there in such overpowering heat? She had risen to her feet, and, opening the door which communicated with the landing, she leant over the banisters, and came back saying: 'It is Madame Félicité.'

Old Madame Rougon [1] came briskly in. Despite her four-

---

[1] The scheming mother of the brothers Rougon, who figures so conspicuously in *La Fortune des Rougon* and *La Conquête de Plassans.—Trans.*

score years she had just climbed the stairs with the light step
of a girl ; and she was still the same dark grasshopper as of
yore, with spare figure and rasping voice. Nowadays very
elegant in her attire, robed in sheeny black silk, she might
yet, from behind, have been taken for some love-stricken or
ambitious woman hurrying to gratify her passion or attain her
ends. Her eyes, too, still shone out with a sparkle from her
withered face, and she smiled with a pretty smile when it
pleased her to do so.

'What! is it you, grandmother ? ' exclaimed Clotilde stepping forward to meet her. 'But this terrible sun is enough
to bake one.'

Kissing her on the forehead, Félicité began to laugh.
'Oh, the sun is a friend of mine,' said she ; and, trotting with
brisk little steps up to one of the windows, she turned the
fastening of the shutters. 'You should open them a bit and
let a little light in,' she resumed ; 'it's too gloomy to live like
that in the dark—I let the sunshine come in at home.'

A stream of fierce, hot light, a flood of dancing sparks
rushed into the room as the shutters were set ajar, and under
the sky of a fiery, violescent blue, the vast, scorched stretch of
country could be seen, asleep, lifeless beneath this furnace-
like annihilation. Above the pink house-roofs on the right
the steeple of St. Saturnin arose—a gilded tower with open
work glistening like polished bone in the blinding glow.

'Yes,' continued Félicité, 'I shall no doubt go on to Les
Tulettes by-and-by ; and I wanted to know if you had Charles
with you, so that I might take him with me. But I see that
he is not here ; I must put it off till another day.'

While she was giving this pretext for her visit, her ferreting
eyes travelled round the room. She did not lay any stress on
the matter, but hearing the rhythmical tap-tap of the pestle,
which went on without ceasing in the adjoining chamber, she
forthwith spoke of her son Pascal : 'Ah! so he's up to his
devil's cookery again. Don't disturb him. I've nothing to
say to him !'

Martine, who had gone back to the armchair, shook her
head by way of signifying that she felt no inclination to dis-

turb her master ; and then came a fresh spell of silence, whilst Clotilde wiped her pastel-soiled fingers on a cloth, and Félicité again began taking little steps about the room with a prying air.

For nearly two years now old Madame Rougon had been a widow. Her husband, after becoming so corpulent that he could no longer stir, had been carried off—stifled by an attack of indigestion—on the night of September 3, 1870, a few hours after hearing of the catastrophe of Sedan. The downfall of the *régime* which he prided himself on having helped to establish, seemed to have crushed him like a thunderbolt. From that time Félicité, for her own part, affected to take no further interest in politics, but lived like some queen who has given up her throne. Nobody was ignorant of the fact that by ensuring the triumph of the Coup d'État at Plassans, in 1851, the Rougons had then saved the town from anarchy, and that they had again conquered it a few years later when they had snatched it from the Legitimist and Republican candidates to place it in the hands of a Bonapartist deputy. Till the advent of the Franco-German war the Empire had remained all-powerful here, so popular that at the time of the Plebiscitum it had obtained an overwhelming majority of votes in its favour. Since the great disasters, however, a Republican spirit had been growing in the town. The Saint-Marc district was certainly relapsing into the same underhand Royalist intrigues that had been prevalent there formerly ; still, both the old and the new town had sent to the Assembly a representative of liberal views, of a vague shade of Orleanism, it is true, but nevertheless quite prepared to range himself on the side of the Republic, should the latter triumph.[1] This was why Félicité, like an intelligent woman, had decided to hold aloof from politics, and content herself henceforth with being merely the dethroned queen of a fallen *régime*.

---

[1] The story opens in the summer of 1872, when efforts were being made to bring about a ' fusion ' between the Legitimist and Orleanist Royalists with the object of placing the Count de Chambord on the throne as King Henri V. As will be remembered, these schemes came to nought, and the Assembly, in spite of its Royalist majority, was compelled to organise a Republican form of Government.—*Trans.*

Even this, however, was still a high position fraught with a gloomy poesy. For eighteen years, at any rate, she had reigned. The legend of her two drawing-rooms—the yellow drawing-room where the Coup d'État had ripened, the green drawing-room which later on had proved the neutral ground on which the conquest of Plassans had been effected—gained increased brilliancy with the lapse of years, especially now that the period it belonged to had disappeared. Then, also, she was very wealthy ; and people, moreover, thought her very dignified in her fall—never giving vent to a sigh of regret, a word of complaint, but carrying along with her in the train of her eighty years so long a succession of frantic yearnings, abominable stratagems, and surfeits of self-gratification, that she became with it all positively august. At present her only pleasure lay in the peaceful enjoyment of her large fortune and past royalty, and she no longer had but one passion—that of defending her career by sweeping aside all that might hereafter besmirch her. Her pride, nurtured by the twofold exploit which the townsfolk still talked of, was ever watching with jealous care—resolved to allow the survival only of that which redounded to her credit—that legend which made the people bow to her as to a fallen sovereign whenever she passed through the town.

She had stepped as far as the door of her son's room, and stood there listening to the obstinate tap-taps of the pestle, which never ceased. Then, with a thoughtful look, she came back to Clotilde : ' Good heavens ! what can he be concocting ? He's doing himself the greatest possible harm, you know, with that new drug of his. I heard that he had again nearly killed one of his patients the other day.'

' O grandmother ! ' exclaimed the girl.

But Félicité was started : ' Yes, quite so. And the women say a good deal more. Go and question them down in the Faubourg. They'll tell you that he pounds dead men's bones in the blood of new-born babes.'

At this even Martine protested, and Clotilde, wounded in her affection, became quite angry. ' O grandmother ! ' said she, ' don't repeat those abominable things ! To think of it !

master, who has so great a heart, whose only thought is for the happiness of all ! '

Seeing that they both became indignant, Félicité realised that she was precipitating matters too fast, and again reverted to blandishment. 'But it isn't I that say these frightful things, my little pussy. I simply repeat the nonsense which people spread abroad, so that you may understand how mistaken it is on Pascal's part not to take account of public opinion. He fancies he has discovered a new remedy ; well and good ; indeed I'm quite willing to admit that he is going to cure everybody as he hopes to do. Only why should he put on these mysterious airs, why shouldn't he speak out openly about it, and, above all, why should he try it on the riff-raff of the old town and the countryside, instead of attempting some cures which would cause a stir, and do him honour, among the townspeople of good position ? But no— your uncle, you see, my little pussy, has never been able to do anything like other people.'

She had assumed an aggrieved tone, lowering her voice to reveal the secret wound which made her heart bleed. ' Men of value, thank heaven, have not been wanting in our family. My other sons have given me ample satisfaction. Your uncle, Eugène, climbed high enough, didn't he ? A Minister for twelve years, almost Emperor ! And your father himself fingered millions enough, was mixed up in all the great building enterprises which made Paris a new city ! Nor need I speak of your brother Maxime, so rich and so distinguished ; nor of your cousins, Octave Mouret, one of the conquering kings of commerce in its new form, and that dear Abbé Mouret, for his part a perfect saint ! Well, why does Pascal, who might have followed the same path as all of them, why does he obstinately live on like this in his hole, like an eccentric old fellow who is half cracked ? '

Then, as the girl again showed symptoms of rebellion, her grandmother closed her lips with a caressing wave of the hand : No, no, let me finish ; I am quite aware that Pascal is not an idiot, that he has done some remarkable work, that the memoirs he has sent to the Academy of Medicine have even won him a reputation among learned men. But is all that of any account in comparison with what I dreamt of for him? Yes! the finest practice in the town, all the rich people as his patients, a large fortune, the red ribbon, honours in fact, and a position worthy of the family. Do you see, my little pussy, that's what I complain of—he does not, he never would belong to the family. Really now, when he was a child I used to say to him, " But where have *you* come from? *You* don't belong to us." For my own part, I have sacrificed everything to the family. I would let myself be cut up into mincemeat if it could only make the family great and glorious for ever ! '

She drew her little figure erect, and grew quite tall in this outburst of the one passion of greed and pride that had filled her life. As she resumed her promenade about the room, however, she was startled by the sight of the number of the *Temps*, which the Doctor had thrown upon the floor, after cutting out the article concerning Saccard and adding it to the batch of documents relating to him. The gap in the paper doubtless sufficed to enlighten her, for she at once stopped short and let herself fall upon a chair, as though she had at last obtained the information she had come in search of.

' Your father is appointed director of the *Époque*,' she abruptly resumed.

' Yes,' said Clotilde, with perfect tranquillity ; ' master told me so ; it was in the paper.'

Félicité gazed at her with an attentive, anxious air, for there was something monstrous about this appointment of Saccard and his adhesion to the Republic. After the collapse of the Empire he had been bold enough to return to France, despite the sentence he had incurred as managing director of the Banque Universelle, the stupendous fall of which [1] had preceded that of the *régime*. New influences, some complicated, incredible intrigue must have set him on his legs again. Not only had he obtained a pardon, but he was once more

---

[1] Recorded in M. Zola's novel, *L'Argent*.

' promoting ' large undertakings, fully launched in journalistic spheres, with a finger in every pie, and a share of every bribe. Reflecting upon all this, his mother recalled the frequent tiffs and ruptures between himself and his brother, Eugène Rougon, whom in former times he had so often compromised, and whom, through the strange turn that things were taking, he would perhaps be called upon to protect, since the ex-Minister of the Empire was now but a simple deputy, resigned to the one task of defending his fallen master with an obstinacy akin to that with which his mother defended their family. She continued submissively obeying the orders of her eldest son, the eagle still, though stricken low ; nevertheless Saccard, with his indomitable resolution to succeed, retained, no matter what he might do, a hold upon her heart. And she was also proud of Maxime, Clotilde's brother, who, after the war, had again installed himself in his mansion in the Avenue du Bois de Boulogne, and was there spending the fortune bequeathed to him by his wife—but in a prudent way, with the enforced restraint, indeed, of a man whose marrow is diseased, and who seeks by artifice to ward off the paralysis threatening him.

' Director of the *Époque*,' she repeated ; ' it's almost a ministerial position your father has conquered. Ah ! I was forgetting to tell you that I have again written to your brother to induce him to come and see us. It would be a change for him, and would do him good. And then, too, there's the child, poor Charles——'

She did not dwell, however, on the subject of this child ; this was another of the wounds which made her pride bleed : a son whom Maxime had had, at seventeen years of age, by a servant girl. The lad, who was now fifteen or so, had a weak brain, was, in fact, half an idiot, and lived at Plassans, passing from one to another member of the family, a burden in turn upon all.

For a few minutes Félicité continued waiting, hoping for some remark from Clotilde, something transitional which would allow her to broach the subject which she desired to arrive at. When she saw, however, that the girl gave her no attention, but busied herself with setting the papers on her

desk in order, she abruptly made up her mind to speak out,
though not before darting a glance at Martine, who still went
on mending the armchair, apparently giving no more heed to
the conversation than if she had been deaf and dumb.

'So your uncle cut out the article in the *Temps* ?' said
Madame Rougon.

'Yes, master put it away among his documents,' Clotilde
calmly answered, with a smile. 'Ah ! the number of notes
that he buries away like that. Everything that concerns the
family—the births, the deaths, the most trifling incidents in
the lives of every one of us. And there's the famous genealogical tree, our genealogical tree, you know, which he carefully keeps up to date.'

A flash darted from old Madame Rougon's eyes. 'You
know what these documents are ?' said she, gazing fixedly at
the girl.

'Oh, no, I don't, grandmother ! Master never talks to me
about them, and he forbids me to touch them.'

Félicité would not believe her, however. 'But they are
here at your elbow, you must have read them ?'

Again smiling in her serene uprightness of heart and
mind, Clotilde simply answered : 'No; when master forbids
anything it's because he has his reasons for doing so, and I
obey him.'

'Ah, my child !' Félicité, no longer able to restrain her
passion, exclaimed in an excited voice : 'Since Pascal is so
much attached to you, he would perhaps listen to you ; so you
should beg him to burn all those things, for if he happened to
die and all the horrors which he has among his documents
were found, we should every one of us be dishonoured !'

Ah ! those hateful documents : she saw them at night-
time in her feverish dreams, recording in letters of fire all the
true stories, all the physiological defects of the family, all the
seamy side of her glory which she would fain have buried for
ever with the progenitors of the race already dead and gone !
She knew that the idea of collecting those documents had
come to the Doctor at the very outset of his great studies on
Heredity, that he had been led to take the members of his

own family as examples, struck as he was by the typical cases
he found among them, cases which confirmed the laws he had
discovered. And was not this a natural field of observation,
well within his reach, and of which he had a minute, particular
knowledge? So, with the superb indifference of the *savant*,
who cares nought for what others may say, he had for thirty
years past been accumulating the most precise data concerning
his relatives, collecting and classifying everything that came
in his way, drawing up that genealogical tree of the Rougon-
Macquarts of which his voluminous portfolios of documents
formed a commentary replete with proofs.

'Yes, indeed,' resumed Madame Rougon, in a passionate
voice; 'to the fire, yes, to the fire with all those wretched
papers which would besmirch us all!' Then, as the servant, seeing the turn the conversation was taking, rose up to
leave the room, she stayed her with a hasty wave of the hand:
'No, no, Martine; don't go, you are not in the way, for you
have become one of the family.' And in a strident voice she
went on: 'A mass of falsehoods and tittle-tattle, all the lies
that our enemies used to spread abroad against us in their
rage at our triumph! Just think of it, my child! Such
horrors about all of us, about your father, your mother, your
brother, about me——'

'Horrors, grandmother? But how can you know that?'

The old woman was momentarily embarrassed: 'Oh, well,
I have good cause for suspecting it! Where is the family, I
should like to know, that never met with mishaps which
might be misconstrued? Thus, hasn't our mother, the mother
of all of us, that dear, venerable Aunt Dide, your great-grand-
mamma, been at the Lunatic Asylum at Les Tulettes for one-
and-twenty years? If God has been pleased to let her reach
the great age of one hundred and four, he has nevertheless
severely stricken her by depriving her of reason. Certainly
there is no shame in that; only what exasperates me, what
mustn't be, is that people should base themselves on that to
say we are all mad! And then, too, there's your Uncle Macquart; deplorable tales have been spread abroad about *him*!
Certainly Macquart did not behave as he should have done,

long ago, and I won't defend him. But nowadays doesn't he live very staidly and quietly at his little place at Les Tulettes, only a few steps away from our afflicted mother, over whom he watches like a good son ? And then, listen, a last instance. Your brother Maxime behaved very wrongly in the matter of that little boy of his, poor little Charles, and it is unfortunately true that the unhappy child's wits are none of the best. No matter; would it please you if people said to you that your nephew is degenerate, that, after the lapse of four generations, certain infirmities reappear in him, those of his great-great-grandmother, the poor dear woman whom we sometimes take him to see, and with whom he is so pleased to be ?   No ! no such thing as a family would be possible should people begin dissecting and analysing this and that—the nerves of one, and the muscles of another. It would disgust one with life.'

Erect in her long black blouse, Clotilde had listened to her attentively. She had become very grave, with eyes fixed on the floor, and arms hanging at her sides. Silence reigned for a moment, and then she slowly said : ' That is science, grandmother.'

' Science ! ' exclaimed Félicité, stamping her foot, ' a pretty affair their science is ; why, it attacks every sacred thing there is in the world ! Will they be any the better off, I should like to know, when they've destroyed everything ? They destroy respect, they destroy family ties, they destroy God—— '

' Oh, don't say that, madame ! ' interrupted Martine, in a grieved tone, sorely wounded as she was in her narrow piety ; ' don't say that Monsieur Pascal destroys God.'

' Yes, he does, my poor girl. And looking at it all in a religious light, it's a crime, do you know, to let him damn himself like this. You cannot care for him, upon my word ; no, you cannot care for him—you two who possess the happiness of Faith—since you do nothing whatever to bring him back into the right path. Ah ! if I were in *your* place, I'd rather split that press to pieces with a hatchet, and make a fine bonfire of all the insults against Providence which are inside it

She had planted herself in front of the huge press, and was measuring it with her flaming eyes as though, despite her eighty years and withered muscles, she would have taken it by assault, have pillaged and annihilated it. Then, with a sweep of the hand expressive of ironical disdain, she exclaimed: 'His science, indeed! As if it could teach him everything!'

Clotilde was still standing there, absorbed, with dreamy eyes. ''Tis true, he cannot know everything,' she resumed in an undertone, as though talking to herself. 'There is always Something Else, yonder. It's that that makes me angry, it's that which sometimes makes us quarrel, for I cannot set the Mystery on one side as he does; it makes me anxious to the point of torture—yes, all the Volition and Action yonder in the quivering darkness, all the unknown forces——'

Her words fell yet more slowly from her lips, dying away in an indistinct murmur.

Then Martine, who for a few moments had been looking gloomy, in her turn intervened: 'If it were true though, mademoiselle, that master is working his damnation with all those horrid papers! Ought we to let him do it? For my part, you know, if he told me to throw myself off the terrace, I'd shut my eyes and throw myself over, because I know he's always in the right. But as for his salvation, oh! if I only knew how, I'd work for it in spite of him, by all means in my power; yes, I'd compel him, for it's too dreadful to me to think that he won't be in heaven with us.'

'Well spoken, my girl,' said Félicité approvingly. 'You at least love your master in an intelligent manner.'

Between these two Clotilde yet seemed irresolute. Her belief did not bend submissively to strict dogmatic rules; her religious feeling did not seek materiality in the form of a Paradise, some spot of delight where one would again meet kith and kin. She simply experienced a need of something beyond what she had, based upon the certainty she felt that the vast universe is not limited to that which we know of by our senses, that there is also another, an unknown world of which we should keep account. But, on the other hand, in her anxious affection for her uncle, she was shaken in her own views by the words of her aged grandmother and that devoted servant. Did they not love him more than she herself did, and in a more enlightened and upright way; they who would have had him spotless, freed from all scientific mania, pure enough in thought and deed to be included among the Elect? Sentences she had read in works of piety came to her mind—the ceaseless battle one must wage against the Spirit of Evil, the glory of contending with the unbeliever, conquering him and converting him to Faith. What if she were to undertake such a holy task; what if she were to save him, despite himself, despite everything? Enthusiasm was gradually gaining upon her mind, already inclined to venture-some enterprises.

'Certainly,' she ended by saying, 'I should be very glad if he would leave off troubling his mind about all those scraps of paper that he heaps up, and come with us to church.'

Seeing her on the point of giving way, Madame Rougon exclaimed that it was necessary to act, and Martine herself brought all the weight of her genuine, authoritative influence to bear upon her. They had drawn near, and now began to indoctrinate her, lowering their voices as though for some plot, whence a miraculous blessing would accrue, a divine delight that would perfume the entire house. What a triumph if the Doctor could only be reconciled with God! And what after-felicity in dwelling together in the celestial communion of a common faith!

'Well, what am I to do?' at last asked Clotilde, vanquished, conquered.

At that moment, however, as the continuous, rhythmical taps of the Doctor's pestle resounded yet more loudly amid the silence, the victorious Félicité, who was on the point of speaking, turned her head anxiously, and gazed for an instant at the door of the adjoining room. Then, in an undertone, she said: 'You must know where the key of the press is?'

Clotilde did not answer, but made a gesture which expressed all the repugnance she felt at thus betraying her master.

'How childish you are! I swear to you that I will take nothing. I will not even disturb anything. Only, since we are alone and Pascal never shows himself again before dinnertime, we might satisfy ourselves—eh?—as to what there is in there. Only just a glance, that's all, upon my word of honour.'

Standing there quite motionless, Clotilde still withheld her consent.

'Besides,' continued Félicité, 'perhaps I may be mistaken after all; perhaps none of the horrid things I have been talking about are there.'

This decided the battle. Clotilde ran to the drawer, took out the key, and set the press wide open. 'There, grandmother, the documents are on the top shelf.'

Martine, without speaking a word, had stationed herself at the door of Pascal's room, lending an attentive ear to the tap-tap of the pestle, while Félicité stood gazing at the portfolios of papers as though rooted to the spot by emotion. At last, so there they were, those terrible documents, the ceaseless dread of which had poisoned her life! She could see them, she was about to touch them and carry them away! She drew herself erect at the thought, passionately striving to lengthen her little legs. 'They are too high up, my little pussy,' she said. 'Help me. Give them to me.'

'Oh! no, grandmother, not that—take a chair.'

Félicité took a chair, and nimbly climbed upon it. But she was still too short. Then, by an extraordinary effort, she raised herself, managed even to make herself taller, so that at last she could touch the stout blue-paper wrappers of the batches of documents with the tips of her nails. And then her fingers strayed hither and thither, clutching and scratching like claws. All at once there was a crash, she had knocked a bit of marble—a geological specimen, placed upon one of the lower shelves—on to the floor.

The taps of the pestle immediately ceased, and Martine, in a stifled voice, exclaimed: 'Take care, here he comes!'

But Félicité, in despair at the mishap, did not hear her, and was still clutching at the documents when Pascal came

in. He thought that a serious accident had happened, that
some one had fallen, and he stopped short, quite stupefied at
the spectacle he beheld : his mother on the chair with her
arms still upraised, while Martine had drawn on one side, and
Clotilde, erect and very pale, awaited him without averting
her eyes. When he understood the situation he also became
as pale as linen. A terrible anger was rising within him.

Old Madame Rougon, however, was in no wise bewildered.
Immediately she realised that the opportunity was lost she
jumped down from the chair without even alluding to the
attempt in which her son had surprised her. ' Oh ! so it's
you,' said she ; ' I did not want to disturb you—I came to
kiss Clotilde. But I've been chattering for nearly two hours
and now I must be off quick. They must be waiting for me
at home, and wondering what can have become of me. *Au
revoir*, till Sunday ! '

Then off she went, quite at her ease, after smiling at her
son, who had remained standing before her, silent and respectful. He had long since adopted this demeanour towards her,
in order to avoid an explanation which he realised must prove
a cruel one, and which had therefore always frightened him.
He knew her, and, with the broad tolerance of the *savant* who
admits the influence of heredity, environment, and circumstances, he wished to forgive her everything. Besides, was
she not his mother ? That alone would have sufficed, for
amidst the many terrible blows which his researches dealt at
the family, he yet retained a great affection for all his kin.

When his mother was gone his anger burst forth and fell
upon Clotilde. He had averted his eyes from Martine, and
kept them fixed on the girl, whose gaze met his own unflinch-
ingly, bravely resolved as she was to accept the responsibility
of her action.

' You ! you ! ' he said at last. He had caught hold of
her arm, and pressed it to the point of making her cry out.
Nevertheless, without sign of submission, she continued looking him in the face, asserting the indomitable will of her own
personality, her own mind. She was at once beautiful and
irritating thus—so slight, so slender, in her black blouse—and

her rebellious mood lent a bellicose charm to her exquisite, blonde youthfulness, her straight forehead, her delicate nose and firm chin. 'You, whom I have made what you are,' continued the Doctor; 'you, my pupil, my friend, my thought, to whom I have given a little of my heart and brain! Yes, indeed, I ought to have kept you entirely to myself, I ought not to have let the best part of you be taken from me by that Providence of yours!'

'Oh! you are blaspheming, monsieur!' cried Martine, who had drawn near, in order to divert some of his anger from Clotilde to herself.

But he did not even see her. For him, at that moment, Clotilde alone existed. And he was as though transfigured, stirred by such passion that between his white hair and his white beard his handsome face was flashing with youth, with immense, wounded, exasperated tenderness. For yet another moment they continued in this wise gazing at one another, with fixed eyes and without a sign of yielding on either side. 'You! you!' the Doctor repeated in his quivering voice.

'Yes, I! Why should I not love you, master, as much as you love me? And why, if I consider you in peril, should I not try to save you? You on your side occupy yourself with what *I* think; you endeavour to make *me* think like you!'

Never before had she resisted him in this fashion. 'But you are only a little girl; you know nothing,' he rejoined.

'No, I am a soul; and you know no more than I.'

He released her arm and made a vague, sweeping gesture in the direction of the sky. Then silence fell, an extraordinary silence, fraught with weighty things, with all that discussion which he deemed futile and would not enter upon. Stepping up to the central window, he had energetically pushed open the shutters; for the sun was setting and darkness was filling the room. Then he came back again.

She, however, with a need of air and space, went up to this open window. The downpour of fiery sunbeams had ceased; from above there now fell nought save the last tremor of the over-heated, paling sky; whilst with the lightened, freer breath of evening warm odours were arising from the still burning soil. Below the terrace came, first of all, the railway-line, with the goods-sheds and other dependencies of the station, the principal buildings of which could be seen in the distance. Then, across the vast, barren plain, a line of trees marked the course of the Viorne, beyond which climbed the hills of Ste. Marthe, hills of ruddy soil forming terraces, up-held by walls of dry stones, and planted with olive trees ; whilst crowning the summits were sombre woods of pines. The whole formed an extensive, desolate amphitheatre of an old-brick-red hue, corroded by the fierce sun, and parted from the sky above by that fringe of sable greenery. On the left opened the gorges of La Seille—heaps of huge yellow boulders that had tumbled with some landslip, strewn over the san-guineous soil and o'ertopped by an immense bar of rocks which resembled the wall of a cyclopean fortress. And over towards the right, at the very entry of the valley where flowed the Viorne, the town of Plassans reared in tiers its roofs of faded, pinky tiles, its old-city-like jumble of close-clustering houses, 'twixt which uprose the crests of ancient elms ; while over tree and house alike reigned the lofty tower of St. Saturnin, solitary and serene, at present, in the limpid gold of the sunset.

' Ah, my God ! ' said Clotilde, slowly ; ' what pride one must have to think that one may take all in one's hand and know everything ! '

Pascal had just climbed upon a chair to make sure that not a single one of his batches of documents was missing. Then he picked up the fragment of marble and replaced it on the shelf, and when, with an energetic turn of the wrist, he had locked up the press, he slipped the key into his pocket.

' Yes,' he replied, ' to seek to know everything, and espe-cially not to lose one's head over what one doesn't know, and, maybe, will know never.'

Martine had again drawn near to Clotilde to support her, and to show that they had taken up a common cause. And the Doctor now saw her also, and felt that the two women were linked together in the same determination to conquer. After years of underhand attempts, here at last was open warfare—the *savant* who beholds those that belong to him turning against his opinions, and threatening them with destruction. There can be no worse torment for a man than to have treason in his home and all around him, to be pursued, beset, dispossessed, annihilated by those whom he loves, and who love him!

This thought had just presented itself to the Doctor's mind. 'And yet you both love me!' he said. He saw their eyes grow dim with tears, and was himself seized with a feeling of infinite sadness amid that peaceful close of a lovely day. All his gaiety, all his good-nature which sprang from his passion for life, were profoundly disturbed. 'Ah! my darling, and you, my poor woman,' he added, 'you are doing this for my happiness, are you not? But alas! how unhappy we shall now be!'

CHAPTER II

THE NEW ELIXIR OF LIFE

At six o'clock on the following morning Clotilde awoke. She had gone to bed on bad terms with Pascal—they were sulking with one another. And now her first feeling was one of discomfort, a covert grief, a need of immediately making peace, so that she might no longer retain on her heart the heavy weight which she still felt there.

Springing briskly out of bed she had gone to set the shutters of both windows ajar. The beams of the sun, which was already high, then darted into the room, throwing two golden bars, as it were, across it. The clear morning air brought a fresh, gentle breath of gaiety into this slumberous chamber, whilst the girl, who had returned to seat herself on the edge of the mattress, remained there for a moment in a thoughtful posture, clad merely in her somewhat tight-fitting chemise, which seemed to render her yet more slender, with long spindle-shaped legs, a slim yet strong trunk, round bosom, round neck, and round and supple arms. And her nape, her lovely shoulders were of a pure milky hue, white, sheeny like silk, and soft as could be. Whilst she was yet growing, during the ungraceful period of life between the ages of twelve and eighteen, she had seemed over-tall, lank and ill-formed; but at last the seemingly sexless creature, that climbed trees like a boy, had blossomed into this delicate young woman, so charming and so lovable.

With dreamy eyes, she continued gazing at the walls of the room. Although La Souleiade dated from the last century, it must have been refurnished about the time of the

First Empire, for the hangings were of a printed cotton stuff, covered with heads of sphinxes encircled by wreaths of oak leaves. Once of a bright red, this stuff was now of a pinky hue, an uncertain pink fading into orange. The curtains both of the windows and the bed still subsisted, but it had been necessary to have them repeatedly cleaned, which again had lightened their colour. And this faded purple, this aurora-like hue of such delightful softness, had really an exquisite effect. As for the bedstead, originally draped with the same stuff, it had fallen into such decay that it had been necessary to replace it by another taken from an adjacent room, another First Empire bedstead, low and broad, in massive mahogany and with brass ornaments, the four posts being surmounted by sphinx's heads, similar to those upon the hangings. The rest of the furniture matched this bedstead; there was a ward-robe with massive column-flanked doors, a white-marble-topped chest of drawers, with a brass cornice, a lofty cheval-glass of monumental proportions, a very large sofa with straight, stiff legs, and several chairs with upright backs, shaped like lyres. However, a counterpane, made out of an old silk skirt, such as was worn under Louis XV., gaily bedecked the majestic bedstead, which was placed so as to face the two windows, and quite a collection of cushions softened the hard-seated sofa; whilst there were yet a couple of whatnots bearing ornaments, and a table covered, like the bedstead, with some old flower-brocaded silk, discovered in a cupboard.

Clotilde at last put on her stockings, slipped into a white *piqué* dressing-gown, and then, having thrust her feet into a pair of grey canvas slippers, ran off to her dressing-room—a back room this, lighted from the other side of the house. She had hung it simply with a twill material, of an *écru* shade with blue stripes; and the articles of furniture—the wash-stand, the two wardrobes, and the chairs—were simply of polished pine. It could here be divined, however, that she was very much a woman; coquettish withal, in a natural, delicate way. This had grown with her, simultaneously with her beauty. Apart from the obstinate, boyish creature which she still showed herself to be at times, she had become a submissive, tender-hearted woman, delighting above all things in being loved. The truth was that she had grown up in freedom, learning no more than to read and to write whilst at school, but afterwards teaching herself and acquiring considerable knowledge in assisting her uncle. There had been, however, no regular plan of study between them; he had not desired to make a prodigy of her, and the only subject to which she had applied herself with a passionate interest was natural history, which had taught her everything concerning man and woman. Yet she retained all her virgin bloom, like a flower, a fruit that no hand has ever touched, and this, doubtless, owing to the ignoring, religious spirit in which she awaited love, the deep-rooted womanly feeling which caused her to reserve the gift that she would some day make of herself, that self-annihilation in the man whom she might come to love.

She caught up her hair, and washed herself; then, giving way to her impatience, she came back, softly opened the door of her bedchamber, and ventured to cross the spacious workroom on tip-toe. The shutters there were still closed, but she could see sufficiently to avoid knocking against the furniture. When she had reached the further end and was at the Doctor's door, she leaned forward and listened, holding her breath the while. Was he already up? What could he be doing? She could distinctly hear him walking about, taking short steps here and there, dressing himself in all probability. For her own part she never entered that room, where he was fond of hiding certain operations he engaged in, and which remained closed to all but himself like some tabernacle. At the idea that he might open the door and find her listening there, a strange feeling of anxiety seized hold of her—a most disturbing sensation, compounded of conflicting elements, a revolt of her pride coupled with a desire to show submissiveness, through all which sped a throb of fever, a shiver she had never known before. For a moment her yearning for reconciliation became so intense that she was on the point of knocking at the door. Then, however, as the sound of the Doctor's footsteps came near, she darted wildly away.

Until eight o'clock Clotilde was very restless, her impatience becoming more and more acute. Hardly a moment passed but she glanced at the clock on the mantelshelf in her room, a First Empire clock of gilt bronze, on which Cupid, leaning against a milestone, was contemplating Time, whom he had sent to sleep. As a rule she went down every morning at eight to partake of the first breakfast with the Doctor in the dining-room. And now, whilst awaiting the hour, she occupied herself in making a very careful toilet, dressing her hair, and putting on first her boots and then a white gown with red spots. After this, finding that she had yet a quarter of an hour to while away, she satisfied an old inclination and sat down to sew a narrow strip of lace, some imitation Chantilly, on her working blouse, the long black garment which she was at last finding too boyish, not womanly enough in character. However, eight o'clock had no sooner struck than she dropped her work, and hastily went downstairs.

'You will have to breakfast alone in the dining-room,' said Martine, composedly.

'How is that?'

'Oh, the Doctor called me and set his door ajar, and I gave him his egg. He's busy again with his mortar and his filter. We shan't see him before noon.'

All the colour had flown from Clotilde's cheeks; she was thunderstruck. She drank her milk standing, and, carrying off her roll, followed the servant into the kitchen. Besides this kitchen and the dining-room there was yet, on the ground-floor, an abandoned drawing-room in which the stock of potatoes was stored, and which had been used by the Doctor as his consulting room at the time when he had been in the habit of receiving patients at home. Some years previously, however, the writing-table and the armchair had been removed to the apartment overhead. And down below there was but one other chamber—the old servant's little bedroom, communicating with the kitchen and looking very clean and tidy with its walnut-wood chest of drawers, and its convent-like bedstead, hung with snow-white curtains.

'Do you think, then, that he has begun making his *liqueur* again?' asked Clotilde.

'Well, it can only be that. You know that he neglects even food and drink when that gets hold of him.'

All the girl's worry and disappointment found vent in a whispered plaint: 'Ah! my God! my God!'

Then, whilst Martine went off to set her room to rights, she took a parasol from the hall stand, and went off into the garden to eat her roll there, quite in despair, and at a loss how to occupy her time until noon.

Nearly seventeen years had already gone by since Dr. Pascal, making up his mind to leave his little house in the new town, had purchased La Souleiade for a score of thousand francs. It was his desire to lead a retired life, and also to provide more space and pleasure for the little girl whom his brother Saccard had then but lately sent to him from Paris. La Souleiade, perched on a plateau overlooking the plain, in the near outskirts of the town, was an old estate, once of considerable extent, but the wide expanse, which it had formerly comprised, had dwindled to some four or five acres, through successive sales and the laying-down of the railway line, which last had carried off its remaining arable fields. The house itself had been half-destroyed by a fire, and only one of the two original blocks of building now remained—a square 'four-walled wing' as folks say in Provence, roofed with big pink tiles, and with five windows lighting its façade. The Doctor, who had bought the place furnished, had contented himself with repairing and completing the walls of the grounds, and this done had felt himself quite at home.

Clotilde was, as a rule, passionately fond of this solitary spot, this tiny kingdom which she could visit from end to end in ten minutes, but which yet retained some vestiges of its ancient grandeur. That morning, however, she entered it with anger in her heart. For a moment she walked along the terrace, at either end of which were planted some century-old

cypresses, huge, dark cierges that could be seen three leagues
away. The slope descended to the railway line, with walls of
dry stones upholding the red soil, the last remaining vines
planted in which were dead; and now on these giant steps
there only grew some sorry-looking olive and almond trees
with scanty foliage. The heat here was already quite oppressive, and as Clotilde walked along she could see the little
lizards scampering across the disjoined flagstones into the
clumps of shaggy caper-bushes.

Then, as though irritated by the sight of the far-spreading
horizon, she crossed the orchard and kitchen-garden, which
Martine, in spite of her age, obstinately insisted on tending,
employing a man only twice a week for the heavier work.
And thence she went up into a *pinède*, a little pine grove on
the right, where stood all that remained of the superb pine
trees which of yore had covered the plateau. But again did
she find herself ill at ease; the dry cones crackled under her
feet, an oppressive resinous odour fell from the branches of
the trees. So she rapidly skirted the boundary-wall, passed
the entrance-gate—which led into the Chemin des Fenouillères at some three hundred yards from the first houses
of Plassans—and came out at last on the threshing-floor, a
spacious threshing-floor with a radius of a score of yards,
which alone sufficed to prove the old-time importance of the
domain. Ah! that ancient *area* paved with round pebbles, as
in the days of the Romans, that vast esplanade-like space
which the short, dry, golden herbage covered as with a tufty
carpet, what bonny times she had once had there, now running hither and thither, now rolling on the ground, now lying
there for hours upon her back when the stars began to peer
forth from the depths of the limitless heavens!

She had opened her parasol again, and crossed the threshing-floor at a slower pace. She now found herself on the
left of the terrace, having completed the round of the property.
So she returned to the rear of the house, and stationed herself
under the huge plane trees which, on that side, threw a deep
shade around. Here were the two windows of the Doctor's
room, towards which she raised her eyes, having indeed only

come back to the house in the sudden hope that she might see him. But the windows remained closed, and she felt hurt that it should be so, as though it were, in fact, an act of harshness towards herself. And only now did she perceive that she was carrying her roll about with her, and forgetting to eat it. Thereupon she dived under the trees and began biting the bread impatiently with her fine, strong, young teeth.

The old quincunx of plane trees, another vestige of the departed splendour of La Souleiade, furnished a most delightful retreat. Under these sylvan giants, whose trunks had grown to a monstrous size, it was scarcely possible to see, and the little light that prevailed was of quite a greeny tinge; it was exquisitely cool there, too, during the very hottest days of summer. In former times there had been a garden laid out hereabouts in the old French style, but all that now remained of it were some borders of box plants, to which the shade had doubtless been congenial, for they had grown very vigorously, and were now tall shrubs. The great charm of this shady nook, however, was a spring, a streamlet of gushing water no bigger than the little finger, which, flowing incessantly, even during the greatest drought, from a leaden pipe protruding from a pillar, fed, at some short distance away, a large mossy basin, the green stonework of which was only cleaned every three or four years. When all the wells in the neighbourhood became dry La Souleiade still had its spring, whose centenarian children those huge plane trees undoubtedly were. Day and night alike, for centuries past, that little streamlet of water, continuous and uniform, had been chanting with a crystalline vibration the same pure song.

After wandering among the box plants, which reached to her shoulders, Clotilde went to fetch some embroidery, and on her return seated herself before a stone table beside the spring. A few garden chairs had been placed at this spot, for they often took coffee there. She now pretended to no longer raise her head, as though, indeed, she were quite absorbed by her work. The occasional glances which she darted between the trunks of the trees seemed to be directed solely towards the blazing distance towards the threshing-floor now as dazzling as a brazier under the scorching sun. But in reality her glance, stealing from behind her long lashes, glided upward to the Doctor's windows. Nothing of him was to be seen there, however, not his shadow even. Then a feeling of sadness and rancour grew more and more intense within her at finding herself left in such seeming abandonment by him, treated with such apparent contempt after their quarrel of the day before. She, who had risen that morning with so keen a desire to make peace at once! He, however, was in no hurry, so it seemed. Didn't he love her then, since he could live on bad terms with her? And little by little she became gloomy, and reverted to thoughts of a struggle, again resolving that she would not give way to him on any point.

About eleven o'clock, before setting the second breakfast on the fire, Martine joined her for a moment, bringing with her the everlasting stocking, which, if not engaged with her housework, she was always knitting, even when she walked about. 'You know,' said she, 'he is still shut up there like a wolf, concocting that precious stuff of his.'

Clotilde shrugged her shoulders, without raising her eyes from her embroidery.

'And if you only knew, mademoiselle, what folks are saying,' continued Martine; 'Madame Félicité was quite right when she declared yesterday that it was enough to make one blush with shame. I've had it cast in my face, yes, in my own face, that it was he who killed old Boutin, that poor old fellow, you know, who used to fall down in fits, and who died on the high road.'

An interval of silence followed; then, as the girl grew yet more gloomy, the servant, plying her fingers with increased activity, resumed: 'I understand nothing about it myself, but those concoctions of his put me in a rage. And you, mademoiselle; do you approve of that cookery of his?'

Clotilde abruptly raised her head, yielding to the flood of passion which rushed upon her. 'Listen,' said she, 'I don't want to understand any more about it than you do; but I

think he is on the high road to very serious worries. He
does not care for us——'

' Oh, yes, mademoiselle, he does ! '

' No, no ; not as we care for him ! If he cared for us, he
would be here with us, instead of ruining his soul, his happiness and ours, up there, in his foolish desire to save everybody.'

The two women gazed at one another for a moment, their
eyes flashing with mutual affection in the fit of jealous anger
that had come over them. Then, enveloped in the deep
shade, they resumed their work, and spoke no further.

Meantime, in his room up above, Dr. Pascal was working
in unclouded, joyful serenity. He had hardly practised more
than twelve years from the time of his return from Paris till
the day when he had retired to La Souleiade. Satisfied with
the hundred and odd thousand francs which he had realised
by the exercise of his profession, and prudently invested, he
had since then devoted himself to little beyond his favourite
studies, retaining only a small circle of friends as patients ;
though when summoned to the bedside of a sufferer he readily
gave his services, for which he never sent in any bill. If a fee
were paid him, he would simply slip the money into a drawer of
his *secrétaire*, and treat it as pocket-money that would enable
him to gratify a fancy, or make an experiment, without need
of encroaching on his income, with the amount of which he
was well satisfied. He scorned the bad reputation which he
had acquired by his eccentric ways, and was only happy
amidst his researches into the matters in which he took such
a passionate interest.

Many were surprised that this *savant*, whose genius was
in some measure spoilt by the over-exuberance of his imagination, should have remained at Plassans, that lonely town,
where it seemed as though everything he needed must be
lacking. He explained very satisfactorily, however, all the con-
veniences that he had discovered there : first, the exceedingly
peaceful retreat in which he had been minded to cloister his
life ; then, too, the unsuspected field for continuous inquiry
into the theory of Heredity—his passionate study—which he

had found in this little town, every inhabitant of which he
knew, and where he was able to watch and follow certain
hidden phenomena over two and three successive generations.
Moreover, he was near the sea-shore, whither he repaired
almost every summer to study the birth, propagation, and
infinite swarming of life in the depths of the mighty waters.
At the hospital of Plassans, also, there was a dissecting
room, which he was almost the only one to frequent—a
large, light, peaceful room, where for more than twenty
years all the unclaimed dead bodies had pássed under his
scalpel. Yet another reason, too, why he did not betake
himself to Paris lay in the circumstance that he was extremely
modest, of a shyly timid temperament, so that he was amply
satisfied with remaining in correspondence with his old masters and new friends with reference to the very remarkable
memoirs which from time to time he sent to the Academy of
Medicine. In active ambition he was wholly wanting.

In dealing with the question of Heredity, Dr. Pascal had
not merely contented himself with dissecting dead bodies,
but had extended his observations to the living, struck as
he was by certain characteristics that constantly recurred
among his patients, and especially placing his own family
under observation, this having become his chief experimental
field, so precise and complete were the instances of hereditary
influence that here presented themselves. And from that
moment, as he went on accumulating and classifying facts
among his notes, he began attempting a general theory of
Heredity which might suffice to explain all cases.

It was a difficult problem, and for years he had been
modifying his solution of it. He had started from the two
principles of invention and imitation : heredity or reproduction on the basis of similarity ; innateness or reproduction on
the basis of diversity. He had admitted but four kinds of
heredity : first, direct heredity, the representment of the
father and mother in the physical and moral nature of the
offspring ; second, indirect heredity, the representment of
collateral relatives—uncles and aunts, and cousins of either
sex ; third, reverting heredity ('throwing back'), the repre-

sentment of progenitors after an interval of one or more generations ; and, finally, influencive heredity, the representment
of a former spouse, as, for instance, in the case of the first
husband who, though dead and gone, is yet represented in
the children borne by his wife after she has married again.
As for innateness, this applied to the new being, or, to be
more precise, to the being that appeared new, in whom the
moral and physical characteristics of the parents were blended
without any apparent sign thereof.

Then, coming back to heredity, he again classified it, in
various divisions : the predominance of the father or the
mother in the child ; the predominance of self, or the commingling of father, mother, and self ; with yet three forms of
adjection—junction, dissemination, and fusion ; the first being
the crudest, and the third the most perfect. As for innateness, this could only affect one form—combination, as in
chemistry, when two bodies uniting constitute a new body
totally different from those that form it.

All this was the result of a considerable mass of observations, not only in anthropology, but also in zoology, pom-
ology, and horticulture. Then the difficulty began with the
task of synthetising the multiple facts yielded by analysis, of
formulating the theory which should explain them all. Here
he felt that he was on the shifting sands of hypothesis which
each new discovery transforms ; and if he could not prevent
himself from offering a solution, through that need of inferring
and concluding which possesses the human brain, he was
yet broad-minded enough to leave the problem open. He had
gone by degrees from the gemmules and pan-genesis of Darwin
to the peri-genesis of Haeckel, taking Galton's stirps on the
way. Then he had had an intuition of the theory which
Weismann was to bring forward so triumphantly later on,
and had adopted the idea of an extremely delicate, complex
substance, the germ-plasm, some portion of which is always
held in reserve in each new being, to be transmitted, invariable and immutable, from generation to generation. This
seemed to explain everything ; but what an infinite mystery
there yet was—all that world of resemblances transmitted

by the reproducing substances in which the human eye
can distinguish absolutely nothing, not even with the aid of
the most powerful microscope. And thus the Doctor fully
expected that his theory would some day become antiquated,
and contented himself with it only as a transitional explanation, which sufficed for the present phase of that perpetual
inquiry into Life, the fount and source of which must, it would
seem, for ever escape our researches.

Ah! that question of Heredity; what a subject of endless
meditation it supplied him with! The unexpected, the prodigious, part of it all was that the resemblance of children to
their parents did not prove complete and mathematical. He
had at first drawn up a genealogical-tree of his own family,
in which, in accordance with strict logic, each parent, from
generation to generation, was credited with an equal share of
influence. But at almost every step the theory was upset by
living facts. Heredity, instead of being resemblance, was but
an effort towards resemblance, counteracted by circumstances
and surroundings. And thus the Doctor had come at last
to an hypothesis which he called 'the failure of the cells
theory.'

Life is but motion; and heredity being transmitted motion,
it ensued that the cells, in multiplying one from another,
pressed both against and upon each other whilst settling into
position, in accordance with the hereditary effort. If during
this struggle some of the weaker cells succumbed, considerable
disturbances arose, and organs became formed quite different
to what they should have been. Did not innateness—the
theory of the constant invention of nature, with which he did
not hold—arise from some such cause as this? If he himself
were so different to his parents, was not this due to such
accidental circumstances as he surmised? Or was it the effect
of latent heredity, in which he had for a moment believed?
Every genealogical-tree has roots, which extend back through
all humanity to the first man; no one can descend from any
one determined ancestor; one may still resemble an ancestor
yet more remote, unknown. Yet the Doctor was doubtful of
atavism; for, despite a singular case in his own family, it

seemed to him that, after two or three generations, resemblance must cease by reason of the many possible accidents, the many intervening circumstances and combinations. So a perpetual change went on, an increasing transformation, due to that transmitted strength and effort, that perturbation, which imbues matter with life, and which is, indeed, life itself in an abstract sense.

Then many questions presented themselves. Was there really a physical and intellectual progress through the ages? Did the human brain, placed in contact with science, ever on the increase, become amplified thereby? Might one hope to attain, *at last*, to a greater sum of reason and happiness? Doubtless, the Doctor only took such a passionate interest in this question of Heredity because it remained so dim, so vast and fathomless, like all the sciences which are yet immature, lisping but their first words, and over which imagination still reigns supreme. Finally, a long study that he had made of the supposed hereditary character of phthisis had lately revived within him his failing faith in the healing art, and, at the same time, imbued him with the wild but noble hope of regenerating humanity.

To sum up, the Doctor had but one belief, a belief in Life. To him Life was the one unique manifestation of the Divinity. Life was itself God, the prime mover, the soul of the universe. And Life's only instrument was heredity; heredity made the world; so that if one only had full knowledge of it, and could seize upon it and dispose of it, one might mould the world according to one's fancy. He had seen illness, suffering and death at near range, and thinking of it all, the active compassion of the physician awoke within him. Ah! if there could be no more illness, no more suffering. . . His dream led him to the thought that the advent of universal happiness, of the future realm of perfection and felicity, might be hastened by intervening and imparting health to all. When all living beings should have become healthy, strong, and intelligent, there would only remain a superior race exceedingly wise and happy. . . Then, since his inquiry into phthisis had led him to the conclusion that the disease in itself was not hereditary, but that all the children of consumptive persons offered a degenerate field in which phthisis developed with rare facility, his mind turned to the one thought of how he might fortify this soil which heredity had impoverished; how he might give it strength enough to resist the destructive parasites, or, rather, ferments, the existence of which in the human organism he had suspected long before the advent of the microbe theory. To impart strength, that was the whole problem; and the imparting of strength meant the bestowal of increased will-power, the enlargement of the brain as well as the consolidation of the other organs.

Reading, about this time, an old medical work of the fifteenth century, the Doctor was greatly struck by an account he found there of a preparation called 'signature.' To cure any ailing organ it sufficed to take the same organ from a sheep or an ox in a perfectly healthy condition, to boil it, and administer the broth it yielded to the patient. The theory was akin to that of the homœopathists—*similia similibus curantur*; and the old book asserted that its application had been particularly successful in liver complaints, in which cures without number had been effected. On this, then, the Doctor's quick imagination set to work. Why not try it? Since he wished to regenerate those whom hereditary influence had weakened, who were deficient in nervous matter, he had but to endow them with an increase of nervous matter in a normal, healthy state. The broth system, however, seemed to him puerile, and he devised the plan of pounding both the cerebrum and the cerebellum of sheep in a mortar, moistening the matter with distilled water, and afterwards decanting and filtering the *liqueur* which he thus obtained.

Mixing this *liqueur* with Malaga wine, he next began experimenting on his patients with it, but without any effective result. He was becoming discouraged when one day, whilst he was administering an injection of morphia with Pravaz's little syringe to a lady suffering from hepatic colic, an inspiration suddenly came to him. What if he were to try hypodermic injections with his *liqueur*? As soon as he got home he began experimenting on himself, trying the effect of a puncture on the loins, which he repeated on the following morning and evening. The first doses of a *gramme*[1] each had no effect, but having doubled and trebled the doses, he was delighted one morning on getting up to find that his young legs had come back to him again. In this wise he increased the dose to five *grammes*, and then found that he could breathe more freely, possessed greater lucidity of mind, and could work with far more ease than he had known for years. A sensation of comfort, a delight with life pervaded him. And then, as soon as a syringe that would hold five *grammes* of his *liqueur* had been made for him in Paris, he was surprised at the favourable results which he obtained among his patients, whom he set on their legs again in a few days, as though he had endowed them with a fresh current of vibrating, active life.

His system was still a tentative, rudimentary one; he divined the presence of certain dangerous features in it, and was especially afraid of provoking embolism, should his *liqueur* not be absolutely pure. Then, too, he suspected that the energy which his convalescents manifested came partly from the fever that his treatment imparted to them. However, he was but a pioneer; the system would be perfected later on; and had he not already wrought prodigies, making the ataxic walk, resuscitating the consumptive, and even endowing the mad with hours of lucidity? A vast hope opened out before him, in presence of this great 'find' of twentieth-century alchemy; he fancied that he had discovered the universal panacea, the elixir of life, which was to stamp out human debility—that one real cause of every evil—a genuine, scientific fountain of youth which, by supplying mankind with strength, health, and will, would create a new and improved humanity.

Upstairs in his room, a chamber with a northern aspect, somewhat darkened by the vicinity of the plane trees, and simply furnished with an iron bedstead, a mahogany *secrétaire*, and a large writing-table, on which were a mortar and

---

[1] Equivalent to 15·4325 grains troy.

a microscope, he was busy that morning completing, with scrupulous care, the preparation of a phial of his *liqueur*. On the day before he had pounded the nervous matter of a sheep in some distilled water, and he had now to decanter and filter it; in this wise eventually obtaining a small bottle-full of an opaque, opaline, iridescent fluid, which he gazed at for a long time in the light, as though it were the regenerating blood that was to save the world.

Some light taps on the door and an importunate voice outside roused him, however, from his dream : ' Why, what are you about, monsieur ; it's a quarter past twelve, don't you want any breakfast ? ' [1]

The breakfast was indeed already waiting in the large, cool dining-room downstairs. During the morning the shutters had been kept closed, and only those of one window had just now been set ajar. It was a bright, gay room, with panelled walls, the mouldings of which, painted a light blue, showed up well on a pearl-grey ground. The table, sideboard, and chairs must have formed part of the same First-Empire set of furniture that figured in the bedrooms ; and all this old mahogany of a deep red stood out vigorously against the light surroundings. A polished brass hanging-lamp, always spick-and-span, was shining like a sun in the centre of the room, whilst on the four walls bloomed four large pastels of flowers —carnations, gilliflowers, hyacinths, and roses.

The Doctor came in smiling, in fact quite radiant : ' Dear me,' he said, ' I had forgotten, I wanted to finish my work— here's some of it, quite fresh, and this time absolutely pure— the kind of stuff to work miracles with ! '

So saying he displayed his phial, which, in his enthusiasm, he had brought downstairs with him. He saw, however, that Clotilde stood there erect and silent, with a grave expression on her face. Her mortification at having vainly waited for him all the morning had again made her thoroughly hostile, and she, who, a few hours before, had yearned to throw her

---

[1] The second breakfast, of course, equivalent to our luncheon, but, the first meal being a very light one, served at an earlier hour.—*Trans.*

arms around his neck, now remained motionless, as though quite chilled, and sundered from him.

'Dear me,' he resumed without losing aught of his gaiety, 'we are still sulking then. That's anything but pretty, I must say. So you don't admire my sorcerer's *liqueur* which awakens the dead.'

He had taken his place at table, and the girl, sitting down in front of him, was at last compelled to answer. 'You know very well, master,' she said, 'that I admire everything you do. Only I want others to admire you too—and there's the death of poor old Boutin——'

'What of that?' he exclaimed, without letting her finish; 'an epileptic who succumbs through a congestive attack! However, since you are in a bad humour, don't let us talk any more about it—you would only grieve me, and then my day would be spoilt.'

The meal consisted of some boiled eggs, cutlets, and a custard. Silence fell, and Clotilde, despite her ill-humour, began eating heartily, for she invariably had a good appetite and was not so foolish as to hide it (as some women do) in an absurd spirit of coquetry. This induced the Doctor to resume, laughing : 'There's one thing that tranquillises me, and that is you have a capital digestion. Martine, give Mademoiselle some more bread.'

The old woman was serving them as usual, watching them eat with an air of quiet familiarity. And now and again, moreover, she would speak to them. 'Monsieur,' said she, when she had cut some bread, 'the butcher has brought his bill—am I to pay it?'

The Doctor raised his head and gazed at her wonderingly. 'Why do you ask me that?' he asked. 'Don't you usually the bills without consulting me?'

It was, in fact, Martine who kept the purse. The money which the Doctor had deposited with M. Grandguillot, the notary at Plassans, yielded, in round figures, an income of six thousand francs[1] a year. Every quarter some fifteen

---

[1] £240.

hundred francs were handed to the servant, who disposed of
the money to the best household advantage, buying and paying for everything, and observing the strictest economy, for
she was inclined to be avaricious, a failing on which the
others were always twitting her, in a jesting way. Clotilde,
in no wise extravagantly inclined, had never dreamt of asking
for an allowance of her own. As for the Doctor, he provided
for his experiments out of the three or four thousand francs
which he still earned every year, and which he put away in a
drawer of his *secrétaire*. This contained quite a little treasure
in gold and bank-notes, the exact amount of which he never
knew.

'No doubt I pay the bills, monsieur,' replied the servant;
'but that's when I buy the goods; and the butcher's bill is
so heavy this time, on account of all those sheep's brains
which he has been supplying you with——'

The Doctor abruptly interrupted her. 'Come, come,' said
he, 'are you going to set yourself against me too? That
would never do! You grieved me very much yesterday, and
I got angry. But there must be an end of it all. I won't
have the house turned into a purgatory. Two women against
me, and they the only ones that care for me a bit! Rather
than that I should prefer to go off at once.'

He did not speak at all angrily; in fact, he was laughing,
but by the quiver in his voice one could guess the anxiety that
filled his heart. And with his gay, good-natured air, he
added: 'If you are afraid of running short, my girl, you had
better tell the butcher to send in my bill separately. And
don't be at all alarmed, you won't be asked to dip into your
own pocket, your own coppers can sleep in peace.'

This was an allusion to Martine's little private hoard.
Earning four hundred francs a year, she had received twelve
thousand in thirty years, and had only spent what was strictly
necessary to provide herself with clothing. In this way her
savings, carefully invested, had now increased to some thirty
thousand francs, which, through some sort of caprice, a desire
to keep her nest-egg to herself, she had not been willing to

deposit with M. Grandguillot, the notary. The money was well invested in the State funds.

'What I may have put by was all honestly earned,' she replied gravely. 'But you are quite right, monsieur, and I will tell the butcher to send in a separate bill, since all those brains are for your kitchen, and not for mine.'

Clotilde, generally amused by any jests concerning Martine's avarice, smiled at this explanation, and the meal ended more gaily than it had begun. The Doctor expressed a desire to take coffee under the plane-trees, saying that he needed a breath of fresh air after remaining cooped up indoors throughout the morning. So the coffee was served on the stone table near the spring. And it was indeed very pleasant there in the shade, in the freshness diffused by the gurgling water, whilst everything around them—the plantation of pines, the threshing-floor, the entire place, in fact—was being scorched by the early afternoon sun.

Pascal had complacently brought his phial of liquefied nervous matter with him and placed it on the table. 'And so, mademoiselle,' said he, as he sat there looking at it, 'you don't believe in my resuscitating elixir, and yet you believe in miracles?'

'Master,' replied Clotilde, 'I believe that we do not know everything.'

'But it is necessary that we should end by knowing it,' he answered, waving his hand impatiently. 'You must understand, you obstinate little thing, that a single departure from the invariable laws which rule the universe has never been scientifically proved. Up to the present time the only intervention in the work of nature has come from human intelligence, and I defy you to find any real manifestation of will-power, any manifestation of intention even, apart from what may be found in Life itself——And, indeed, everything is there —there is no other will save that one force which urges everything to life—to life on a more and more developed and higher plane.'

He had risen to his feet, waving his arms; and such faith upbuoyed him, that, as the girl gazed at him, she was sur-

prised to see how young he looked under his white hair.
'Shall I tell you my belief,' said he, 'since you reproach me
for not accepting yours? I believe that the future of
humanity lies in the progress of human reason through
science. I believe that the pursuit of truth through science
is the divine ideal which man should have in view. I believe
that, apart from the treasure of scientific truths which we
possess—so slowly acquired but never more to be lost—everything else is but illusion and vanity. I believe that these
truths, ever increasing, will end by endowing mankind with
incalculable power and serenity, if not happiness. Yes, I
believe in the final triumph of Life.'

As he spoke, his sweeping gestures travelled round the vast
horizon as though he were taking all that blazing countryside, teeming with the germs of life in every form, to witness
what he said. 'And as for miracles, my child,' he added, 'the
one continual miracle is life. Open your eyes and look——'

She shook her head. 'I do open them, but I do not see
everything. It is you, master, who are obstinate, when you
refuse to admit that there is an unknown realm beyond, into
which you will never penetrate. Oh! I know that you are
too intelligent to be ignorant of it. Only, you will not
take it into account; you set the Unknown on one side,
because it would hamper you in your researches. It is all
very well for you to tell me to brush the Mysterious on one
side. I cannot. It immediately claims me, and makes me
anxious.'

He listened smiling, pleased to see her grow so animated,
and stroked the short curls of her golden hair. 'Yes, yes, I
know,' said he, 'you are like the others, you cannot live without illusions and lies. Well, no matter, we will understand
one another despite it all. Keep in good health, that is the
first half of wisdom and happiness.' Then, changing the conversation, he added: 'At all events you must come and help
me on my round of miracles. To-day is Thursday, you know,
my visiting day. When the heat has subsided a little we will
go out together.'

She at first refused, so that he might not think her always

ready to give way to him ; but seeing how distressed he was
she ended by consenting. She did as a rule accompany him
on his visits.

For some time longer they remained together under the
plane-trees, but at last the Doctor betook himself upstairs to
dress, and when he came down again, buttoned up in a frock
coat and with a broad-brimmed top hat on his head, he talked
of having Bonhomme harnessed to the trap. Bonhomme was
the horse with whom for five-and-twenty years he had gone
his rounds through the streets and outskirts of Plassans. But
the poor animal was now becoming blind ; and out of gratitude for his past services and affection for his person, he was
in these later days seldom disturbed. That evening, on going
together to the stable, they found him quite sleepy, with
dreamy eyes and legs woefully stiffened by rheumatism. So
they contented themselves with kissing him heartily on either
side of his nostrils, and bade him rest on a truss of straw
which the servant brought. And then they made up their
minds to go off on foot.

Retaining her red-spotted, white linen dress, Clotilde
simply placed on her head a large straw hat decked with a
spray of lilac ; and, shaded by the broad brim, she looked
remarkably charming, with her large eyes and her face all
milk and roses. When she went abroad in this wise, leaning
on Pascal's arm—she herself slight, slender, and so youthful
in appearance, and he radiant, with his face illumined, as it
were, by the whiteness of his beard, and yet so vigorous that
if need were he could lift her over the puddles—folks smiled
at them as they passed by, and turned round to gaze after
them, so good and so handsome did they look. That afternoon, as they were turning out of the Chemin des Fenouillères, to enter Plassans, a group of gossiping women stopped
short in their chatter to watch them. The Doctor looked like
one of those old kings whom one sees in pictures, a venerable,
mighty, yet gentle king, who never ages any more, and whose
hand rests for support on the shoulder of a girl as lovely as
sunshine, whose dazzling, submissive youth is the prop of his
old age.

They were crossing the Cours Sauvaire to reach the Rue de la Banne, when a tall, dark young fellow, some thirty years of age, accosted them. ' You have forgotten me, master,' he said, ' I am still waiting for that note on consumption which you promised me.'

The speaker was Dr. Ramond, who for a couple of years past had taken up his abode at Plassans, and had already secured a very fine practice there. Extremely handsome, and in the smiling prime of his virility, he was an especial favourite with women. Fortunately, too, he was possessed of much intelligence and good sense.

' What, is it you, Ramond ; how are you ? ' said Pascal. ' You are mistaken, my dear friend, I've not forgotten you. It's this little girl here who, as yet, has done nothing with the note, though I gave it her to copy out yesterday.'

The two young people had shaken hands with an air of cordial intimacy.

' Good afternoon, Mademoiselle Clotilde.'

' Good afternoon, Monsieur Ramond.'

During an attack of fever—a slight attack, fortunately— from which the girl had suffered the previous year, Dr. Pascal had become so distracted as to doubt his own powers and acumen ; and he had then insisted on having the assistance of his young *confrère*. In this way a kind of intimacy, of com- radeship, as it were, had sprung up between the three of them.

' I can promise that you shall have your note to-morrow morning,' resumed Clotilde, laughing.

Ramond, however, accompanied them on their way for a few minutes, until, indeed, they had reached the end of the Rue de la Banne, at the entry of the old town whither they were bound. And by the manner in which he leant forward to smile at Clotilde one could divine a discreet affection, a slow- gathering love, which was patiently biding its time till it were meet to seek the most reasonable of all solutions. Whilst smiling at the girl, however, he also listened deferentially to Dr. Pascal, whose researches he greatly admired.

' Just now, my dear friend,' said Pascal, ' I'm on my way to Guiraude's—that woman, you know, whose husband, a tanner, died cf consumption five years ago. The widow was left with two children—a girl, Sophie, who will soon be sixteen, and whom, four years before the father's death, I was fortunate enough to be able to send into the country near by, where she lives with one of her aunts. The mother, however, in her obstinate affection, and despite the frightful results with which I threatened her, insisted on keeping her other child, a son named Valentin, who is now just one-and-twenty. Well, by what has happened you will see that I am right in contending that phthisis is not hereditary, but that consumptive parents simply transmit a degenerate soil, in which the disease develops at the slightest contagion. At present Valentin, through having lived in daily contact with the father, has become consumptive, whilst Sophie, after growing up in the open air, enjoys wonderful good health.'

He was quite triumphant, and added laughing : ' Still, that is not to say that I sha'n't save Valentin, for he is visibly improving, even putting on flesh, since I have been puncturing him. Ah ! Ramond, you yourself will come to my system at last.'

The young doctor shook hands with them both. ' Oh ! I don't say the contrary,' he replied. ' You know very well that I am on your side.'

Then they parted, and Pascal and Clotilde, left to themselves, hastened their steps, and turned into the Rue Canquoin, one of the narrowest and blackest streets of the old town. In the torrid sunshine which illumined all around, there here prevailed a livid light, a damp coolness like that of a cellar. The woman Guiraude lived with her son Valentin, on a ground floor. It was she who came to open the door. Slight of build, exhausted, worn out, indeed, by a slow decomposition of the blood, she spent her time from morning till night in breaking almond shells with a mutton-bone, on a big paving-stone, which she held tightly between her knees. This labour was their only resource, the son having had to give up work entirely. Nevertheless, the woman smiled that afternoon on seeing the Doctor, for Valentin had just eaten a cutlet with appetite—a thing which had not happened to him for several months past. Of stunted growth, with sparse hair and beard, and projecting cheek-bones which bloomed like roses on either side of his waxy face, the young fellow had promptly risen by way of showing that he felt more active. And Clotilde was quite moved by the reception that Pascal met with, as though he were some saviour, some long-expected Messiah. These poor folks pressed his hands, would have kissed his very feet, and gazed at him with grateful, glittering eyes. So he could do everything; he was a personification of Providence, since he could resuscitate the dying! He himself burst into an encouraging laugh on noticing the patient's promising condition. The young fellow was not cured by any means; all this was possibly a mere fillip; indeed, when the Doctor examined him he could only detect that he was excited and feverish. Still, was it not already something to gain time? Then, whilst Clotilde, turning her back, went and took her stand at the window, he again punctured the young man; and as they went off she saw that he had left a twenty-franc piece lying on the table. It often happened, indeed, that he paid his patients instead of being paid by them.

They made three other calls in the old town, and then went off to the new town to see a lady there. When they found themselves in the street again: 'Do you know,' said he, 'if you were a plucky girl, we might walk as far as La Séguiranne to see Sophie at her aunt's, before calling at Lafouasse's. It would please me if you would come.'

The distance being little more than a couple of miles, the promenade promised to be a delightful one in such charming weather. So Clotilde gaily accepted the proposal, no longer sulking, but pressing close to Pascal, happy at being on his arm. It was five o'clock, and the oblique sunlight was transforming the whole stretch of country into a vast golden lake. As soon as they had emerged from Plassans, however, they had to cross a portion of the barren, parched plain on the right of the Viorne. The recently excavated canal, whose irrigating stream was to transform the thirsty district, did not as yet water this part of the plain, and the red and yellow ochreous fields stretched far away under the oppressive sun, planted merely with stunted almond and dwarf olive trees, which were continually being pruned and cut down, and whose branches were turned and twisted in positions expressive of suffering and revolt. Afar off, on the bare, stripped hills, there were only the light dots of the white-walled *bastides*,[1] each flanked by the usual dark, bar-like cypresses. The vast expanse, destitute of greenery, possessed, however, with the broad folds and hard, clearly defined tints of its desolate fields, some fine classic outlines of a severe grandeur. And the road was covered with a layer of dust, eight inches deep, a snow-like dust which the faintest breath of air sufficed to carry up in flying smoke-clouds, and which powdered the fig-trees and brambles on either side of the way as though with flour.

Clotilde, as amused as a child at hearing all this dust crunch under her little feet, wished to shelter Pascal with her parasol. ' The sun comes in your eyes,' she said ; ' you should walk on my left hand.'

He ended, however, by taking the parasol from her in order to carry it himself. ' It's you who don't hold it properly,' he asserted ; ' and, besides, it tires you. However, we haven't much farther to go.'

An ait of foliage, quite a large clump of trees, could already be seen at a short distance across the scorched plain. This was La Séguiranne, the place where Sophie had grown up in the charge of her aunt Dieudonné, the *méger's*[2] wife. Wherever there was the smallest spring, the smallest streamlet, this blazing land burst forth into powerful vegetation, and then a dense shade prevailed, and the paths were deep and delightfully cool. Plane-trees, horse-chestnuts, and elms grew vigorously. The Doctor and Clotilde for their part turned into an avenue of evergreen-oaks which had thriven beautifully.

They were drawing nigh to the farm, when a girl who was haymaking in a meadow threw down her fork and ran up to

---

[1] The name given to small country-houses in Provence.—*Trans.*

[2] *Méger* is the Provençal name for a farmer who shares the expenses and profits of his farm with the owner of the land. Men of this class, now a very small one, are called *métayers* in other parts of France.— *Trans.*

them. This was Sophie, who had recognised the Doctor and the demoiselle, as she was wont to call Clotilde. She was most attached to them, and approached gazing at them with confusion, unable to give utterance to all the affectionate feelings which were overflowing from her heart. She resembled her brother Valentin, for, like him, she was short of stature, with the same prominent cheek-bones and the same light hair ; but country life, far from the contagion of the paternal home, had put flesh upon her, set her erect on sturdy legs, filled out her cheeks, and dowered her with abundant hair. And she also had very beautiful eyes, which gleamed with health and gratitude. Her aunt Dieudonné, who had been haymaking with her, now came forward in her turn, calling out and jesting in the somewhat rough Provençal style : 'Oh ! we don't want you here, Monsieur Pascal ! We've got nobody ill.'

The Doctor, who had simply come thither that he might feast his eyes on this fine picture of healthfulness, replied in the same fashion : ' I hope not, indeed. All the same, here's a lassie who owes a pretty penny to you and me.'

' That's really the truth. And she knows it, too, Monsieur Pascal. She is always saying, that but for you she would now be in the same state as her poor brother Valentin.'

' Oh ! we'll save him too. He is better, is Valentin. I have just seen him.'

Sophie caught hold of the Doctor's hands, and big tears came into her eyes. ' O Monsieur Pascal ! ' was all that she could stammer.

How deeply he was loved ! Clotilde felt that her own love for him was increased by all these scattered affections. They lingered there for a little while longer, chatting amid the healthy shade of the holm-trees. Then they retraced their steps towards Plassans, having yet another call to make.

This was at a common wine-shop, which stood at the corner of two roads, and whose roof and walls were quite white with all the dust that had blown upon them. With a view to utilising the old buildings of an estate called the Paradou,[1]

[1] Described by M. Zola in *La Faute de l'Abbé Mouret.—Trans.*

dating from the last century, a steam-mill had been set up just over the way; and Lafouasse, the landlord of the wine-shop, contrived to do a little business, thanks to the millers and the peasants who came to the place with their grain. On Sundays, too, he had a few more customers—the folks of Les Artauds, a neighbouring hamlet. But ill-luck had overtaken him some three years previously, since when he had been dragging himself about complaining of 'rheumatics,' in which the Doctor had at last detected symptoms of ataxia. Still the obstinate fellow would not engage a servant, but continued dragging himself here and there, holding on to the furniture, and somehow contriving to serve his customers, despite the state he was in. Less than a dozen injections of the Doctor's *liqueur*, however, had lately set him on his legs again, and he was already proclaiming his cure far and wide.

As Pascal and Clotilde approached they saw him standing at his door, tall and sturdy, and with a blazing face under a thick crop of flaring red hair. 'I was expecting you, Monsieur Pascal,' he said; 'do you know, I was able to bottle two casks of wine yesterday without tiring myself.'

Clotilde remained outside, seated on a stone bench, whilst Pascal entered the shop in order to puncture Lafouasse. They could be heard talking, and the landlord, very susceptible to pain, despite his big muscles, complained that the puncture hurt him, though after all, said he, one might very well put up with a little suffering if it was to bring one good health. Then he all at once pretended to get angry, and did not rest till he had prevailed on the Doctor to accept a glass of something. The demoiselle, too, he added, would certainly not do him such an affront as to refuse a little currant syrup. And so saying, he brought a table outside, and it became absolutely necessary to chink glasses with him.

'To your health, Monsieur Pascal, and to all the poor devils whom you bring back to health and appetite!'

With a smile on her face, Clotilde thought of all the tittle-tattle which had reached her through Martine, of poor old Boutin, whom the Doctor was accused of having killed. But it now appeared that he did not kill all his patients, and that this preparation of his accomplished real miracles. In the glowing love which mastered her heart she recovered all her faith in her master, and when they started off again she had once more become wholly his; he might take her, carry her wheresoever he would, dispose of her as he pleased.

A few minutes previously, however, whilst seated on the stone bench, looking at the mill, she had bethought herself of a story she had vaguely heard. Had not those buildings yonder, once as black as coal, now white with flour, been the scene of a strange drama of passion? The tale gradually came back to her mind—the particulars which Martine had related to her, the allusions which the Doctor himself had made to the affair—a tragic, amorous adventure it had been—shared by her cousin, the Abbé Serge Mouret, when priest of the hamlet of Les Artauds, with a wild, passionate, lovely girl, living at the Paradou.

They were again following the road when Clotilde all at once stopped short, and pointing to the vast mournful expanse of stubble, seedplots, and land still lying waste, inquired: 'Was there not once a large garden over yonder, master—did you not tell me some story of it?'

Amid all the joy that this happy day had brought him the Doctor experienced a quiver of emotion. With a smile of very mournful tenderness he answered: 'Yes, yes, the Paradou, an immense garden, groves, meadows, orchards, parterres, fountains, springs, streamlets that ran into the Viorne—a garden which had been abandoned for a century, the garden of the Sleeping Beauty, where nature had become sovereign once more. And you see they have cleared it of all its trees, rooted up and levelled everything, so as to cut it up into lots and sell it by auction. The very springs have dried up; and now, over yonder, there is only that poisonous marsh. Ah! I feel sore at heart every time I pass by here!'

She ventured to question him further. 'Was it not in the Paradou that my cousin Serge and your great friend Albine loved one another?'

But he had already forgotten that she was beside him, and

with his eyes wandering away, peering dreamily into the past, he continued : ' Albine, ah me ! I see her still, in the blazing sunlight in the garden, looking like some large, strong-scented bouquet, with her head thrown back, her bosom expanding with mirth, so happy amid her flowers, the wild flowers garlanding her fair hair, decking her neck, her corsage, her bare, gilded, slender arms—— And when she suffocated herself among her flowers—ah ! I see her still, lying there dead, quite white, with joined hands, sleeping with a smile upon her couch of hyacinths and tuberoses—a victim of love ! Ah ! how fondly Albine and Serge loved one another in that great garden, fraught with temptation, in the midst of nature, love's accomplice ! What a stream of Life was there, carrying all false trammels away—what a triumph of Life, indeed ! '

Profoundly disturbed by these ardent mutterings, Clotilde gazed steadily at him. She had never dared to speak to him of another rumoured story, the discreet, unique love that he had borne a lady now dead. It was said he had attended her without ever daring to kiss even the tips of her fingers. Though nigh to his sixtieth year, study and timidity had kept him away from women. Yet it could be divined that he was reserved for love, and possessed a heart still fresh and overflowing with tenderness, beneath his long white hair.

' And she who is dead,' said Clotilde, ' she who is mourned——' But she abruptly checked herself, her voice trembling, her cheeks flushing, though she knew not why— ' Did not Serge love her, then, since he let her die ? ' she resumed.

Pascal seemed to awaken, quivering at finding her beside him, so young, with such lovely, clear, burning eyes, shining forth in the shadow cast by the broad brim of her hat. Something had passed, the same quiver had sped through both of them. They did not take one another's arm again, but walked on side by side.

' Ah, my dear,' said he, ' things would be too beautiful if men did not mar them. Albine is dead, and now Serge is parish priest at Saint-Eutrope, where he lives with his sister

Désirée, a good creature, who's lucky enough to be half an idiot. He is a holy man. I have never said the contrary——'
And then, still with his gay smile, he went on speaking plainly of existence, talking of the blackness and hatefulness of certain portions of humanity. He himself loved life, and showed how incessant and calmly valiant was the effort it made, despite all the evil and anguish that it might contain. Life, indeed, might appear frightful, yet it must assuredly be something good and great, since all beings displayed such a tenacious determination to live, with the object, doubtless, of exercising that same determination, and of furthering the great secret labour which it accomplished. For his part, like the perspicacious man of science he was, he did not believe in an idyllic humanity living amid a nature of milk and honey. On the contrary, he was fully aware of all the ills that flesh is heir to, of all the stains and blemishes disfiguring humanity; for during thirty years he had busied himself in bringing them to light, investigating and cataloguing them. Yet his passion for life, his admiration for the forces of life sufficed to fill him with a perpetual delight, whence sprang, it would seem, his affection for his fellow-creatures, his fraternal, compassionate tenderness—all the sympathy, in fact, that could be divined beneath his professional roughness and the affected impersonality of his studies.

'*Bah!*' he concluded, as he turned to take a last look at the far-stretching, mournful fields. 'The Paradou no longer exists; they pillaged it, polluted it, destroyed it; but, no matter, vines will be planted there, corn will grow there, new crops will spring from the soil; and even as they loved of yore, so will men and women go on loving in the far-away days of vintage and of harvest. Life is eternal; its one task is to begin again and again and again, and to grow and spread as it does so.'

He had once more taken Clotilde's arm, and thus, walking close together in mutual affection, they betook themselves homeward through the sunset, now slowly fading away in the heavens, which looked like some vast calm lake of pink and violet water. And seeing them again pass by together—the venerable, mighty yet gentle king leaning on the shoulder of a charming, submissive maiden whose youth served as the prop of his old age—the women of the Faubourg, seated at their doors, gazed after them with a tender smile.

Martine was on the watch for them at La Souleiade, and waved her arm to them from afar off. What! were they not going to have any dinner that day? Then, when they had drawn near to her, she said: 'Well, you will have to wait a quarter of an hour—I didn't dare to begin cooking the leg of mutton till rather late.'

They waited outside in the waning light which charmed them. The pine grove, where all had grown dark, was exhaling a balsamic, resinous odour, and a quiver arose from the heated threshing-floor, where the last pinky reflection of the sunset was expiring. A sigh of relief and contentment seemed to ascend from all the restful surroundings, from the lank almond and twisted olive trees, rising up under the vast paling heavens so perfectly serene. And behind the house, the clump of platanes was now but a black impenetrable patch of darkness, where one heard only the spring, ever chanting the same crystalline refrain.

'Why, Monsieur Bellombre has already dined,' said the Doctor at last. 'There he is, taking an airing.' So speaking, he pointed to a tall old man of seventy, with a long, deeply-furrowed face and large fixed eyes, who, correctly attired in a frock-coat and tight-fitting stock, could be seen resting on a bench in the grounds of an adjacent house.

'He is a sage,' murmured Clotilde. 'He is happy.'

'He?' protested Pascal. 'I sincerely hope he is not.'

The Doctor hated nobody, and of all men the only one who had the power of exasperating him was this same Monsieur Bellombre, a superannuated seventh-class professor, living in a little house close by, with no other companion than a deaf and dumb gardener, older than himself. 'A fellow who has always been afraid of life,' added Pascal; 'afraid of life, you hear? Yes, an egotist, a tyrant, and a miser! If he has banished woman from his existence, it has only been because he was afraid of having to keep her in shoe-leather. And the only children he has ever known have been the children of others—who have made him suffer. Thence his hatred of children, whom he considers only fit for punishment. Ah! the fear of life, the fear of its burdens and its duties, its worries and its catastrophes—that fear of life which, through dread of its griefs, makes a man even refuse its joys—such cowardice, do you know, my dear, altogether exasperates me; I cannot forgive it! One must live, live wholly, entirely, live life out from beginning to end, and I would rather have suffering, suffering alone, than this renouncement, this death of all that is alive and human within us.'

M. Bellombre had meantime risen to his feet, and was slowly, quietly pacing along one of the paths in his garden. Then Clotilde, who had been silently contemplating him, at last replied: 'Yet there is the joy of renouncing. Did not the great happiness of the saints lie in renunciation, in a refusal to live, a resolve to keep themselves in reserve for the Mystery?'

'If they did not live,' cried Pascal, 'they cannot have been saints!'

He felt, however, that she was rebelling, that she was again on the point of escaping him. Deep hidden in the anxiety for the realms beyond, there lurks fear and hatred of life. And so he suddenly indulged in his wonted good-natured laugh, so affectionate and conciliatory. 'No, no, that is quite enough for to-day,' he exclaimed; 'don't let us quarrel again, but rather love one another as much as we can. And besides, there's Martine calling us. Let us go in to dinner.'

CHAPTER III

SOME FAMILY SKELETONS

DURING the ensuing month life became more and more uncomfortable in the Doctor's household, and that which above all else caused Clotilde acute suffering was to see that Pascal now kept his drawers carefully locked. He no longer had the same tranquil confidence in her as of yore, and she was so deeply hurt by this, that had she only found the old press open she would have flung the collections of documents it contained into the fire, as her grandmother Félicité urged her to do. Moreover, the fallings-out began again, and two days often went by without a word being exchanged between herself and the Doctor.

One morning, during one of these tiffs, which had begun a couple of days previously, Martine, whilst serving breakfast, exclaimed: ' While I was crossing the Place de la Sous-Préfecture just now, I saw a gentleman, whom I thought I recognised, going in to Madame Félicité's. I shouldn't be at all surprised, mademoiselle, if it were your brother.'

These tidings at once prompted Pascal and Clotilde to speak to one another. ' Your brother ! ' said the Doctor. ' Was grandmother expecting him ? '

' No, I hardly think so. There has been a talk of his coming for six months and more. But I know that grandmother wrote to him again a week ago.'

Thereupon they began to question Martine.

' Well, monsieur,' she replied, ' I can't say for certain, for Monsieur Maxime has perhaps changed a good deal since I saw him four years ago, when he stopped here for a few hours while on his way to Italy. Still I thought I recognised the gentleman, though I only saw his back.'

The conversation went on, Clotilde being, to all appearance, well pleased that the heavy silence should have been broken by this incident. 'Well,' remarked Pascal at last, 'if it is Maxime, he will certainly come to see us.'

The person whom Martine had seen was indeed Clotilde's brother, who, after the lapse of many months, had at last complied with the pressing entreaties of old Madame Rougon. She desired his presence at Plassans that she might take steps to rid the family of a sore for which he was responsible. It was a very old story, and matters were now growing worse and worse every day.

Fifteen years previously Maxime, then a lad of seventeen, had had a son by a servant-girl of his acquaintance. Saccard, his father, had simply laughed at the affair, and if his stepmother Renée had displayed any vexation, it was solely on account of what she deemed his unworthy choice. The servant, a gentle, docile, fair-headed girl of precisely the same age as the young man, was named Justine Mégot. She came from a village near Plassans, and the upshot of the affair was that she was sent home again provided with an annuity of twelve hundred francs, which was to enable her to bring up her boy, called Charles. Three years later, she had married a saddler of the Faubourg, one Anselme Thomas, a steady, hardworking, sensible fellow, whom her annuity tempted. It must be said, however, that her conduct had meantime become exemplary ; and moreover she had grown quite plump, and was cured of a nasty cough which had formerly prompted a suspicion of hereditary weakness, due to alcoholism among her progenitors. Two children, born to her since her marriage, a boy of ten and a girl of seven, both of them fat and rosy, enjoyed the finest health, and she would have been the happiest woman alive but for the worries occasioned by Charles. In spite of the annuity, Anselme Thomas execrated this other man's son, and treated him very harshly, much to the grief of the lad's mother, though she concealed her feelings like the silent, submissive wife she was. Under these circumstances, albeit very fond of the boy, she would willingly have handed him over to his father's family.

At fifteen years of age, Charles looked scarcely twelve, and possessed merely the lisping intelligence of a child of five. Of an extraordinary resemblance to his great-great-grand-mother, the inmate of the Asylum of Les Tulettes, he was endowed with a slender, delicate gracefulness like one of those little white-blooded kings, the last scions of their race; and like them he was crowned with long fair hair, as fine and as soft as silk. His big clear eyes were empty, expressionless, and the shadow of death lurked behind his alarming beauty. Destitute of either brains or heart, he had developed into a vicious puppy. His great-grandmother Félicité, won over by his handsome looks, in which she pretended to recognise her blood, had at first sent him to college at her own expense, but six months later his conduct had led to his being expelled. Three times had Félicité obstinately sent him to other schools, but on each occasion with the same scandalous result. Then as he would not, in fact could not, learn anything, it had become necessary that the family should keep him in idleness, and in this wise he had gone from one to another in turn. Dr. Pascal, compassionating his condition, and thinking he might be able to cure him, had kept him during nearly a year, when finding that cure was impossible, he had got rid of him —in some measure on Clotilde's account, for he did not desire that she should remain any longer in contact with the lad. And now, when Charles was not at his mother's—where indeed he lived but little—he was to be found either at Félicité's, or at some other relative's, always coquettishly dressed, and abundantly provided with playthings—living, in fact, like some little effeminate Dauphin of an ancient, dethroned race.

Nevertheless, the presence of this urchin, with the same long fair hair as some scion of royalty, caused old Madame Rougon intense suffering, and in order that he might no longer furnish a subject for gossip among the scandal-mongers of Plassans, she had devised the plan of prevailing on Maxime to take charge of him and keep him in Paris. In this way another blot on the family history would be wiped

out. Maxime, however, had long turned a deaf ear to her
entreaties, through the continual dread he experienced of
introducing any element of worry into his existence. A
wealthy man through the death of his wife, he had returned
to Paris after the war, again taking up his abode in his mansion in the Avenue du Bois de Boulogne, where he now lived
in a staid, sober way, tormented as he was by the hereditary
influences which were to bring him to an early grave, and
having contracted, through precocious debauchery, a salutary
dread of a so-called life of pleasure. He, at present, fled all
emotions and responsibilities, in order that he might prolong
his life. Acute pains in his legs—rheumatism so he thought
—had been worrying him for some time past, and he already
pictured himself infirm, rooted to his arm-chair. Then, too,
his father's sudden return to France, the fresh activity which
Saccard was displaying, put the finishing-touch to his terror.
He knew that man, whose *rôle* in life was to devour millions,
and trembled at finding him at his side again, so eager and
cordial, with the same old friendly sneer on his face. Would
not he, Maxime, be torn to pieces and devoured, if he some
day found himself at that man's mercy, bedridden by the
pains which were invading his limbs? And then such intense
dread at the idea of solitude took possession of him, that he
at last fell in with the suggestion of seeing his son again. If
the lad should appear gentle, intelligent, and healthy, why
should he not take charge of him? In that way he would
have a companion, a heir who would protect him from his
father's designs. Little by little, this egotist pictured himself
loved, petted and defended ; and yet he would perhaps not
have ventured on so long a journey if his medical man had
not ordered him to Saint-Gervais to take the waters there.
Only a few leagues then separated him from Plassans, and
so, that morning, he had unexpectedly presented himself at
Madame Félicité's, determined to take the train back that
same evening, after he had questioned the old lady and seen
the child.

Pascal and Clotilde were still sitting near the spring, under
the plane-trees, where they had taken coffee, when at about

two o'clock in the afternoon Madame Félicité made her appearance with Maxime. 'I have such a surprise for you, my dear,' said she; 'I've brought your brother to see you.'

The girl had risen to her feet wonder-struck at the sight of that yellow-skinned, emaciated stranger, whom she could scarcely recognise. Since their separation in 1854 she had seen him twice, once in Paris and once at Plassans. She had retained, however, a distinct recollection of him as he had then appeared—young, active, and elegant. And now his cheeks were hollow and his hair was falling and becoming grey. Still, she was at last able to identify his delicate, handsome features, which, even in his precocious decrepitude, retained an unnatural feminine gracefulness.

'How well you are looking!' he said, as he kissed his sister.

'It is because I live in the air and the sunlight,' she replied; 'I am so glad to see you.'

With a keen professional glance, Pascal had at once taken stock of his nephew. He kissed him in his turn, and welcomed him, adding: 'Your sister is right; one can only obtain good health by living in the air and the sunlight, like the trees.'

Félicité meantime had gone hastily into the house. 'Isn't Charles here, then?' she exclaimed, as she came out again.

'No,' replied Clotilde; 'we saw him yesterday. Uncle Macquart came to fetch him, and he has gone to spend a few days at Les Tulettes.'

Félicité was in despair. She had hastened to Pascal's so fast simply because she had felt certain that she would find the lad there. What could she do now? The Doctor, in his quiet way, suggested that they should write to Macquart, who would bring the boy over on the following morning. Then, on hearing that Maxime was determined to leave that same evening by the nine o'clock train, another plan occurred to him. He would send to the livery stables for a landau, and they would all four of them go to see Charles at Uncle Macquart's. Besides, it would be a very pleasant outing. The distance from Plassans was not more than three leagues; it would not take them more than an hour to go and an hour to return, and they would be able to stay at Les Tulettes for a couple of hours, and be back by seven o'clock, when Martine would have some dinner ready. Maxime would thus have ample time to dine and reach the station before his train was due.

Félicité, however, was quite upset by this plan, visibly anxious at the thought of what a visit to Macquart might entail. 'But I can't go there in such weather as this,' said she; 'we shall be having a thunderstorm. It would be far better to send someone to bring Charles back to us.'

Pascal shook his head. It was not always easy to do as one wished with Charles. He was an unreasoning child, and when some fancy or other took possession of him he would gallop off like an untamed colt. Opposed in this manner, old Madame Rougon, furious that she had not been able to make any preparations, was at last compelled to give way and trust to what chance might bring about. 'Well, all right, since you wish it we will go,' said she, 'but I certainly don't like the turn that things are taking.'

Martine thereupon ran off to fetch the landau, and three o'clock had not struck when the horses turned into the road to Nice, trotting down the slope which descends to the bridge over the Viorne. They then turned to the left, and for a mile and a half skirted the wooded banks of the river. The road afterwards passed through the gorges of La Seille, a narrow *défilé* between giant walls of rocks, which the blazing sun had baked and gilded. Pines had sprung up in the clefts; plumes of trees, looking from below no larger than tufts of herbage, fringed the crests, and waved above the chasm. This was a perfect chaos; it looked like some spot rent by the bolts of heaven, some passage of the infernal regions with its many sudden turns and twists, its streams of blood-red soil pouring from each gash in its sides, its desolation and its solitude disturbed only by the eagles winging their flight on high.

With her brain actively at work, and to all appearances overcome by her reflections, Félicité did not open her lips during the entire journey. The heat moreover, was most oppressive, the sun was blazing fiercely behind a veil of livid clouds. Pascal was almost the only one to talk, giving vent to his passionate affection for that wild, ardent scenery, an affection with which he sought to imbue his nephew; but vainly did he talk on, in an admiring strain, pointing out the obstinate tenacity with which the olives, fig-trees and brambles grew amid all those rocks, calling attention, too, to the life of the rocks themselves, to the life of all that colossal, mighty carcase of the world whence a quiver as of breathing seemed to rise. Maxime still remained cold, experiencing a secret anguish at the sight of all those blocks of stone, so wildly majestic, and the very hugeness of which overwhelmed him. And accordingly he preferred to turn his eyes on his sister, who sat in front of him. She was gradually charming him, so healthy and happy did she look, with her pretty round head and straight brow betokening a well-balanced mind. Every now and again their eyes met, and her features would then relax into a tender smile, which penetrated to his heart like balm.

The gorge, however, at last became less wild in aspect, the walls of rocks fell lower and lower, and then on either side there were peaceful hillocks with gentle slopes overgrown with thyme and lavender. 'Twas still the wilderness, however, a bare, greeny, violescent expanse across which the slightest breeze wafted a pungent perfume. Then, all at once, after a last turn in the road, they dipped down into the valley of Les Tulettes, whose running waters rendered it fresh and cool. At the bottom lay the meadows, parted by lofty trees. The village was perched on the hillside, among the olives, and Macquart's *bastide* stood at some little distance from the others on the left, facing the south. To reach it the landau had to turn into the road leading to the Lunatic Asylum, whose white walls could be seen ahead.

Félicité's silence had become yet more gloomy, for she did not like to show Uncle Macquart to anyone. This was another relative whom the family would be well rid of, when he should be taken from them. It would have been better for the glory of all of them if he had long since been sleeping underground. But he was tenacious, and carried the burden of his three-and-eighty years like some dram-saturated drunkard, whom alcohol preserves. He had left terrible souvenirs behind him at Plassans, where he had led the life of an idler and a bandit, and the old folks would relate in whispers the abominable story of blood and death that linked him to the Rougons — the treacherous plot which they had devised together in the troublous times of December, 1851, the ambush into which he—Macquart—had led his comrades, to leave them lying, riddled with bullets, on the blood-stained paving-stones. Later on, when he had returned to France, in lieu of the comfortable appointment which he had exacted a promise of, he had preferred that little domain at Les Tulettes, which Félicité had purchased for him. And since then he had been living there in comfortable style, with no remaining ambition save that of adding to his land, with which design he had watched his opportunities for a good stroke, and had at last found a means of acquiring some long-coveted field or other by rendering himself useful to his sister-in-law, at the time when she was wresting Plassans from the Legitimist party. This again was a frightful story, which men spoke of with bated breath—a madman stealthily let out of an asylum, wandering about by night intent on vengeance, and at last swooping down, setting fire to his own house, and burning four people alive. Fortunately, however, all this had happened long ago, and Macquart, having settled down, was no longer the alarming bandit who had made the whole family tremble. Nowadays he comported himself like other people, seeking to obtain his ends solely by diplomatic cunning, and of his old ways he had only retained his jeering laugh, which always seemed to imply that he cared not a rap for anybody.

'Uncle Macquart is at home,' exclaimed Pascal, as they drew near to the *bastide*.

This was one of those single-storied Provençal buildings roofed with faded tiles and with walls coloured a bright yellow. In front of it was a narrow terrace shaded by ancient mulberry-trees, stretching out thick, twisted branches which had been bent so as to form a kind of arbour. Here it was that Uncle

Macquart smoked his pipe in the summer. On hearing the carriage approach he had stepped to the edge of the terrace, and, drawing his lofty figure erect, stood there, respectably clad in a blue cloth suit, whilst on his head was the everlasting fur cap which he wore from one end of the year to the other. As soon as he recognised his visitors he began to jeer, and called to them : ' Here's a fine company and no mistake ! This is really very kind of you ; you must take some refreshment.'

However, Maxime's presence perplexed him. Who could that stranger be ? Why had he come there ? He was told his name, and at once checked the explanations which were added by way of guiding him through the labyrinth of relationship : ' Charlie's father, I know, I know. My nephew Saccard's son, of course ! The one who made such a fine marriage, and whose wife is dead.'

So saying, he scrutinised Maxime, and appeared extremely pleased to find that he was already wrinkled at two-and-thirty, and that his hair and beard were plentifully streaked with silver. ' Ah well,' he added, ' we are all of us getting old. For my own part, I haven't much ground for complaint. I'm hearty yet.'

Erect on his legs he gazed at them triumphantly, with his face flaring, looking in fact as if it had been boiled, and as brightly red as a brazier. For a long time past ordinary brandy had seemed pure water to him, and only *trois-six*[1] would now tickle his hardened throat. And such quantities of it did he imbibe that he was fairly saturated with it, his flesh absorbing it like a sponge. Alcohol oozed out through the very pores of his skin, and whenever he opened his lips to speak his mouth exhaled an alcoholic vapour.

' Yes, certainly, you are a sturdy fellow, uncle,' said Pascal, marvelling at the old man's appearance. ' Yet you have done nothing yourself to make it so. You can well afford to laugh

[1] The common alcohol of commerce, marking 33 deg. on Cartier's scale, and containing therefore 84·4 vol. per cent. of absolute alcohol. As the percentage of alcohol by volume in proof spirit, as we know it, is only 57·06, the reader will be able to form some idea of what fiery tipple it was that Uncle Macquart was in the habit of swallowing.—*Trans.*

at us. There is only one thing I fear for you, which is that
some day, when you are lighting your pipe, you'll set yourself
alight just like a bowl of punch.'

Macquart, who felt flattered by this prediction, laughed
noisily: ' Oh! you may joke, you may joke, little one, but a
glass of cognac is worth a deal more than your horrid drugs.
And now you are all going to chink glasses with me, eh ? So
that it may really be said that your uncle is a credit to all of
you. For my part, I don't care a fig what the gossips may
say. I've corn, and olive-trees, and almond-trees, and vines,
and lands, just as much as any *bourgeois* has. In the summer
I smoke my pipe under my mulberry-trees ; in the winter I
go and smoke it over yonder, against the wall, in the sunlight.
And there can be no cause to blush for an uncle like that, can
there ? I've got some currant syrup, Clotilde, if you'd like it.
As for you, Félicité, my dear, your preference I know is for
anisette. And I've some of that, too ; in fact, I may tell you,
there is never anything wanting here.'

So saying, he indulged in sweeping gestures, as though to
embrace all the comforts he possessed, now that after living
the life of a rascal he had become a hermit in his old age.
Félicité, however, whom he had frightened by the enumera-
tion of his belongings, kept her eyes fixed on him, ready to
interrupt him at the first opportunity. 'Thank you, Macquart,' she said, ' but we won't take anything; we are in a
hurry. Where is Charles ? '

' Charles, Charles ; he's all right, we'll see to him by-and-
by. I understand matters. The papa has come to see his
boy. However, that won't prevent us from having a glass
together.'

Upon their positively declining to drink with him, he put
on an offended air, and said with his evil laugh : ' Charles is
not here. He is at the Asylum with the old woman.' Then
leading Maxime to the end of the terrace, he pointed towards
the large white buildings of the Asylum, whose inner gardens
looked like so many prison yards. 'There, nephew, you see
those three trees in front of you. Well, beyond the one on
the left there is a fountain in a yard. Look along the ground-

floor wall; the fifth window on the right hand is Aunt Dide's. And that's where the lad is. Yes, I took him there a little while ago.'

This was an arrangement tolerated by the officials. During the twenty-one years which she had spent in the Asylum the old woman had never caused her nurse the slightest worry. Very calm and very gentle, she spent her days sitting motionless in her armchair, and gazing straight before her; and as the child was pleased to be there, and she herself seemed to take an interest in him, the officials closed their eyes to this infraction of the regulations, and Charles was allowed to stay there, sometimes two or three hours at a stretch, occupied the while in cutting out picture scraps.

This fresh *contretemps*, however, had brought Félicité's ill-humour to a climax. And she almost flew into a passion when Macquart proposed that they should all five of them go to the Asylum to fetch the child. 'What an idea!' she exclaimed; 'go yourself and make haste back! We have no time to lose.'

The quiver of rage which she sought to restrain seemed to afford Uncle Macquart considerable amusement; and from that moment, divining how obnoxious he was making himself to her, he insisted on his own plan in that jeering way of his. 'Well,' said he, 'it would be an opportunity for all of us to see our dear old mother—the mother of all of us, you know. For there is no saying the contrary; we have all come from her, and it wouldn't be at all polite not to go and bid her good-day, especially as my grand-nephew here has come from such a distance, and has perhaps never seen her since he went away from us when a boy. For my part, I don't deny her—oh dear no! She is certainly mad; but it is not often that one sees a granny of her age—over a hundred years old— and, to my mind, a woman as aged as that deserves a little attention.'

A pause ensued. A little icy shiver had sped through his listeners. And it was Clotilde, hitherto silent, who, in a voice fraught with emotion, at last responded: 'You are in the right, uncle; we will all of us go there.'

Félicité herself had to consent, and they got into the landau again, Macquart taking the box-seat beside the driver. A sensation of discomfort had rendered Maxime's tired face quite pale, and during the few minutes that they spent on the road he questioned Pascal respecting Charles with an air of paternal interest, which concealed a feeling of increasing disquietude. Troubled by his mother's imperious glances, the Doctor toned down the truth. '*Mon Dieu !*' said he ; ' the child did not enjoy very good health ; in fact, it was for this reason that he was left for weeks together at his uncle's in the country ; however, he did not suffer from any definitely characterised disease.'

Pascal concealed the fact that he had at one moment dreamt of giving him brains and muscles by administering to him injections of nervous matter. In making these attempts he had on each occasion been confronted by the same complication—the slightest punctures provoked hæmorrhage, which it was necessary to arrest by compressive dressings. Degenerateness displayed itself in a laxness of the tissues, beads of blood oozed to the surface of the skin, and the lad was so liable, moreover, to sudden and abundant bleedings from the nose that they dared not leave him by himself for fear lest he should some day lose all the blood in his veins. The Doctor did not acquaint Maxime with all this ; he simply wound up by saying that, although the boy's intelligence had so far remained sluggish, he hoped that it would develop more rapidly in a sphere of livelier mental activity.

They had now reached the Asylum, and, on alighting from the box-seat, Macquart, who had been listening, exclaimed : ' He is a very gentle little fellow, very gentle indeed. And besides, he's so handsome, quite an angel ! '

Maxime, who had grown yet paler than before, and was still shivering despite the suffocating heat, did not ask any further questions, but gazed at the vast buildings of the Asylum, at the wings forming the various wards, divided one from another by gardens. There were the men's wards, the women's wards, the wards in which the harmless maniacs, quiet and peaceful, were lodged, and those where the raving

lunatics, frenzied and violent, were confined. **Extreme clean-**
liness prevailed throughout the mournful solitude, which was
traversed now and again by the clatter of the keepers' footsteps and the jingle of their keys. Old Macquart knew all
the keepers personally, and, besides, the doors were readily
opened for Dr. Pascal, who had been authorised to attend
some of the inmates. After going down a gallery they came
out into a courtyard, and here, on the ground-floor, was the
old woman's room, its walls covered with a light tinted paper,
and its furniture consisting of a bedstead, a wardrobe, a table,
an armchair, and two chairs. The nurse, who, by the regulations, should have never left her charge alone, had, all the
same, just taken herself off, and there was no one there save
the mad woman, sitting rigidly erect on her armchair at one
end of the table, and the boy, who, on a chair at the other
end, was giving all his attention to a sheet of coloured figures,
which he was cutting out, one by one.

'Go in, go in,' repeated Macquart; 'there's no danger,
she's quite nice and quiet.'

Adélaïde Fouque, the ancestress, on whom her grand-
children, all the swarming brood in fact, had bestowed the
caressing nickname of 'Aunt Dide,' did not even turn her
head at the noise they made on entering her room. Already
in her youth her mental balance had been upset by hysteric
disturbances. Of an ardent, passionately amorous temperament, she had, although shaken by repeated attacks, attained
to the great age of eighty-three, when a frightful grief, a
terrible mental shock, had rendered her insane. One-and-
twenty years had gone by since then, and the sudden lapse of
her intelligence, the abrupt weakening of her faculties had
rendered all cure impossible. And now, at the venerable age
of one hundred and four, she lived on there like one forgotten
—a harmless lunatic, with an atrophied brain, whose dementia
might remain stationary for an indefinite period without provoking death. Senility had come, however, with atrophy of
the muscles; her flesh was as though eaten away by extreme
old age; in fact, she had none left, only her skin remaining
on her bones; and such was her helplessness that it was

necessary to carry her from her bed to her armchair. Dry and yellow skeleton that she was—like some centenarian tree whose bark alone remains—she, nevertheless, sat up very erect against the back of her armchair, with nothing alive in her long thin face save her eyes, which were staring fixedly at little Charles.

Trembling slightly, Clotilde had drawn near. 'It's we who have come to see you, Aunt Dide—don't you recognise me? Your great-granddaughter who comes every now and then to kiss you?'

The madwoman did not seem to hear her, however. Her eyes did not stray from the child, who, scissors in hand, had just finished cutting out one of the personages on his sheet of figures—a purple king in a gold mantle.

'Come, mammy,' said Macquart in his turn; 'don't play the stupid. You can surely look at us. Here's a gentleman, a great-grandson of yours, who has come all the way from Paris to see you.'

At the sound of Macquart's voice Aunt Dide ended by turning her head. She slowly rested her clear, expressionless eyes on all of them in turn, and then bringing them back to Charles, she fell into the same contemplation as before. No one spoke any further.

'Since the terrible shock she had,' Pascal at last explained, in an undertone, 'she has always been like this—all intelligence, all memory seems destroyed. She more frequently remains quite silent, but occasionally stammers forth a stream of indistinct words. She laughs and weeps without rhyme or reason—she is like a thing which nothing henceforth can affect. And yet I would not undertake to say that the night in which she is plunged is absolutely complete, that no recollections whatever remain stored up in the far depths of her mind. Ah! poor old woman, how I pity her, if she has not yet attained to the final stage of mental annihilation—for if she *does* remember, what can she have been thinking of during the last one-and-twenty years?'

He waved his hand as if to sweep aside the frightful past, which he knew too well. He pictured her as she had appeared in her younger days, a tall, pale creature with wild eyes, a widow after fifteen months of married life with Rougon, that lubberly gardener whom she had insisted on taking as her husband. And then, even before her term of mourning had expired, she had thrown herself into the arms of Macquart, the smuggler, whom she had loved with the passion of a she-wolf, and had not even married. And for fifteen years, with one legitimate and two illegitimate children, she had lived as that man's mistress, leading a noisy, capricious life, disappearing for weeks at a stretch, and then returning home one mass of bruises, with her arms all black and blue. Then Macquart had died, shot dead like a dog by a gendarme; and this first shock seemed to have curdled her blood. Already at that period she had become quite lifeless, save for those eyes of hers, which, clear like spring water, shone out in her ashy face. Withdrawing from the world into the hovel which her lover had left her, she had there for forty years led the life of a nun, traversed by terrible nervous attacks. But the second shock was destined to finish her off and drive her to madness; and Pascal well remembered the atrocious scene, for he had himself witnessed it: A poor child that the old woman had taken to live with her, her grandson Silvère, a victim of the family's sanguinary struggles and hatreds, whose brains a gendarme had blown out with his pistol, during the repression of the insurrectionary movement of 1851. And his blood, like that of Macquart, had bespattered her.

However, Félicité had drawn near to Charles, who was so intensely absorbed in his picture-scraps that the presence of all these people failed to disturb him. ' My darling,' she said, ' this gentleman here is your papa. You must give him a kiss.'

Thereupon they all turned their attention to Charles. He was very prettily dressed in a black velvet jacket and breeches; and pale like a lily, with large light eyes and streaming fair hair, he really seemed to be the son of one of those kings that he was cutting out. But that which at this moment was most striking about him was his resemblance to Aunt Dide— the close resemblance which manifested itself, after the lapse of three generations, between that worn and withered cen-

tenarian visage and his own delicate childish face, about
which there was a certain indefiniteness, as though racial
wear and tear had aged, exhausted, well-nigh effaced its lineaments. Seated there face to face, the idiot child, with his
deathlike beauty, looked like the *finis* of the forgotten, neg-
lected ancestress.

Maxime stooped to imprint a kiss on the child's forehead,
and, as he did so, he felt a chill at his heart, for the lad's
strange beauty alarmed him. Besides, his discomfort had
been greatly increased by finding himself in that room, that
abode of madness, where the atmosphere reeked of human
woe, the legacy of time long past. ' How handsome you are,
my pet! Do you love me a little?' he asked.

Charles looked at him, failed to understand, and then again
turned to his pictures.

But the others stood by in consternation. Without the
slightest apparent change on her expressionless face, Aunt
Dide had begun to weep—a stream of tears was coursing
from her living eyes on to her dead cheeks! Her stare was
still intently fixed upon the child, and she went on weeping,
slowly, infinitely.

Then an extraordinary emotion took possession of Pascal.
He had caught hold of Clotilde's arm, and was pressing it
tightly, but without being able to convey his meaning to her.
The fact was it had suddenly dawned upon him that there,
before his eyes, was the whole race, both the legitimate branch
and the bastard branch that had sprung from that one trunk
when it was already impaired by neurosis. The five generations were there face to face, the Rougons and the Macquarts
—Adélaïde Fouque, at the root, then the old bandit uncle,
then himself, then Clotilde and Maxime, and finally Charles.
Félicité filled the place of her dead husband. There was no
gap, the chain of logical, implacable heredity spread out complete. And what a century it was that he thus evoked, in the
tragic depths of that madhouse, where the atmosphere reeked
of far-descending human woe, amid such a seizure, too, of
fright and awe that every one of them stood there shivering,
in spite of the oppressive heat!

'What is it, master?' whispered Clotilde, trembling.

'Nothing, nothing,' murmured the Doctor; 'I will tell you later on.'

Macquart, alone sufficiently at his ease to jeer and jest, then began to scold the old woman. That was a fine idea, and no mistake, to receive people with tears when they put themselves out of the way to pay you a visit! It certainly wasn't polite. And then, reverting to Maxime and Charles, he exclaimed: 'Well, nephew, there's your boy, you see. Isn't he a pretty little fellow, eh? Doesn't he do you credit all the same?'

Félicité, very displeased at the turn which things were taking, and with no desire now but to leave the place as soon as possible, thereupon intervened: 'Yes, he's certainly a handsome child, and by no means so backward as one thinks. See how clever he is with his fingers! And you'll see what a change there will be in him when you have got him to Paris, eh? You will sharpen his wits much more easily there than we have been able to do at Plassans.'

'No doubt, no doubt,' muttered Maxime, 'I don't say no —I will think it over.' He displayed considerable embarrassment, and added: 'I only came just to see him, you know. I can't possibly take him now, since I am going to spend a month at Saint-Gervais. But as soon as I get back to Paris, I will think it over, and write to you.' Then, pulling out his watch: 'The deuce! Why, it's half-past five. I wouldn't miss the nine o'clock train, you know, for anything in the world.'

'Yes, yes, let us get off,' said Félicité; 'there is nothing more for us to do here.'

Macquart vainly endeavoured to delay them by relating all sorts of stories about Aunt Dide. He spoke of the occasions when she chattered, and asserted that he had even found her one morning singing an old song of her youthful days. Then, as regards going back in the landau, he added that he had no need of a lift. He could very well return home on foot with the lad, since the latter was to be left with him.

'Kiss your papa, my boy,' he said in conclusion, 'We know very well when we meet, but there's never no telling when we may see each other again.'

Charles raised his head in the same surprised, indifferent way as before, and Maxime, still ill at ease, imprinted a second kiss on his forehead. 'Be a good boy, my pretty pet,' he said, 'and try to love me a little.'

'Come, come, we have no time to lose,' repeated Félicité.

Just then, however, the nurse came in. She was a strong, strapping wench, specially charged with attending on the old woman, whom she carried to her armchair, put to bed, fed and cleaned, just as though she had been a child. And now the nurse at once entered into conversation with Dr. Pascal, who began to question her. One of the dreams in which the Doctor had most willingly indulged was that of treating and curing the inmates of the Asylum by his system of injections. Since it was the brain which failed these poor folk, might not injections of nervous matter endow them with resistive strength and will, and repair the injuries sustained by the mental organ? For a moment he had even thought of trying his treatment on his old grandmother; but certain scruples had assailed him, a kind of sacred terror, without mentioning the fact that insanity, at such an advanced age as hers, meant total, irreparable ruin. Accordingly he had selected another subject for his experiments, a journeyman hatter, named Sarteur, who for a year past had been an inmate of the Asylum, whither he had come of his own free will, begging the officials to shut him up so that he might be prevented from committing a crime. In the attacks to which he was subject, he was possessed by such an irresistible desire to kill that he would have thrown himself on the passers-by and murdered them. Short of stature, and very dark, with a retreating forehead and a beaklike countenance—his nose being extremely prominent and his chin very short—he was further disfigured by having the left side of his face much larger than the right. The experiments which the Doctor had made on this impulsive madman had yielded a miracu-

lous result; for a month past Sarteur had not been troubled
with any delirious access. And now the nurse, on being
questioned concerning him, replied that he was quite calm and
visibly improving.

' Do you hear, Clotilde ? ' exclaimed Pascal in his delight
at the news. ' I haven't time to see him this evening, but we
will come back to-morrow. It is my visiting-day. Ah! if I
only had the courage ; if she were only younger ! '

Whilst speaking, his glance had again fallen on Aunt
Dide. However, Clotilde, smiling at his enthusiasm, gently
responded : ' No, no, master, you cannot re-create life. Come,
we must go, we are the last.'

The others had indeed already left the room. Standing
outside, Macquart, with the customary contemptuous snigger
on his face, was watching Félicité and Maxime as they
walked away. And Aunt Dide, the forgotten one, horribly
emaciated, remained there in her armchair quite motionless,
with her eyes again staring at little Charles, who looked very
effete and pale under his long regal hair.

The drive home was a very uncomfortable one. The
landau rolled along heavily in the heat ascending from the
soil, whilst the sunset slowly spread over the stormy sky with
the coppery glow of dying embers. At first a few trifling
words were exchanged ; but, as soon as they entered the
gorges of La Seille, the awe inspired by the threatening
masses of rock, whose giant walls seemed to be closing in
upon them, put an end to all conversation. Was not this the
end of the world ? Would they not presently be hurled into
the unknown depths of some yawning abyss ? An eagle flew
by, overhead, raising a piercing cry.

The willows were in view again, and they were once more
skirting the banks of the Viorne, when Félicité, without any
transition—as though she were indeed continuing a conversation but lately begun—remarked to Maxime : ' You need not
fear any refusal on the mother's part. She is fond of Charles,
but she is a very sensible woman, and she fully understands
that it would be for the child's good for you to take him. I
must admit, also, that the poor little fellow is not very happy

at home, for the husband naturally enough prefers his own
boy and girl. I say this because it is as well that you should
know everything.'

And she continued chattering in this strain, desirous, no
doubt, of enchaining Maxime, of inducing him to give her a
formal promise. Until they had got to Plassans she never
ceased. Then, while the landau was jolting over the paving-
stones of the Faubourg, she all at once exclaimed: ' But
there, as it happens, is the lad's mother ! Do you see her ?
That fair buxom woman by that door.'

On the threshold of a saddler's shop, where halters and
pieces of harness were hanging, Justine sat knitting a stocking, by way of occupation whilst she took an airing; and her
younger children, a little girl and a little boy, were playing
on the ground at her feet. Behind them, in the dim light
prevailing inside the shop, one could perceive Thomas, her
husband, a stout, dark man, who was busy repairing a
saddle.

Without any feeling of emotion, simply inquisitive, in
fact, Maxime craned his neck forward. And he was very
surprised by the sight of this sturdy woman of two-and-thirty,
with such a staid, *bourgeois* air, in whom naught remained of
the flighty girl whom he had known long years before. And
perhaps, too, he felt a pang at finding her so calm, so much
improved in every way, so plump, whereas he himself was
exceedingly ill, and already very aged.

' I should certainly never have recognised her,' he said.

Then the landau, rolling along, turned into the Rue de
Rome. Justine disappeared, and all that vision of the past—
ah ! so different—faded away in the vague glow of the sunset,
together with Thomas, the children, and the shop.

At La Souleiade they found the cloth already laid. Martine had provided an eel from the Viorne, a rabbit stew, and
a leg of mutton. Seven o'clock was only just striking, so
that they had ample time to dine comfortably.

' Don't worry,' Dr. Pascal repeated to his nephew. ' We
will accompany you to the station, it is less than ten minutes'
walk from here. Since you haven't any luggage with you,

you will merely have to take your ticket and jump into the train.'

Then finding Clotilde in the hall, where she was hanging up her hat and parasol, he said to her in an undertone : ' I am anxious about your brother.'

' How is that ? '

' I've had a good look at him. I don't like the way he walks. There are symptoms that have never deceived me— in fact he is threatened with ataxy.'

She became very pale. ' Ataxy ! ' she repeated. A cruel memory rose up before her, that of a neighbour, a man still young in years, whom she had seen a servant dragging about in a bath-chair, day by day, during ten long years. Could any worse misfortune befall humanity than this infirmity, this crushing blow which severs a living creature from life ? ' But he only complains of rheumatism,' she muttered.

Pascal shrugged his shoulders, and after placing his finger on his lips, went into the dining-room, where Félicité and Maxime were already seated.

They were all very cordial and friendly at dinner. The sudden anxiety which had sprung up in Clotilde's heart made her most affectionate towards her brother, who was seated beside her. She looked after his wants in a gay, good-natured way, insisted on his helping himself to the tit-bits, and twice called Martine back because she passed the dishes round too quickly. On his side, Maxime became more and more fascinated by this kind, healthy, sensible sister of his, who diffused such a caressing charm around her. So complete a conquest did she make of him that a new plan, vaguely outlined at first, gradually took shape in his mind. Since his son, little Charles, had so frightened him with his deathlike beauty, his regal air of sickly imbecility, why should he not take his sister Clotilde to live with him instead ? The idea of having a woman in his house usually terrified him, for he had come to hold all women in dread ; still this one seemed to be quite motherly. Moreover, the presence of a virtuous woman in his home would be a pleasant change, and do him good. At any rate his father would then no longer dare to pester

him with wenches, with the object, so he suspected, of finishing him off more quickly, and seizing upon his property.
His hatred and terror of his father determined him to speak
out.

' But don't you mean to 'marry ? ' he inquired by way of
finding out how matters stood.

' Oh ! there is no hurry,' the girl replied, laughing. And
then, assuming a whimsical air, and looking at Pascal, who
had raised his head, she added : ' Besides, who can tell ?—
but no, I shall never marry.'

At this Félicité began protesting. Finding Clotilde so
deeply attached to the Doctor, she had often desired that she
might marry, and thus be separated from her son, who would
then be left in loneliness in a desolate, wrecked home, where
she herself would thenceforth exercise a sovereign sway.
And so, in this conjuncture, she invoked his own testimony to
further the ends she had in view. Was it not really a woman's
duty to marry ? was not perpetual spinsterhood unnatural ?
Without taking his eyes off Clotilde, the Doctor gravely
assented. ' Yes, yes, one ought to marry—she is too sensible
to do otherwise ; she will marry some day.'

' But are you sure it would really be the best course ?'
interrupted Maxime. ' It might simply make her unhappy
for life. So many marriages turn out badly.' Then making
up his mind, he added : ' Shall I tell you what you ought to
do ? Well, you ought to come and live in Paris with me.
I've been thinking, and I'm frightened at the idea of taking
charge of a child, in my state of health. Am I not a child
myself, a sick man in need of being nursed ? You would take
care of me, I should have you with me, if I should at last
unhappily lose the use of my legs.'

In his pitying sorrow for himself his voice had become
quite tearful. He pictured himself infirm, and saw her at his
bedside tending him like a sister of charity ; and if she would
but consent to remain unmarried he would willingly leave her
his fortune, so that his father might not have it. His dread
of solitude, the necessity he might soon be in of securing a
nurse, rendered his appeal quite touching. ' It would be very

kind of you,' he added, 'and I assure you that you would not regret it.'

Martine, however, who was handing the mutton, stopped short in blank amazement, and all round the table the suggestion caused the same surprise. Félicité was the first to approve of it, realising that Clotilde's departure would help her plans. She looked at the girl, who still remained silent, as though bewildered; whilst Dr. Pascal sat there, waiting, with his face extremely pale.

'O brother, brother!' stammered the girl at last, finding no words to express her feelings.

Her grandmother thereupon intervened : 'Is that all you have to say? But your brother's proposal is a very proper one. If he's afraid of taking Charles with him just now, there's nothing to prevent you from going ; and by-and-by we can send you the boy. Come, come, all this fits in beautifully. Your brother appeals to your affection. Doesn't she owe him a favourable answer, Pascal?'

The Doctor with an effort had regained his self-possession; still one could divine the chill that had come over him. 'I repeat,' he slowly said, 'that Clotilde is a sensible girl, and if she feels that she ought to accept, she will do so.'

At this, amid all the confusion she was in, a spirit of rebellion seized upon the girl: 'Do you want to send me away then, master? Maxime is certainly very kind, and I thank him with all my heart. But to leave everything, *mon Dieu!* To leave all that loves me, all that I have hitherto loved——' She finished her sentence with a wild wave of the hand which embraced the whole of La Souleiade, both the things and the beings that it contained.

'If, however,' said Pascal, looking fixedly at her, 'if, however, Maxime should positively need you——'

Her eyes became moist, and for a moment she sat there quivering. She alone had understood the Doctor's meaning. The cruel vision had again appeared to her—Maxime infirm, wheeled about hither and thither in a bath-chair like the neighbour she had so often met. But her passion protested against her pity. Could it be said that she had any duty to fulfil with regard to a brother who for fifteen years had remained a stranger to her? Did not her duty lie there, where her heart had fixed its abode?

'Listen, Maxime,' she ended by saying; 'let me think it over on my side. I will see. You may be certain that I am very grateful to you. And if some day you should really have need of me, no doubt I should make up my mind.'

They could not prevail on her to bind herself more explicitly than this. Félicité, ever in a fever, wore herself out with her efforts to obtain a more positive decision; whilst the Doctor affected to consider the discussion closed, saying that she had given her word. Martine served the custard without seeking to hide her contentment. Take Mademoiselle away! No, no, indeed. What an idea! So that Monsieur might die of sadness and loneliness, no doubt? The incident led to the meal being prolonged, and they were still at dessert when the clock struck half-past eight. From that moment Maxime became restless and anxious, eager to take his departure.

At the railway station, whither they all accompanied him, he gave his sister a parting kiss. 'Remember,' said he.

'Oh! have no fear,' declared Félicité, 'we are here to remind her of her promise.'

The Doctor smiled, and all three of them began waving their handkerchiefs as soon as the train was set in motion.

When they had seen Félicité to her door, Dr. Pascal and Clotilde walked back slowly to La Souleiade, where they spent a delightful evening. The discomfort of the previous weeks, the covert antagonism which parted them, seemed to have flown away. Never had they experienced anything so sweet as now, feeling themselves to be so united, so inseparable. It was as though they had just recovered from some sickness and were awakening to health, and hope and the delight of living. For a long time did they linger in the warm night air, listening under the plane-trees to the delicate crystalline song of the spring. And they did not even converse, deeply wrapt as they were in the delight of being together.

CHAPTER IV

THE NEW HOLY ALLIANCE

EIGHT days later discomfort once more prevailed in the house. Pascal and Clotilde again spent entire afternoons without speaking to one another; and the fits and starts of bad temper were continual. Even Martine was in a state of perpetual irritation. The little household was becoming a hell once more.

Then, all at once, the situation of affairs became yet worse. A Capuchin, one of those very holy men who frequently pass through the towns of Southern France, had come to preach at Plassans, and his voice rang out from the pulpit of St. Saturnin. He was a sort of apostle, with a vivid, popular style of eloquence, a gift of flowery language, fertile in imagery. He preached upon the vanity of modern science, soaring into mysticism in the most marvellous way, denying the reality of the world, and revealing the Unknown, the mystery of the realms beyond. All the devout women of the town were quite upset by it.

Already, on the very first evening, Pascal perceived how feverish Clotilde was on returning from the sermon, which she had been to hear in company with Martine. On the following days she grew quite impassioned, and came home much later, after kneeling in prayer for an hour or more in a dark corner of some side-chapel. She could scarcely bring herself to leave the church, and came from it utterly crushed, with glittering eyes, like one in a mesmeric trance. And the Capuchin's ardent words incessantly haunted her. She now seemed to feel but hatred and contempt for men and things.

Pascal, rendered anxious, resolved to have an explanation with Martine. Accordingly, one morning he went down early whilst she was sweeping out the dining-room. 'You know,' said he, 'that I leave you and Clotilde quite free to go to church whenever it pleases you. I do not wish to interfere with anybody's conscience. But I won't have you making her ill.'

Without pausing in her work, the servant answered in a low voice : 'The folks that are ill are perhaps those who think there is nothing the matter with them.'

She spoke these words with so convinced an air that he began to smile. 'Yes,' said he, 'I'm the one with the ailing mind, the one whose conversion you implore, whilst you others are possessed of sound health and perfect wisdom. If you two continue torturing me and torturing yourselves in this fashion, you will end by making me angry.'

He uttered these last words in so despairing, so harsh a voice, that the servant abruptly ceased sweeping and looked up at him. A flash of infinite tenderness, of overwhelming desolation, passed over the worn face of this aged spinster, who had cloistered her life in the Doctor's service ; tears rushed into her eyes, and she ran off stammering: 'Ah! monsieur, you do not care for us.'

Thenceforth Pascal remained disarmed, a prey to growing sadness. His remorse increased at the thought that he had shown himself so tolerant, instead of despotically enforcing his own views with regard to the rearing and education of Clotilde. Believing, as he did, that trees grow straight when they are not interfered with, he had, after teaching her how to read and write, allowed her to grow up as she listed. It was without any predetermined plan—taking, indeed, things as they came in the natural course of their everyday life— that she had ended by reading pretty well everything ; and while helping him in his researches, correcting his proofs, recopying and classifying his manuscripts, had begun to take a passionate interest in natural science. But how bitterly the Doctor now regretted his heedlessness ! How powerfully he might have directed and influenced that clear young mind, so ardently thirsting for knowledge, instead of letting it stray and lose itself in that longing for something beyond life which both Grandmother Félicité and worthy Martine now favoured ! Whilst he limited himself to facts, and strove to prevent his thoughts from straying beyond phenomena—in which he succeeded, thanks to the discipline which scientific training imparts—he found her invariably preoccupied with regard to the Unknown, the Mysterious. She was beset by an instinctive curiosity which became intensified to the point of torture when she failed to satisfy it. And such were her yearnings that she was never sated; she always heard an irresistible call to that which was inaccessible, that which could not be known.

Already in her childish, and more especially in her youthful days, she had invariably gone straight to the why and wherefore, the *ultima ratio* of things. If a flower were shown to her, she would ask him why this flower would produce seed, and why this seed would germinate. Then came all the mystery of sex, birth and death, all the mystery of the unknown forces, of the Deity, of everything. In four questions she would corner him, bring him invariably to the same fatal confession of ignorance ; and when he no longer knew what or how to answer, but rid himself of her with a gesture of comical fury, she would indulge in a hearty, triumphant laugh, and again fly distractedly to her dreams, to the limitless vision of all that one does not *know*, but that one may *believe*. She would often stupefy him by the explanations she gave of things. Fed upon science, her mind would start from proven truths, but with so swift a spring, that it would soar at once to the very heaven of the ancient legends. Mediators would pass before her mind—angels, saints, supernatural currents, which transformed matter and endowed it with life ; or else there would be but one force, the Soul of the World, toiling so that things and beings might mingle in a final kiss of love after the lapse of fifty centuries. That was the space of time required—she had calculated it, she would say.

Never, however, had Pascal seen her so disturbed as now. She had been following the Capuchin's service for a week past, and it was evident that she spent all her time during the day in waiting for the evening sermon. To this she betook herself with the all-absorbing excitement of a girl repairing to her first love-meeting. Then, on the morrow, everything about her betokened how detached she was from ordinary life, from her wonted existence ; as though, indeed, the visible world, the necessary actions of each moment, had become but delusions and snares. She had thus virtually given up her usual occupations, surrendering to an idleness from which nothing could rouse her, remaining for hours with her hands lying in her lap, her eyes blank, wandering far away into dreamland.

She, as a rule so active and matutinal, now got up late and scarcely showed herself before the second breakfast ; and she could hardly have spent the long morning hours on her toilet, for she was losing all her feminine coquetry, and would go about with her hair barely combed, clad in any old gown, and even with that fastened all awry, but nevertheless still looking very charming, thanks to her triumphant youth. And she no longer indulged in those morning walks which she had been so fond of ; those walks through La Souleiade from the top to the bottom of the olive and almond planted terraces ; those visits to the pine grove, so balmy with resinous odours ; those long halts on the burning threshing-floor where she had been wont to take baths of sunshine. Now she preferred to immure herself in her room, where she kept the shutters closed, and where she could not even be heard stirring. Then, in the work-room during the afternoon, came a long spell of languishing idleness ; she would drag herself from chair to chair doing nothing, wearied, irritated with everything that had formerly interested her. Pascal had to renounce obtaining any help from her. A memorandum which he gave her to copy out remained for three days unnoticed on her desk. She no longer classified anything ; she would not even have stooped to pick up a fallen paper. And she had altogether forsaken her pastels, those minute, careful drawings of flowers which were to supply the plates for illustrating a work on artificial fecundation. Some large red

mallows, of a new and singular hue, had faded in their vase
before she had finished copying them. Yet throughout one
long afternoon she worked passionately at one of those wild,
imaginative designs of hers—limning the flowers of dreamland, a fantastic florescence bursting into bloom under the
warmth of some miracle-working sun—a spurting of golden
rays in the form of spikes of grain, darting hither and thither
from among large purple corollas, which resembled open
hearts, and whence, in lieu of pistils, shot a shower of stars,
myriads of worlds streaming over the sky like some milky
way.

'Ah, my poor girl,' the Doctor said to her that day, ' is
it possible that you can lose your time in such fancies ! I,
who was waiting for the copy of those mallows which you
have now let die ! And you will make yourself ill. There is
no health, no beauty even, possible, if we live out of reality.'

She often refrained from replying to him, immuring herself in her fierce convictions, bent upon not engaging in any
discussion. But these last words of his had doubtless touched
her to the quick, for she answered flatly : ' There is no
reality.'

Amused at seeing this big child assume the dogmatic air
of a philosopher, the Doctor began to laugh : ' Yes, yes, I
know. Our senses are liable to err ; it is only through our
senses that we know the world, hence it may be that the
world does not exist. But in that case let us open the door
to madness, accept the most extravagant chimeras as possibilities, and betake ourselves right away into dreamland, far from
all known laws and facts. Cannot you see, however, that if
you suppress Nature there will be no rule of life left, and
that the only interest in living lies in believing in life, in loving it, and in striving with all the strength of one's intelligence
to know it better ? '

She made a gesture of mingled indifference and bravado,
and the conversation fell. She was now slashing away at
her pastel with a blue crayon, so that the flowers seemed to
be blazing amid the limpid sky of a lovely summer's night.

Two days later, after a fresh discussion, matters became

still worse. On rising from the table in the evening after dinner, Pascal went upstairs again to continue his work, whilst Clotilde strolled out of the house and sat down on the terrace. Several hours went by, and the Doctor became both surprised and anxious at not having heard her return to her room. To reach the latter she must needs pass through the work-room, and he was quite certain that she had not done so whilst his back was turned. Going downstairs he found that Martine was fast asleep, and that the hall-door was not yet locked. Clotilde must have remained forgetfully outside. She did so at times when the nights were warm; but never before had she lingered so late as this.

The Doctor's disquietude increased when he noticed on the terrace that the chair, on which the girl must have long remained seated, was now unoccupied. He had hoped to find her asleep on it. Since she was no longer there, why had she not come in? whither could she have gone at such an hour? It was a splendid September night, still very warm, and the infinite, dark, velvety expanse of sky was studded with a profusion of large stars, shining forth so brilliantly from the depths of those moonless heavens that they sufficed to light up the earth. The Doctor began by leaning over the balustrade of the terrace and inspecting the slopes, the giant steps of dry stones which descended to the railway line; but nothing stirred there. He could only see the motionless, rounded tops of the stunted olive-trees. Then it occurred to him that she might be under the plane-trees, near the spring, lulling herself with the everlasting quiver of the murmuring water. He hastened thither and plunged into the darkness, which was here so dense that, although he knew each tree-trunk, he had to advance with outstretched arms to avoid hurting himself. Next, fumbling and groping, he explored the black depths of the pine grove, but still without meeting anyone. And at last, in a stifled voice, he began to call: ' Clotilde ! Clotilde ! '

The night remained deep and silent. By degrees he raised his voice : ' Clotilde ! Clotilde ! '

Not a soul, not a sound. The very echoes seemed to be

slumbering; his call died away, stifled amid the soft, bluey darkness. And then he began calling with all the power of his lungs, again plunging under the plane-trees, again groping through the pinewood, growing at last utterly distracted, and exploring the entire place. In this way, he all at once found himself upon the threshing-floor.

This extensive threshing-floor, this vast circular space, was now slumbering like all else. During the long years that had gone by since any grain had been winnowed there, grass had sprung up wherever it could, grass which, as soon as it showed itself, was scorched, gilded, cropped close, like the wool of a carpet, by the fiery sun. And the round pebbles lying between the tufts of this soft vegetation were never cool, but began steaming as soon as the twilight fell, exhaling throughout the night all the heat they had absorbed for years and years, during the overpowering noontide glow.

Amid the quiver of its exhalations, the threshing-floor spread out apparently bare and deserted under the peaceful sky; and Pascal was crossing it to hasten into the orchard when he narrowly missed stumbling over a prostrate body, stretched at full length upon the ground. He had previously failed to notice it. 'What, you are here?' he exclaimed, quite scared.

Clotilde did not even deign to answer. She was lying on her back with her arms bent, her hands clasped together behind her neck, and her face turned towards the sky; there was no sign of life in her pale visage save for the glittering of her large eyes.

'Why, I have been in the greatest anxiety, calling you everywhere for the last quarter of an hour,' said the Doctor; 'you must surely have heard me call.'

She at last opened her lips. 'Yes,' she said.

'Then how stupid of you! Why didn't you answer me?'

But she had relapsed into silence, and refused to explain herself, lying there with an obstinate brow, and with eyes soaring into the sky.

'Come! go to bed, you naughty child! You shall tell me all about it to-morrow.'

She still refrained from moving, however. Although he begged her to come in a dozen times, she did not stir. He had ended by sitting down beside her on the close-cropped grass, and could feel how warm the pebbles were beneath him.

'So you want to sleep here?' he resumed. 'You might at any rate answer me. What are you doing here?'

'I am looking,' she answered; and as she spoke the gaze of her large motionless eyes—fixed and dilated—seemed to ascend yet higher, to reach indeed the very stars. She was roaming far away among the planets, in the limpid Infinite of that summer night.

'Ah, master!' she resumed at last, speaking slowly but without a pause, in a monotonous voice which neither rose nor fell, 'how limited, how little is all that you know, by the side of that which must surely be up yonder! Ah! if I did not answer you, it was because I was thinking of you and feeling very grieved. You must not think me wicked, unkind——'

Such a quiver of affection sped through her words that he was deeply stirred. In his turn he stretched himself on his back, beside her. Their elbows touched. And in this wise they continued talking. 'I very much fear, my dear,' said he, 'that your sorrows are unreasonable ones. You think of me and you feel grieved. Why is that?'

'Oh, because of certain things which it would be difficult for me to explain to you. I am not a learned woman. True, you have taught me many things, and I have myself learnt many more since I have been living with you. But I refer to things that I feel—perhaps I will try to tell you what they are since we are quite alone, and it is so lovely here.'

After long hours of reflection in the peaceful privacy of that delightful night her heart was now full to overflowing. For his part he did not speak for fear lest he might intimidate her, but patiently awaited whatever she might desire to confide to him.

'When I was a little girl,' said she, 'and heard you talk of science, it seemed to me that you were talking of God, so full you were of faith and hope. In your eyes nothing seemed to be any longer impossible. By means of science one was to unravel the secret of the world, and bestow perfect happiness upon mankind. According to you, we were marching towards this goal with giant strides. Not a day but brought its discovery, its certainty. Another ten years, another fifty years, another hundred years possibly, and the heavens would be opened to our gaze and we should find ourselves face to face with Truth. Well, the years go by, and nothing opens, and still and ever Truth recedes.'

'You are impatient,' he quietly answered; 'if ten centuries be necessary, one must wait for them.'

'It is true that I am impatient. I cannot wait. I long to know; I long to be happy, now, at once. And I must know all, not by degrees, but at one stroke, and I must be made perfectly, absolutely happy. Oh! it is that, do you know, it is that which makes me suffer; to find that I cannot climb at one bound to perfect knowledge, and cannot rest in perfect felicity, free from all doubts and scruples. Is this living, to crawl through the darkness no faster than a tortoise, to be unable to enjoy even an hour's peace without trembling at the idea of the coming anguish? No, no, I would have perfect knowledge and perfect happiness without delay! Science has promised them to us, and if she gives them not, we may pronounce her bankrupt.'

At this he himself began to feel impassioned. 'But what you say, my child, is senseless! Science is not revelation. Science proceeds at the only pace possible to humanity: its very glory is in the unremitting effort it must make. Besides, what you say is not true; science has never promised happiness.'

She hastily interrupted him: 'Not true, indeed! Why, open your books upstairs. You know very well that I have read them. They overflow with promises! To read them it would seem that one were marching to the conquest of earth and heaven. They throw everything down, and vow that they will replace everything, and replace it both solidly and wisely, guided by the light of pure reason only. No doubt I am like a child. When something has been promised me I wish to have it. My mind sets to work, and the gift, to satisfy me, must prove a beautiful one. But then it is so easy to promise me nothing! And now that I am pained and exasperated with desire, it would be wrong to tell me that nothing was ever promised me.'

He again waved his arm through the deep, serene night, with a gesture expressive of protest and impatience.

'At all events,' she continued, 'science has swept everything away, the earth is bare, the heavens are empty, and so what is to become of me, even supposing that science be not responsible for the hopes I have conceived? In either case I cannot live without certainty and without happiness. Where am I to find a firm foundation on which I may build my house, since the old world has been demolished and such little speed is shown in forming the new one? The catastrophe wrought by examination and analysis has rent the ancient places of habitation, their denizens wander through the ruins, not knowing on what stone to rest their heads, but camping under the storm, and clamouring for the definitive, unshakeable place of refuge where they may begin life anew—so you must not be surprised at our discouragement and impatience. We can wait no longer. Since science is too slow, and does not yield the results we had hoped for, we prefer to turn back —yes, to plunge anew into the beliefs of former times, which during long, long centuries sufficed for the happiness of the world.'

'Yes, indeed! That's just what it is!' he cried; 'we have reached that turning-point, the end of the century, wearied, enervated by the frightful mass of knowledge that the century has stirred and sifted. And now the everlasting need of lies, the everlasting need of illusions, is again tormenting humanity and leading it backward to the lulling charm of the Unknown. Since we shall never know everything, why seek to know more than we know already? Since the conquest of truth does not yield immediate and certain happiness, why not remain content with ignorance, and repose in the darkness on the same couch on which humanity slumbered so soundly during its younger years? Yes, the Mysterious is returning to the attack;

this is the reaction after a hundred years of experimental
inquiry. And this was bound to be ; and desertions must be
expected when one cannot satisfy all needs at once. But
there is merely a halt; believe me, the forward march will
continue up yonder, far from our eyes, in the infinity of space.'

For a moment they remained silent without moving, their
glances wandering among the myriads of worlds which
glittered in the sombre sky above. A shooting star darted
like a flash of fire across the Cassiopeian constellation. And
the illumined universe on high slowly turned upon its axis
with a holy splendour, whilst from the shadowy earth around
them there ascended but a faint quivering like the warm and
gentle breath of a sleeping woman.

'Tell me,' the Doctor asked, with a good-natured air, 'it is
that Capuchin of yours, is it not, who has turned your head
like this ? '

'Yes,' she answered frankly ; 'the things he says in the
pulpit thoroughly distract me; he preaches against all that you
have taught me, and it is as though the science which I owe
to you had become a poison and were destroying me. My
God, my God ! what will become of me ? '

'My poor child ! It is terrible that you should prey upon
yourself, devour yourself like this ! True, I feel pretty confident with regard to you, for, after all, as I have often told
you, you have a nice, clear little head. And by-and-by you
will grow calm again. But what mental havoc this Capuchin
must be causing, since even you, healthy as you are, are
disturbed by it all ! Are you not possessed of Faith then ? '

She did not speak, but sighed.

'Certainly,' he continued, 'so far as happiness is concerned, Faith is a strong staff, and when one is lucky enough
to possess it the march through life becomes an easy and
peaceful one.'

'Ah ! I no longer know,' she answered ; 'there are days
when I believe, and there are others when I am with you and
your books. If I am in this distracted state it is your doing;
if I suffer it is through you. And all my suffering perhaps
is caused by the fact that I love you and yet cannot help

rebelling against you. No, no, tell me nothing, do not say that I shall grow calmer later on. It would only increase my irritation now. You deny the supernatural. In your eyes the mysterious is only the unexplained. You grant, however, that we shall never know everything; and so the only interest of life lies in for ever and ever attempting the conquest of the Unknown, in for ever and ever striving to know more than we know already. But, ah ! I myself already know too much to be able to indulge in a quiet belief; you have already conquered me too far, and there are times when it seems to me that I shall die of it all.'

He had taken hold of her hand and pressed it tightly in the warm grass. 'But it is life that frightens you, child,' said he. 'But how right you are in saying that the only happiness lies in incessant effort, for henceforth it will be impossible to rest and slumber in ignorance. No halt can be hoped for, no tranquillity is ever to be purchased again by shutting one's eyes. One must march on, march on, despite everything, with life which is always on the march. And all the expedients that are proposed, turnings back, dead religions, religions patched and mended, modified in the hope of making them suit new requirements—all these are mere delusions ! Learn to know life, love it, live it as it should be lived ; there is no other wisdom.'

But with a sudden jerk she freed her hand, and in a voice which quivered with disgust replied: 'Life is an abomination ! How can you expect me to live peacefully and happily ? The light which your science throws upon the world is a terrible one ; analysing and analysing, you penetrate to every human sore and lay it bare in all its horror. And whatever you find you reveal, you speak out, say everything without disguise, and leave us utterly disgusted both with men and things, with no consolation possible.'

He interrupted her with a cry of ardent conviction : 'Speak out, say everything, yes, so that all may be known, and all may be cured ! '

Roused by anger, she sat up : ' If there were only the consolation of equality and justice in nature. But you **yourself** admit it, life belongs to the strongest; the weak fatally perishes because he is weak. In the whole world there are no two beings that are equal, either in health, or in beauty, or in intelligence—it all comes, too, in a chance, haphazard way. And the last hope crumbles if there be no great and holy justice.'

'There is no equality, 'tis true,' he said in an undertone, as though speaking to himself; 'no society that might be based on equality could live. For centuries men have thought that they might remedy the evil by charity, but the old world has cracked, and now justice is suggested. Is Nature just? I rather think that she is simply logical. Logic is perhaps a natural, superior justice, having only the great final labour in view, the sum-total of our common toil.'

'And so,' she cried, 'justice in that case consists in crushing the individual so that the race may be happy, in destroying some weak species so as to fatten the species that conquers it? No, no, all that is crime! There is nothing here below but filth and murder. He was right in what he said in church: The world is rotten; science simply lays its rottenness bare; and it is up above, yes, upon high that we should all seek refuge. . . O master! I beg of you, let me save myself, and let me save you too!'

She had just burst into tears, and her sobs rose wildly into the pure night. Vainly did he strive to calm her; her voice rang out above his own. 'Listen, master, you know whether I love you; you, who are all that I have in the world. And my torment comes from you; I feel as though I should stifle with grief when I think that we are not of one mind, and that, if we were both to die to-morrow, we should be parted for evermore. Why will you not believe?'

He again tried to reason with her. 'Come, come; you are losing your head, my darling!'

But she had risen to her knees and caught hold of his hands, clinging to him with a feverish grasp. And she sobbed yet more loudly, with such a clamorous despair that all the black countryside afar quivered at the sound.

'Listen, this is what he said in church: One must change

one's life and do penance, put aside, destroy, burn all one's past errors—yes, your books, your documents, your manuscripts—make this sacrifice, master, make this sacrifice, I implore it on my knees ! And then you will see what a delightful life we will lead together ! '

But at last he was rebelling. ' No, no, I won't listen to you ; be quiet.'

' Yes, you *will* listen to me, master ; you *will* do what I desire. I assure you that I am horribly wretched, even loving you as I do love you. There is something wanting in our affection. So far it has been great but useless, and I have an irresistible yearning to fill it—oh ! with everything that is divine and eternal. What can we lack unless it be God ? Kneel down there, and pray with me.'

In his turn irritated, he freed himself with a movement of some violence. ' Be quiet ; you have lost your head. I have left you free ; leave me free also.'

' Master, master ! what I desire is our happiness. I will carry you far, far away. We will fly to some solitude, and lead a holy life together.'

' Be quiet. I will not—never.'

They remained for a moment face to face in silence, and with threatening mien. Around them La Souleiade spread out in its nocturnal silence, with the slight shadows cast by its olive-trees, and the dense darkness prevailing under its pines and its plane-trees, where the spring sang on in a saddened voice ; and up on high, above them, it seemed as though the vast heavens, studded with stars, had suddenly quivered and turned pale, although the dawn was yet far off. Clotilde raised her arm as if to point to the infinity of quivering sky, but Pascal promptly caught hold of her hand again and kept it in his own, pointing towards mother earth. And not another word was spoken between them ; they were beside themselves, violent, inimical. It was rupture fiercely wrought.

All at once she withdrew her hand and sprang aside like some proud, untamable animal ; and then she darted off through the night towards the house. The clatter of her little boots resounded for a moment over the pebbles of the threshing-floor, then died away as she reached a sanded path. He, already in great distress, pressingly called to her to return. She, however, would not listen, would not answer, but still ran on. Seized with fear, with his heart oppressed, he darted after her, and turned the corner of the clump of plane-trees just in time to see her whirl like a tempest into the hall. He plunged into it behind her, and sprang up the stairs to find himself, however, face to face with the door of her room, the bolt of which she was violently pushing to. And he calmed himself, stayed himself by means of a mighty effort, resisting the desire he felt to cry out, to call her yet again, to burst the door open so that he might convince her, win her, and keep her wholly to himself. For a moment he remained motionless, noting the deathlike silence of the room, whence there came not even a sound of breathing. Doubtless she had thrown herself across the bed, and, with her face close-pressed to the pillow, was there stifling her cries and sobs. At last he made up his mind to go down and close the hall door. When he came up again it was as softly as possible, to listen if he could hear her moaning; and the daylight was breaking when at last he went to bed, in despáir, and choking with sobs.

From that night forward a pitiless warfare went on. Pascal felt that he was being spied upon, beset, threatened. He was no longer at home, no longer had a house of his own : the enemy was ever there, and he was exposed to every fear, forced to lock up everything. Two phials of liquefied nervous matter which he prepared were in turn found shattered to pieces, and he had to barricade himself in his room, where he remained pounding away with his pestle and mortar all day long, not even showing himself at meal-time. He no longer took Clotilde with him when he went to see his patients, for she discouraged them by her aggressively incredulous demeanour. Only, he no sooner went out than he was in all haste to get back again, fearing lest he should find his locks forced and his drawers pillaged on his return. He no longer employed the girl to classify and copy out his memoranda, since several of them had disappeared as though carried off by the wind.

He no longer dared to give her his proofs to read for literal errors, having found, on one occasion, that she had actually cut a passage out of one article, the views embodied in it being offensive to her Catholic belief. And so she remained idle, prowling about the rooms, having all the leisure necessary to wait and watch for an opportunity that might put the key of the large press in her possession. This must have been her dream—the plan which with glittering eyes and feverish hands she concocted during her long spells of idle silence—to secure that key, open the press, take everything out of it, destroy everything in an *auto-da-fé* which would be agreeable to God. One day, whilst he had just gone to wash his hands and put on his frock-coat, a few pages of a manuscript which he had forgotten on the corner of a table disappeared, leaving no trace beyond a few ashes in the fireplace. One evening, whilst he was returning home in the twilight, having stayed longer than he intended with a patient, a mad terror took possession of him before he was out of the Faubourg, at the sight of a great whirling cloud of smoke which was blurring the pale sky. Was not La Souleiade blazing from garret to basement, set alight by a bonfire of his papers? He hastened back at a run, and was only tranquillised when he saw that the smoke came from a slowly kindling fire of old roots in a neighbouring field.

Ah! what a frightful suffering, this torment of the *savant*, who feels that it is his intelligence, his work, that is thus threatened! The discoveries he has made, the manuscripts he means to leave behind him, these are his pride; they are beings, the blood of his veins, his children, and to destroy them, burn them, would be to burn some of his flesh. That which distressed Pascal the most was that he could not rid himself of the enemy who was installed in his house, the enemy who was incessantly lying in wait to pounce upon the work of his brain, for she had secured an abode in his very heart; he loved her still, despite everything. Thus he was disarmed, without weapon of defence, unwilling to act, with no resource at his disposal save vigilant watching. And, moreover, he was being beset more closely than ever; it seemed to him that little thieving fingers dived into his pockets, he failed to secure peace of mind even when his door was locked, for he feared lest he might be robbed through every crack and chink.

'But you unhappy child!' he one day exclaimed, 'you are the only being I love in the world, and it is you who are killing me. Yet you love me, and do all this because you love me. It is abominable, and it would be better to end it all by drowning ourselves at once.'

She made no answer in words, but her brave eyes eagerly declared that she was quite willing to face death if it were with him.

'And if I were to die suddenly to-night,' continued the Doctor, 'what would happen to-morrow? You would empty the press, empty the drawers, make a big pile of all my work and burn it! That's it, is it not? But, do you know, it would really be murder—just as though you assassinated someone? And what abominable cowardice, to kill Thought!'

'No,' she answered, in a husky voice, 'to kill Evil, and prevent it from spreading and being revived!'

All their explanations together—and some were terrible—threw them back into anger. One evening old Madame Rougon made her appearance during one of these quarrels, and remained alone with Pascal after Clotilde had rushed away into her own room. An interval of silence followed. Despite the afflicted air which the old lady had assumed, delight was perceptibly gleaming from the depths of her bright eyes. 'But your poor house has become a perfect hell,' she said at last.

The Doctor simply waved his hand to avoid answering. Behind the girl he had always divined the presence of his mother; she it must be who goaded Clotilde's religious fervour to exasperation, availing herself of this ferment of revolt in order to bring trouble into his home. He had no illusions, and was perfectly well aware that the two women had seen each other during the day, and that he owed the frightful scene which had just taken place, and which still made him tremble, to this meeting, to the poison which the old woman had artfully instilled into her granddaughter's mind. And if his mother had come to La Souleiade that evening, it was, doubtless, in order that she might be able to judge of the havoc wrought, and ascertain whether the end of it all was now not near at hand.

'Matters cannot go on like this,' she resumed. 'Why don't you separate, since you no longer agree together? You ought to send her to her brother Maxime—he wrote to me the other day, again asking that she might come.'

The Doctor had drawn himself erect, pale and energetic. 'Part in anger? Ah! no, no, that would mean everlasting remorse, incurable suffering. If she must go away some day or other, I would rather that it should be under such circumstances that we might continue loving one another from afar. But why should she go? Neither of us complains.'

Félicité felt that she had spoken too precipitately. 'Of course, if it pleases you to quarrel and fight together, nobody has a right to object to it. Only, in that case, my poor fellow, you must allow me to tell you that I do not think Clotilde altogether in the wrong. You compel me to tell you that we saw each other this afternoon—after all it is better that you should know it, though I promised her I would not speak of the matter. Well, the fact is, she is not happy, and complains bitterly. As you may imagine, I scolded her, and advised her to be more submissive. Nevertheless, I must say that I do not altogether understand you, and that to my mind you do all you can to make yourself unhappy!'

She had taken a chair, compelling him also to sit down in a corner of the work-room, where she seemed delighted to have him, all alone, at her mercy. She had several times already wished to force an explanation which, on his part, he had always avoided. Still, although she had been torturing him for years, and he was ignorant of nothing concerning her, he invariably treated her with deference, vowing that he would never depart from a stubbornly respectful demeanour towards her. Accordingly, as soon as she broached certain subjects, he was wont to seek refuge in perfect silence.

'Come,' said she, 'I can understand very well that you

won't give way to Clotilde, but perhaps you will to me? If I were to beg you to sacrifice those abominable documents which you keep in the press there! Suppose, for a moment, that you suddenly died, and that those papers fell into a stranger's hands! We should all of us be dishonoured. Surely you do not desire that, eh? Then what is your object? why do you play such a dangerous game? Promise me that you will burn them.'

For a while he remained silent, but at last he was obliged to answer: 'I have already begged it of you, mother; do not let us ever talk of that—I cannot comply.'

'But, come, give me a reason at any rate,' she cried. ' One might say that you looked on our family with as much indifference as though it were that drove of oxen passing along the road yonder. Yet you belong to it. Oh! 1 know very well that you do all you can *not* to belong to it. I, myself, am often astonished, and wonder where you can have come from! All the same, it is none the less very wrong on your part to expose yourself to the risk of besmirching us. No thought even of the grief which you must cause me, your mother, seems able to stop you. To my mind it is simply wicked! '

In spite of his resolution to remain silent, he could not refrain from resenting her words, from yielding for a moment to a desire to defend himself. ' You speak harshly; you do wrong,' he answered; ' I have always believed in the necessity, the absolute efficacy of truth. It is a fact that I say everything which I may know of others and of myself, but it is simply because I firmly believe that in saying everything I do the one good work that is possible. First of all, those documents are not intended for the public; they are simply private memoranda, and it would be painful for me to part with them. Moreover, I understand very well that it is not only those documents that you desire to see destroyed. All my other writings would have to be flung into the fire, eh? And that, understand me, is a thing that shall not be. Whilst I live not one line of writing here shall be destroyed.'

But he was already regretting that he had said so much,

for he saw her draw near to him to press, urge him, drive him to the cruel explanation that he desired to avoid.

'Well, speak out, make a clean breast of it all,' she said; 'tell me what it is you reproach us with—yes, for instance, what do you reproach *me*, your mother, for? It can't be for having brought you all up with so much difficulty? Ah! it took us a long time to rise to fortune. If we enjoy a little happiness nowadays we certainly earned it. Since you have seen everything and noted everything in your papers, you can bear witness to the fact that the family has rendered far more services to others than it has ever received from them. On two occasions Plassans would have been in a pretty pickle but for us! And it's merely natural that we should have only reaped ingratitude and envy as our reward—to such a degree, indeed, that even nowadays the whole town would be delighted with any scandal that might besmirch us. You cannot desire that, and I am sure you do me the justice to admit that my conduct has been sufficiently dignified since the fall of the Empire and the disasters from which France will very likely never recover.'

'Let France alone, mother!' he said, again compelled to speak, so deeply did her words wound him in what she knew to be a tender part. 'France has plenty of life in her yet, and to my thinking she is astonishing the world by the rapidity of her convalescence. Certainly there are many rotten elements in her yet. I have not hidden them, possibly I have revealed them too freely, but you do not understand me if you imagine that I believe in a final downfall, simply because I point out the cracks and crevices. I believe in life which is incessantly engaged in eliminating all that is hurtful, which fills up wounds with new flesh, which, even in the midst of impurity and death, still marches on towards health and a continuous renewal.'

He was growing excited, and, becoming conscious of it, made a gesture of anger and ceased speaking. His mother had thought it best to cry, and was slowly shedding some little tears, which oozed with difficulty from her eyes, and dried at once. And, meantime, she reverted to the fears which saddened her old age, and, in her turn, entreated him to make his peace with God, if only out of regard for the family. Did not she herself give an example of courage ? Did not the whole of Plassans, the St. Marc district, the old town, the new town, render homage to the nobility of her demeanour ? All she asked for was help ; she demanded that all her children should make an effort similar to her own. And she brought forward the example of Eugène, that great man who had fallen from such a height, and was now content to be a mere deputy, defending to his very last breath the vanished *régime* to which he owed his glory. She was also full of praise for Aristide,[1] who never despaired, but was acquiring by dint of efforts quite a fine position under the new *régime*, and this in spite of the undeserved catastrophe which had momentarily buried him under the ruins of the Banque Universelle. And would he, Pascal—he who was so intelligent, so affectionate, so kind—would he alone stand on one side, doing nothing in order that she might die in peace, in the joy of beholding the final triumph of the Rougons ? Come, come, surely it was impossible ! He would go to mass on the ensuing Sunday, and he would burn all those wicked papers, the mere thought of which sufficed to make her ill. She entreated, ordered, threatened. But he no longer answered her, calmed as he now was, not to be moved from the extremely deferential demeanour that he had assumed. He was unwilling to enter into any discussion ; he knew her too well either to have any hope of convincing her or to dare to discuss the past with her.

' Ah ! ' she said, when she realised that he was unshakeable, ' you don't belong to us. I always said so ! You dishonour us.'

He bowed. ' You will reflect, mother,' said he, ' you will forgive me.'

Félicité went off that day in a perfect rage ; and, meeting Martine just outside the house, in front of the clump of plane-trees, she began to ease her mind, unaware that Pascal had

---

[1] Saccard, Clotilde's father.

just gone into his bedroom, the windows of which were open,
and could therefore hear everything. She openly aired her
resentment, and swore that since he would not willingly
sacrifice those papers she would end by securing them and
destroying them, in spite of everything. But what froze the
Doctor's heart was the manner in which Martine strove
to pacify her. The servant was evidently an accomplice;
she repeated that they must bide their time, precipitate
nothing, that she and Mademoiselle had vowed that they
would never give Monsieur a moment's rest, and that in
this way they would end at last by conquering him. It
was sworn, he would be reconciled with Providence, since
it was not right, not possible that a man like Monsieur, in
all other things a perfect saint, should remain without religion. And then the two women lowered their voices, and
soon only whispering could be heard, a stifled murmur made
up of tittle-tattle and plotting, of which he could merely distinguish a word or two here and there—some mention of
orders that had been given, measures that had been taken,
all with a view to hamper his freedom of action. When his
mother at last decided to take herself off he saw her walk
away well satisfied, with the slim, erect figure and light step
of a young girl.

Then an hour of weakness, of absolute despair overtook
Pascal. He had let himself fall upon a chair, and sat there
asking what use there could be in struggling, since the only
beings he cared for had allied themselves against him. To
think that Martine, who would have flung herself into the
fire, had he only bidden her do so, was thus betraying him—
for his salvation's sake! And Clotilde was in league with
the servant, plotting with her in every corner, securing her
help to set traps for him! Ah! he was now altogether
alone—he had only traitresses about him; the very air he
breathed was being poisoned. These two women certainly
loved him, and, had they been alone, he might possibly have
managed to soften them and have turned them from their
intention; but knowing, as he now did, that his mother was
behind them, he understood their implacable tenacity, and no

longer hoped to win them back. Timid, like a man whose life has been spent in study, and who has had but little to do with women, the idea that there were three of them resolved to capture him and bend him to their will quite overwhelmed him. He always felt one of them behind him; when he shut himself in his room he divined their presence on the other side of the wall, and they haunted him filled him with a ceaseless dread of being robbed of his very thoughts—even before he expressed them—should he only allow their presence in his brain to be divined.

This was certainly the unhappiest period of Dr. Pascal's life. The state of defence in which, without a moment's cessation, he was forced to live, wore him out; and it seemed to him as though the very floor of his house were sinking beneath him. He then acutely regretted that he had never married, that he had no child. Had he himself then been afraid of life? Was he not punished for his egotism? The regret that he had no child developed at times into positive anguish, and his eyes would fill with tears when little girls with clear bright glances smiled at him as he passed them on the roads. Doubtless Clotilde was there, but his love for Clotilde was a different love, fraught with tempests; it was not a calm, gentle affection, the love which he would have felt for a little child, and in which his lacerated heart might have found repose. And, moreover, that which he desired, now that he could feel the end of his being near at hand, was a continuation of it, some offspring that would have continued, perpetuated him. Such was his faith in life, that the more he suffered the greater would have been the consolation of bequeathing his suffering. He believed himself to be free from the physiological defects of his family; but even the thought that heredity sometimes misses a generation, and that the disorder of his forerunners after escaping himself might appear again in any son that he might have, did not deter him. In spite of the rotten roots of his genealogical-tree, in spite of the long succession of loathsome relatives, he still some days found himself longing for a son, in the same way as one longs for some unexpected gain, some rare happiness, some stroke of fortune which will console and enrich one for ever. And, amid the tottering of his other affections, his heart bled because it was now too late.

One heavy, sultry night, towards the close of September, Pascal was unable to sleep. He opened one of the windows of his room; the sky was black, a storm was doubtless travelling by in the distance, for a continuous rolling of thunder could be heard. The Doctor could but imperfectly distinguish the sombre mass of the plane-trees, which every now and then, when illumined by the reflections of the lightning, stood forth, of a dull green hue amid the encompassing darkness. Pascal was frightfully distressed in mind. He was living all his recent unhappy days over again—days of fresh quarrelling, days which suspicion and treachery had filled with increased torture—when, all at once, a recollection flashed upon him and made him start. In his fear lest he might be robbed he had ended by always carrying the key of the large oak press in one of the pockets of his coat. That afternoon, however, finding the heat intolerable, he had taken his jacket off, and he now remembered that he had seen Clotilde hang it on a nail in the work-room. A sudden terror darted through him; if she had felt the key lying in his pocket she must have stolen it. He rushed to his jacket, which he had just thrown upon a chair, and searched it. The key was no longer there. At that very moment he was being robbed, he felt it clearly. Two o'clock in the morning was striking; he did not tarry to dress himself again, but simply clad in his night-shirt and trousers, and with slippers on his bare feet, he violently threw the door open and sprang into the work-room, candlestick in hand.

'Ah, I knew it!' he cried. 'Thief! Murderess!'

And it was true—Clotilde was there, disrobed, her feet in her canvas slippers, with legs bare, arms bare, shoulders bare, wearing nothing, indeed, but her chemise and a short petticoat. Out of prudence she had brought no candle with her, but had contented herself with opening the shutters of one window; the illumination furnished by the storm passing across the cloudy sky southward, the swift recurring flashes of lightning which threw a livid phosphorescent glow upon everything, sufficed her for her work. The deep old press stood wide open. She had already taken everything from the topmost shelf, removing armfuls of documents at a time, and throwing them upon the long table in the middle of the room, where they now lay heaped up in confusion. And fearing that she might not have time to burn them, she was feverishly making packages of them—packages which she thought she might hide and afterwards send to her grandmother—when, all at once, the light of Pascal's candle falling full upon her brought her to an abrupt pause in an attitude which betokened both surprise and a spirit of resistance.

'You rob me and you murder me!' Pascal furiously repeated.

She was still holding one of the batches of documents in her bare arms and he wished to take it from her. But she pressed it to her bosom with all her strength, stubbornly bent on accomplishing the work of destruction, evincing, indeed, neither confusion nor repentance, but comporting herself like a combatant whose cause is the good one. Then he, blinded, maddened by anger, rushed upon her, and they fought. He caught hold of her, scantily clad as she was, and ill-treated her.

'Kill me then,' she stammered; 'kill me, or I'll tear everything to pieces.'

But he held her with such an overpowering grasp that she could scarcely breathe. 'When a child steals,' he cried, 'she must be chastised!'

She was scratched in the struggle, and a few drops of her crimson blood began trickling over the white, silky skin of her round shoulder. Pascal saw them and released her, having with a final effort torn the portfolio of documents from her arms.

'And now you must help me to put them back again,' he shouted. 'Come here; begin by putting them in order on the table. Obey me, do you hear?'

'Yes, master.'

She drew near and began helping him, like a wild animal

suddenly tamed, overcome as she was by that masculine grasp which seemed to have penetrated her very flesh. The candle, burning with a tall flame in the sultry night air, lighted them; and the distant rolling of the thunder never ceased; the open window, facing the storm, seemed to be on fire.

CHAPTER V

THE GENEALOGICAL-TREE [1]

FOR a moment Pascal looked at the batches of documents, lying in a huge pile upon the long table in the middle of the work-room. Flung carelessly, hastily upon it, several of the stout blue paper wrappers had opened, and all sorts of documents, letters, newspaper cuttings, legal instruments and memoranda were slipping out of them.

In order to re-classify the collection he was seeking the names, written in large letters upon the wrappers, when, with a violent gesture, he roused himself from his sombre, reflective mood. And turning towards Clotilde, who stood there waiting, erect, silent and pale, he said to her : 'Listen, I have always forbidden you to read these papers, and I know that you have obeyed me. Yes, I felt certain scruples—not that you are an ignorant girl like others, for I have let you learn all that is needful concerning man and woman ; and it is only to evil natures that such knowledge can seem evil. However, I asked myself what good it would do to bring you, at such an early age, face to face with all the terrible truths of life. So I spared you the history of our family, which is indeed the history of all families, the history of all humanity—much evil and much good.'

He paused, strengthened himself apparently in his resolution, having grown quite calm again and supremely energetic.

---

[1] In this chapter M. Zola vigorously defends the various works that have come from his pen.—*Trans.*

' You are now five-and-twenty, however,' he resumed, ' and it is fitting that you should know. Besides, it is no longer possible to continue leading the life we lead now. Carried away by your dream, you live yourself and make me live in a perpetual nightmare. I prefer that reality—however hateful it may be—should be spread out before us. Perhaps the blow which the knowledge of it will deal you will make you the woman you should be. We will re-classify these documents together, run through them and read them ; it will be a terrible lesson of life.'

Then, as she still stood there motionless, he added : ' We must be able to see clearly. Light those two candles which are there.'

A desire for plenty of light possessed him ; he would have liked the blinding glow of the noontide sun ; and the three candles failing to satisfy him, he stepped into his bedroom to fetch a pair of candelabra. Seven candles then flared upon the table, yet Pascal and Clotilde—both of them still imperfectly clad, he with his shirt open and his chest bare, she with naked arms and shoulders—did not even see each other. It was past two o'clock, but neither of them was conscious of the hour, or felt any need of sleep, passionately intent as they were on spending the night in examining that great problem, Life, with never a thought of either time or place. And meanwhile the storm, which was still raging on the horizon, visible through the open window, thundered yet more loudly than before.

Never had Clotilde previously seen Pascal with such ardent, feverish eyes. He had been overtaxing himself for some weeks, and moral anguish had at times made him abrupt and harsh in spite of his fund of conciliatory good nature. Now, however, that he was about to plunge into the terrible truths of life, it seemed as though a feeling of infinite tenderness, fraught with fraternal compassion, were penetrating his heart ; a very lofty feeling of indulgence, impelling him if not to justify at least to condone all the terrible facts that he must let loose and spread out before the girl. He was resolved upon it : he would say all, since to cure all it is needful that all should be revealed. Was not the entire fatal evolution, the supreme argument summed up in the history of those beings so closely allied to him? Their careers typified life, and such as it was it was necessary to live it. Doubtless Clotilde would come forth from the explanation, tempered like steel, and full of courage and tolerance.

'You are being urged on against me,' he resumed; 'you are persuaded to do abominable things, and I wish to restore your conscience to you. When you have learnt the truth you will be able to judge and act for yourself. Come near and read with me.'

She complied. It is true that these documents, which her grandmother never mentioned without an outburst of anger, frightened her a little; but, on the other hand, a feeling of curiosity was now dawning, nay, growing within her. And besides, although physically subdued by that explosion of masculine authority that had grasped and overpowered her, she had not abdicated her right to think. Surely, therefore, she might listen to him and read with him, since she would be free to draw her own conclusions afterwards, and accept or refuse his views. So she drew near and waited.

'Come, are you willing?' he asked.

'Yes, master, I am!'

He then began by showing her the genealogical-tree of the Rougon-Macquart family. He did not keep this document in the old press, but in the *secrétaire* in his bedroom, whence he had taken it when fetching the candelabra. For more than twenty years he had been keeping this genealogical-tree up to date, making entries of all the births and deaths, marriages and other important family events, and briefly noting upon it the main characteristics of each member of the family in accordance with his theory of heredity. The whole covered a large sheet of paper, yellow with age and worn at its folds. Upon this paper was boldly outlined a symbolical tree, whose branches, spreading out and dividing, displayed five rows of large leaves; and each of these leaves bore a name followed by brief biographical particulars in small handwriting.

It was with a *savant's* delight that the Doctor gazed at this document—the work of twenty years—in which the hereditary laws that he had laid down were so precisely, so completely exemplified.

' Look, my child,' said he, ' you know quite enough, you have copied out sufficient memoirs of mine to understand it all. Is it not beautiful to have succeeded in obtaining such an *ensemble* as this, so complete and final a document, free from the slightest gap ? It is like a mathematical problem worked out in full detail. Down here, you see the trunk, the stock common to us all—Aunt Dide.[1] From this trunk spring three branches—the legitimate one, Pierre Rougon, and the two bastard ones, Ursule Macquart and Antoine Macquart. From these, other branches climb up and ramify. On one side Saccard's three children, Maxime, Clotilde, and Victor, and Sidonie Rougon's daughter, Angélique. On the other side, Lisa Macquart's daughter Pauline ; and Gervaise Macquart's four children, Claude, Jacques, Étienne, and Anna.[2] Jean, the brother of Lisa and Gervaise, is yonder on the furthest branch. And here in the centre you will observe what I call the knot, the legitimate and illegitimate branches uniting in the persons of Marthe Rougon[3] and her cousin François Mouret,[4] whom she marries. And from them three fresh boughs ascend—Octave, Serge, and Désirée Mouret. Springing from Ursule Macquart and Mouret the hatter, there are also Silvère—with whose tragic death you are acquainted—and Hélène and her daughter Jeanne. Finally, right at the top, are the last twigs, so to say ; poor Charles, your brother Maxime's son, and two other little fellows, both dead —Claude Lantier's boy, Jacques-Louis, and Anna Coupeau's son, Louiset. In all we have five generations. With the sap of eternal life rising within it our human tree has thrown

[1] All the persons now to be enumerated are characters figuring in the Rougon-Macquart series of novels. Farther on M. Zola explains the purport of each work.—*Trans.*

[2] Nana.

[3] Daughter of Pierre Rougon and Félicité Puech.

[4] Son of Ursule Macquart by Mouret senior, a hatter.

out new branches at five fresh springtides, five successive
renewals of humanity ! '

He was growing animated, and began pointing out the
cases of hereditary influence on the old sheet of yellow paper
as though it had been some anatomical plate. ' And I repeat,'
said he, ' that all is here. In the direct hereditary line we
have cases where the mother's prepotency is manifest—for
instance, in Silvère, Lisa, Désirée, Jacques, Louiset, and yourself ; whilst here, in the cases of Sidonie, François, Gervaise,
Octave, and Jacques-Louis the prepotency is invariably on the
father's side. Then there are the three forms of the adjection
of characteristics—simple junction in Ursule, Aristide, Anna,
and Victor ; dissemination in Maxime, Serge, and Étienne ;
and fusion in Antoine, Eugène, and Claude. I have also had
to specify a fourth and very remarkable form—an equilibrious
blending of characteristics in Pierre and Pauline. Then come all
the many varieties, the moral nature of the mother in a child
physically resembling the father, or *vice versâ* ; whilst, in the
different blendings, one or the other parent is physically or
morally predominant according to circumstances. Then we
come to indirect or collateral heredity, and here I have only
one good example—the striking physical resemblance between
Octave Mouret and his uncle Eugène Rougon. I also have
only one example of influencive heredity : Anna, the daughter
of Gervaise and Coupeau, was, especially in her childhood,
remarkably like Lantier, the lover by whom long previously
her mother had been seduced. I am well provided, however,
with instances of reverting heredity. Here I have three
remarkably fine cases—Marthe, Jeanne, and Charles in turn
resembling Aunt Dide, and the resemblance missing either
one, two, or three generations. This is assuredly exceptional,
for I hardly believe in atavism. It seems to me that the new
elements introduced into a family by marriage with strangers,
the many chance circumstances which may occur, and the
infinite variety of successive blendings must rapidly efface any
particular characteristics and bring the individual back to the
general type. Then comes innateness, of which I have ex-

amples in Hélène, Jean, and Angélique. This is combination, a chemical blending in which the physical and moral natures of the parents are so amalgamated that nothing of them seems to subsist in the offspring.'

An interval of silence followed. Clotilde had listened to him with deep attention, desirous as she was of understanding everything. And he, with his eyes still fixed on the genealogical-tree, seemed absorbed in his reflections, striving to pass an equitable judgment on his work. After a moment he continued slowly, as though speaking to himself: 'Yes, it is as scientific as could be. I have only put down the members of the family, it is true; I might have given equal importance to those whom the family has married, the fathers and mothers of different extraction whose blood, mingling with ours, has modified it. I did draw up a mathematically arranged tree, in which each parent was put down as contributing one half of each child's nature, in such a way that in Charles's case, for instance, Aunt Dide's share of influence was only one-twelfth. But this was absurd, for the physical resemblance between them is absolute. So I thought it sufficient just to indicate the extraneous elements introduced into the family, the various marriages, and the new factors which these brought with them. Ah! these infantile sciences, these sciences in which one can only proceed timidly by hypothesis, and over which imagination still reigns supreme, they are assuredly the domain of poets quite as much as of *savants*. The poets go forward in the advance guard as pioneers, and often discover virgin lands, and point out the solutions which are near at hand. Between the acquired truths, those that are completely established, and the Unknown, whence the truth of to-morrow will be wrested, there is a space which fairly belongs to the poets. And what a huge fresco might be painted, what a colossal human comedy and tragedy might be written on heredity, which is the very genesis of families and societies, of the world itself!'

A vague expression had come into his eyes; he was following his thoughts, losing himself among them. Then all at once, pushing the genealogical-tree on one side, he came back to the batches of documents, saying : 'We will take the tree in hand again by-and-by; for, in order that you may understand things, it is needful that facts should now be brought before you, and that you should see all the personages whom we have just glanced at, against whose names, on the tree, there are only a few memoranda summarizing their characters and careers. It is necessary, I say, that you should see all these at work. I will show you, tell you what each portfolio contains, before they are all put back on the shelf again. I won't take them in alphabetical order, but in the order in which the events they are connected with occurred. I have long been wishing to classify them in that manner. Come, look for the names on the wrappers. Aunt Dide, first of all.'

At this moment some of the fringing clouds of the storm, which was setting the horizon afire, drifted obliquely over La Souleiade, and burst above the house. A torrential rain poured down, still they did not even close the window. They heard, in fact, neither the bursts of thunder nor the continuous roll of the deluge beating upon the roof. Clotilde had passed the portfolio, on which Aunt Dide's name was written in big letters, over to the Doctor, who drew from it various papers, old memoranda long since written by himself, which he began to read.

'Give me Pierre Rougon,' he called; 'give me Ursule Macquart; give me Antoine Macquart.'

She silently obeyed his instructions with a fresh pang at her heart at each name she heard. And, passing from her to him in due order, the portfolios displayed their contents in turn, and were then once more piled up on the shelf of the old oak press.

First of all came the origin of the family [1]—its founder, Adélaïde Fouque, the tall, demented creature from whom had come the first nervous lesion and with whom had originated both the legitimate branch, Pierre Rougon, and the two

---

[1] All the volumes of the Rougon-Macquart series are now passed in review. The first is *La Fortune des Rougon* ('The Fortune of the Rougons').

illegitimate branches, Ursule and Antoine Macquart. Here was a sanguinary middle-class tragedy with the Coup d'État of December 1851 as its setting; the Rougons, Pierre and Félicité, ensuring the 'triumph of order' at Plassans, but staining their dawning fortunes with the blood of poor Silvère; whilst Adélaïde, already aged, already the wretched Aunt Dide, was shut up at Les Tulettes, there to remain as a spectral personification of expiation and death deferred.

Then the appetites of the family were let loose, and the supreme craving for power was personified by Eugène Rougon, the great man, the eagle of the family, full of disdain, above all petty motives, loving force for its own sake, conquering Paris in his shabby clothes in company with all the adventurers of the coming Empire, rising from the Corps Législatif to the Senate, quitting the Presidency of the Council of State for a Ministerial portfolio, raised to power by his 'band,' the hungry pack that carried him along and preyed upon him.[1] And, although momentarily defeated by a woman, the lovely Clorinde, for whom he had felt an insane desire, he had proved himself so strong, so firm of purpose, that by abandoning every principle of his past life he had yet again victoriously risen to power, marching on to the triumphal, princely position of Vice-Emperor.

Then came Aristide Saccard,[2] personifying the ravenous appetite for low enjoyment, in hot pursuit of money, woman and luxury, possessed by an all-devouring hunger which had thrown him on the streets at the very moment when the juggling with millions began; when the mad whirlwind of speculation swept through Paris, laying entire districts of it low so that they might be built anew; when within six months huge fortunes were made unblushingly, spent to the last penny, and made again; when men got drunk with their longing for gold, when he himself grew so intoxicated with desire that the body of Angèle, his first wife, was barely cold before he sold his name in order to obtain the first needful hundred thousand francs by marrying Renée. And it was the same maddening

---

[1] *Son Excellence Eugène Rougon* (' His Excellency Eugène Rougon ').
[2] *La Curée* (' The Rush for the Spoil ').

thirst that led him later on, at a moment of pecuniary difficulties, to shut his eyes to the abominable intrigue which
his second wife carried on with his son Maxime amid all the
flaring brilliancy of Paris *en fête*.

Saccard it was, too, who a few years afterwards[1] set in
motion that huge machine for squeezing millions out of
people's pockets, that machine called the Banque Universelle;
Saccard who was never conquered ; Saccard who had grown,
raised himself to a higher level, to the intelligence and bravery
of the great financier, to a comprehension of the fierce civil-
ising *rôle* that money plays in the world ; Saccard who fought,
won, and lost battles at the Bourse like Napoleon at Austerlitz
and Waterloo, who submerged a world of poor folks beneath
the downfall of his enterprise, whilst his illegitimate son,
Victor, disappeared through the black night into the hidden
spheres of crime, and he himself, as though protected by
unjust and impassive nature, was loved by that adorable
Madame Caroline, as a reward, no doubt, for all the evil that
he had wrought.

And then a large, immaculate lily sprang up from the
hotbed of vice.[2] Sidonie Rougon, the complaisant helpmate
of her brother Saccard, the foul go-between with a hundred
shady callings, had brought that pure, divine creature
Angélique into the world : Angélique, the little fairy-fingered
embroideress, who, with the gold thread for her chasubles,
wove such an entrancing dream of Prince Charming, ever far
away with the saints her companions, and of a nature so ill
adapted to stern reality, that it was vouchsafed to her to die of
love upon her wedding-morn, under the first kiss of Félicien
de Hautecœur, even whilst the pealing bells were proclaiming
the glory of her regal nuptials.

Then were the two branches—legitimate and illegitimate—
grafted upon one another.[3] Marthe Rougon became the wife
of her cousin, François Mouret—a peaceful household at first,
then slowly sundered, and overtaken at last by the most awful
catastrophes—a sad, gentle woman caught in, utilised and

---

[1] *L'Argent* (' Money ').   [2] *Le Rêve* (' The Dream ').
[3] *La Conquête de Plassans* ('The Conquest of Plassans ').

crushed by the huge war-machine set in position to effect the conquest of a town. And her three children were, so to say, torn from her, and even her heart was wrenched away by the fierce hand of the Abbé Faujas ; and the Rougons saved Plassans yet a second time ; whilst she, unhappy woman, lay upon her death-bed amid the glow of the conflagration in which her husband, maddened by heaped-up rage and vengeance, was devoured together with the priest.

Of the three children, Octave Mouret proved the audacious conqueror, the man with a clear head. Bent on becoming the sovereign of Paris through woman's instrumentality, he had, on his arrival in the capital, tumbled into the midst of the rotten Parisian middle classes,[1] among whom he underwent a terrible *éducation sentimentale*, and became steeped in the mire of adultery. But fortunately he retained his active, industrious habits and his warlike spirit of enterprise, and, despite everything, rose above circumstances, gradually freeing himself from all the low tricks and subterfuges of that rotten world, whose crack of doom could already be heard. And Octave Mouret, victorious, had then set to work to revolutionise the spheres of commerce, annihilating the little shops where old-fashioned traders plied their callings with so much prudence, and rearing in the midst of fevered Paris a colossal Temple of Temptation,[2] ablaze with the light of countless chandeliers and overflowing with velvets, silks and laces. Here he had gained a king's fortune in exploiting woman— woman whom he continued treating with a smiling contempt, till a mere girl, but an avengeress — simple and virtuous Denise—mastered him and kept him at her feet, distracted with suffering—despite the apotheosis of his Louvre and the gold that rained incessantly into his cash-boxes—so long as she, poor though she was, would not accord him the boon of her hand in marriage.

There remained Serge and Désirée Mouret—the other two children of Marthe and François ; Désirée, as witless but as healthy as a happy young animal ; and Serge, of a refined

[1] *Pot-Bouille* (' Piping Hot ').
[2] *Au Bonheur des Dames* (' The Ladies' Paradise '

nature and mystical disposition. By some nervous, racial accident he had become a priest, destined, however, to enact the Adamic adventure over again in the legendary Paradou, where he was born anew that he might love Albine, possess her and lose her in the bosom of accomplice nature.[1] Reconquered by the Church, he had again waged the everlasting war against life, struggling for his own sexual death, casting, as officiating minister, the symbolical pinch of earth upon Albine's lifeless form, and this at the very hour when Désirée, the animal's good friend, was exulting with delight over the fecundity of her poultry-yard.

Later on began a gentle, tragic sketch of life : [2] Hélène Mouret, living peacefully with her little girl Jeanne on the heights of Passy, overlooking Paris, that limitless, bottomless human ocean, in full view of which the love episode unfolded itself—Hélène's sudden passion for a stranger, a chance doctor who had been called at night to her daughter's bedside ; Jeanne's sickly jealousy, the instinctive jealousy of an *amoureuse*, seeking to prevent her mother from loving elsewhere, and so consumed by the sufferings of passion that when the sin was committed it killed her. A terrible price to pay for a single hour's forgetfulness in an otherwise blameless life—the loss of that poor dear little girl, lying all alone under the cypresses of the silent cemetery, facing eternal Paris.

The bastard branch began with Lisa Macquart, who, full of strength and life, with the plumpness born of prosperity, stood in her spotless white apron on the threshold of her pork-butcher's shop, smiling at the Central Markets, where the hunger of an entire people growled, and where the century-old battle of the Fat and the Thin was waged so bitterly.[3] The Thin personified by her lean brother-in-law Florent, so execrated, so mercilessly hunted down by the fat fishwives, by the fat tradeswomen, by even fat Lisa herself, who, strictly honest but altogether unforgiving, caused him to be arrested on the score that he was a Republican escaped from captivity, in the

---

[1] *La Faute de l'Abbé Mouret* ('The Abbé Mouret's Transgression ').
[2] *Une Page d'Amour* ('A Love Episode ').
[3] *Le Ventre de Paris* ('Fat and Thin ').

belief that by doing so she was contributing to the peaceful
digestion of all decent folks.

From Lisa came the healthiest, most human of girls—
Pauline Quenu,[1] the virgin with a well-balanced, sensible
mind, who knew what life was and accepted it ; so passionate
in her love for others that, despite the revolt of nature, she
relinquished her betrothed Lazare to her friend Louise, and,
saving the child of the sundered pair from death, became its
real mother. And, albeit always sacrificed and eventually
ruined, she yet remained triumphant and gay in her mono-
tonously solitary nook facing the great ocean, amid a small
circle of suffering beings who shrieked their pain aloud, yet
would not die.

And then came Gervaise Macquart with her four children ;[2] Gervaise, lame, pretty, industrious, cast by her lover
Lantier on to the pavement of the Faubourgs, where she
came across Coupeau, the plumber, the steady workman,
whom she married. And right happy was she at first, employing three girls in her little laundry shop, but soon, like
her husband, sinking low under the fatal influence of her
surroundings—he slowly conquered by drink, to the point
even of furious madness and death ; she perverted, rendered
lazy, finished off by the return of Lantier, by the igno-
minious life which she then led between him and her husband, and thenceforth becoming the prey of accomplice
misery, which wore her away and ended one night by laying
her prostrate—dead of starvation.

Claude, her eldest son, had the pain-fraught genius of a
great painter mentally unhinged, driven mad by his powerlessness to produce the masterpiece[3] which he felt within
him, but which his fingers were unable to transfer to canvas.
A struggling giant he was, a giant ever conquered, one of
the crucified martyrs of art, adoring woman, sacrificing his
wife Christine, so loving and for a time so loved, to the
increate woman, whose divinity he pictured in his mind's
eye, but whom his brush could never rear erect in her

---

[1] *La Joie de Vivre* ('How Jolly Life is ! ').   [2] *L'Assommoir.*
[3] *L'Œuvre* (' His Masterpiece ').

sovereign nudity. His was the devouring passion to bring forth, the insatiable desire to create, a desire so frightfully distressful when it cannot be satisfied, that he ended at last by hanging himself.

His brother Jacques [1] brought crime into the family. In him the hereditary virus turned to an instinctive appetite for blood—young, fresh blood, flowing from the gashed throat of some woman, the first comer, the first creature passing along the street. An awful and abominable disease it was, and though he struggled against it, it seized upon him, mastered him during his amours with submissive, sensual Severine, whom one night, in a paroxysm of his ailment, infuriated by the sight of her white bosom, he stabbed to death. . . . And all this bestial savagery, the savagery of the human animal swept hither and thither among express trains, amid the roar and rattle of the engine he drove, the engine which he loved so well, and which one day crushed him to pieces, and then, driverless, unrestrained, rushed furiously onward to the unknown dangers ahead.

In his turn came Étienne, [2] dismissed from his employment, astray in the world, reaching the black country one icy night in March, descending into the voracious pit, there meeting and loving that sorry creature Catherine, whom a brute robbed him of, living with his mates the miners their mournful life of misery and low promiscuity, until a day came when hunger breathed forth revolt, and carried hither and thither over the bare and level plain the whole howling swarm of wretches, clamouring for bread amid conflagrations and crumbling buildings—undeterred by the threatening presence of the soldiers, whose guns went off spontaneously. . . . A terrible convulsion it was, premonitory of the end of a world, for the avenging blood of the Maheux would assuredly rise up later on. Alzire had been killed by starvation, Maheu had been killed by a bullet, Zacharie had been killed by an explosion of fire-damp, Catherine had been entombed underground, and only La Maheude survived,

---

[1] *La Bête Humaine* (' The Human Animal ').   [2] *Germinal.*

bewailing her dead, but, nevertheless, descending into the pit again to earn her beggarly thirty sous [1] a day; whilst Étienne, the defeated leader of the band, haunted by the thought of the revendications which the future held in store, took himself off one balmy April morning, listening as he went to the subdued, covert travail of the new world, which in germinating would rend the earth.

And then came Nana, the low-born harlot, who had grown up on the social dung-heap of the Faubourgs—Nana, the *revanche* of the humble, the golden blowfly that darts upward from the rottenness below, that is tolerated, concealed, and carries with it in its flight the ferment of destruction, soaring aloft and rotting the aristocracy, poisoning men by merely alighting upon them in the palaces which it enters through the windows, and unconsciously accomplishing a mighty work of ruin and death. Vandœuvres roasting in the conflagration he had so furiously kindled; Foucarmont in deep melancholy roaming the China seas; Steiner sucked dry and forced to live an honest life; La Faloise with his self-satisfied imbecility; the Muffats and their tragic downfall; George, shot dead by his own hand and lying there a white corpse, watched over by his brother Philip, discharged from prison the day before—these were some of Nana's victims; and such was the contagion wafted on the pestilential atmosphere of the period that she herself became putrefied, perished of the black-pox—which she had caught beside the deathbed of her son Louiset—whilst under her windows streamed Paris, drunk, stricken with madness—the madness for war which urged it onward to the Downfall of everything.

At last appeared Jean Macquart,[2] the artisan and soldier, who had again become a peasant, contending with the hard ground which exacts a drop of sweat for every grain of wheat that it yields; struggling above all things with the country folk, the peasantry, in whom the slow and laborious conquest of the soil fosters an intense desire, a galling need of possession; as witness the aged Fouans parting with their fields

---

[1] 1s. 2d.   [2] *La Terre* ('The Soil').

as though they were parting with their flesh ; the exasperated Buteaus impelled even to parricide in order that they might the sooner inherit a field of lucern ; that obstinate creature Françoise, ripped up by a scythe, and dying in stubborn silence, unwilling that a single clod of earth should go out of the family's possession—all that tragedy, indeed, enacted by simple, instinctive folk barely raised above the savage state of ancient times, that tragedy enacted by all those specks of human dirt cast upon the far-stretching surface of the earth, which alone remains immortal, the Mother whence we come and whither we must return, she whom we so love that we recoil not from crime to win her, and who, ever and ever, continues recreating life even out of the misery and abominableness of human beings, in order that she may achieve her unknown ends !

And Jean it was again who, having become a widower, and re-enlisted at the first rumour of war, supplied in the hour of need the inexhaustible reserve fund, the fund of eternal rejuvenescence which the earth is careful to preserve. Jean the humblest, firmest soldier of the supreme smash-up ;[1] Jean carried along by the frightful and fatal tempest, which, whilst it rushed from the frontier to Sedan, sweeping away the Empire, threatened also to destroy the country itself; Jean, full of a fraternal affection for his comrade Maurice, the crazed progeny of the middle-class, the holocaust destined for the expiation ; Jean, shedding tears of blood when inexorable fate selected him to lop off that rotten limb ; and then, at the end of all, after the continual defeats and the frightful civil war, when the provinces were lost and the milliards had to be paid, Jean, despite everything, setting out on the march once more, returning to the soil which was waiting for him, betaking himself to the great and the laborious task of building up a new France.

Pascal paused. Clotilde had passed him all the batches of documents in turn, and he had run through them all, reclassified and replaced them on the topmost shelf of the old

---

[1] *La Débâcle* ('The Downfall').

press. He was out of breath, exhausted by his rapid survey of all that living humanity; whilst the girl, without a word, without a gesture, bewildered by the overflowing torrent of life that had rushed past her, still remained waiting, incapable as yet of reflecting or forming a judgment. The storm continued beating the black countryside with its ceaseless downpour of diluvian rain. A thunderbolt had just thrown a tree near by to the ground, with a horrible noise of cracking and breaking; and the candles flared and flickered in the gusts of wind which were darting in through the open window.

'Ah!' the Doctor resumed, again pointing to the documents, 'they form a world, a society, a civilisation. All life is there, with its good and its evil manifestations, amid the forge-like glow and labour which leaven the whole. Yes, our family might now suffice as an example to science, which hopes that it will some day be able to determine mathematically all the nervous and sanguineous accidents to which a race becomes liable after the first organic lesion—accidents which, according to circumstances and environment, bring about in each individual of the race all the various sentiments, desires and passions that he may feel, all those human, natural, and instinctive manifestations which are denominated vices and virtues. And our family, moreover, serves the purpose of an historical document, for its history is that of the Second Empire, from the Coup d'État to Sedan. Rising from among the people, our kith and kin have spread through the whole of contemporary society, fought their way into every kind of position, urged on by that outburst of ravenous appetite, that impulsion peculiar to modern times, that lashing whipstroke which sets the lower orders on the march through the entire social system, seeking the various satisfactions that they may desire. The origin of the family, as I have told you, was at Plassans, and here we are, back at Plassans again.'

He paused afresh in a dreamy mood, amid which the words fell more slowly from his lips: 'What a frightful mass it all makes! how many episodes of love, how many terrible adventures; how many joys, how many sufferings there are

in this huge pile of facts ! There is history pure and simple :
the Empire founded in blood, at first bent on self-enjoyment,
sternly authoritative, subduing the rebel towns, then slowly
becoming disorganised, and at last toppling over in blood—
in such a sea of blood, indeed, that the entire nation was well-
nigh submerged. Then there are social studies, commerce on
a large and a small scale, prostitution, crime, the soil, money,
the middle classes, the working classes—those who rot in the
mire of the Faubourgs, those who revolt in the great centres
of labour, the whole growing impulsion of Socialism, which is
pregnant with the century to come. And there are simple
studies of humanity, pages of quiet domestic life, tales of love,
the contests in which the mind and the heart engage with
unjust nature, the crushing of those who shriek aloud under
their overpowering task, the cry of compassionate goodness
which sacrifices itself and triumphs over pain. And there is
fantasy, too, flights of imagination beyond the realms of
reality, vast gardens flowering at all seasons, cathedrals with
tapering spires exquisitely carved, marvellous tales wafted from
Paradise, ideal affections ascending to Heaven in a kiss. There
is something of everything—of that which is excellent and
that which is most vile, the vulgar, the sublime, flowers, filth,
sobs and laughter—the very torrent of life itself, which for
ever and ever bears humanity upon its bosom ! '

He again took up the genealogical-tree, which alone had
remained on the table, and having spread it out there, he
once more ran over it with his finger, enumerating in turn
the various members of the family who were still alive.
Eugène Rougon, the discrowned potentate, now a member of
the Assembly, there impassively defended the old order of
things which the Downfall had swept away. Aristide Saccard,
having changed his skin, had fallen on his feet again, a
Republican for the nonce, directing a leading newspaper, and
once more making piles of money, whilst his natural son,
Victor, had altogether vanished, living no doubt in the shady
haunts of crime—since he was in no penitentiary—let loose
upon the world like some brute foaming with the hereditary
virus, whose every bite would enlarge the existing evil—free

to work out his own future, his unknown destiny, which was perchance the scaffold. Sidonie Rougon, after long disappearing from the scene, weary of the shady callings she had plied, and now of a nunlike austerity, had just retired to the gloomy shelter of a conventual kind of establishment, holding the purse-strings of the Œuvre du Sacrement, an institution founded with the object of assisting seduced girls, who had become mothers, to secure husbands. Octave Mouret, the proprietor of that huge repository, 'The Ladies' Paradise,' and whose colossal fortune was still increasing, had, towards the end of the previous winter, been presented with a second child by his wife, Denise Baudu, whom he still adored, though he was not quite so steady as formerly. The Abbé Mouret, parish priest at Saint Eutrope, in the depths of a marshy gorge, had there cloistered himself with his sister Désirée, leading a life of great humility, refusing all preferment from his bishop, waiting for death like a holy man, averse to remedies, although he was already in the early stage of phthisis. Hélène Mouret and her new husband, M. Rambaud, were living, very happily and in a very secluded way, on a small estate they owned upon the seashore near Marseilles. Hélène had no children by her second marriage. Pauline Quenu was still at Bonneville, at the other end of France, face to face with the mighty ocean, all alone with little Paul since Uncle Chanteau's death, and determined that she would never marry, but devote herself entirely to the son of her cousin Lazare. Lazare, on his side, having become a widower, had betaken himself to America in search of fortune. Étienne Lantier, returning to Paris after the Montsou strike, had subsequently taken part in the rising of the Commune, whose principles he had defended with passionate violence. Condemned to death but reprieved, he had been transported, and was now at Noumea, New Caledonia. It was said that he had married immediately on his arrival there and already had a child, but the latter's sex was as yet unknown to the Doctor. Finally, Jean Macquart, receiving his discharge after the Bloody Week, had returned to Provence and fixed his abode at Valqueyras, near Plassans, where he had been lucky enough to marry a sturdy girl, Mélanie Vial, the only daughter of a peasant farmer in easy circumstances, whose land he cultivated. His wife, who had only given birth to a boy in May, was already expecting another child; it was one of those instances of rich fertility which do not even allow mothers the time to suckle their offspring.

'Yes, certainly,' Pascal resumed in an undertone, 'races degenerate. One can here trace a veritable exhaustion, a rapid decline. It is as though, with their furious enjoyments and the gluttonous gratification of their appetites, they had burnt themselves out too quickly. Louiset dying in his cradle; Jacques-Louis half an idiot and carried off by a nervous malady; Victor relapsing into a state of pristine savagery, rushing into the black depths of some unknown abyss; our poor Charles, so handsome and so feeble—these are the last boughs of our tree, the last white twigs to which the powerful sap of the large branches seems unable to ascend. The worm was in the trunk, and now it is in the fruit and devouring it. But one must never despair; families represent eternal change. They plunge back—far beyond the common ancestor, through the inexplorable strata of races that once existed—to the very first human being; and they will grow and spread, branch out endlessly through all the future ages. Look at our tree, it only comprises five generations, and amidst the vast, black, human forest, of which nations are the centenarian oaks, it has not even the importance of a blade of grass! But think of its immense roots extending right through the soil to its lowest depth; think of its leaves on high for ever shooting forth and mingling with other leaves, with the whole sea of crests, waving incessantly under the everlasting, fructifying breath of life! Yes, the hope is there—in the constant modification and reconstitution of the race by the fresh blood that comes to it from without. Each marriage introduces new elements, either good or bad, whose effect in any case is to prevent mathematical, progressive degeneration. Gaps are filled up, stains, blemishes are effaced, equilibrium is reestablished after the lapse of a few generations, and it is always *the average man* who ends by emerging — indeterminate humanity obstinately intent on its mysterious labour, and ever marching onward to achieve its unknown end.'

He paused and sighed deeply. 'Our family!' he exclaimed, 'ah! what will become of it—what being will spring from it at last?' And then he went on talking—no longer counting on the survivors whom he had enumerated, for he had classified them and knew what they were capable of—but full of curiosity with regard to the children, who were yet in infancy. He had written to a fellow-practitioner at Noumea for precise information respecting the woman whom Étienne had married there and the child that she was said to have given birth to; but hitherto he had received no reply, and greatly feared that on this side the tree would remain imperfect. He was better informed with regard to the two children of Octave Mouret, for he had remained in correspondence with the latter. The little girl, it appeared, was growing up lean and sickly; whilst the boy, who greatly resembled his mother, was, on the contrary, becoming a superb child with sound health and a well-balanced intelligence. The Doctor's firmest hope, however, centred in the children of Jean, whose firstborn was a magnificent boy, in whom one could divine all the young, revivifying sap of the races which acquire renewed vigour by returning to the soil. Pascal occasionally went over to Valqueyras and returned delighted with the happy fecundity he beheld there: the father calm and sensible, always at his plough; the mother gay and simple, broad-hipped, well built for the functions of maternity. Who could tell whence the healthy branch would spring? Perhaps it was there that the sensible, strong-minded being he longed for would germinate. Unfortunately for the beauty of his genealogical-tree, these lads and lassies were still so young that he could not classify them. Resting, as he did, his hope for the future on their curly pates, his voice, in speaking of them, quivered with affection— affection tinged with the secret regret he felt at his own celibacy.

Still looking at the genealogical-tree spread out before him, he at last exclaimed: 'See how complete, how decisive it is! I repeat that every kind of hereditary case is to be found there.

To determine my theory indeed, I merely had to base myself on all those facts. And the marvellous part of it all is that we here see that human creatures belonging to the same stock may appear radically different one from another, though they simply typify so many logical modifications of their common ancestors. The trunk explains the branches, and the branches explain the leaves. Although your father, Saccard, and your uncle, Eugène Rougon, are so different in temperament and mode of life, it was the same impulsion that produced the former's ravenous appetites and the latter's sovereign ambition. Angélique, a spotless lily, came from an equivocal creature like Sidonie, for the same influence determines either mysticism or sexual passion according to environment. Then take Mouret's three children—the inspiration which makes an intelligent fellow like Octave a millionaire dealer in finery for women, also causes Serge, a believer, to become a poor country priest, whilst Désirée, a witless creature, develops into a handsome, happy girl. But the most striking example of that which I wish to point out occurs among Gervaise's children — the neurosis passes to them, and Nana sells herself, Étienne rebels, Jacques murders, and Claude is endowed with a measure of genius; whilst near at hand, Pauline, their cousin-german, becomes the personification of victorious honesty, the woman who combats and sacrifices herself. This is heredity, life itself, which produces imbeciles, madmen, criminals, and great men. Certain cells collapse, others take their place, and you have a rascal or a raving lunatic in place of a man of genius or a simply honest man. And meantime humanity continues rolling onward, carrying all along with it.'

Then, his thoughts taking another turn, he added: 'And linked with all this there's the animal creation—the animal which suffers and loves, which is, so to say, the *rough-draft* of man. I should have liked to include in my system all those brotherly household animals which share our life—I should have liked to give them a place in our family, showing how often they become mingled, blended with ourselves, completing, as it were, our lives. I have known cats to whose presence a house owed all its mysterious charm, dogs that were positively adored, whose deaths were lamented with tears, and who left inconsolable grief in their masters' hearts. I have known goats, cows, donkeys who have been important factors in the existence of human beings, who played such preponderant parts that their history ought really to be written. For instance, take our old Bonhomme, our poor old horse who has served us for a quarter of a century—don't you think that his blood has mingled with ours, and that he has now become a member of the family? We have influenced him in the same way as he has slightly influenced us, and we all end by being made after much the same image. And so true is this, that nowadays, when I see him half-blind, with dim eyes, and legs stiffened by rheumatism, I kiss him on either cheek as I might kiss some poor aged relative who had fallen to my charge. Ah! the animal world, all the creatures that drag themselves about, that suffer and sorrow by the side of man, what a large space, what a large share of sympathy should be meted out to them in any history of life!'

This last exclamation was fraught with all Pascal's passionate affection for the living creature. He had gradually grown excited, and had come at last to his confession of faith, his belief in the continuous, victorious labour of living nature. And Clotilde, who had hitherto remained without speaking, as pale as linen beneath the blow dealt her by all that she had heard, at last opened her lips to ask: 'And what of me, master, what of me?'

She had placed one of her slender fingers on the leaf of the genealogical-tree upon which she saw her name inscribed. He had invariably passed that leaf by while giving his explanations. 'And I?' she insisted, 'what am I? Why did you not read the documents concerning me?'

For a moment he remained silent as though surprised by the question. 'Why?' he said at last, 'oh, for nothing. And really I have nothing to hide from you. You can see what is written there: "Clotilde born in 1847. Takes after her mother. Reverting Heredity: the mental and physical characteristics of her maternal grandfather preponderant." Nothing could be clearer. You take after your mother; you have her good appetite, and you have also a good deal of her coquetry, and even occasionally of her indolence and submissiveness. Yes, without being aware of it, you are very feminine, as she was. I mean, that you like to be loved. Your mother, too, was much addicted to reading novels; she was a fantastical creature, and adored lying in bed for days at a stretch, poring and dreaming over some book or other. She delighted, also, in old woman's tales; she would have her fortune told her by cards, and consult somnambulists. I have always thought that your preoccupation with regard to the Mysterious, your anxiety respecting the Unknown, has come from all that. But what completes you, what imparts a dual character to your nature, is the influence of your grandfather, Major Sicardot. I knew him; he was not an eagle certainly, but at least he possessed a large fund of rectitude and energy. Frankly, if it were not for him, I fear you would not be worth much, for the other ancestral influences are hardly favourable. To him, then, you owe the best part of your being, your courage, pride and frankness.'

She had listened to him attentively, and now slightly nodded her head as if to say that it was indeed so, and that she did not feel hurt at hearing it, albeit her lips had quivered as these new particulars concerning her mother fell upon her ears. 'Well,' she resumed, 'and you, yourself, master?'

This time he did not hesitate for a moment, but exclaimed: 'Me? Oh! what is the use of speaking of me? I don't belong to the family. You can see what is written there. "Pascal born in 1813. Innateness. A combination in which the physical and moral characteristics of the parents are so blended that nothing of them appears manifest in the offspring." Ah! yes, your mother has repeated often enough that I didn't belong to the family, that she could not tell where I had sprung from.'

These words came from him like a cry of relief, instinct with an involuntary delight. 'Yes,' he added, 'folks make no mistake about it. Have you ever heard the townspeople call me Pascal Rougon? No, they have never called me otherwise than mere Dr. Pascal. That is because I am so unlike the others. It is not very affectionate of me, perhaps, but I am delighted at it, for there are some hereditary influences which are really too hard to bear. I certainly love them all, but none the less my heart beats with delight when I feel that I have nothing in common with them, but am absolutely different. Not to belong to them, not to belong to them! Ah, my God! it is like a puff of pure air, it is that which gives me the courage to keep them all there, to lay them bare in all those papers of mine, and yet, at the same time, retain courage enough to live!'

He spoke no further; silence ensued. The rain had now ceased falling, the storm was passing away, the thunderclaps were becoming more and more distant, whilst from the refreshed countryside, where all was still black, a delightful odour of moist soil ascended, entering the room through the open window. And now that the atmosphere was becoming so much calmer the partially consumed candles burned with steady, erect flames.

'Ah,' said Clotilde, with a gesture of overpowering despair, 'what will become of me?'

She herself had declared it one night on the threshing-floor: Life was abominable. How could one live peacefully and happily? Science cast a terrible light upon the world, analysis penetrated to every human sore and bared its horror. And now he had spoken yet more bluntly, increased all her nausea for creatures and things, laying even his own family bare on the slabs of the dissecting-room. For nearly three hours the torrent of mire had been rolling past before her eyes, and it was the most awful of revelations, the truth, sudden and terrible, concerning all her kith and kin, the dear ones, those whom it was her duty to love. Her father had battened amid the crimes that money engenders, her brother had been an adulterer—nay, worse; her grandmother had shown herself utterly unscrupulous, and was stained with the blood of the just; and in almost all of the others there was something evil—drunkenness, vice, murder, the whole monstrous florescence of the human tree. So brutal was the

shock, so painful was her stupor at learning the whole of life
so suddenly and in such a fashion, that she knew not where
or what she was. Nothing evil, however, had come to her
from it all; she had felt her face lashed as by a briny sea-
breeze, the wind of the tempests, whence one emerges with
dilated and healthy lungs. He had said everything, speaking
freely of his own mother, though without departing from the
deference of the *savant*, who expounds facts and does not
judge them. To say everything so that everything might be
known, everything cured, was not that the cry which he had
raised on the threshing-floor one lovely summer's night?
The excessiveness of what he had taught her had shaken her;
she was blinded by the violent light that his words had shed;
still she now, at last, understood him and acknowledged that
he was attempting a mighty work. Despite everything, his
was an appeal for health, a cry of hope in the future. He
spoke as a benefactor who, given the circumstance that
heredity makes mankind, wished to determine its laws so that
he might be able to dispose of it and recreate a happy world.

Moreover, was there merely mire in that overflowing river
whose floodgates he had opened? How much gold had there
not floated by, mingling with the weeds and flowers on the
banks? Hundreds of living creatures were still galloping
before her, figures typical of charm and goodness haunted
her—girls with delicate profiles, women of serene beauty.
There passion in all its phases bled, the entire human heart
opened and soared in flights of love. The Jeannes, the
Angéliques, the Paulines, the Marthes, the Gervaises, the
Hélènes were numerous. A breath of fraternal humanity
rose both from them and from the others, even from the
sorriest of them all, even from the most terrible of the men,
the vilest scoundrels of the entire band. And it was that
breath which she had felt passing by, that current of broad
sympathy with which he had imbued his otherwise precise
and scientific lesson. He had not appeared moved, he had
preserved the impersonal demeanour of the demonstrator; but
what a fund of sorrowful compassion, of feverish devotion, of
self-sacrifice for the happiness of others, could be divined in

the depths of his being! His entire work, built up so mathematically, was, even when keenly ironical, fraught with this
grief-stricken fraternity. Had he not spoken of animals like
an elder brother of all that lives and suffers? Suffering exasperated him; if he spoke out so loudly and openly, it was
because he could not silence the anger born of his dream; if
he was brutal, it was only by reason of the hatred he felt for
the artificial and the transitory, for he dreamt of working—
not for the polished society of any brief period—but for the
whole of humanity, and for all the critical phases of its
history. Perhaps it was indeed his feeling of revolt against
current triteness that had rendered him so audacious in pro-
pounding and working out theories. And, whatever might be
said of his work, it remained instinct with human feeling,
overflowing with the endless sob that ascends from creatures
and things.

Besides, was not this life? There is no absolute evil. No
man is ever bad in everybody's eyes; he always makes the
happiness of some one; so when one does not obstinately
look at mankind from one sole point of view, one ends by
understanding the utility of each living creature. Those who
believe in a Deity must say to themselves that if their Deity
does not immediately crush and annihilate the wicked, it is
because his eyes are fixed upon the march of his work taken
in its entirety, because he cannot or will not bestow attention upon individuals. The labour that ends begins anew;
the vast majority of the living display, despite everything,
admirable courage and industry, and the love of life leavens
the whole lump. The gigantic labour that men perform, their
stubborn resolve to live, is the excuse of their being, their
redemption. And so, from on high, the glance of the Deity,
it may be, takes account only of this continual struggle, and
of the existence of much good even if there also be much
evil. Mankind is entering upon an era of universal indulgence and forgiveness, all else is if slowly yet surely giving
way to infinite pity and ardent charity. And surely the
haven is there, awaiting those who have lost their faith in
dogmas, who desire to understand why they live, given all

the apparent iniquity of the world. One must live for the effort that life requires, one must live to contribute one's share to the mysterious work whose accomplishment may be yet far distant; and the only peace of heart possible in the world lies in the joy of having made this effort, of having accomplished one's share of toil.

Another hour had slipped by, the whole night had been spent in that terrible lesson of life, without either Pascal or Clotilde being conscious of where they were or of the flight of time. And at last—overtaxed as he had been for several weeks past, wearied with the life of suspicion and grief that he had been compelled to live—the Doctor rose up shivering nervously, as if suddenly awakened.

'Come,' said he, 'you now know everything—is your heart firm, has truth penetrated it, is it full of forgiveness and hope? Are you with *me*?'

Under the frightful mental shock that she had sustained, however, she herself was quivering, unable to regain her self-possession. Within her there was such a smash-up of the old beliefs, such an evolution towards a new world, that she dared not question herself and come to a conclusion. She felt herself caught, carried off by the almightiness of truth, but she suffered it instead of accepting it, being yet unconvinced— 'Master,' she stammered, 'master——'

For a moment they remained face to face, looking at one another. The day was breaking, a dawn of delicious purity was rising in the vast clear heavens washed clean by the storm. At present not a cloud blurred the pale azure, over which rose a pinky tinge. The gay awakening of the moist countryside penetrated through the open window, whilst the flames of the candles, now nearly consumed, grew pale in the growing daylight.

'Answer me—do you still wish to destroy and burn everything here? Are you with me, entirely with *me*?'

At that moment he thought that she was about to fling herself weeping on his neck. A sudden impulse seemed to urge her to it. But all at once they perceived each other as they were. She, who hitherto had not given the matter a thought, became conscious that she was clad merely in her chemise and petticoat, that her arms were bare, her shoulders bare, scarcely screened by the wavy curls of her unbound hair; and as she lowered her glance she beheld, near her left arm-pit, a few stains of blood, the marks of the scratch she had received during the struggle when, in order to subdue her, he had caught her in a brutal grasp. And thereupon a feeling of extraordinary confusion came over her, a conviction that she was fated to be vanquished, as though he had indeed, by that grasp, become her master in all things and for ever. The sensation lasting, she felt her will power leaving her, seized, transported as she was by an irresistible need of surrendering.

But, all at once, she drew herself erect, determined to reflect upon it all. She had crossed her arms tightly over her bare bosom. All the blood in her veins rushed to her skin in a stream of purple modesty, and she turned and darted away, crying : ' Master, master, let me think—I will see.'

With a nimble step she sought refuge in her room as once before, and he could hear her hastily shutting the door and locking it. He remained alone, and suddenly overcome by immense discouragement and sadness, asked himself if he had, after all, done well in saying everything, if truth would ever germinate in the heart and mind of that dear loved one, to grow and blossom forth, some day, in a harvest of happiness.

CHAPTER VI

SEVERAL days went by, the month of October was at first delightful, without a cloud in the sky : it was a hot burning autumn, all the warm passion of summer mingling with the maturity of the later season. But before long the weather changed, terrible winds began sweeping by, a last storm gullied the slopes ; and as the winter drew nigh an infinite sadness invaded that dreary house, La Souleiade.

It was again a hell, but of another kind. There was no more lively quarrelling between Pascal and Clotilde. The doors were no longer slammed, angry shouting no longer compelled Martine to run upstairs every hour or so. At present they scarcely spoke together, and not a word had been said respecting the scene of the night. Through a scruple which remained unexplained, a singular feeling of modesty which the Doctor did not seek to understand, he was not inclined to renew the discussion, or to ask for the reply that he awaited—a word of submission and of faith in himself. Clotilde, on her side, after the great mental shock which had wholly transformed her, continued reflecting, hesitating, and struggling, brushing the solution aside in the instinctive feeling of revolt which she experienced. And so the misunderstanding continued amid the heavy mournful silence of that wretched house, where there was no happiness left.

For Pascal this was a period during which he suffered frightfully, yet without complaining. The seeming peacefulness did not reassure him, far from it. He was still the prey of gloomy suspicion, ever imagining that the others were still lying in wait for him, and that if they pretended to leave him in peace, it was only that they might plan the blackest plots against him in the dark. His anxiety indeed had even increased, and not a day passed but he expected a catastrophe; his papers would be swallowed up in some abyss that would suddenly open, the whole of La Souleiade would be razed to the ground, would be carried off or fly away in shreds; and now that the persecution directed against his thoughts, against his moral and intellectual life, was in this wise concealing itself, it worried him yet more than before, and became in fact so intolerable that at night time, when he went to bed, he would be in a high fever. He would often start and turn, thinking that he was on the point of surprising the enemy plotting some piece of treachery behind him; but there was no one, nothing indeed but the quiver of his own fears, stirring in the depths of the darkness. At other times, seized with suspicion, he would remain watching during long hours, hiding behind his shutters, or crouching in ambush in some passage. However, not a soul moved; he could hear no sound save the throbbing of his own temples. It all ended by driving him to distraction, and he no longer went to bed until he had searched each room. Even when he was stretched between the sheets, he could not sleep; at the slightest noise he awoke, panting with anxiety and ready to defend himself.

Pascal's sufferings were aggravated by the incessant and ever-growing thought, that he was being thus wounded in heart and mind by the only being that he loved in the whole world—by that adored creature Clotilde, whose growth in charm and beauty he had been watching for twenty years, and the blossoming of whose life had hitherto imparted a perfume to his own. To think that it was she—she, *mon Dieu*, who filled his heart with an absolute tenderness which he had never analysed, she who had become his joy, his courage, his hope, the new youth in which he felt himself live once more. When he saw her pass him, with her delicate, round, young neck, he felt as it were refreshed, healthful, and blithesome as at the return of spring. His life explained how it was that she had thus taken possession of him, how it was that his entire being had been penetrated by this young creature, who, when yet but a child, had already secured a place in his affections, and had ended by appropriating them entirely. Since he had definitely fixed himself at Plassans, he had been leading the life of a Benedictine, cloistered among his books, and far from women. He was only known to have had one passion, a passion for that lady who was dead, and whose finger-tips he had never even kissed. Doubtless he went at times to Marseilles, and slept away from home, but these trips were few and far between, and without consequence. In point of fact, he had not lived, and now, at the approach of old age, all the virility within him was asserting itself. He would have lavished affection on any animal, on any dog picked up in the street, that would have licked his hands; and now it was Clotilde, whom he loved so dearly —that little girl now suddenly become a woman—who possessed his whole heart, and tortured him by remaining his enemy.

Pascal, once so kind and so gay, grew unbearably harsh and ill-tempered. He flew into a passion over the most trifling matters, and was ever hustling Martine, who, greatly astonished, gazed at him with the submissive eyes of a beaten animal. From morning till night, he carried his distress about the dreary house, with so stern a look upon his face, that they dared not speak to him. He never took Clotilde out with him now, but went alone to visit his patients. And in this wise he came back one afternoon in a state of utter distraction, with a man's death upon his conscience. He had gone to puncture Lafouasse, the landlord of the little wineshop near Le Paradou, whose ataxy had suddenly made such progress that the Doctor deemed him lost. Nevertheless he obstinately continued his efforts to save him, persevering with the same treatment; but unfortunately that afternoon some particles of impure matter, which, despite the filtering, had entered into his *liqueur*, passed from the phial into the little syringe, whilst, to complete the misfortune, in making the puncture he pricked a vein, and a drop of blood oozed forth. He immediately felt very anxious, for he saw Lafouasse turn pale, perspire, and catch his breath. Then when death came like a lightning flash, and the man lay

there with his lips blue and his face black, he understood everything. It was a case of embolism, the responsibility of which
rested with the crude nature of his preparations, the as yet
raw character of his entire method. No doubt Lafouasse
could never have been cured, he could hardly have lived
another six months, and then only amidst atrocious sufferings; nevertheless the brutal fact—that frightful death—was
there, and in presence of it the Doctor's despair was intense ;
all his confidence in himself was shaken, he was angered
beyond measure with science—science powerless to cure and
swift to slay. He came home quite livid, and did not show
himself again until the following day—having in fact remained
for sixteen hours shut up in his room, motionless, scarce
breathing, stretched in his clothes across the bed.

That afternoon, as Clotilde sat sewing near him in the
workroom, she at last ventured to break the heavy silence.
Raising her eyes, she watched him as he worked himself into
a state of nervous agitation, turning and turning the pages of
a book in search of some information which he was unable to
find in it. 'Are you ill, master?' she asked. 'If so, why
don't you tell me? I would nurse you.'

Without taking his eyes off the book, he muttered in a
husky voice, 'Ill! what does it matter to you? I have no
need of anybody.'

'If you have any worries and could tell me of them,' she
resumed in a conciliatory way, 'it would perhaps ease you to
do so—you seemed so sad when you came home yesterday.
You must not let yourself give way like that. I spent a very
anxious night. I went three times to your door to listen,
worried by the thought that you were perhaps in pain.'

She had spoken very gently, still her words lashed him
like a whip. Bowed though he was by suffering, a sudden
outburst of anger now made him push the book aside, and
spring, quivering, to his feet. 'And so you spy on me!' he
cried. 'I can't even go into my room but you must come and
press your ears to the walls—my very heart-beats are listened
to, my death is being watched and waited for, so that everything here may be pillaged and burnt!'

His voice rang out, and he exhaled all his unjust sufferings in words of complaint and menace. ' I forbid you to busy yourself about me,' he continued. ' Have you anything else to say to me ? Have you reflected, can you put your hand in mine, loyally, and tell me that you are of the same mind as myself ? '

She did not answer, but simply continued looking at him with those clear eyes of hers, which frankly expressed her desire to remain mistress of her own mind. Her demeanour heightened his exasperation, and, casting aside all restraint, he waved his arm to drive her away and stammered out : ' Be off, be off with you ! I won't have you remain near me. I won't have enemies beside me. I won't have people staying with me and trying to drive me mad ! '

She had risen to her feet, looking extremely pale, and, rigidly erect, she took herself off, carrying her sewing and not once looking round.

During the ensuing month Pascal sought a refuge in desperate, incessant work. He would now remain all day long in the workroom, quite alone there, and would even sit up all night, going through old documents of his, and re-arranging the whole of his writings upon heredity. It might have been thought that a raging desire now possessed him to convince himself that his hopes were justifiable, to compel science to make it quite certain that humanity might be remoulded, restored to complete health and raised to a higher plane. He no longer went out, but, abandoning his patients, lived solely among his papers, without a thought of fresh air or exercise. And when he had overtaxed himself in this way, wearing himself out without alleviating his domestic worries, he fell into such a state of nervous exhaustion, that illness, which for some time had been germinating, declared itself with alarming violence. When he arose in the morning he felt overwhelmed with fatigue, heavier, more wearied even than he had been on going to bed the previous night. It was a distressful sensation pervading his entire being ; his legs felt tired after five minutes' walking, the least effort exhausted him, he could no longer make a movement but acute suffering

followed. At times the ground seemed to oscillate beneath
his feet. A continual buzzing in the ears made him feel
giddy, showers of sparks seemed to flash before his eyes and
compelled him to close them. He acquired a disgust for
wine, ate scarcely anything, and suffered from indigestion.
Then, amid the apathy of increasing indolence, he would
have sudden useless spurts of foolish activity. Physical and
mental equilibrium were destroyed; in the weak, irritable
state in which he found himself, he rushed without rhyme
or reason from one extreme to the other. At the slightest
emotion, his eyes filled with tears, and he ended by shutting
himself up in such crises of despair that he would weep and
sob for long hours, without any immediate cause of grief, but
simply by reason of the utter dreariness of things. His complaint became much worse after a sudden trip he made to
Marseilles, whence he returned bowed down, overwhelmed
like a man who finds all his virility departed from him. He
seemed utterly distracted with wretchedness, and even
thoughts of suicide flashed through his mind. In the early
days of December he began suffering from acute neuralgic
pains. It seemed to him as though the bones of his skull
were cracking, as though his head would suddenly split. Old
Madame Rougon, having been apprized of his condition, made
up her mind one day to come and enquire-after him. Wishing, however, to speak with Martine first of all, she slipped
into the kitchen on entering the house, and there, Martine,
with a scared, afflicted expression on her face, told her that
Monsieur was of a certainty going mad. In proof thereof she
gave an account of his singular behaviour, of the way he
tramped up and down his room, of the care with which he
kept every drawer locked, and of the incessant rounds which
he made through the house up to two o'clock in the morning.
Tears came into her eyes as she told all this, and she ended by
expressing an opinion that an evil spirit had taken up its abode
in Monsieur's body, and that it might be advisable to communicate with the priest of St. Saturnin. 'To think of it!'
said she, 'so good a man, a man for whom I'd let myself be
chopped to pieces. How unfortunate it is that we cannot

persuade him to go to church, for that would surely cure him at once.'

Just then, Clotilde, having heard her grandmother's voice, came into the kitchen. She also wandered about the empty rooms, spending most of her time in the disused drawing-room on the ground floor. She did not speak, but stood by listening to the others with that reflective, waiting air now peculiar to her.

'Ah! it's you, darling! how are you?' said old Madame Félicité. 'Martine tells me that an evil spirit has lodged itself in Pascal. And that is my own opinion, too, only the name of the spirit is Pride. He believes that he knows everything, he is pope and emperor all in one, and so, of course, it exasperates him when others don't say the same as himself.' She shrugged her shoulders, full of infinite disdain, and then went on: 'It would really make me laugh if it were not all so sad, a man who in point of fact knows nothing at all, who has never lived, who has foolishly remained all his life shut up with his books. Take him into a drawing-room, and he shows himself as much an innocent as a new-born babe—and besides, what does he know of women?' Forgetful to whom she was speaking—that girl and that old spinster servant—she lowered her voice to add with a confidential air: 'A man may be too virtuous. No wonder his brain has become affected.'

Clotilde did not stir; the only sign she gave was to slowly lower the lids of her large pensive eyes; then she raised them again, retaining the demeanour of one who hides her thoughts, or who cannot as yet tell what is passing within her. And indeed, her mind was still in confusion, undergoing an evolution, the purport of which she herself was doubtless unable to realise. 'He is upstairs, is he not?' resumed Félicité. 'I came to see him, for there must be an end of all this, it is altogether too foolish.'

Thereupon she went up, whilst Martine returned to her saucepans, and Clotilde again began wandering through the empty house.

In the workroom upstairs, Pascal sat like one stupefied, with his eyes fixed upon an open book. But he could no longer read, the words seemed to dance away from him, to vanish, to have no sense. Yet he obstinately persevered, suffering sorely at the thought that he was losing even his faculty for work, hitherto so powerful. And his mother immediately began scolding him, tearing the book out of his hands, and flinging it upon a table, whilst she exclaimed that, when a man was ill, he ought to take care of himself, nurse himself properly. Pascal had risen to his feet with an angry gesture, intent on driving her away just as he had done with Clotilde. By a final effort of will, however, he succeeded in reacquiring his wonted deferential demeanour. 'You know very well, mother, that I have never desired to have any discussions with you; leave me, I beg you,' he said.

She would not give way, however, but began tackling him with regard to his incessant suspicions. If he were in a feverish state like that, it was his own fault, it was the result of his foolish fancy that he was surrounded by enemies who were ever laying traps for him, and watching and waiting to pillage him. But could any man in his senses believe in such persecution? Moreover, she reproached him with having unduly excited himself over that discovery of his, that wonderful scheme for curing all diseases. Then, too, it never did a man any good to refuse to believe in God. Deceptions then proved cruel indeed; and thereupon she alluded to Lafouasse, the man whom he had killed. She could understand very well, said she, that this had been very unpleasant to her son: it was, in fact, enough to make anyone take to his bed.

Still restraining himself, and keeping his eyes turned towards the floor, Pascal contented himself with repeating: 'Leave me, mother, I beg of you.'

'No, no, I won't leave you,' she retorted with all the impetuosity she was wont to display in spite of her great age. 'I came expressly to stir you up a bit, to rid you of that low fever which is consuming you—Things cannot go on like this, I don't want the family to become the talk of the whole town again, through these affairs of yours—I am determined to make you take care of yourself.'

Pascal shrugged his shoulders, and, in a low voice, as

though speaking to himself, as though anxiously diagnosticating his own case, replied : 'I am not ill.'

At this, Félicité started up quite beside herself: 'Not ill? Not ill, indeed! Really, only a doctor could be so blind to his own condition—why, my poor fellow, everyone who comes near you is struck by it. You are going mad with pride and fear!'

On hearing this, Pascal quickly raised his head, and looked her straight in the eyes, whilst she continued : 'That's what I came to tell you, since nobody else would undertake to do so. And assuredly you are old enough to know what you ought to do. You must bring about a reaction, think of something else. it does no good to let a fixed idea secure possession of one's mind, especially when one belongs to such a family as ours. You know it well, so be warned and take care of yourself.'

He had turned pale, and was still gazing at her fixedly, as though trying to fathom her, to ascertain how much of her, his mother, there might be in himself. And by way of reply, he contented himself with saying, ' You are right, mother, thank you.'

When he found himself alone, he sank down upon a chair in front of his table, and wished to resume the perusal of his book. But he was no better able now than before to concentrate his attention upon it, or to understand the words, whose letters intermingled and faded away from before his eyes. His mother's warning was still buzzing in his ears, and a feeling of anguish, which had been rising within him for some time already, now expanded, and became more precise, shaping itself into a haunting dread of a well-defined and imminent danger. Only two months previously, he had triumphantly prided himself on not being one of the family, and were events now about to belie his words in the most cruel way possible?

Was the grief of finding the family taint in his own marrow reserved to him? Was he fated to feel himself in the awful clutches of the hereditary monster? His mother had declared that he was going mad with pride and fear. And, after all, what could that supreme idea of his be, that enthusiastic conviction that he would be able to abolish suffering, endow mankind with increased will power, remould humanity, imbue it with health, and set it on a higher level—what could all this be indeed but the premonitory symptom of that form of madness called *la folie des grandeurs*? And then too, in his fears of an ambush, in the need he felt of incessantly watching for the foes whom he believed intent on destroying him—in these things he recognised the symptoms of the mania of persecution. And that granted, all these racial accidents could only have one terrible ending, madness within a brief period, then general paralysis and death.

From that day forward Pascal was like one possessed. The state of nervous exhaustion, to which he had been reduced by overwork and grief, plunged him, without possible means of resistance, into a haunting dread of insanity and death. All the morbid sensations he experienced, his intense weariness on rising, the buzzings he heard in his ears, the dizziness which came over him, even his attacks of indigestion, and his fits of weeping, helped, one by one, to pile up the agony as it were, like so many certain proofs of the approaching mental collapse with which he believed himself to be threatened. So far as his own condition was concerned he had entirely lost his delicate, penetrating power of diagnosticating; and if he continued reasoning his case, it was only in a confused and perverse way amid all the moral and physical depression in which he now dragged out his life. He no longer had any control over himself; he grew mad, as it were, in seeking at every moment to convince himself that mad he must assuredly become.

He spent every one of those pale December days in plunging yet deeper and deeper into his malady. Every morning he felt a desire to escape from his haunting thoughts, but, despite everything, he once more came and shut himself up in the workroom, there to take up the same tangled skein as on the day before. His long studies on heredity, his vast researches, all his scientific labours indeed, helped to poison his mind, incessantly supplying him with fresh reasons for disquietude. His batches of documents furnished every possible kind of answer to the question which he was always asking with reference to his case from the hereditary point of view. So manifold were the possibilities that he now fairly lost himself among them. If he had indeed been mistaken, if he could not set himself entirely apart as a remarkable instance of innateness, ought he to put himself down among the cases of reverting heredity, those which skipped one, two, or even three generations ; or, was his case merely an instance of latent heredity, supplying a fresh proof in support of his theory of the germ-plasm ; or, on the other hand, ought he only to see in it the peculiarity of successive resemblances, the sudden appearance of some unknown ancestor in his nature ? From the moment when these thoughts assailed him, he no longer knew any rest, but set out on a search to identify his case, rummaging among all his memoranda and reading his books afresh. And he began to analyse himself, to watch and note the slightest of his sensations, in order that he might acquire data that would enable him to pass judgment on himself. On the days when his mind was more indolent than usual, when he fancied that he experienced peculiar phenomena of vision, he inclined to a belief in some predominance of the original nervous lesion ; whereas if he fancied himself attacked in the legs and his feet seemed heavy and painful, he imagined that he was experiencing the indirect influence of some forerunner who had married into the family. Amid all the imaginary symptoms which dealt such shocks to his distracted system, he ended at last by fairly losing himself, so intricately did these symptoms mingle together. Still every evening he came to the same conclusion, the same alarm bell sounded in his brain : heredity, the terror of heredity, the dread of going mad.

During the early days of January, Clotilde, without desiring it, witnessed a scene which sorely distressed her. Hidden by the lofty back of an armchair, she was seated reading at one of the windows of the workroom, when she saw Pascal, who had remained cloistered in his bedchamber since the previous day, come in. With both hands he was holding, open, before his eyes, a large sheet of yellow paper, which she recognised to be that of the genealogical-tree. He was so profoundly

absorbed, his eyes were so intently fixed upon the paper, that
she might have shown herself without being noticed by him.
Laying the document open on the table, he continued for a long
time examining it with a terrified, questioning expression,
which gradually became humble and prayerful, whilst tears
coursed slowly down his cheeks. Why was this, *mon Dieu*?
Would not the genealogical-tree answer him, tell him which
ancestor it was that he took after, so that he might note down
his own case beside the others on the leaf bearing his name?
If he was destined to become mad, why did not the tree declare
it plainly and distinctly?

He fancied that this would have calmed him, imagining
indeed that it was simply uncertainty that caused his sufferings.
His tears obscured his sight, still he continued gazing at the
paper, humbling himself in his desire to *know*, that pressing
desire which was now, at last, making his brain fairly reel.
All at once, Clotilde felt compelled to hide herself, for she saw
him step up to the old press and throw its doors wide open.
He caught hold of the batches of documents, and flinging them
on the table began searching them in a feverish way. It was
a repetition of the scene of the terrible, stormy night—the
distracting gallopade, the *défilé* of all the phantoms rising up
as at the touch of a wizard's wand, from among that mass of
old papers. And as each visionary form passed before him
he asked a question, raised an ardent prayer, demanded to
know the origin of his sufferings, as though in reply there
would come some word, some murmur which would bring
him certainty. At first he simply stammered in an indistinct,
unintelligible fashion, then words fell from his lips, snatches
of sentences, clearly articulated. 'Is it you? Is it you? Is
it you? You, old grand-dame, the mother of us all—is it
your madness that is to be transmitted to me? Is it you, the
guzzling uncle, the old bandit uncle, is it your chronic
drunkenness that I shall have to pay for? Is it you, nephew,
the ataxic, or you, nephew, the mystical, or you, niece, the
idiot, who will bring me the truth and show me the lesion
from which I suffer? Is it not rather one of you cousins—
you who hanged yourself, or you who murdered, or you who

perished of putrefaction—one of you whose tragic end presages my own—a miserable death in some cell, the abominable decomposition of one's being?'

And whilst he spoke the gallop past continued; they all reared themselves erect, and swept by like a tempest blast. The batches of documents became animated, assumed human forms, jostling one another like a tramping mob of suffering beings.

'Ah! who will tell me?' he continued. 'Is it the one who died mad? Is it the one who was carried off by phthisis? The one whom paralysis stifled? The one who succumbed in childhood to the poverty of his organism? What is the poison that is to kill me? What is it—hysteria, alcoholism, tuberculosis, scrofula? What will it make of me — an epileptic, an ataxic, or a madman? A madman! Who said a madman? Ah! they all say it—a madman, a madman, a madman!'

His sobs were choking him. He let his dizzy head sink on the table amid the documents, and wept on and on, shuddering violently. And then Clotilde—seized with a kind of religious terror at this vision of the fatality which governs races—stole softly away, holding her breath as she went, for she fully divined that he would have experienced great distress and shame had he known her to be there.

A long period of deep despondency followed. January was very cold. Still the sky remained beautifully serene; every day the sun shone forth from the limpid azure; and the three windows of the workroom facing the south made the apartment a kind of conservatory, maintaining a delightfully mild temperature in it. They did not even light any fire in the room, for the sun never left it, but filled it from dawn till dusk with a pale golden light, in which the flies, spared by the winter, flew hither and thither. And no sound was now heard there save the quivering of their wings. It was a warm, sleepy, closed nook—a glimpse of springtide, as it were, abiding amid winter in the old house.

And there it was, one morning, that Pascal in his turn heard the end of a conversation which sorely aggravated his sufferings. He now scarcely ever left his bedchamber till the second breakfast, and Clotilde had therefore received Dr. Ramond in the workroom, where, seated close to one another, they had begun talking softly in the bright sunshine.

This was the third time that Ramond had called within a week. Personal considerations, and especially the necessity of definitely establishing his professional position at Plassans, required that he should no longer defer his marriage; and so he was desirous of obtaining a decisive reply from Clotilde. On the two previous occasions he had been prevented from speaking out by the presence of third parties, and so he had come back again. Desirous as he was of obtaining her hand from herself alone, he had resolved upon explaining himself to her direct, in the course of a frank conversation. Their comradeship, the good sense and honourable feelings common to them both, allowed him to take this step. And accordingly he spoke his mind, and having done so, added smiling, with his eyes peering into hers, 'I assure you, Clotilde, that this is the most sensible conclusion. You are aware that I have long loved you—I indeed feel deep affection and esteem for you—still that of itself would perhaps not be sufficient, but I am certain that we shall understand one another perfectly, and be very happy together.'

She had not lowered her eyes whilst he was speaking, but on her side continued gazing at him frankly and with a friendly smile. He really looked very handsome, as he sat there near her, in all the pride and strength of early manhood. 'And why,' asked she, 'why do you not marry Mademoiselle Lévêque, the solicitor's daughter—she is prettier, richer than I am, and I know that she would be very pleased? I am really afraid, my good friend, that you are acting foolishly in choosing me.'

He listened without any sign of impatience, with an air of conviction, indeed, that his resolve was a sensible one. 'But I don't love Mademoiselle Lévêque,' he answered, 'and I love you. Besides I have thought everything over, and repeat that I am well aware what I am doing. So I pray you say yes; you yourself can have no better course to take.'

She suddenly became grave, a shadow as it were passed over her face—the shadow of those reflections, those internal struggles which she was scarce conscious of, but which had kept her silent during so many long days.

'Well, my friend,' she answered, 'since it is altogether serious, you must suffer me not to answer you to-day—allow me a few weeks longer. Master is really very ill, I am myself worried, and you would not care for me to give you an inconsiderate promise. On my own side, I can assure you that I have a deal of affection for you. Still it would be wrong for me to come to a decision just now; we are too unhappy here. So it is agreed, is it not? I will not keep you waiting long.' Then, changing the conversation, she added: 'Yes, Master alarms me. I wanted to see you to tell you of it. The other day I found him weeping bitterly, and to my mind it is certain that he is haunted by the dread of going mad. I noticed that you were examining him when you were chatting together on the day before yesterday. So tell me frankly, what do you think of his condition? Is he in danger?'

Dr. Ramond began protesting: 'No, no,' said he, 'he has overtaxed himself, broken down, that is all. How can a man of his attainments, who has busied himself so much with nervous complaints, how can he fall into such errors concerning his own condition? Really, it is distressing to think that the clearest and most vigorous minds can have such lapses. That discovery of his—the hypodermic injections—would be a sovereign specific in his case. Why does he not puncture himself?'

Then, as the girl with a gesture of despair replied that she was no longer listened to, that she could no longer even muster up courage to speak to him, he added: 'Well, then, I will tell him myself.'

It was at that moment that Pascal, attracted by the sound of the conversation, emerged from his bedroom. But seeing them seated there, so near to one another, so animated, so young, so handsome in the sunlight, which seemed to clothe them in radiant garb, he stopped short upon the threshold, and his eyes dilated, while an expression of deep suffering came over his face.

Wishing to detain Clotilde a moment longer, Ramond had taken hold of her hand. 'It is promised, eh ?' he said. 'I much wish the marriage to take place this summer—you know how I love you : I shall be waiting for your answer.'

'Certainly,' she replied, 'within a month all will be settled.'

A dizzy feeling came over Pascal, and made him stagger. So now this young fellow, a friend, a pupil, slipped into his house to rob him of his belongings ! He ought to have looked forward to this climax, and yet the sudden tidings that a marriage was possible surprised him, overwhelmed him like some unforeseen catastrophe wrecking his life for ever.

So that creature whom he had moulded, whom he had believed to be his own, would take herself off without regret, and leave him to suffer all alone in his dreary nook. Only the day before she had caused him so much anguish of mind that he had asked himself whether he should not part from her and send her to her brother, who was constantly asking for her. For a moment even he had quite resolved upon separating, both in his interest and hers. But now, all at once, finding her there with that man, hearing her promise an answer, and thinking that she would marry and leave him before long, he felt as it were stabbed to the heart.

With a heavy tread he came forward, and the young couple, turning round and perceiving him, experienced some little embarrassment. 'O Master! we were talking about you,' Ramond said at last in a cheery voice. 'Yes, we were plotting together, but not with the intention of hiding anything from you. Come, why is it that you won't nurse yourself ? There is nothing serious the matter with you : you would be all right again in a fortnight.'

Pascal, who had let himself sink upon a chair, continued gazing at them. He had strength enough to master himself, and no sign of the wound he had received appeared upon his face. It would most surely kill him, and not a soul in the world would know what hurt it was that carried him off. It

was a relief, however, to be able to fly into a tantrum, and
passionately to refuse to drink as much as a glass of *tisane*.
'Nurse myself!' he said vehemently, 'why, what's the good
of it? Isn't it all over with my old carcass?'

Ramond insisted, however, with the quiet smile of a self-
possessed man: 'You are sturdier than any of us. It's a mere
accident, and you know very well that you have a remedy at
hand. Puncture yourself——'

He was unable to continue, for this proved the climax.
Pascal flew into a passion, and asked if they wanted him to
kill himself as he had killed Lafouasse. His punctures,
indeed! There was a fine invention to be proud of, and no
mistake! He denied the power of medicine, and vowed that
he would never touch a patient again. When a man was no
longer good for anything, he died, and that was the best for
everyone. And, moreover, that was what he himself intended to do as soon as possible, so as to have done with
it all.

'Pooh, pooh,' said Ramond at last, making up his mind to
leave, in the fear lest he might yet further increase Pascal's
excitement. 'I feel quite at ease since I leave Clotilde with
you—she will attend to all that.'

Nevertheless Pascal had indeed received the supreme blow
that morning. He took to his bed at dusk, and throughout
the following day refused to open the door of his room.
Clotilde grew anxious, but in vain did she hammer on the
door with her fist; no answer was given her. Martine herself came, and, speaking through the keyhole, begged Monsieur
to tell her at any rate if he needed anything.

A death-like silence still prevailed, it seemed as though
the room were empty. Then, on the morning of the second
day, when the girl chanced to turn the handle, the door
at once opened; possibly it had already been unlocked for
several hours. And then she was at liberty to enter that
room in which she had never yet set foot, a spacious room,
cold on account of its northern aspect, and where she only
perceived a small, curtainless iron bedstead, a shower-bath in
a corner, a long black table, some chairs, and numerous

objects suggestive of alchemy, mortars, chemical furnaces, machines, apparatuses, cases of surgical instruments, placed on the table, and on shelves running along the walls. Pascal, up and dressed, was seated at the edge of his bed, quite exhausted with having made it.

'Won't you let me nurse you, then?' asked Clotilde, who felt both affected and afraid, and dared not advance very far into the room.

He waved his hand in a dejected way: 'Oh! you may come in,' said he. 'I sha'n't hurt you, I haven't the strength to do so.'

And so from that morning forward he suffered her to be near him, and to wait upon him. However, he still showed himself capricious, and, influenced by a kind of sickly modesty, would not allow her to come in whenever he was in bed. He then compelled her to send Martine to him. Still this did not happen often, for he remained but little in bed; he more often dragged himself from chair to chair, powerless to attempt any work. His condition had become yet worse; he had sunk into a state of absolute despair, and was worn out with sick head-aches and vertigo, lacking, as he said, even sufficient strength to set one foot before the other, and awaking every morning with the conviction that he would go to bed that evening at Les Tulettes stark mad. He was getting very thin too, and ever had a pained expression on his face, which looked tragically handsome under his long, wavy white hair, which he continued combing, through a last feeling of coquetry. And although he allowed them to attend on him, he roughly refused to take any remedies, doubting as he did the efficacy of medicine.

He was now Clotilde's sole preoccupation. She became detached from everything else. At first she had attended low mass at an early hour, then she altogether gave up going to church. Amid all her impatience to acquire certain knowledge and happiness, it seemed as though she were beginning to content herself with thus employing every minute in ministering to one whom she loved, whom she would have liked to see gay and kindly as of yore. She devoted herself, forgot her-

self, felt a need of making her own happiness out of the
happiness of another, and all this in an unconscious way,
impelled to it simply by her woman's heart, amid the crisis
through which she was passing, and which was profoundly
modifying her nature though she did not reason on it.   She
still remained silent concerning the differences which had
parted them ; so far she had no idea of flinging her arms
around his neck and calling to him that she was his, that he
might live afresh since she surrendered ; to her own thinking
she was but a loving daughter, watching over him like any
other relative might have done.   And everything was very
pure and very chaste—the most delicate ministerings, constant
attentions and forethought, such encroachments on her existence indeed, that now her days flew swiftly by, full of the
one desire to cure and save him, and free from all torturing
thoughts of the realms beyond.

To prevail upon him to puncture himself, she had to
engage in a perfect struggle.   He became excited, denied his
discovery, called himself a fool.   And then she on her side
began to shout.   It was she at present who evinced faith in
science, who waxed indignant at seeing him doubt his own
genius.   He resisted for a long time ; then, greatly weakened,
surrendering to the authority she was acquiring over him, he
consented, simply with a view, however, to avoid the loving
quarrels which she sought with him every morning.   After the
very first punctures he experienced great relief, although he
declined to admit it.   His mind became more clear, strength
slowly returned to him ; and thereupon she became quite
triumphant, feeling proud of him, praising his system, growing
indignant because he did not admire himself as an example of
the miracles he might work.   He smiled, he began to understand his condition : Ramond had spoken the truth, it could
only have been a question of nervous exhaustion ; and possibly,
after all, he might manage to get over it.

' It's you, little one, that are curing me,' he would say, unwilling to acknowledge his hopes.   ' All the effect of remedies,
you see, depends on the hand that administers them.'

His convalescence was a protracted one, lasting throughout

the month of February. The weather remained bright, and
though it was cold in the shade, not a day passed but the
sun warmed the workroom with its pale beams. There were,
however, occasional relapses into deep despondency, times
when the sufferer was again plunged into a state of terror, and
when his nurse, sorely afflicted, found it necessary to go and
seat herself at the far end of the room, so that he might have
no cause for an increase of irritation. At these times he
again despaired of ever getting well again, grew bitter and
aggressively ironical.

Stepping up to a window on one of these unfavourable
days, Pascal caught sight of his neighbour M. Bellombre, the
superannuated professor, who was inspecting his trees to
ascertain if they bore many fruit-gems; and the sight of this
old man, so correctly attired, so upright, so superbly calm
in his natural egotism, and apparently so far removed from
the reach of illness—suddenly drove the Doctor quite wild.

'Ah!' he growled, 'there's a fellow who'll never overtax
himself, who'll never risk his skin by letting himself give way
to grief.' And thus launched, he began in ironic strains to
sound the praises of egotism. To be all alone in the world,
unhampered by any friend, any wife, any offspring, what
delightful happiness it was!

Did not that stern old miser, who for forty years had only
had to box the ears of other people's children, who had gone
into retirement without even a dog of his own, with no
companion indeed save a deaf and dumb gardener older than
himself—did not that man typify, as it were, the greatest
happiness that could exist under the sun? No one to provide
for, not a duty to perform, not a preoccupation of any kind
save his own dear health! Verily he was a sage, and would
live a hundred years.

'Ah!' said Pascal, 'the fear of life—decidedly, there is no
better cowardice. To think that I sometimes regret having
no child of my own here. But has anyone the right to bring
wretches into the world? Noxious heredity must be killed,
life must be killed. The only truly worthy man, you see, is
that old coward.'

M. Bellombre was still peacefully going the round of his pear-trees in the March sunshine. He was never so imprudent as to risk a hasty movement, but carefully husbanded his vigorous old age. Encountering a pebble on the path, he moved it aside with the tip of his walking-stick, and then went slowly by.

'Just look at him !' continued Pascal. 'See how well preserved, how handsome he is ; aren't all the blessings of Heaven combined in his person ? I know nobody happier than he !'

Clotilde had hitherto remained silent ; this irony of Pascal's made her suffer, for she divined that it was fraught with pain. She, who as a rule defended M. Bellombre, was conscious of a feeling of protest arising within her. Tears moistened her eyelids, and in a low voice she simply answered : ' Yes, but he is not loved.'

This at once brought the painful scene to a close. As though he had received a shock, Pascal turned and looked at her. A sudden emotion was moistening his own eyes, and he walked away in order that he might not weep.

Several more days went by, with good and evil hours alternating. The Doctor's strength returned to him but slowly, and he was quite in despair at finding that he could not apply himself to work without experiencing abundant perspirations. If he had obstinately persevered he would assuredly have fainted. Still he felt that, so long as he did not work, his convalescence would progress but slowly. True, he again took an interest in his accustomed researches, reperused the last pages he had written ; and, as the *savant* awoke anew within him, all his former anxieties returned. He had at one moment sunk into so depressed a state, that the house seemed to have vanished ; it might have been pillaged, everything might have been taken, destroyed, without his even being conscious of the disaster. But now he was on the watch again, and felt his pockets to make quite sure that he had the key of the old press about him.

One morning, however, having lingered late in bed, he came out of his room at about eleven o'clock, and perceived Clotilde in the workroom, quietly engaged on a very precise ρastel drawing of a branch of blossoming almond. She raised her head smiling; and taking up a key which lay near her on her desk she offered it to him. ' Here, master,' said she.

Astonished, not understanding her as yet, he examined the object she held out to him. 'What is it ? '

' The key of the press, which you must have dropped yesterday, for I found it here this morning.'

Thereupon Pascal took it, experiencing an extraordinary emotion. He looked at it and looked at Clotilde. Was it all over then ? So she no longer persecuted him, was no longer savagely intent on stealing and burning everything. And seeing that she was still smiling, that she herself appeared moved, he felt a deep joy penetrating his heart. He caught hold of her and kissed her : ' Ah ! little girl ! ' said he, ' if we could only manage not to be too unhappy together ! ' Then, going to his table and opening a drawer, he flung the key into it, as in former days.

From that time forward he recovered strength, and his convalescence progressed rapidly. Relapses were still possible, for he was yet badly shaken. He was, however, now able to write, and his days proved less heavy, less wearisome. The sun, also, had acquired more vigour ; and so warm was it at times in the workroom that it became necessary to close the shutters. Pascal refused to receive any visitors, he rarely suffered Martine to be near him, and on the infrequent occasions when his mother came to inquire after him, he gave instructions that she should be told he was asleep. He only felt happy in that delightful solitude, nursed by her who yesterday had been a rebel and an enemy, but who was now an all-submissive pupil. Long spells of silence reigned between them, but brought them no embarrassment. They reflected, basked in dreams of infinite sweetness.

One day, however, Pascal looked very grave. He was now quite convinced that his ailment had been due to a purely accidental cause, and that hereditary questions had nothing to do with it. Still he none the less felt full of humility. ' *Mon Dieu*,' he murmured, ' what paltry things we are ! I who fancied myself so strong, who felt so proud of my healthy mind! And yet a little grief and a little fatigue all but drove me mad!' He ceased speaking and again reflected, his eyes slowly brightening as he completed the conquest of himself. And, at last, in a moment of good sense and courage he made up his mind and said: 'It is especially for your sake that I am pleased to feel in better health.'

Clotilde, who did not understand him, raised her head. 'Why is that?' she asked.

'Why, on account of your marriage, of course. We shall now be able to fix a date.'

She could not recover from her surprise: 'Ah, yes! my marriage, it's true——'

'Shall we now at once select, say, the second week in June?'

'Yes, the second week in June—that will do very well.'

They spoke no further; she had again turned her eyes to the sewing which she was engaged upon; whilst he sat there motionless, his gaze wandering afar, his face very grave.

CHAPTER VII

LOVE

On reaching La Souleiade that day old Madame Rougon perceived Martine planting some leeks in the kitchen garden. Profiting by the circumstance, she directed her steps towards the servant with the view of having a chat and extracting some information from her before entering the house.

Time was going on, and she lamented what she called Clotilde's desertion. She fully recognised that she would never more gain possession of the documents through the girl, who was ruining herself, drawing closer and closer to Pascal since she had been nursing him; becoming perverted, indeed, to such a point, that she, Félicité, had not seen her at church for several weeks past. And so the old lady was reverting to her original idea—to get rid of Clotilde first of all, and then, when her son was alone and weakened by solitude, to conquer him. Since she had not been able to prevail on the girl to go and join her brother, she had grown passionately desirous of bringing that marriage about, and, sorely vexed with the prolonged delay, she would gladly have thrown Clotilde into Dr. Ramond's arms forthwith. That afternoon she had come to La Souleiade with a feverish desire to hasten matters.

'Good day, Martine; and how are you all here?' she asked.

The servant, who was kneeling on the ground with her hands full of mould, raised her pale face, which she shielded from the sun by means of a handkerchief tied over her coif, and answered: 'Oh, the same as usual, madame, only so-so.'

Then they talked. Félicité treated her as a confidant, as a devoted helpmate, now become one of the family, to whom everything might be told. She began by questioning her, inquiring if Dr. Ramond had not called that morning. Yes, he had called, but it was pretty certain that the conversation had been confined to matters of no importance. On hearing this, Félicité began to despair, for she had herself seen the young doctor on the previous day, and he had confided in her, expressed his vexation at having so far obtained no definite reply, eager as he was to secure at least a promise from Clotilde. Matters could not go on like this; the girl must be forced to engage herself.

'Raymond is too timid and delicate,' exclaimed the old lady. 'I told him so; I knew very well that he would not dare, even this morning, to bring her to a stand. However, I mean to interfere in it myself. We'll soon see if I can't compel her to come to a decision.' Then, recovering her composure, she added: 'My son is now on his legs again, and does not need her.'

At this Martine, who, bending double, had again begun planting her leeks, quickly drew herself erect: 'Oh! certainly not,' said she.

Her face, whitened and worn away by thirty years of domestic service, was now all aglow. To tell the truth, her heart had been bleeding for some time past; it hurt her that her master would scarcely suffer her to be near him. Throughout his illness he had kept her at a distance, less and less frequently availing himself of her services, till at last he had closed the door of his room to her. She was vaguely conscious of what was going on, an instinctive jealousy tortured her amidst her adoration of her master, whose slave, whose thing she had remained during so many long years.

'Most certainly we don't need Mademoiselle,' she said. 'I can do everything that Monsieur may require.'

Thereupon she, as a rule so discreet, began talking of her gardening work, saying that she tried to find time to attend to the vegetables so as to avoid having to pay a man for his labour. The house was a large one no doubt, but when a woman wasn't afraid of work, she ended by getting through it. Then, too, when Mademoiselle was gone there would be a person less to wait upon. And quite unconsciously her eyes glittered at the idea of the deep solitude, the profound and happy peacefulness, in which she and the Doctor would live after that departure.

'It will grieve me,' she said, lowering her voice, 'because Monsieur himself will certainly be very grieved at it. I should never have thought that I could desire such a separation. Only I think like you, madame, that it's necessary, for I am very much afraid that Mademoiselle will end by ruining herself here, and that another soul will be lost. Ah! it is very sad; it distresses me so much that I often fear my heart will burst.'

'They are both of them upstairs, are they not?' asked Félicité. 'I'm going up to them, and I'll undertake to make them end it all.'

When she came down an hour later, she again found Martine in the kitchen garden, dragging herself upon her knees over the loose soil, and finishing her planting. At the very first words that Félicité had spoken upstairs—as soon as she mentioned that she had seen Dr. Ramond, and that he was impatient to know his fate—she found Pascal approving her. He was very grave, and nodded his head as though to say that Ramond's impatience seemed natural to him. Clotilde herself ceased smiling, and listened with apparent deference. Still, she manifested some surprise. Why should she be hurried? Master had selected the second week in June for the wedding, so she still had two long months before her. Very shortly she would speak to Ramond on the subject. Marriage was such a serious matter that assuredly she ought to be allowed to reflect; there was no necessity for her to engage herself till the last moment. She said these things with that sensible air of hers, like a person who has resolved to come to a decision; and Félicité had to content herself with the evident desire which they both manifested that the affair should terminate in the most reasonable way.

'I really think that it's settled,' she concluded, after telling everything to Martine. 'He doesn't seem disposed to put any obstacle in the way, and on her side she only appears desirous of not doing anything in a hasty manner. She simply behaves like a girl who wishes to question her heart fully before entering into a lifelong engagement. I will allow her another week's reflection.'

Martine, crouching on her heels, gazed fixedly at the ground, with a dark look upon her face. 'Yes, yes,' she muttered in a low voice. 'Mademoiselle has been reflecting a great deal for some time past—I'm always finding her in some corner or other. When you speak to her she doesn't answer you. She's like a person nursing an illness, with her eyes all topsy-turvy. Something's going on, sure enough; she's no longer the same, no longer the same.' Thereupon, obstinately intent on her work, the servant took up her dibber again, and stuck a leek into the ground, whilst old Madame Rougon went off tranquillised, quite sure, she declared, that the marriage would eventually come off.

Pascal, indeed, seemed to look upon Clotilde's marriage as a matter resolved upon, inevitable. He had had no further conversation with her respecting it; the infrequent allusions to the subject which occurred during their wonted chats left both of them quite calm. It was simply as though the two months which they had yet to spend together would prove endless—an eternity whose limit they would never see. She would look at him with a smile on her face, postpone all worries and resolutions with a pretty, indefinite kind of gesture, as though leaving everything to the decision of beneficent life. He, who was cured, and acquired additional strength every day, only grew sad when he returned into the solitude of his own room at night, after she had retired to bed. He felt cold; a shiver came over him at the thought that the time was approaching when he would always be alone. Was it old age beginning that made him shiver like that? Old age—it seemed to him as it were a land of darkness, in which he could already feel all his energies departing. And then regretfulness for woman, the regret that he had no child, filled him with a feeling of revolt, wrung his heart with intolerable anguish.

Ah! Why had he not lived? On certain nights he would curse science, accusing it of having robbed him of the best

part of his manhood. He had allowed labour to devour him ;
it had eaten away his brain, eaten away his heart, eaten away
his muscles. And all his lone passion had merely given birth
to books, to paper blackened with ink, which the wind some
day would doubtless sweep away, and whose cold leaves even
now froze his hands when he turned them over. And there
was no woman's breast that he might press to his own, no
child's warm hair that he might cover with kisses ! He had
lived alone, on the *savant's* icy couch, and there, alone, he
would die. Was he really fated to die like that ? Would no
share of the happiness that fell to the lot of mere porters,
mere carters who passed cracking their whips under his
windows—ever belong to him ? At any rate he must make
haste, for before long it would be too late. All his unspent
youth, all his amassed desires, coursed at the thought through
his veins in a tumultuous flood : vows that he would yet
love, that he would live anew to taste that cup of passion from
which he had never drunk. Then on the morrow, when he
came out of his room after washing himself in cold water, all
his feverishness subsided, the burning visions faded away, and
he relapsed into his natural timidity. But when night came
again, the fear of solitude threw him once more into the same
insomnia, and he experienced afresh the same despair, the
same rebellion, the same need of not dying without experience
of the love of woman.

With his eyes wide open in the darkness during those ardent
nights he ever indulged in the same dream. A girl passed
by, a girl of twenty, divinely beautiful, who entered and knelt
before him with an air of submissive adoration ; and he married
her. She was one of those pilgrims of love whom one reads
about in the old-time stories, who follow the guidance of a star
that they may come and restore health and strength to some
aged and very powerful king covered with glory. He was the
old king, and she adored him, miraculously imbuing him with
some of the youth of her own twenty years, and restoring to
him all his former faith in life. He possessed an old fifteenth-
century Bible, illustrated with quaint woodcuts, one of which
especially interested him. It represented old King David

returning into his chamber with his hand resting on the shoulder of Abishag, the young Shunammite.

The shiver which had come over David in his old age was it not the same which now froze him, Pascal, as soon as he laid himself down to rest in his lonely, dreary room? And the pilgrim of love that he beheld in his dreams, was she not another devoted, docile Abishag? He pictured her before him, a happy slave, attentive to do his bidding, of dazzling beauty, and so sweet that near her it seemed as if he were anointed with perfumed oil. Then, whilst he sometimes turned the leaves of his old Bible, other engravings passed before his eyes, and his imagination strayed afar into all that vanished world of patriarchs and kings. What faith was there manifested in the longevity of man, in his creative power, in his sovereign authority over woman! There was Abraham, a hundred years old, father of Ishmael and Isaac, husband of his sister Sarah, submissively obeyed by his bond-woman Hagar. There was the delicious idyll of Ruth and Boaz, the young widow coming to Bethlehem in the beginning of barley-harvest, laying herself down at the feet of the master, who understood the right she claimed, and as a kins-man took her to wife, in accordance with the law. And through it all one traced the free growth of a strong, long-lived race whose labour was destined to conquer the world, a stubborn, teeming racial continuity, athwart crime and sensuality in every form. Whilst he gazed at the old naïve woodcuts, Pascal's own dream seemed at last to become a reality: Abishag, the Shunammite, entered his dreary room, illumined, and embalmed it with her presence.

Ah! youth, youth, how keenly he hungered for it! This passionate desire coming to him in his declining years was fraught with a feeling of rebellion against the old age threat-ening him, with a despairing longing to retrace his steps, and begin life anew. And in this desire of his there was not merely regretfulness for early happiness, the inestimable value set upon vanished hours, to which memory imparts a charm, but there was also the well-fixed determination to profit by health and strength, and lose nought of the joys of life. Ah,

youth! How desperately he longed to live it over again!
Anguish wrung his heart when he pictured himself as he
had been at twenty, slim, healthily vigorous, like a young
oak-tree, with sheeny white teeth and thick black hair. How
he would have welcomed those gifts, once treated with disdain, could a prodigy now have restored them to him! And
youth in woman, the sight of a young girl passing by plunged
him into deep emotion. Often, too, there was nothing personal
in his feeling; he beheld but a typical picture of youth, diffus-
ing a pure scent and radiance around—youth with clear,
bright eyes, healthy, ruddy lips, fresh cheeks and dainty
rounded neck—a neck sheeny like satin, and with wavy,
downy curls casting a shadow over the nape. And youth
always seemed to him to be tall, delicate, and divinely slender.
His eyes would wander away after the vision, infinite longings
to be young himself would fill his heart. Youth alone was
good, desirable; youth was the flower of the world, the only
beauty, the only joy, the only true gift, with health, that nature
can bestow upon mankind. Ah! to begin life afresh, to be
young again!

Now that the fine April weather was bringing the fruit-
trees into bloom, Pascal and Clotilde had resumed their morning promenades through La Souleiade. These were the first
outings of the Doctor's convalescence; Clotilde led him to
the threshing-floor, where it was already very warm, took him
along the paths of the pine-grove, and brought him back to
the terrace, where all was bright, save for the two bars of
shadow thrown across it by the centenarian cypresses. The
old flagstones looked very white under the hot sun, and all
the vast horizon spread out before them, under a dazzling
sky.

One morning, when Clotilde had been running about, she
came in very animated, vibrating with laughter, so gaily giddy,
indeed, that she made her way upstairs into the workroom
without taking off her garden hat, or the strip of lace which
she had wound about her neck. 'Ah!' said she; 'how hot
I am! How foolish of me not to have taken off my things in
the hall! I'll take them down by-and-by.' She had flung

the lace upon an armchair, and began impatiently pulling at
the strings of her large straw hat. 'There now!' she exclaimed; 'I've got the bow in a knot. You must come and
help me; I shall never be able to undo it myself.'

Pascal, to whom the pleasant walk had also imparted some
excitement, felt quite merry at seeing her look so charming
and so happy. He stepped forward, came close to her. 'Wait
a moment,' said he, 'raise your chin. But you don't keep
still. How can I do anything?'

She laughed yet more gaily, and he could see her bosom
heaving with a sonorous wave of merriment. His fingers met
under her chin, involuntarily touching the warm satin of her
neck. Her person exhaled the pure scent of youth, and all at
once his eyes became dizzy, and he thought he was about to
faint. 'No, no,' he gasped, 'I can do nothing if you won't
keep still.'

A rush of blood was making his temples beat, as with
fumbling fingers he strove to unfasten the knot. His vision
of regal youth had taken shape; there before him were the
clear, bright eyes, the healthy, ruddy lips, the fresh cheeks,
the delicate, rounded neck, sheeny like satin, and with wavy,
downy curls casting a shadow over the nape.

'There, it is done!' she all at once exclaimed.

Somehow or other, he had managed to unfasten the strings.
The walls were revolving around him; for another moment
he beheld her, bare-headed now, and with a star-like face,
laughing and shaking the curls of her golden hair. Then he
was afraid lest he might catch her in his arms and kiss her
wildly, madly; and so, carrying away the hat which he still
held in his hand, he rushed from the room, stammering: 'I'll
hang it up in the hall, I sha'n't be long, I want to speak to
Martine.'

When he got down the stairs he ran and hid himself in
the abandoned drawing-room, locking himself inside it,
trembling at the thought that she might grow anxious and
come in search of him. He was distracted and haggard, as
though he had committed a crime. He spoke aloud, and
shuddered at the first cry which burst from his lips: 'It is

she that I love, that I have always loved!' And now, all at
once he saw clearly, beheld her as she was, realised that from
the seemingly sexless creature who had climbed trees like a
boy there had emerged a charming and lovable woman.   It
was monstrous, no doubt, but none the less it was true, it was
she that he loved, she, her pure, soft-scented youth that he
adored.

Then Pascal, who had sunk upon an old, broken chair,
with both hands pressed to his face, as though unwilling to
gaze any more on the light of day, burst into tumultuous sobs.
What would become of him, O God! A child whom his
brother had confided to him, whom he had reared paternally,
and who now had become a temptress of five-and-twenty
summers—woman in all her sovereign might! He felt less
resourceful, weaker than a child.

And above all things else he loved her with immense
tenderness for her moral and intellectual gifts, for her frank
uprightness of feeling, for her brave, clear mind.   Even their
differences of views—that anxiety respecting the Mysterious,
which tormented her—helped to make her more precious to
him, a being different from himself, in whom he would find
some of the Infinite of things. She pleased him even when
she rebelled and made a stand against him.   She was at once
companion and pupil; he beheld her as he had made her,
with her large, open heart, her passionate frankness, her
victorious good sense.   And, in his mind, she ever remained
necessary and present; he could not imagine that it would be
possible for him to breathe an atmosphere that she would not
share.   He needed her breath, the rustle of her skirts around
him, her thoughts, her affection, which he could feel enveloping him, her glances, her smile, all her daily womanly life
which she had hitherto given him, and which she would
surely not be so cruel as to deprive him of.   At the thought
that she was going to betake herself elsewhere, it seemed to
him as though the heavens were falling upon his head, as
though the end of everything were nigh—black and eternal
night.   She alone existed in the world, she alone was good
and lofty, intelligent and sensible, beautiful with the beauty

of the miraculous. And why then, since he adored her, and was her master, why did he not go and take her in his arms, and embrace her like an idol? They were both free; she was a woman of an age to love. 'Twould be happiness.

Pascal, who was no longer weeping, rose up, about to walk towards the door. But all at once he fell upon the chair again, overcome by a fresh outburst of sobbing. No, no, it was abominable, impossible! He had just felt upon his head, his hair as white as icicles; and horror seized him as he thought of his own age, his nine-and-fifty years beside her five-and twenty. The old shudder of terror had come over him once more; a certain conviction that she possessed him, and that he would be strengthless against the temptation of every day and hour. He pictured her again asking him to untie the ribbons of her hat, calling him, compelling him to lean over her that she might show him her work; and he pictured himself blinded, maddened, printing kiss after kiss upon her neck. He was transported with anger at the thought of the *dénouement* that might, that must come if he did not muster courage enough to separate. It would be the vilest of crimes, an abuse of confidence. And so intense was his feeling of revolt that he now rose up bravely, and found strength to return to the workroom, fully resolved upon a struggle.

Upstairs Clotilde had quietly set herself to finish one of her drawings. She did not even turn her head when he came in, but contented herself with saying: 'How long you have been! I thought at last that there must be a mistake of ten sous in Martine's accounts.'

This familiar old jest respecting the servant's avarice made him laugh; and he, too, went and seated himself quietly at his table. They spoke no further until breakfast time. A sweet, comforting feeling came over him and calmed him now that he was near her. He ventured to look at her, and was filled with gentle emotion at sight of her delicate profile, her serious, attentive air. Was it merely a nightmare, an evil dream that had come over him downstairs? Would he after all be able to conquer himself so easily?

'Ah!' he exclaimed, when Martine called them; 'I feel awfully hungry; you'll see how fast I'll pick up strength.'

She stepped up to him gaily, and took his arm: 'That's right, master; one must be merry and strong.'

When the night came, however, and he was once more alone in his chamber, his agony began afresh. At the idea of losing her he had to bury his face in the pillow so as to stifle his cries. At the thought that she would soon marry, belong to another, he was tortured by an atrocious jealousy. He would never have the heroism to consent to such a sacrifice. All sorts of plans clashed together in his feverish brain. He would turn her from marriage, keep her near him, never letting her so much as suspect his passion; he would go away with her, travel from town to town, occupy his mind and hers with endless study, so that they might remain on their old footing of comradeship as master and pupil; or, if it were necessary, he would even send her to her brother, so that she might nurse him; he would, indeed, rather lose her in that way than give her to a husband. At each solution that his mind suggested, however, he could feel his heart rending and shrieking with anguish, so imperious was the desire, the need which he experienced that she should become his own for all in all.

Nevertheless, when he rose up on the morrow, wearied by a sleepless night, Pascal had taken a resolution. After his customary shower-bath he felt strengthened, sound in mind once more. The decision he had come to was that he would compel Clotilde to plight her troth. It seemed to him that when she had formally promised to marry Ramond he himself would feel relieved. This solution, once irrevocably resolved upon, would prevent him from indulging in any insane hopes. It would constitute another barrier, an insurmountable one, between him and her; a weapon which would protect him from himself.

When he explained to her that morning that she could no longer delay matters, that she owed the good fellow, who had been waiting so long, a decisive answer, Clotilde at first appeared to be astonished. She looked Pascal in the face, in the eyes; and he found strength enough to show no perturbation, simply insisting on the point with a slightly sorrowful air, as though it worried him to have to say these things to her. At last with a faint smile she turned away her head.

'So you want me to leave you, master!' she said.

He did not give her a direct answer. 'I assure you,' he rejoined, 'that it is becoming ridiculous. Ramond would have a right to complain.'

She went up to her desk and began setting some papers in order. An interval of silence followed; then she said, 'It's funny, but here you are, now, on the same side as grandmother and Martine. They persecute me with their entreaties that I should finish matters. I thought I should still have a few days before me. But really, if all three of you urge me on——'

She did not finish, and on his side he did not compel her to explain herself more explicitly. 'Well, when shall I tell Ramond to call?' he asked.

'Oh! he can come when he likes; his visits have never displeased me. You need not worry about it. I will let him know that we shall be expecting him one afternoon.'

A couple of days later there was a repetition of the scene. Clotilde had not moved in the matter, and this time Pascal became quite violent. He was suffering too intensely; anguish overcame him as soon as she was no longer by his side, calming him with her fresh, smiling youth. And he roughly insisted that she should behave like a serious girl, and not play any longer with an honourable man who loved her. 'Come now,' he said; 'since the thing is to be, let's have done with it. I warn you that I am about to write a line to Ramond, and that he will be here at three to-morrow afternoon.'

She listened in silence, with downcast eyes. Neither of them seemed desirous of broaching the question whether the marriage was really decided upon or not; they spoke, however, as though a decision had been previously arrived at. When she raised her head again he trembled; he had felt something passing, a breath, a sigh, as it were, and he believed that she

was on the point of saying that she had questioned her
heart, and refused to contract that marriage. In that case
what would have become of him, what could he have done,
mon Dieu? Immense joy and mad terror were already
gaining possession of him. But she gazed at him with the
discreet, tender smile, which now never departed from her
lips, and answered, with an obedient air: 'As you please,
master. Send him word to be here to-morrow at three
o'clock.'

Pascal spent such an abominable night that he rose late,
giving as a pretext that his headache had come upon him
again. It was only the cold water of his shower-bath that
now brought him any relief. At about ten o'clock he went
out, saying that he would himself call upon Ramond, but in
reality he had another purpose. He knew of a *corsage* in old
point d'Alençon which a second-hand dealer of Plassans had
for sale—a marvel which had long been lying in a drawer
waiting to be purchased by some lover in a moment of
generous folly; and, amid the tortures of the night, the idea
had come to him to make a present of it to Clotilde, that she
might use it to adorn her bridal gown. The bitter idea of
adorning her himself, of making her very beautiful for the
occasion on which she would bestow herself upon another,
deeply stirred his heart, already exhausted by sacrifice. She
knew the *corsage* and had admired it one day in his company,
wonderstruck by its exceeding beauty, and coveting it only
for the purpose of setting it upon the shoulders of the Virgin
at St. Saturnin—an antique, wooden statue of the Virgin
which the faithful deeply reverenced. The dealer having
handed the *corsage* to Pascal in a small cardboard box, he
carefully hid it away in his *secrétaire* as soon as he returned
to La Souleiade.

When Dr. Ramond arrived at three o'clock he found
Clotilde and Pascal in the workroom, where they had been
waiting for him, feverish and unnaturally gay, but avoiding
any further mention of his visit. On his arrival there were
smiles and laughter—a greeting, indeed, of exaggerated
cordiality.

' Why, you are quite well again, master,' said the young man. ' You never looked stronger.'

Pascal shook his head. ' Strong, perhaps so,' said he ; ' still, the heart isn't right.'

This involuntary avowal made Clotilde start, and she gazed at them both as if the force of circumstances impelled her to compare them together. Ramond, the young doctor so greatly admired by women, had a superb smiling face, with black beard and hair of powerful growth—all the glow indeed of manly youth ; whilst Pascal with his white hair and white beard, all his abundant snowy fleece, still possessed the tragic comeliness imparted by the six months of torture through which he had been passing. His sorrowful face had somewhat aged ; of his former self he now only retained his large infantile eyes, brown, bright, and limpid. At this moment, however, his features expressed so much gentleness, such lofty kindliness, that Clotilde let her glance dwell upon him with a feeling of deep affection. A moment of silence ensued ; a little quiver sped through their hearts.

' Well, my children,' resumed Pascal heroically, ' I believe that you want to have a talk together. For my part, I have something to attend to downstairs. I will come up again by-and by.' And thereupon he went off, smiling at them.

As soon as the others were alone, Clotilde frankly approached Ramond with both hands outstretched, and taking hold of his own, retained them in her grasp whilst speaking.

' Listen, my friend,' said she ; ' I am going to pain you deeply, but you must not be too angry with me, for I swear to you that I feel deep friendship for you.'

He had immediately understood her, and turned pale. ' I beg of you, Clotilde,' he said, ' don't give me an answer now ; take longer to think it over, if you like.'

' It would be useless, my friend. I have made up my mind.' She was gazing at him with her lovely, loyal eyes, still holding his hands in order that he might feel she was both composed and affectionate.

' So you say no ? ' he resumed in a low voice.

' I say no, and I assure you that it deeply grieves me to say it. Ask me nothing now, you will know everything later on.'

He had seated himself on a chair, overcome by the emotion which he was restraining like a strong man of well-balanced mind, whose equilibrium no suffering could entirely upset. Never had any grief disturbed him to such a point before. He sat there speechless, whilst she, erect, continued : 'And above all things, my friend, don't think that I have played the coquette with you. If I allowed you to hope, if I kept you waiting for my answer, it was because I did not really know my own mind. You can have no idea of the crisis through which I have been passing, a perfect tempest in the dark, and even now I scarcely know where or what I am.'

He was at last able to speak. 'Since you desire it I will ask you nothing,' said he ; 'though it would suffice that you should answer one question. You do not love me, Clotilde ? '

She did not hesitate, but, with a compassionate sympathy, which softened the frankness of her words, gravely responded : 'It is true, I do not love you. I only feel sincere affection for you.'

He had risen to his feet again, and, with a gesture, stayed the kindly words which she would yet have spoken : 'It is over ; we will never speak of it again,' said he. 'I wished to make you happy. Do not trouble yourself about me. At this moment I am like a man whose house has just fallen on his head. However, I must needs pull through it somehow.'

A rush of blood was suffusing his pale face ; he was stifling. He went up to the window, and then came back again with heavy steps, seeking to regain his self-possession ; and in the painful silence which had fallen, Pascal was heard coming up the stairs noisily, by way of announcing his return.

'Pray do not say anything to Master,' said Clotilde, swiftly, in an undertone. 'He is ignorant of my decision, and I wish to break it gently to him—for he desired this marriage.'

Pascal paused upon the threshold. He was staggering,

out of breath, as though he had been walking too fast.
However, he still had the strength to smile at them.

' Well, my children, are you agreed ? '

' Yes, doubtless,' responded Ramond, who also was
quivering.

' Then it is settled ? '

' Completely,' in her turn said Clotilde, who felt as
though she would faint.

Leaning upon the articles of furniture, Pascal managed to
reach his writing-table, and sink into his armchair. ' Ah !
ah ! ' he exclaimed : ' my legs, you see, are of no account.   It's
this old carcase of mine.   However, I've still a strong heart.
And I feel very happy, very happy, my children ; your happiness will set me right again.'

Nevertheless, when Ramond had taken himself off after a
few minutes' conversation, and Pascal again found himself
alone with Clotilde, his anguish of mind seemed to return to
him.   ' It's finished ? ' he asked, ' quite finished ; you swear it ? '

' Oh, absolutely finished,' she responded.

He thenceforth spoke no further, but nodded his head as
though repeating that he was delighted, that everything was
for the best, and that they would now be able to live in peace.
Then he shut his eyes and feigned sleep, but in reality his
heart was beating as though it would break, and his eyelids,
so obstinately closed, were restraining his tears.

That evening, Clotilde having gone downstairs to give some
order or other to Martine, Pascal profited by the opportunity to
place the cardboard box containing the lace *corsage* in her
room.   She came up again, wished him good-night as usual,
and he himself had for twenty minutes or so retired into his
own room, when an outburst of sonorous gaiety resounded at
his door.   A little fist was knocking on it, and a fresh voice
was laughingly calling : ' Come and see, come and see ! '

Her joyfulness gained him ; there was no resisting that
call of youth, and at last he opened the door.

' Oh ! come and see, come and see what a little bird has
brought me,' she repeated.   And thereupon she led him away,
powerless to resist her.

'Do you know,' she resumed, 'I did not see the box at first, and when I came upon it I was so surprised and delighted that my heart was quite upset. I felt that I should never be able to wait till to-morrow, so I came and knocked at your door.' She had caught hold of his hands, and was pressing them caressingly in her own. 'How kind of you, and how I thank you! Such a marvel, such a lovely present for a nobody like me! And you remembered—you remembered that I admired this old relic. I told you that only the Virgin at St. Saturnin was worthy of wearing it on her shoulders. I am pleased, yes very pleased—for it's true, I'm coquettish—so coquettish, do you know that at times I should like impossible things—dresses woven of sunrays, impalpable veils made out of the azure of the sky. Ah! how beautiful I shall be! how beautiful I shall be!'

Radiant with gratitude she gazed at the *corsage*, and compelled him to join her in admiring it. Then in a sudden access of curiosity, she exclaimed: 'But tell me, why have you made me this beautiful present?'

Since, in an outburst of sonorous gaiety, she had gone to seek him, Pascal had seemed transported into dreamland. Her loving gratitude moved him to tears. At her last question, however, an expression of surprise came over his face, and he answered: 'That present, my dear, is for your wedding gown.'

She, in her turn, remained for a moment astonished, as though she could not understand. Then her face again brightened with the strange, gentle smile which it had worn for some days past. 'Ah, yes, it's true; my marriage!' And becoming serious again, she asked: 'So you are getting rid of me? You are so desirous that I should marry, because you don't want to have me here any longer. Do you still think me your enemy, then?'

He felt his anguish returning to him, and no longer looked at her, desirous as he was of proving heroic. 'My enemy, no doubt; is it not so? We have both suffered so much through one another of recent months. It is better that we should separate. Besides I am ignorant of what you think; you never gave me the answer I was waiting for.'

She vainly sought his eyes, and began talking of that terrible night when they had gone through the documents together. It was true, the shock she had then experienced had so overwhelmed her, that she had not yet told him if she were with him or against him. It was right that he should ask for a reply.

She caught hold of his hands again and compelled him to gaze at her. 'So it is because I am your enemy that you send me away,' she said. 'But I am not your enemy, I am your servant, your work, your own. Do you hear, I am with you, I am yours, yours alone.'

He was radiant; immense joy was kindling in the depths of his eyes.

'Yes,' she continued; 'I will wear that lace, yes, for I wish to be beautiful, very beautiful—for you. Have you not understood me? *You* are my master, it is *you* that I love!'

With a frantic gesture he sought to close her lips, but she finished with the cry: 'Yes; you are the man I love!'

'No; no, be silent,' he gasped; 'you madden me. You are betrothed to another, you have given your word; such madness is happily impossible.'

'The other! I compared him with you, and it is you whom I have chosen! I dismissed him; he has gone, and will never more return. There are only we two left, and it is you whom I love, and you love me, I know it, and I am yours—yours for all in all.'

CHAPTER VIII

WHEN, on the following day, Martine learnt what the situation was from Clotilde's own lips, she staggered and almost fell to the floor. The shock seemed to rend her heart, and an expression of poignant grief came over her poor pallid face, so expressive of nun-like renunciation under her white coif. She did not speak a word, but, turning on her heels, betook herself to the kitchen, where she sat down, with her elbows resting on her chopping-board, whilst she sobbed aloud between her clasped hands.

Clotilde followed her, anxious and sorrowful, and strove to understand and console her. 'How foolish you are,' said she; 'what is the matter with you? We still love you, master and I; we will always keep you with us. Because we love one another, I and he, there is no reason why you should be wretched. On the contrary, the house will now be gay from morn to eve.'

Martine, however, only sobbed the louder, utterly distracted.

'Answer me at all events,' continued Clotilde. 'Tell me why you are angry and why you weep—I shall end by calling master, and he will know how to make you answer.'

At this threat the old servant hastily rose up and sprang into her room, which communicated with the kitchen. With a gesture of fury she shut and locked the door violently behind her, and Clotilde vainly exhausted herself with knocking and calling. Hearing the noise, Pascal himself at last came down. 'What is the matter?' he inquired.

Clotilde told him of what had happened, and then he also called and knocked, in turn becoming grieved and angry. One after the other they began again and again, but there was no reply —a death-like silence prevailed inside the room. In his mind's eye Pascal could picture the little chamber, so scrupulously clean and tidy, with its walnut-wood chest of drawers and its white-curtained, nun-like bed, across which, no doubt, Martine had now flung herself, biting the bolster and striving to stifle her sobs.

'Well, so much the worse,' said Clotilde at last with the egotism born of her happiness; 'let her sulk!' And clasping Pascal's face with her fresh hands, and raising her own charming head to his, she added: 'I'll be your servant to-day, master.'

He kissed her gratefully, and she at once began busying herself with the breakfast, turning the kitchen topsy-turvy with her preparations. She had draped herself with a large white apron, and looked delicious with her sleeves rolled up, displaying her delicate arms as though for some mighty task. It happened that there were already some cutlets in the house, and these she cooked very nicely, adding to them some poached eggs and some fried potatoes, with which she was equally successful. It proved, indeed, a delightful meal, interrupted a score of times whilst with zealous haste she ran to fetch some bread, some water, or a forgotten fork. If he had allowed it, she would have served him on her knees. Ah! to be all alone together in that dear large house, far from the world and free to laugh and love one another in peace!

Throughout the afternoon they loitered about, sweeping and tidying the place. Pascal insisted upon helping her. It was a game, so to say, and they amused themselves at it like a pair of laughing children. Still now and then—at rather long intervals—they came back to knock at Martine's door. Really it was senseless on her part—she was surely not going to let herself die of hunger! However, their knocks still resounded amid a dreary void. Night fell at last, and they had to get themselves some dinner, which they ate, seated side by side, out of the same plate; and then, making a final effort, they threatened to burst open the servant's door. But their ears, close-pressed to the woodwork, were still unable to distinguish the faintest sound. On the morrow they became seriously anxious on finding that nothing stirred ; that the door of Martine's room still remained hermetically closed. For four-and-twenty hours the servant had given no sign of life.

On returning to the kitchen, however, after a short absence, they were stupefied to find her there, sitting at the table and preparing some sorrel for the second breakfast. She had quietly returned to her wonted occupations.

'Why, what has been the matter with you?' exclaimed Clotilde. 'Will you speak now?'

Martine raised her sad face, which still bore traces of her tears. However, it had become very calm, and now only expressed the resignation of dreary old age. She looked at Clotilde with an air of deep reproach ; and then, without speaking, again lowered her head.

'Are you angry with us, then?' asked the girl.

Martine still remained silent, whereupon Pascal inter-vened : 'You are angry with us, my good Martine?' said he.

The old servant at once looked at him with her old-time expression of adoration, as though indeed she loved him well enough to put up with everything, and still remain with him. And at last she spoke : 'No, I am not angry with anyone,' she said. 'The master is free. All is well if he is pleased.'

From that time forward the new life began. Clotilde, who had remained childish so long, now bloomed like some exquisite flower of love, in all the radiance of her five-and-twenty summers. And Pascal, too, under love's influence, had become handsome again, with the serene comeliness of the man who has remained sound and vigorous, despite the whiteness of his hair. He no longer had the sorrowful face that he had acquired during the months of grief and suffering through which he had lately passed. His former pleasant face came back to him, with large, bright, childish eyes and delicate features, smiling with kindliness ; whilst his white hair and his white beard grew fast and thick, with leonine abundance, imparting to him yet a younger look, snowy though they were. He was as though awakened, transported ;

a youthful ardour now upbuoyed him, manifested itself in his gestures, in his speech, in a continual desire to exert himself and live. Everything became new and delightful to him once more; the tiniest nook of the vast encompassing landscape enraptured him; the simplest flower threw him into a perfumed ecstacy; the most commonplace term of affection which through constant repetition had formerly lost all significance, now touched him to tears, as though it were some new invention of the heart, and had not long since withered under the breath of many millions of lips. Those old familiar words, 'I love you,' when spoken by Clotilde were like a wondrous caress, the superhuman charm of which was known to none but himself. And, together with health and comeliness, gaiety also had come back to him, that tranquil gaiety which he had once owed to his love of life, and which was now brightened by his passion, by all his present reasons for finding life still better than he had ever found it before.

With youth in its flower on the one hand, and ripe strength on the other, both of them, moreover, healthy, gay and happy, they formed a truly radiant couple. During an entire long month they did not once stir from La Souleiade. They would remain all day long in the spacious workroom, where everything spoke of past habits and affections, but seldom did they even attempt any work. The large carved oak press, with its doors closed, slumbered like the bookcases; books and papers, moreover, littered the tables in piles, without ever being disturbed. Both Clotilde and Pascal seemed to have forgotten their wonted occupations, to be transported beyond the realms of reality. The hours seemed all too brief, absorbed as they were in the delight of being together in this their own domain —a domain destitute of luxury, all in disorder, but full of familiar objects, and enlivened from morn till evening by the pleasant, increasing warmth of the April sun. Whenever he now and then remorsefully spoke of work, she would laughingly throw her arms around his neck and silence him with a kiss, unwilling, she said, that he should make himself ill again by overtaxing his strength. And they were likewise very fond of the dining-room, downstairs, so gay did it seem with its light-coloured panels set off with blue mouldings, its old mahogany furniture, its large pastels of flowers, and its brass hanging lamp always so clean and bright. They ate there with hearty appetites, and only took themselves off, after each meal, to return to their delightful solitude upstairs.

Then, when the house seemed to become too small for them, they had the garden, the whole of La Souleiade at their disposal. The spring advanced as the sun climbed the heavens, and when April was drawing to a close the roses began to bloom. And how delightful the place was, so well enclosed with walls that nothing occurring beyond it could disturb them. Long did they linger at times on the terrace, face to face with the vast horizon where the shady course of the Viorne and the hills of Ste. Marthe spread out, from the bar-like rocks of La Seille to the dusty, distant vista of the valley of Plassans. There was no other shade there, save such as was cast by the two centenarian cypresses planted at either end like two huge, vernal cierges which could be seen three leagues away. At times they went down the slope for the sole pleasure of climbing up those giant steps, clambering over the little walls of dry stones which upheld the soil, and examining the stunted olive and meagre almond trees, to see if they were shooting. More frequently, however, they in-dulged in delightful walks under the tapering spires of the pine-grove, which was impregnated with the warmth of the sun and exhaled such a powerful resinous odour ; or else they would again and again skirt the wall of the grounds beyond which they could only, and at infrequent intervals, hear the heavy rumbling of some waggon passing along the Chemin des Fenouillères. Then, too, they would linger enraptured on the antique threshing-floor whence such an expanse of sky could be discerned, and where they loved to stretch them-selves on the grass, with a tender recollection of the tears that they had once shed there, when their love, as yet unknown to themselves, had burst forth disputatiously under the stars.

But the retreat which they preferred, in which they in-variably ended by hiding themselves, was the quincunx of plane-trees, with its dense, shady foliage, now of a light, tender green, and resembling lacework. The huge box-plants beneath it, the old borders of the vanished French garden, formed a kind of labyrinth, the end of which they could never find. And the streamlet of water from the spring, the pure incessant crystalline vibration seemed to sing within their hearts. Hand in hand they would remain seated near the mossy basin, letting the twilight fall, slowly shrouded by the dense shade cast by the trees, whilst the water, no longer visible, still and ever sounded its flute-like note.

In this wise did Pascal and Clotilde sequester themselves, without once crossing the threshold of their retreat, until May had half run its course. Then, however, one morning he disappeared, and on returning home an hour later decked her ears with a pair of brilliants which he had gone in all haste to purchase on remembering that it was her birthday. She was passionately fond of jewels, and his gift enraptured as well as surprised her, so beautiful did she find herself with those white stars flashing beside her cheeks.

From that time forward not a week went by but he once or twice made his escape of a morning and came back bringing her some gift. Any pretext served his purpose—a fête day, a whim, a mere feeling of joyfulness. In this wise he successively brought her rings and bracelets, a necklace and a slender diadem. And taking all the jewels from their cases, he would amuse himself by decking her with every one of them, so that with a golden bow in her hair, gold upon her arms, and gold upon her neck and bosom, she looked at last like an idol, divine and effulgent with jewels and precious metal. It afforded a delicious satisfaction to her feminine coquetry, and she let herself be loved like this on bended knee, feeling that it was after all but an exaggerated form of passion.

Nevertheless, she ended by scolding him somewhat, by addressing some sensible remonstrances to him, for, in point of fact, it was absurd that he should lavish all these gifts upon her, for she could only put them away in a drawer, never making any use of them since she went nowhere. After the momentary pleasure which their bestowal afforded, the feeling of gratitude which they kindled in her breast, they were fated to be put away and forgotten.

But he would not listen, madly intent as he was upon ever and ever showering gifts upon her, and incapable of resisting his impulse to purchase any object as soon as the idea of giving it to her had once seized hold of him. It was the largess of a bounteous heart; an imperious desire to prove to her that she was ever present in his thoughts; a proud resolve to make her the most magnificent, the most envied, and the happiest; and yet a deeper feeling than all these—a longing, indeed, to sacrifice everything to her, to despoil himself, to retain for his own use neither a copper of his money nor a moment of his life. And besides, how delightful it was, when she blushingly threw her arms about his neck and expressed her gratitude in kisses. After the jewellery came dresses, finery, all sorts of toilet articles. Her room became quite littered with his gifts; the drawers were soon full to overflowing.

One morning she felt obliged to get angry. He had brought her yet another ring. 'But since I never wear them!' she exclaimed. 'And look at them all; why, if I were to put them on they would reach to my finger tips! Come, you must be reasonable.'

He was quite confused. 'Then you are not pleased with me?' he said; and so great was his distress that to relieve him she had to kiss him fondly, and swear with tears in her eyes that she was very happy. When he spoke, however, of decorating her room, of having the walls decked with hangings, and of laying a carpet on the oaken floor, she again found it necessary to protest. Her room, she said, recalled so many happy memories; she would rather he would leave it as it was.

Meantime, Martine, by her stubborn silence, passed condemnation on Pascal's exaggerated and useless expenditure. She had now assumed a less familiar demeanour, as though, under the new order of things, she had fallen from the position of friendly housekeeper to her old station as a mere serving woman. Especially did she change in her manner towards Clotilde, whom she treated like a mistress—one who is less loved, but more scrupulously obeyed. As a rule, her face retained its

wonted expression of submissive resignation—a commingling
of adoration for her master, and of indifference for everything
else. But now and then, of a morning, there would be a woe-
ful look on her face, and her eyes would be swimming in tears,
though when questioned on the subject she invariably refrained
from giving a direct answer, saying that it was nothing, that
she had simply caught a cold. And she never made any
remark concerning the presents which were filling the drawers;
indeed, she scarcely seemed to see them. She wiped or
dusted them, and put them away without a word of either
praise or blame. But in reality her whole person revolted
against this mania for giving, the comprehension of which was
assuredly beyond her capabilities. She protested against it in
her own way, by exaggerating her own economy, reducing the
expenses of the household, managing it in so strict a fashion
indeed, that she found a means of cutting down the most
trifling expenses. Thus she retrenched a third of the milk
which she had been in the habit of buying, and provided no
more sweet *entremets* excepting on Sundays. Pascal and
Clotilde, who did not dare complain, laughed together at her
extreme avarice, indulging afresh in the jests which had
amused them for ten years past, and relating that whenever
she added any butter to the vegetables she would toss the
latter in a cullender so as to get the butter back again in a
dish placed underneath.

That quarter, however, she insisted upon handing in her
accounts. As a rule she herself went every three months to
receive from the notary, Maître Grandguillot, the fifteen hundred francs which periodically fell due ; and she would afterwards dispose of the money as she pleased, entering the sums
she expended in a book which the Doctor had ceased verifying
for several years past. She now, however, brought it to him,
and insisted that he should look through it. He was in no
wise inclined to do so, but declared that everything must be
quite correct.

'But the fact is, I've been able to save some money this
quarter, monsieur,' she said. ' Yes, three hundred francs—here
they are,'

He looked at her in stupefaction. As a rule she only made both ends just meet. By what miracle of niggardliness had she been able to save such an amount ? He ended by bursting into a laugh. 'Ah ! my poor Martine,' he said, 'so that's why we've been eating so many potatoes lately ! You are a pearl of economy, but, really now, you ought to spoil us a little more.'

This discreet reproach wounded her so deeply that she at last ventured to allude to what was going on. 'Well, monsieur,' she said, 'when so much money is being thrown out of the window on one side, it's only fit one should be prudent on the other.'

He understood her, but evinced no anger ; on the contrary, the lesson amused him. 'Ah ! ah ! so you are picking holes in my accounts,' said he. 'But you know very well, Martine, that I also have my savings put by.'

He alluded to the money which he still at times received from patients, and which he was in the habit of throwing into a drawer of his *secrétaire*. For more than sixteen years he had in this wise been putting away nearly four thousand francs each twelvemonth, and the whole would have formed quite a little treasure of gold and notes, mingled indiscriminately together, had he not every now and then freely helped himself to fairly large amounts to defray the cost of his experiments or to gratify his whims. All the money that he had expended on gifts for Clotilde had come from that drawer, which he was now always opening afresh. Moreover, he deemed its contents to be inexhaustible ; he was so accustomed to take whatever he wanted from it, that no fear of ever getting to the bottom entered his mind.

'A man may surely enjoy himself a little with his savings,' he continued gaily. 'Since it is you that go to the notary's, Martine, you are well aware that I've got an income apart from all this.'

Thereupon, in the sharp, cutting voice of the miser, who is ever haunted by the threatening dread of disaster, she retorted : 'And if you hadn't got it ?'

Pascal gazed at her in amazement, and simply responded

by a vague sweeping gesture, for the possibility of any misfortune was far from his mind. He fancied that avarice was turning Martine's head, and during the evening jested about it with Clotilde.

The many presents purchased by the Doctor also supplied a subject for endless tittle-tattle in Plassans. Rumours of the situation at La Souleiade had been noised abroad, had been carried over the walls of the grounds, how one could scarcely tell, by that expansive force which feeds the keen, restless curiosity of little towns. The servant certainly said nothing, but perhaps her demeanour sufficed; at all events, the rumours flew about—doubtless the lovers had been spied upon from over the walls. And then came the purchasing of the presents, fully corroborating and aggravating everything. When the Doctor roamed the streets early in the morning, and entered the jewellery, drapery, and bonnet shops, eager eyes would peer at him from neighbouring windows, his most trifling purchases would be carefully watched, and in the evening the whole town would know that he had given Clotilde an India-silk hood, or some lace-trimmed chemises, or a bracelet enriched with sapphires. And, of course, it all developed into a crying scandal; the most extraordinary stories began to circulate, and folks would point out La Souleiade to one another as they passed it.

But especially did old Madame Rougon wax indignant and exasperated. She had ceased visiting her son on hearing of Clotilde's refusal to marry Dr. Ramond. So they played the fool with her, did they; they would do nothing in accordance with any wish of hers! Then, when the rupture had lasted an entire month, during which she had wholly failed to understand the pitying airs, the discreet condolences and vague smiles which greeted her everywhere, she all at once suddenly learnt everything. The news fell upon her like a blow from a bludgeon. Living alternately in moods of pride and dread, she had but recently, during Pascal's illness, that wehrwolf affair, been obliged to shout and scold, in order to avoid becoming, as in days gone by, the talk of the whole town! And this time it was far worse; the greatest scandal possible.

Once more was the legend of the Rougons in peril; decidedly her unhappy son knew not what to devise to annihilate the glory gained by the family at such hard cost. And so, in her angry emotion, having constituted herself the guardian of this glory, resolved as she was upon purifying the family legend by all means in her power, she straightway put on her bonnet and rushed off to La Souleiade with all the juvenile vivacity that she still retained, despite her eighty years. It was ten o'clock in the morning when she arrived.

Pascal, who was delighted with the breach between himself and his mother, was fortunately absent. An hour or so previously he had started in search of an old silver buckle, which he wished to give Clotilde for some sash or belt. Thus Félicité fell upon the girl, whom she found at her toilet, with bare arms and unbound hair, as bright and as fresh as a rose. The first onset was full of violence. The old lady emptied her heart, poured forth all the vials of her wrath. ' Why,' she at last concluded, ' why have you behaved in such an abominable way? Answer me! '

Clotilde had listened to her with a smiling albeit respectful air. ' Why?' she answered. ' Because it pleased us, grandmother. Are we not free? We are only accountable for our actions to ourselves. We owe no duty to anyone! '

' No duty, indeed! not to me, not to the family! Yet now we shall again be trailed through the mire. Do you imagine that is likely to please me? '

All at once, however, her indignation fell. She gazed at Clotilde, and saw how beautiful and radiant she looked. In her heart she was not so surprised at what had happened, and her only desire was to arrive at a fitting solution so as to silence the scandalmongers. Accordingly, in a conciliatory way she exclaimed: ' Then marry! Why don't you marry? Have you lost all shame? '

Without any sign of revolt, still as gentle as ever, Clotilde waved her hand as though to say that she could feel no shame. —Ah! *mon Dieu*, with life so full as it is of corruption and weakness, what harm had she done in following the dictates of her heart? Still she evinced no determined obstinacy on the question of marriage. 'Certainly, we will marry since you desire it, grandmother,' she said. 'He will do whatever I may ask. Later on, I will see.'

With this vague promise old Madame Rougon was forced to content herself, and thereupon she went off, and from that time forward gave out through the town that she had altogether ceased to have any intercourse with the inmates of La Souleiade. Indeed, she did not set foot there again, but in a very dignified way went into public mourning for this fresh affliction. Still, she in no wise renounced hostilities. With that tenacity which had always ended by bringing her victory, she remained on the watch, ready to profit by any circumstance that would enable her to return to the attack.

And now it was that Pascal and Clotilde ceased cloistering themselves. There was no provocation on their part, no desire to make a public display of their happiness in answer to all the evil things that were rumoured abroad. It was, so to say, a natural expansion of their love. They had gradually experienced a need of increased freedom and space, which had first of all led them out of the house into the garden, and now brought them out of the garden into the town, and carried them thence all over the vast horizon. Everything seemed filled with their love; it bestowed the world upon them. So the Doctor quietly resumed his visits, taking Clotilde with him; and they went off together across the promenades and along the streets, she leaning on his arm, in a light-coloured dress, with a spray of flowers on her head, and he buttoned up in his frock-coat and wearing his broad-brimmed silk hat. He was quite white, and she quite golden. They stepped forward, erect and smiling, with their heads uplifted, amidst such radiant felicity that a halo seemed to envelope them. At first the emotion was intense, prodigious; the shopkeepers came to their doors, women leaned out of the windows, passers-by paused to gaze after them. Folks whispered together, laughed and pointed at them. It seemed, indeed, as though the explosion of hostile curiosity would gain the urchins, and lead to their being pelted with stones. But they were both so handsome, he superb and triumphant, she so

young, so submissive yet so proud, that little by little a feeling
of indulgence came upon everyone, a feeling so delightfully
contagious that none could refrain from envying them and
loving them. They seemed to diffuse a charm which affected
every heart.

The new town, with its middle-class population of officials
and enriched tradespeople, was the last to be conquered. The
St. Marc district, its rigorism notwithstanding, at once showed
itself accessible, discreetly tolerant, as soon as they began
threading its deserted grassy footways, past the old silent
mansions which exhaled a lingering perfume of the loves of
long ago. But it was more particularly the old town that
welcomed them—the old town inhabited by the humble, who
instinctively realised what a graceful legend, what a profound
myth they personified—the beauteous damsel serving as
support to the regal master who was growing young again in
his old age. The Doctor was here adored for his kindness,
and his companion speedily became popular, greeted with
gestures of admiration and praise as soon as she appeared.
And, on their side, if they had seemed to be ignorant of the
hostility of the first few days, they readily realised the tender
forgiveness and friendship that now encompassed them; and
it seemed to render them yet handsomer; their happiness
smiled upon the entire town.

One afternoon, as Pascal and Clotilde were turning the
corner of the Rue de la Banne, they perceived Dr. Ramond on
the footway opposite. They had learnt on the previous day
that he had at last made up his mind to marry Mademoiselle
Lévêque, the solicitor's daughter. This was assuredly the
most sensible course he could take, for the requirements of
his position did not allow him to delay his marriage any
longer, and moreover, the girl, who was very pretty and well
off, was in love with him. On his side he would certainly
love her, Clotilde felt sure of it, and she was well pleased at
being able to smile at him by way of cordial congratulation.
Pascal, on his side, had waved his hand affectionately, whilst
Ramond, experiencing some little emotion at the meeting,
remained for a moment perplexed. His first impulse had

certainly been to cross the street, but a feeling of delicacy
must have restrained him; the thought, no doubt, that it
would be brutal to break in upon their dream, to penetrate the
solitude in which they yet isolated themselves amid all the
traffic in the streets; and so he, too, contented himself with
a friendly salutation, a smile with which he forgave them
their happiness. And to all three of them it was very sweet.

About this time Clotilde amused herself during several
days by working at a large pastel drawing which represented
old King David and Abishag, the young Shunammite. It
was an evocation from dreamland, one of those soaring
compositions in which her other self, the imaginative creature
within her, satisfied her passion for the Mysterious. The old
King stood with his hand resting on the shoulder of Abishag,
against a wildly luxuriant background of scattered flowers.
He looked very great, she very pure, and both seemed to diffuse
a star-like radiance.

Until the last moment, however, Clotilde left the faces of
either figure indistinct, shrouded by a kind of cloudy veil.
Pascal twitted her about it as he stood behind her watching,
in a state of agitation, for he guessed what she intended to
do. And, indeed, it was so. With a few crayon strokes she
finished the faces, and then old King David was himself,
whilst she was Abishag, the Shunammite. But both figures
remained enveloped in the glow of dreamland, poetised,
deified, as it were, with their white and their golden locks
covering them as with imperial robes, and with features
elongated by ecstacy, as though elevated to the beatitude of
the angels, endowed with smiles and glances of immortal
love.

'Ah! my dear,' he exclaimed, 'you have made us too
handsome. You have flown away to dreamland again, as in the
old days when, as you will remember, I used to reproach you
for all those chimerical flowers over there.' So saying he
pointed to the walls, on which bloomed a fantastic parterre of
pastels, the work of other days, an increate flora such as
might spring up in some imaginary paradise.

She gaily protested, however: 'Too handsome? We

cannot be too handsome. I assure you it is thus that I feel, see us, thus that we indeed are—here, look, see if it is not really so—'

With these words she took up Pascal's old fifteenth-century Bible which lay near her, and pointed to a naïve woodcut depicting King David and his handmaiden. 'You see,' she said, 'it is just the same.'

In answer to this quiet but extraordinary statement he began laughing gently.

'You laugh,' said she, 'you concern yourself with details of drawing. But it is the spirit of the thing that one should penetrate. And look at the other engravings, see if they are not the same. I will draw Abraham and Hagar, Ruth and Boaz; I will draw all of them, all the prophets, shepherds and kings, whom humble handmaidens dowered with their youth. They all look handsome and happy. You can surely see it.'

Then they leaned together over the old book, whose pages she turned with her slender fingers, whilst all the naïve woodcuts passed in turn before their eyes. A vision of the whole biblical world arose from the yellow leaves, the free growth of a strong-lived race, whose work was destined to conquer the world, the men ever vigorous, the women ever fruitful—a stubborn, teeming, racial continuity, athwart crime and sensuality in every form.

When Martine saw Clotide's new pastel nailed on the wall she gazed at it for a moment in silence, and then, with much solemnity, made the sign of the cross. A few days prior to Easter she had asked Clotilde to accompany her to church, and on the girl answering her 'No,' she had momentarily set aside the mute deference which she had for some time past observed. Nothing in the new situation of affairs astonished, upset her more than her young mistress's sudden irreligion. Accordingly she ventured to revert to her old remonstrating ways, and scolded her as she had done when she was a child and would not say her prayers. Had she no fear of God, then? Did she not tremble at the idea of going to hell, and burning there through all eternity?

Clotilde could not restrain a smile. ' Oh ! ' said she, ' you know very well that hell has never troubled me much. But you are mistaken in thinking that I have become irreligious If I have ceased going to church, it is because I say my prayers elsewhere, that's all. Cannot one pray without going to church ? '

Martine gazed at her, gaping, unable to understand. Ah ! thought she, it was all over. Mademoiselle was altogether lost. And never afterwards did she ask her to accompany her to St. Saturnin. Her own piety, however, became yet more intense, developed into a kind of mania, so to say. She was no longer to be met in her spare moments strolling about and knitting that everlasting stocking of hers. She no sooner had a moment's liberty than she hastened to the church, where she gave herself up to endless orisons. One day, when old Madame Rougon, ever on the watch, found her crouching behind a pillar, where she had already seen her an hour previously, she began to blush and apologise like a servant discovered idling away her time. ' I was praying for Monsieur,' she said.

Meantime, Pascal and Clotilde were enlarging their sphere of life, lengthening their daily walks, roaming beyond the town through all the far stretch of country around them. And one afternoon, while on their way to La Séguiranne, they experienced a feeling of acute emotion as they skirted the dreary expanse of cleared land where the enchanted garden of the Paradou had once flowered. A vision of Albine had arisen before Pascal's eyes, he had again beheld her blooming like the spring. Never in past times, when he already thought himself very old, and was wont to enter the Paradou to smile at that gay young girl—never would he then have imagined that she would already have been dead long years, when the time came for that good mother life to bestow on him such spring-like rejuvenescence. Clotilde, who felt the vision pass between them, raised her face to his, the need of affection again rising within her. Was she not indeed another Albine, the eternal *amoureuse ?* He kissed her ; and though they did not exchange a word, a great quiver swept over the level

expanse, now sown with wheat and oats, where the Paradou
had once rolled its waves of wondrous greenery.

And then Pascal and Clotilde went on across the dry, bare
plain, crunching the dust of the roads under their feet. They
loved that ardent scenery, those fields planted with meagre
almond and dwarf olive trees, those horizons of bare stripped
hills where the light-coloured *bastides* stood out whitely between
dark, bar-like, centenarian cypresses. The scene recalled those
ancient classical landscapes that figure in paintings of the old
schools—landscapes hard in tone, but with well-balanced, majestic lines. For ages past the fierce sun had been baking the
entire stretch of country, through every vein of which its heat
now coursed, imbuing each vista with increased life and beauty
under the unchanging blue of the sky, whence fell the bright
flame of a perpetual passion. Slightly shaded by her parasol,
Clotilde walked on, blooming, well pleased with this bath of
light, like a plant requiring a southern aspect ; whilst Pascal,
rejuvenescent, felt the warm sap of the soil ascending into his
limbs, in a stream of joyous vigour.

That walk to La Séguiranne had been proposed by the
Doctor,—whom Aunt Dieudonné had lately informed of
Sophie's approaching marriage to a young miller of the
neighbourhood—as he wished to ascertain if they were all
quite well and happy in that remote nook. A delightful
coolness refreshed them as soon as they found themselves in
the lofty avenue of evergreen oaks. The parent springs of all
that shady foliage coursed endlessly on either side. And when
they reached the *mégers'* house, the first persons that they
came upon were the two sweethearts—Sophie and the miller,
who were composedly kissing one another near the well, for
Aunt Dieudonné had just gone to the washhouse, over yonder,
behind the willows skirting the Viorne. For a moment the
young folks stood there blushing, in great confusion ; but as
the Doctor and Clotilde laughed good-naturedly, they became
emboldened, and related that their marriage was fixed for
St. John's Day—a long time to wait, no doubt, though it would
end by coming at last.

Of recent times Sophie had certainly gained in health

and good looks. Saved from the hereditary disease, she had grown sturdily, like one of those trees which spring from among the moist grass beside the rivulets, and rear their crests in the full sunlight. Ah! that vast, ardent sun, with what powerful life it endowed both beings and things! The girl now had but one cause of sorrow—her brother Valentin; and tears stood in her eyes when she began to speak of him, for he would perhaps not live another week. She had received news of him only the day before—he was lost. The Doctor had to prevaricate somewhat with the view of consoling her; he himself was in hourly expectation of the inevitable end. When he and Clotilde quitted La Séguiranne they retraced their steps towards Plassans at a slower pace—moved by that happiness of healthy love mingling with the faint quiver of death.

Whilst they were passing through the old town a woman whom Pascal attended came up to tell him that Valentin had just expired. Guiraude had thrown herself upon her son's body, shrieking, half mad, and two neighbours had been obliged to carry her away. The Doctor went into the house whilst Clotilde waited at the door. Then they wended their way back to La Souleiade in silence. Since Pascal had begun visiting again he seemed to be influenced solely by a sense of professional duty, and no longer extolled the miraculous effects of his treatment. With regard to Valentin's death, however, he was only surprised that it should have been so long delayed; he was convinced that he had prolonged the poor fellow's life for a year. Despite the extraordinary results which he obtained, he knew very well that death remained inevitable, the master. Yet the fact that he had held it in check during long months ought to have pleased him, and have helped to alleviate the poignant regret which he ever felt at having involuntarily killed Lafouasse a few weeks before he would have succumbed in the ordinary course of nature. But to all appearance it was not so, indeed a grave expression sat on his contracted brow as he and Clotilde returned to their dear solitude.

Here a fresh emotion awaited them. Seated under the plane-trees, whither he had been sent to wait by Martine, was

Sarteur, the journeyman-hatter, the inmate of the Asylum at Les Tulettes, whom Pascal had punctured for so long a time; and in this case his impassioned experiments certainly seemed to have been successful. Those injections of nervous matter undoubtedly imparted will-power, since there the madman was, discharged from the Asylum that same morning, declaring that he now had no more attacks, that he was quite cured of that homicidal mania which, a few months before, would have impelled him to throw himself on any passer-by and strangle him. The Doctor looked at his visitor. Short, very dark, with a retreating forehead, a beak-like countenance, and the left side of his face much larger than the right, Sarteur now displayed great gentleness and perfect sense, brimming over with gratitude, and fain to kiss his benefactor's hands. The Doctor felt quite moved at last, and dismissed him in an affectionate way, advising him not to remain idle, but to revert to his old life of steady work—wherein lay the best mental and physical hygiene. Then, as soon as Sarteur had gone, Pascal became calm again, and sat down to table, talking gaily of other things.

Clotilde looked at him, astonished and even somewhat indignant : ' What ! are you no longer satisfied with yourself, master ? ' she asked.

He began jesting. ' Oh, no ! I'm never satisfied with myself, and, as for science, you know, it all depends.'

That same evening, and on this very subject, they had their first quarrel. She was indignant that he had no pride left, and reproached him for not being elated over Sarteur's cure, for not being pleased, even, at having prolonged Valentin's life. It was she who now took a jealous interest in his glory. She began to remind him of his cures. Had he not cured himself ? Could he deny the efficacy of his treatment ? She quivered as she evoked the great dream in which he had formerly indulged ; to combat weakness, the one cause of all evils ; to cure suffering humanity, to make it sound, to raise it to a higher plane ; to hasten the advent of happiness, the era of perfection and felicity, by intervening and imparting health to all ! And he possessed the elixir of life, the universal panacea which justified the mighty hope !

For a time Pascal remained silent. But at last he answered : ' It is true, I cured myself, and have cured others, and indeed I still believe that my system is efficacious in many cases. I do not deny the power of medicine : the remorse I feel in connection with that unhappy accident—the death of poor Lafouasse—does not render me unjust. . . . Besides, work was always my great passion, work preyed upon me, consumed me, until quite recently ; it was in trying to prove to myself the possibility of endowing humanity with renewed vigour and intelligence in its old age—it was in trying to prove this that I nearly killed myself not long ago—Ah ! it was a dream, a beautiful dream ! '

' No, no,' responded Clotilde ; ' it was no dream, but reality, the fruit of your genius, master.'

Speaking in a faint whisper, as though he were timidly confessing some fault, he replied : ' Listen ; I will tell you what I would not tell anyone else in the world, what I do not even acknowledge aloud to myself. Is it a praiseworthy task to correct nature, to intervene, modify it, and seek to turn it from the purpose it has in view ? To cure, to delay the death of any human being, simply for that being's personal gratifi-cation or advantage, to prolong his life to the detriment no doubt of the species as a whole—is not this undoing all that nature seeks to do ? And, moreover, have we the right to dream of a healthier, stronger humanity, modelled in accord-ance with our ideas of health and strength ? Why attempt the realisation of such a dream—what business have we to interfere in the labour of life, whose ways and whose purposes are unknown to us ? Possibly all is well as it is. Possibly we run the risk of destroying love, genius, life itself. You hear me ; I confess it to you alone : *I doubt*, I tremble at the thought of my twentieth-century alchemy, and end by believ-ing that it is wiser, healthier not to thwart the natural evolution.'

He paused for a moment, and then gently added : ' Do you know, very often in puncturing my patients, I now only inject water. You yourself have remarked that I prepare no nervous matter for days and days together. I told you that I had

some *liqueur* in reserve. Well, water alleviates their sufferings
—the effect is doubtless simply a mechanical one, still there it
is. Ah! to alleviate and prevent suffering—yes, certainly I
still wish to arrive at that. It is possibly my last remaining
weakness, but I cannot bear to see anybody suffer. Suffering
transports me with anger, it seems to me monstrous, useless
cruelty on the part of nature. And now all I seek with the
patients whom I attend is to prevent suffering.'

'In that case, master,' said Clotilde, 'if you no longer seek
to cure, you must no longer reveal and say everything, for the
only excuse for displaying sores lies in the hope of healing
them.'

'But yes, but yes—despite everything it is still necessary
that one should know—know all and hide nothing. Everything appertaining to creatures and things must be revealed
and acknowledged. Happiness in ignorance is no longer
possible ; certainty alone can bring tranquil life. When men
know more than they know now they will certainly accept
everything. Cannot you understand that to seek to cure and
regenerate all is a mistaken ambition, the outcome of our
egotism, a revolt against life which we declare to be bad, simply
because we judge it from the standpoint of our personal
interests ? I feel that my serenity is more complete, that I
have enlarged my brain, raised it to a higher level since I
have come to respect the natural evolution. It is my passion
for life which is triumphing to the point that I no longer
cavil as to its purport, but surrender myself to it altogether,
willing to be absorbed in it and to disappear, and no longer
feeling at all anxious to alter it in accordance with my own
ideas of good and evil. Life alone is sovereign ; life alone
knows what it does and whither it tends ; all that I myself
can do is to strive to know it better, in order that I may live
it as it should be lived. And do you know I have only understood this since I have won your love ? Before I had won it
I sought truth elsewhere, struggling with the fixed idea of
saving the world myself. But now your heart is mine and life
is full. And the world is saved, saved from hour to hour by
love—for love brings life, impeccable, almighty, immortal life !'

Then, again in a faint voice, he schemed out an idyllic life, an existence of peace and vigour in the heart of the country. All the physician's experience ended in that simple prescription of a bracing atmosphere. He cursed towns. One could only enjoy health and happiness on the far-spreading plains, in the broad sunlight. And it was needful also that one should renounce wealth, ambition, even the vainglorious excesses of intellectual labour, and rest content with living and loving, rearing one's children and tilling the soil.

CHAPTER IX

So through the town and all the encompassing stretch of country Dr. Pascal continued his professional visits. And almost always Clotilde was on his arm, and accompanied him into the homes of his humble patients.

But, as he had lately confessed to her in a whisper, his visits henceforth had seldom any other object than to bring a little relief and consolation. If, already in former times, he had ended by practising only with repugnance, 'twas because he was conscious of the vanity of therapeutics. Empiricism distressed him. Assuming medicine to be not an experimental science but an art, he grew anxious at the thought of the infinite complications of disease and remedy according to the varying nature and circumstances of the patient. Treatment changed with hypothesis, and how many people must have been killed by the methods nowadays abandoned! Professional scent became everything; the healer became a mere diviner, gifted, it is true, but having to feel his way, and only accomplishing cures by chance strokes of genius. It was on account of all this that, after a dozen years' practice, Pascal had virtually forsaken his patients to seclude himself in study pure and simple. Then, when his profound researches into heredity had momentarily brought him back to the hope of intervening to some advantage, of curing sufferers by means of his hypodermic punctures, he had again taken a passionate interest in practice, till the day came when his faith in life, which had been impelling him to assist its action, brought him the supreme conviction that life sufficed for its own purposes and alone created health and strength. And so, with a quiet smile on his face, he simply continued visiting

those who urgently implored his services, and whose sufferings he miraculously alleviated even when he simply injected
pure water into their systems.

Clotilde would now occasionally venture to jest at it all.
In the depths of her being she still had a fervent belief in
the Mysterious, and she would gaily exclaim that if he thus
wrought miracles, it was because he was endowed with the
power to do so. He, however, as gaily rejoined that all the
efficacy of his treatment was due to her presence beside him,
maintaining that he never cured anybody when she was
absent, and that it was she who brought with her an inspiration from the realms beyond, the unknown, necessary power
of invigorating.   Thus his wealthier, middle-class patients,
whose rooms she did not venture to enter, continued complaining, quite unable to obtain any relief. These affectionate
disputes amused them ; they would start from La Souleiade
as on a voyage of discovery, and exchange meaning glances
in the houses they entered, according as they found some
patient improved or not. Ah ! that horrid suffering, which
made their hearts revolt, which alone they now sought to
assuage ; how happy they felt when they deemed it conquered !
It seemed as though a divine reward were bestowed on them
when some cold perspiration ceased, when some shrieking
mouth was quieted, when a gleam of life appeared on some
death-like face. Assuredly it was the love they diffused, the
love they brought with them, that calmed the sufferers they
tended.

'To die is nothing ; it is in the order of nature,' Pascal
would often say. 'But to suffer—why should one suffer ? It
is abominable and idiotic.'

One afternoon the Doctor went off with Clotilde to visit
a patient at the little village of Ste. Marthe. With the view
of sparing old Bonhomme, they decided to go by rail, and
accordingly repaired to the station at Plassans, there to take
a train coming from Les Tulettes ; Ste. Marthe being the
first station beyond Plassans in the direction of Marseilles.
The train had just come in, and they were darting forward
to open a carriage door, when they saw old Madame Rougon

alight from the compartment, which they had thought to be
empty. She no longer spoke to them, but jumped out with
a light spring despite her age, and walked away, stiff and
dignified.

'It is the first of July,' said Clotilde, when the train had
started. 'Grandmother had just returned from Les Tulettes,
after paying her usual monthly visit to Aunt Dide. Did you
notice how she looked at me?'

Pascal was in reality well pleased at being on bad
terms with his mother, for it freed him from the anxiety
which her presence near him always entailed. '*Bah!*' said
he, 'when folks don't agree it is best that they shouldn't
associate.'

The girl, however, remained grieved and thoughtful, till
at last, speaking in an undertone, she said: 'I thought
grandmother looked changed and pale. And didn't you
notice that she had a green glove on her right hand and none
on her left—she who, as a rule, is always so careful and
particular! I don't know why, but the sight of her quite
upset me.'

He, also feeling disturbed, thereupon made a vague gesture.
His mother would certainly end by becoming old like everybody else. She bestirred herself too much, still took too
passionate an interest in things for a woman of her years.
He had heard, he related, that she proposed bequeathing
her fortune to the town of Plassans for the erection and
endowment of some almshouses which were to bear the
Rougon name. They both began smiling at this, but all
at once the Doctor exclaimed: 'By the way, we ourselves
have got to go to Les Tulettes to-morrow, to see our patients.
And you know, too, that I have promised to take Charles to
Uncle Macquart's.'

As Clotilde had surmised, Félicité, when met at the
station, was indeed returning from Les Tulettes, whither she
repaired regularly on the first of each month to ascertain the
condition of Aunt Dide. For long years she had been taking
a passionate interest in the madwoman's health; stupefied at
finding that she lasted so long, infuriated by her obstinacy in

still surviving, with such prodigious longevity, long beyond
the usual allotted span. What relief she would experience
on the morning when she was at last able to bury that
troublesome witness of the past, that spectral image of lingering expiation, at sight of whom arose the memory of all the
abominations in which the family had been concerned! Many
of the others had passed away, but death seemed to have
forgotten this madwoman, who still lingered on and on,
though only a faint spark of life now gleamed in the depths
of her expressionless eyes. Again that afternoon Madame
Rougon had found her seated erect, motionless, as withered as
ever, in her armchair. As the nurse said, there was really no
reason now why she should ever die. She was one hundred
and five years old.

On leaving the Asylum, Félicité felt utterly incensed. And
then she suddenly remembered Uncle Macquart. Another one
who lingered on with exasperating obstinacy! Although he
was merely eighty-four, but three years older than herself, he
seemed to her to be ridiculously old, to have exceeded indeed
all allowable limits. And to think, too, that he lived a life
of excesses; that for sixty years past he had been dead
drunk every night! Those who lived soberly and staidly
were carried off, whilst he still flowered and bloomed, full
of health and gaiety. In former times, when he had first
taken up his abode at Les Tulettes she had made him presents
of wine, liqueurs, and brandy, in the unconfessed hope of
ridding the family of a dirty rascal, from whom only worry
and shame were to be expected. But she had soon perceived
that the alcohol she lavished upon him merely helped to keep
him in a mirthful mood, with a beaming face and roguish
eye. Accordingly she ceased making him such presents, since
instead of poisoning they only fattened him. The failure of
her design filled her, however, with a terrible spite against
him; she would have killed him, had she dared, when she
saw him more erect than ever on his drunkard's legs, openly
sneering at her, well aware as he was that she was watching
for his death, and quite triumphant at being able to baulk her
of the pleasure of burying, not only himself, but also the

dirty linen of the past—all the blood and the mire of the two
Conquests of Plassans.

' Do you see, Félicité,' he would often say with that fright
fully mocking air of his, ' I'm here to take care of the old
mother, and when we two make up our minds to die, it will
only be out of regard for you—yes! simply to save you the
trouble of coming to see us, as you now do so lovingly every
month.'

To spare herself repeated deceptions she had of late times
altogether refrained from visiting him. She obtained any information she needed concerning his condition at the Asylum.
On this occasion, however, having learnt there that he was
passing through a most extraordinary fit of drunkenness, not
having been sober for a day during the past fortnight, intoxicated
in fact to such a point that he could no longer go out, she was
curious to see with her own eyes in what condition he had put
himself; and accordingly, instead of taking the direct road
back to the station, she went somewhat out of her way in order
to call at the *bastide*.

It was a lovely day, a warm, beaming, summer afternoon.
On either side of the narrow pathway which she had to follow,
Félicité beheld the fields which Macquart had formerly
insisted upon having—all the fertile land which he had exacted as the price of his discretion and good conduct. The
house, with its roof of pinky tiles, and its walls roughly be-
daubed with yellow paint, rose up before her gay and
smiling in the sunlight. Then she enjoyed the delightful
coolness prevailing under the ancient mulberry trees, and
feasted her eyes upon the lovely panorama that stretched
around. What an acceptable, appropriate retreat; what a nook
of happiness and peace for an old man, after a long life of
kindliness and duty !

However, she neither saw nor heard Macquart. The
silence was profound. Only the bees flew humming around
the tall mallows. And on the terrace there was only a
little yellow dog—a *loubet*, as the breed is called in Provence
—stretched at full length on the bare soil, in the shade. He
knew the visitor, and at sight of her raised his head growling,

as though about to bark. But without doing so he once more stretched himself out, and did not stir again.

Then, amidst this deep solitude and gay sunshine, a faint, strange shudder came over Félicité. ' Macquart! Macquart! ' she called.

There, under the mulberry-trees, was the door of the *bastide*, wide open. Still she did not dare to go in. That gaping, seemingly empty house alarmed her. And again she called ' Macquart! Macquart! '

Not a sound, not a breath. The heavy silence fell once more, the bees alone hummed in a louder key around the tall mallows.

At last, however, she felt ashamed of her fright, and resolutely went in. On the left, in the little hall, was the door of the kitchen, where Macquart was generally to be found. This door was shut. She opened it, and on entering was at first unable to distinguish anything, for the old fellow had closed the shutters, doubtless to keep out the heat. Her first sensation was one of oppression at the throat, so violent was the smell of alcohol that filled the room. Each article of furniture seemed to be reeking with this smell, the whole house was impregnated with it. Then, as her eyes grew accustomed to the semi-obscurity, she at last ended by perceiving Macquart. He was seated near the table on which were a glass and a bottle of *trois-six* completely empty. He was sleeping soundly—dead drunk—huddled up on a chair. The sight revived all her anger and contempt.

' Come, Macquart,' she exclaimed, ' how senseless and ignoble to put oneself in such a state! Wake up; it's shameful! '

So profound was his slumber, however, that he could not even be heard breathing. In vain did she raise her voice and clap her hands : ' Macquart! Macquart! Macquart!—oh! you won't stir— You are disgusting, my dear fellow, you really are! '

Thereupon she ceased trying to rouse him ; and, no longer restraining herself, walked hither and thither, pushing whatever was in her way aside. An ardent thirst had come upon

her during her walk along the dusty pathway leading from
the Asylum. Her gloves hampered her, and taking them
off she laid them on a corner of the table. Then she was
lucky enough to find the water-pitcher, and having rinsed
a glass she filled it to the brim, and was on the point of
emptying it when she set it, still full, upon the table again
—deeply stirred by an extraordinary spectacle which she now
beheld.

As the minutes went by she could see more and more
distinctly in the room, which was illumined by some slender
sun-rays penetrating through the cracks and chinks of the
old, disjointed shutters. And thus she could now clearly
distinguish Macquart, who, as usual, was neatly clad in a suit
of blue cloth, his head covered with that everlasting fur cap,
which he wore from one end of the year to the other. He
had been growing stout during the last five or six years, and,
now huddled together on that chair, he formed quite a pile
of flesh, with bulging folds of fat. And she noticed that he
must have fallen asleep whilst smoking, for his pipe, a short,
black clay, was lying on his knees. Then, all at once, stupefaction rooted her to the spot quite motionless. The lighted
tobacco had fallen out of the pipe-bowl, setting his trousers
on fire. There was a hole in them—a hole already as large
as a five-franc piece, and through this aperture she could see
the bare flesh of his thigh—red flesh, from which a little blue
flame was arising.

She had, at first, thought some garment was burning, his
drawers or his shirt. But no ; doubt was impossible—it was
really his bare flesh that she beheld, and the little blue flame
arose from it, volatile, flickering like the roving flame on the
surface of a bowlful of punch. As yet it was barely taller
than a night-light, so gentle and so unstable too, that the
faintest puff of air sufficed to displace it. Rapidly, however,
did it grow and spread, till at last the skin of the thigh
cracked, and the fat commenced to melt.

Then a cry burst involuntarily from Félicité's throat :
' Macquart ! Macquart !! '

But he still remained motionless. His insensibility must

have been complete, intoxication must have plunged him into a sort of coma, a complete paralysis of the senses. He was still alive, that was certain, for at regular intervals his chest slowly rose and fell with the action of breathing.

'Macquart! Macquart!' cried Félicité, again.

The fat was now oozing forth through the cracks in his skin, feeding the flame which was beginning to lick his stomach. Félicité realised that he was igniting like a sponge soaked in brandy. For years past he had been saturating himself with spirit of the strongest, most inflammable kind. So, by-and-by, he would doubtless flare from head to foot.

Finding that he was sleeping so soundly she ceased trying to awaken him. For quite a minute, scared though she was, she had courage enough to gaze at him, slowly coming, meantime, to a resolution. She was stifling; her hands, too, had begun to tremble with a slight shiver which she was unable to restrain, and she needed both of them to again take up the glass of water, which she emptied at a draught. And she was already going off when she suddenly remembered her gloves. Coming back and fumbling nervously, she took both of them, as she thought, from off the table, and then at last slipped out of the room, closing the door carefully, gently, as though she feared that she might disturb someone.

When she again found herself on the terrace, in the gay sunlight and pure atmosphere, facing the vast expanse of sky over the horizon, she heaved a sigh of relief. The countryside was deserted; of a certainty no one had seen her either enter or leave the house. And the only creature there was still the outstretched yellow *loubet* who did not even deign to raise his head. So off she went, with her quick little step, and the customary slight swaying of her girlish figure. A hundred paces away, although she strove to withstand it, an irresistible impulse caused her to turn round and glance for a last time at the house, still looking so quiet and gay, midway up the slope. Only in the train, when she wished to put on her gloves, did she suddenly notice that one of them was missing. She felt certain, however, that she must have dropped it on the platform in getting into the carriage. She fancied herself

very calm, yet she remained with one hand gloved and the
other bare—which, with such a woman as herself, could only
be a visible sign of great inward perturbation.

On the morrow Pascal and Clotilde in their turn took the
three o'clock train to Les Tulettes. Charles's mother, the
saddler's wife, had brought them the youngster, since they were
willing to take him to his uncle's, where he was to stay during
the week.

Fresh quarrels had been disturbing the saddler's household;
Thomas altogether objected to be burdened any longer with
the presence of that other man's child—that prince's son, who
was both drone and idiot. As it was Grandmother Rougon
who provided him with clothing, he was again that day clad
in gold-braided black velvet, like some young lord, some page
of ancient times on his way to Court. They were alone in
their compartment of the train, and during the quarter of an
hour which the railway journey occupied Clotilde amused
herself by taking off the lad's cap and stroking his beautiful,
fair, regal hair, which fell in curls over his shoulders. She
had a ring on her finger, however, and while she was passing
her hand over the nape of the lad's neck she was surprised to
see that her caress left a sanguineous mark. He could not be
touched, indeed, without beads of blood oozing to the surface
of his skin; there was a laxness of the tissues, which degenerateness had aggravated to such a point that the slightest
bruise brought on hæmorrhage. Seeing the mark on his neck,
the Doctor in his turn became anxious, and asked him if he
still bled so frequently from the nose. Charles seemed scarcely
able to answer him; his first reply was ' No,' but at last, his
memory returning, he said that he had bled a great deal a
few days back. It seemed as though the lad were becoming
weaker, relapsing into infancy again as he grew older; as
though his intelligence were fading away without ever having
fully awakened. This boy of fifteen, so handsome, so girlish
in appearance, with the pale complexion of a flower that has
grown in the shade, did not look even ten years old.

On reaching Les Tulettes, Pascal decided that they would
first of all take Charles to Uncle Macquart's; and forthwith

they began climbing the somewhat steep pathway leading to
the little house. The latter, with its pinky tiles, its yellow
walls, its green mulberry trees stretching out their twisted
branches, and covering the terrace with a thick roof of leaves,
was smiling in the sunlight as on the day before. A delightful peacefulness prevailed in this secluded nook, this retreat
worthy of a sage, where nought was to be heard save the
humming of the bees as they flew around the tall mallows.

'Ah! that rascally uncle,' muttered Pascal smiling, 'how
I envy him!'

He was surprised, however, at not yet seeing Macquart,
erect as usual, at the edge of the terrace. And Charles, taking
it into his head to run off, carrying Clotilde away to see the
rabbits, the Doctor finished the ascent alone, still astonished
at perceiving no one. The shutters were closed, the house-
door was gaping wide open. And on the threshold there was
only the yellow *loubet*, who with legs stiffened and coat brist-
ling, was howling continuously in a low, gentle, plaintive key.
On seeing this visitor, whom he doubtless recognised, he became quiet for a moment, stationed himself farther away, and
then began softly moaning again.

Seized with a sudden fear, Pascal could not restrain
the anxious call which rose to his lips: 'Macquart! Macquart!'

There was no reply; the house retained its death-like
silence, with its one doorway wide open, like a black gaping
cavity. The dog still continued whining.

The Doctor grew impatient, and called yet louder: 'Macquart! Macquart!'

Nothing stirred save the bees humming from flower to
flower. The vast, serene sky peacefully enveloped the solitary
nook. Then Pascal made up his mind. Perhaps his uncle
was asleep. But as soon as he had opened the door on the
left hand, a frightful stench poured out of the kitchen, an unbearable odour as of bones and flesh that have fallen on a
brazier. Inside the room he could scarcely breathe, stifled as
he was, blinded, too, by a kind of thick vapour, a stagnant,
nauseous cloud. The slender rays of light which stole in

through the cracks in the shutters were not powerful enough to enable him to see things plainly. Still he instinctively darted towards the fireplace, for his first idea was that the place was burning. But no ; there was no fire, and all the articles of furniture around him appeared to be uninjured. Then, at a loss to understand what had happened, feeling as though he would soon faint in that poisonous atmosphere, he rushed to the window and violently pushed back the shutters. A flood of light at once poured into the room.

He was altogether amazed at what he then beheld. Each article of furniture was in its place. The glass and the empty bottle of *trois-six* were on the table ; there were no traces of fire save on the chair which Macquart must have occupied, and the front legs of which were blackened, whilst the rush seat was partially burnt. But what had become of the uncle ? Where could he have gone ? A pool of grease had spread out over the tiled floor, and just in front of the chair there was a small pile of ashes, beside which lay Macquart's pipe, a blackened clay that had not even broken in falling. And all Macquart was there—in that handful of fine ashes, in that ruddy cloud streaming out of the open window, in that layer of soot which had covered the entire kitchen.

It was the finest case of spontaneous combustion that ever medical man had observed. The Doctor had certainly read of some surprising ones, in sundry medical treatises, and among others of that of a bootmaker's wife, a drunken creature who had fallen asleep on her footwarmer, and of whom only a foot and a hand had afterwards been found ; but for his own part he had hitherto had his doubts, unwilling to admit, as his forerunners had done, that the human body, when saturated with alcohol, diffuses a mysterious gas, capable of igniting spontaneously, and devouring both flesh and bones. Now, however, he no longer denied the theory, but explained everything by recapitulating the various stages of the tragedy—first, the coma of drunkenness, absolute insensibility ; then the pipe falling on the clothes and setting them on fire ; the body, saturated with drink, gradually igniting, and finally sinews, organs and bones alike being consumed. All of Uncle

Macquart was there, including both his blue cloth suit and the fur cap which he had so long worn from one end of the year to the other. No doubt, he must have fallen forward on to the floor when he had thus begun burning like a bonfire. This would explain how it was that his chair was scarcely charred. And at present nothing remained of him—not a bone, not a tooth, not a nail—nothing save that little pile of grey ashes which the draught from the door seemed anxious to sweep away.

However, Clotilde now entered the room, whilst Charles remained outside, interested by the continuous moaning of the dog. 'Ah! good heavens, what a smell!' said she; 'what is the matter?'

When Pascal had explained the extraordinary catastrophe to her, she shuddered. She had already taken hold of the bottle to examine it; but promptly placed it on the table again, quite horrified at finding it damp and sticky. It was impossible to touch anything; every object was coated with yellow grease which adhered to the fingers.

A quiver of disgust and affright sped through the girl, who began to weep, stammering: 'Oh! what a sad death! What a frightful death!'

Pascal, who had recovered from his first shock of surprise, stood there almost smiling. 'Frightful,' said he; 'why frightful? He was eighty-four years old, and did not suffer. For my part, I think such a death a superb one for that old bandit uncle, who led, we may now freely acknowledge it, a life of little credit to himself or others. You remember the documents relating to him; he had some really terrible things upon his conscience, though these did not prevent him from settling down later on and growing old amid every comfort, like a worthy man reaping the reward of the virtues that he never possessed. And now he dies in royal style, like a prince of drunkards, flaring spontaneously, his own body supplying the burning pyre that consumed him!'

With a sweeping wave of the hand, the Doctor, still full of admiring wonder, spread the scene out before her: 'Do you see? To be drunk to such a point that one cannot feel one is burning, to ignite like some bonfire on St. John's eve, and disappear, to one's very last bone, in smoke ? Eh, do you see him vanishing into space, at first spreading through the room, wafting on the atmosphere in a state of dissolution, hovering over all the goods and chattels that once belonged to him, then sallying forth in a dusty cloud through that window, when I opened it, flying away into the sky, and stretching across the horizon ! Why, it is an admirable death —to vanish and leave nothing of oneself behind, save a little pile of ashes and a pipe beside them ! '

With these words he stooped and picked up the pipe, in view, he said, of securing a relic of the uncle. And meantime Clotilde, who fancied that she could divine a touch of bitter raillery beneath his fit of lyrical admiration, again with a shudder gave vent to all her fright and nausea.

She had, however, just noticed something, some remnant possibly, lying under the table. 'Look,' she exclaimed, 'that shred ——'

Pascal stooped again, and, to his surprise, the object proved to be a green kid glove—a woman's glove.

'Ah ! ' cried Clotilde, ' it is grandmother's glove—the glove, you remember, that I noticed she wasn't wearing when we met her yesterday.'

They looked at one another, and the same explanation rose to the lips of both of them. Félicité had certainly been there on the previous day, and a sudden conviction penetrated the Doctor's mind—a certainty that his mother had seen Macquart igniting and had not extinguished the flame. Numerous indications pointed to this conclusion, the perfect coolness now prevailing in the room, the number of hours needful for such combustion. Pascal could plainly see the same conviction dawning in Clotilde's terrified eyes. However, as it seemed impossible that they would ever ascertain the truth, he contented himself with giving what seemed to him the simplest explanation of the incident. 'No doubt,' he said, ' on her way back from the Asylum your grandmother must have called to wish your uncle good day before he began tippling.'

'Let us go, let us go!' cried Clotilde, in reply; 'I am stifling, I can stay here no longer!'

On his side Pascal was desirous of notifying the death to the authorities. Accordingly, he went out behind her, locked the door of the house and put the key in his pocket. And, once outside, they again heard the little yellow *loubet* who had not ceased whining. He had taken refuge between Charles's legs, and the child was pushing him with his foot, amused by his behaviour, and at a loss to understand it all.

The Doctor now went straight to the house of M. Maurin, the notary of Les Tulettes, who, so it happened, was also mayor of the commune. A widower for ten years past, living with his daughter, on her side a childless widow, he had been on good neighbourly terms with old Macquart, and had, at times, taken care of little Charles for days together; his daughter evincing a compassionate interest in this child, who was so handsome and so much to be pitied. Quite scared by the information which Pascal brought, M. Maurin insisted upon returning with him to the *bastide* so as to verify the accident, and promised to draw up a certificate of death in proper form. As for any religious ceremony, any funeral, that was a different matter; for when Pascal had re-entered the kitchen with the notary, the draught from the door had sent the ashes flying; and in piously seeking to collect them, they had mainly got together some of the dust on the tiled floor, a lot of old dirt in which there could have been but little of Macquart's remains. That being the case, what were they to bury? It was best to renounce the idea; and they did renounce it. Moreover, Macquart had never paid much attention to religious rites, and, in the result, his relatives contented themselves, later on, with having a few masses said for the repose of his soul.

The notary, however, had at the first tidings exclaimed that there was a will, deposited at his own office. And forthwith he had convoked the Doctor for the next day but one, when he promised that he would communicate the document to him officially. He had reason to believe, he said, that

Pascal had been appointed an executor. Finally, like the good-natured man he was, he offered to take care of Charles in the meantime, for he understood that the youngster, so ill-treated at his mother's, would be very much in the way amid all these distressing worries. Charles, who appeared delighted with the proposal, was accordingly left at Les Tulettes.

Clotilde and Pascal were only able to return to Plassans very late, by the seven o'clock train in fact, after the Doctor had at last visited the patients whom he had come to see. Two days later, when he and the girl returned to Les Tulettes to keep the appointment which they had made with M. Maurin, they were disagreeably surprised to find old Madame Rougon installed in the notary's office. She had naturally learnt that Macquart was dead, and had thereupon vivaciously hastened from Plassans, brimming over with expansive grief. Having then heard of the will, she had now again returned to Les Tulettes in order to ascertain its contents. The reading of the document was a very simple affair, unmarked by any incident : Macquart left instructions that the portion of his little fortune which the law authorised him to dispose of should be entirely spent in building him a tomb—a superb marble tomb, at either end of which there was to be a weeping angel with folded wings. It was an idea that had come to him, the recollection of a similar tomb which he had seen abroad—in Germany, possibly, at the time when he was a soldier. And he had appointed his nephew Pascal to attend to the erection of the monument, he being the only member of the family, so the will recited, who was possessed of any taste.

Whilst the document was being read Clotilde remained seated upon a bench, in the shade of an old horse-chestnut tree, in the notary's garden. When Pascal and Félicité came out of the house again there was considerable embarrassment for a moment, for they had not spoken to one another for several months past. The old lady, however, promptly assumed an air of perfect ease, not making the slightest allusion to the new position of affairs, but letting it be understood that

in her opinion they might very well meet and appear united
before other people, although in reality they still remained
unreconciled. She made the mistake, however, of laying too
much stress upon the great grief that Macquart's death had
caused her; and at this Pascal could not restrain his impatience, the feeling of revolt which stirred him, for he keenly
suspected that her heart was in reality leaping with joy, that
she was experiencing infinite gratification at the thought that
another family sore, the abomination which the uncle personified, was now at last on the point of being healed. With
these thoughts uppermost in his mind his eyes involuntarily
turned upon his mother's gloves, which were black.

Precisely at that moment she was sorrowfully repeating,
in a very gentle voice: 'Besides, was it prudent of him, at
his age, to live all alone like a wolf? If he had only had a
servant with him.'

Thereupon the Doctor, imperfectly conscious of what he
was doing, but urged to it by an irresistible impulse, spoke
out, and in such a strain that he was quite scared by his own
words: 'But since *you* were there, mother, why did you not
put him out?'

Old Madame Rougon turned frightfully pale. How could
her son know? She looked at him for a moment gaping,
whilst Clotilde, like herself, grew white, for her suspicion of
crime had now become a positive certainty. That terror-
fraught silence which had fallen between mother, son, and
grand-daughter, that quivering silence in which families bury
their domestic tragedies—was equivalent to an avowal. On
their side, the two women found nothing to say. The Doctor,
in despair at having spoken, he who so carefully avoided
entering upon unpleasant and useless discussions, began trying, distractedly, to recall his words, when all at once a fresh
catastrophe extricated them from their terrible embarrassment.

Anxious not to abuse M. Maurin's kind hospitality,
Félicité wished to take Charles away with her; and the
notary, having sent the youngster to the Asylum after breakfast, so that he might spend an hour or two with Aunt Dide,

had despatched a servant thither with instructions to bring the child back at once. They were awaiting this servant's return in the garden; and at that very moment she reappeared, perspiring, breathless, quite beside herself, and calling out to them from a distance: '*Mon Dieu! Mon Dieu!* make haste—Monsieur Charles is covered with blood!'

Quite terrified by these tidings they all three started for the Asylum.

It happened that this was one of Aunt Dide's good days, when, very calm and very gentle, she sat stiffly erect in that armchair of hers, in which for the last two-and-twenty years she had spent so many long hours, gazing fixedly into space. She seemed to have become yet thinner of recent times, every sinew had disappeared—her arms, her legs were now mere bones covered with parchment-like skin. It was necessary, too, that the sturdy fair-haired girl, her nurse, should carry her, feed her, treat her in all things like some inanimate object which you lay down and take up. The ancestress, that tall, knotty, ghastly, forgotten one, remained ever motionless, with only her eyes alive, those eyes as clear as spring water, gleaming in her slender, dried-up face. Early that morning, however, a sudden flood of tears had once again streamed down her cheeks, and she had afterwards begun to stammer a few disjointed words. This seemed to indicate that, despite senile exhaustion and the irreparable numbness of dementia, the slow induration of the brain was not as yet complete : certain recollections remained stored up within her, gleams of intelligence were still possible. After this access, however, she had relapsed into her wonted silence, indifferent to things and beings, occasionally laughing at some accident, some fall, but more generally seeing and hearing nothing amid her endless contemplation of the void.

When Charles arrived the nurse at once sat him at the little table in front of his great-great-grandmother. She kept several sheets of coloured figures expressly for his amusement —soldiers, captains, kings, clad in gold and purple—and some of these she now gave him with her pair of scissors. 'There, amuse yourself quietly, like a good boy,' she said. 'You see that grandmother is very nice and quiet to-day, and you must be the same.'

The child raised his eyes to the mad woman's face, and they gazed at one another. The extraordinary resemblance between them was at this moment very apparent. Their eyes especially, their empty limpid eyes seemed to intermingle, identical. Then, too, they were much alike in physiognomy; the worn features of the centenarian, skipping three generations, appeared afresh on that child's delicate visage—the lineaments of which also seemed, as it were, effaced, aged, exhausted by racial wear and tear. They did not exchange smiles, but gazed at each other profoundly, with an expression of imbecile gravity.

'Well, well,' resumed the nurse, who had acquired the habit of talking aloud by way of enlivening the dreary hours which she spent with her mad charge, 'they can't deny one another. Whoever made one made the other. They are as like as two peas. Come, laugh a bit and amuse yourselves, since it pleases you to be together.'

Any prolonged attention, however, tired Charles, who was the first to lower his head. To all appearance he became interested in his coloured figures, whilst Aunt Dide, who possessed extraordinary fixity of vision, continued gazing at him for a long, long time without a single beat of her eyelids.

For a moment the nurse busied herself in tidying the little room, which was full of sunshine and looked quite gay with its light-coloured wall-paper, spangled with blue flowers. She made the bed which she had been airing, and put some linen away on the shelves of the wardrobe. As a rule, however, she profited by the youngster's presence to take a little time to herself. According to the regulations she ought never to have left her charge; but she had ended by entrusting her to the lad whenever he happened to be there.

'Listen to me,' she said; 'I've got to go out, and if she should move, if she should want me, you will ring the bell, call me at once, won't you? You understand me, eh? You are surely big enough to know how to call anyone?'

Again raising his head, he made a sign that he understood her and would call. Then, on finding himself alone with Aunt Dide, he again quietly turned to his pictures. This lasted for a quarter of an hour amid the deep silence of the Asylum, which was only disturbed by occasional, vague, prison-like sounds, a furtive footfall, the jingling of a bunch of keys, and at times a loud cry, at once silenced. It was a burning hot day, however, and the child must have felt tired; sleepiness gained upon him, and his lily-white face soon seemed to droop beneath the weighty, helmet-like burden of his regal hair. At last he let his head sink gently down among the picture-figures, and fell asleep with one cheek resting on the gold and purple kings. The lashes of his closed eyelids cast a shadow upon his cheeks, life throbbed but feebly in the little blue veins beneath his delicate skin. His was the beauty of an angel, but with the undefinable corruption of an entire race spread over the softness of his visage. And meantime Aunt Dide gazed at him with her blank stare, which expressed neither pleasure nor grief—the stare of eternity as it were, fixed upon the universe.

After a few minutes, however, a gleam of interest seemingly awoke in her clear eyes. Something occurred, a rosy drop gathered and developed at the edge of the child's left nostril. This drop fell, then another formed and followed the first. It was blood—the oozing dew of blood, which this time, without pressure or bruise, but simply through organic laxness, the result of racial degeneracy, was trickling forth, flowing away of its own accord. The drops became a narrow streamlet, which meandered over the gold of the picture figures, and, expanding into a little lake, submerged them; then took its course towards a corner of the table. There the dripping began afresh, the drops fell thick and heavy, bursting one upon the other on the tiled floor of the room. And still the lad slept on, with the divinely calm expression of a cherub, unconscious even that his life was trickling away. Meantime the mad woman continued watching him, with an air of increasing interest. She gave no sign of alarm, however; she appeared rather to be amused; it furnished something for her contemplation, like the flight of the bluebottles which she would often watch for hours together.

A few more minutes went by, the little red streamlet grew broader, the drops followed one another more rapidly, falling with a gentle, monotonous stubborn splash. And at one moment Charles bestirred himself, opened his eyes, and beheld himself in the midst of blood. But he evinced no terror, for he was accustomed to see that bloody source trickling forth from him at the slightest hurt. The plaint he raised was expressive rather of worry. And yet instinct must have warned him, for a moment afterwards he became quite scared, complained in yet a louder tone, stammered a confused call:

'Mamma! Mamma!'

His weakness must have already been too great, however, for an invincible torpor seized hold of him again. Once more he let his head drop, closed his eyes, seemed to fall asleep; and then again he raised that plaint, that gentle moan, but with increased shrillness and feebleness, as though he were repeating it in his dreams:

'Mamma! Mamma!'

And now the lad's sheets of coloured figures were inundated: his gold-braided, black velvet jacket and breeches were stained with long stripes of blood; and the little red streamlet had again begun flowing, stubbornly, incessantly, from his left nostril, coursing through the purple lake upon the table, and falling with a splash upon the floor where it now formed quite a pool. A loud shriek from the mad woman, a call of terror might have sufficed to save him. But she did not shriek, she did not call; motionless, with fixed eyes, she, the ancestress, gazed at the accomplishment of destiny as though dried up, spell-bound, destitute both of will and power of action, her limbs and tongue alike shackled by her hundred years, her brain atrophied by dementia. And yet the sight of the little red stream began to move her somewhat. A quiver had already passed over her death-like face, some warmth was rising to her cheeks. And, at last, a final plaint quite reanimated her:

'Mamma! Mamma!'

At this, visibly enough, a frightful combat took place in Aunt Dide. She raised her skeleton-like hands to her temples as though she could feel her skull cracking. She had opened her mouth quite wide, but no sound emerged from it ; the frightful tumult ascending within her paralysed her tongue. She strove to rise, and hurry away ; but she had no muscles left, and remained riveted as it were to the chair. The whole of her poor frame trembled in the superhuman effort which she made to call for help, without managing to burst the prison bonds of senility and dementia. With her face distorted, her memory aroused, she must have beheld and have understood everything.

Several long minutes elapsed before it was over. It was a slow and very gentle death. Charles, who was now quite silent—asleep again, it might have been thought—ended by losing the last drop of blood in his veins, which with a faint sound went on emptying and emptying. His lily-like whiteness became more pronounced, turned to the pallor of death. His lips lost their colour, faded to a pale pink, then became white like his face. And just before he expired, he opened his large eyes and fixed them on his great-great-grandmother, who could see their last gleam fade away. All else of his wax-like face was already dead, while his eyes survived, still retaining a measure of limpidity and light. Then all at once they also emptied, *went out.* That was the end—the death of the eyes. Charles had died without a shock, without a struggle, exhausted like some spring from which all the water has departed. Life throbbed no longer in the veins under his delicate skin, only his eyelashes now cast a shadow upon his white face. But he remained divinely beautiful, with his head resting in the blood, amid his fair regal hair spreading around him—similar to one of those bloodless little dauphins who are unable to bear the hateful heritage of their race, and, overcome by old age and imbecility, sink into the last sleep when only in their fifteenth year.

The lad had just exhaled his last faint breath when Pascal entered, followed by Félicité and Clotilde. ' Ah ! *mon Dieu !* ' the Doctor exclaimed, as soon as he had seen the quantity of blood that flooded the tiled floor. 'It is what I feared. Poor little fellow! Nobody was there. It is all over!'

All three of them, however, remained terrified at the extraordinary spectacle which they then beheld. Aunt Dide, whose superhuman efforts seemed to have made her taller, had almost succeeded in rising from her chair; and her eyes, fixed upon the dead child's face, now very white and peaceful, were lighting up with a sudden thought after a slumber of twenty years' duration. The terminal lesion of dementia, the enshrouding of the intelligence in black and irreparable night, was doubtless not as yet sufficiently complete to prevent a distant memory, stored in some recess of her cranium, from suddenly awakening, under the terrible blow that was falling upon her. And thus the forgotten one again lived, emerged from nihility, erect, wasted, like some spectre of grief and horror. For a moment she remained panting. Then a shudder seizing her, she was only able to repeat the words:

'The gendarme! the gendarme!'

Pascal and Félicité and Clotilde had understood. They involuntarily looked at one another and shuddered. Before their eyes arose a vision of the whole violent life of the old mother, the mother of them all: the exasperated passion of her youth, the long sufferings of her ripe age. Two mental shocks had already terribly shaken her; the first in the midst of a wild, ardent existence, when her lover, the smuggler Macquart, had been shot dead like a dog by a gendarme; the second, many years afterwards, when another gendarme had, with his pistol, blown out the brains of her grandson, Silvère. Blood had ever besmeared her. And now a third shock was finishing her off; blood was bespattering her yet again—that impoverished blood, the blood of her own race, which she had seen flowing forth during so long a while, and which now covered the floor, whilst the white, kingly child that it had belonged to, slept the last sleep, his veins and his heart empty.

Three times in succession—once more beholding her whole life, her life red with passion and torture, above which uprose the image of the expiatory law—three times did she stammer:

' The gendarme ! the gendarme ! the gendarme ! '

Then she fell in a heap upon her armchair. They thought her dead, killed as by a thunderbolt.

But here at last was the nurse coming back again, seeking excuses, already certain of her dismissal. When Dr. Pascal had helped her to place Aunt Dide on the bed he found that the old woman was yet alive. She was only destined to die on the morrow, at the age of one hundred and five years three months and seven days, from the effects of cerebral congestion due to the last shock that she had received.

Pascal immediately foretold it to his mother. ' She won't last four-and-twenty hours,' he said ; ' she will be dead to-morrow. Ah ! what wretchedness and mourning : the uncle, next that poor child, then the old mother fast following one upon the other ! ' He paused, and added in a lower tone : ' The family is thinning, the old trees fall, the young ones are nipped in the bud.'

Félicité must have thought that this remark concealed a fresh allusion. She was sincerely afflicted by the tragic death of little Charles. Still, despite everything, an immense feeling of relief was rising within her. Next week, when the weeping was all over, with what a sense of quietude would she be able to reflect that all the abominations of Les Tulettes no longer existed : that the family glory might at last freely ascend and beam forth with the splendour of a legend.

Then she suddenly remembered that she had returned no answer to her son's involuntary accusation at the notary's, and, in a spirit of bravado, she again spoke of Macquart. ' You see very well,' said she, ' that servants are not a bit of use. There was one here, but she prevented nothing : and even if the uncle had had himself looked after, he would, none the less, be now in ashes.'

Pascal bowed with his customary air of deference. ' You are right, mother,' said he.

Clotilde had fallen on her knees. In that chamber of blood, madness and death, her old beliefs—the beliefs of a fervent Catholic—had just awakened within her. Tears were streaming from her eyes, her hands were clasped, and she was praying ardently for the dear ones who had departed. O God, might their sufferings now for ever cease, might their sins be forgiven them, might they be resuscitated only for a life of eternal felicity! She interceded for them with all the fervour of her heart, terrified at the thought of a hell which, after such wretched lives as they had led, might make their sufferings everlasting.

And, from that sad day forward, Pascal and Clotilde went to visit their patients in a more pitiful mood, pressing close to one another as they walked along. In the Doctor's mind, perhaps, the thought of his powerlessness in the presence of necessary disease had become still more acute. The one wise course was to let nature accomplish its evolution, eliminate all dangerous elements, and busy itself only with its great final labour of health and strength. But the relatives you lose, the relatives who suffer and who die, leave in your heart a feeling of spite and rancour against the evil, an irresistible longing to combat and conquer it. And thus never before had the Doctor experienced so much joy when by means of a puncture he succeeded in calming an attack, in pacifying some shrieking patient and sending him to sleep. And Clotilde, on their return home, adored him fondly, full of pride, as though their love supplied the relief, which they carried as a viaticum to unhappy, suffering folks.

CHAPTER X

RUIN !

ONE morning Martine, as was her habit every quarter, obtained from Dr. Pascal a receipt for the sum of fifteen hundred francs, with the view of taking and handing it to Grandguillot, the notary, in exchange for what she was wont to call 'our income.' The Doctor seemed surprised that quarter-day had come round so soon again; he now paid no attention whatever to money matters, but entrusted all arrangements to the servant. And he and Clotilde were still sitting idly under the plane-trees, absorbed in the one thought of enjoying life, while the eternal song of the spring rang with delightful freshness in their ears, when all at once, Martine came back from Plassans, looking utterly scared, distracted by some extraordinary emotion.

To such a point did her breath fail her, that at first she was quite unable to speak. 'Ah! *Mon Dieu*!' she at last managed to gasp, 'Ah! *Mon Dieu*! . . . Monsieur Grandguillot has gone !'

For a moment Pascal failed to understand her. 'Well, my girl,' said he, 'there's no hurry, you can go back another day.'

'No! no! he's gone, you understand, gone for good!' And then, as though she were suddenly freed from the impediment that had restrained her voice, words began spurting swiftly from her lips, and she vented all her violent emotion: 'I got to the street and saw a crowd of people at the door—a chill came over me at once, for I felt there must be something wrong—and the door was shut fast, not a shutter was open, you might have thought some one belonging to the house had just died. But the people at once told me that he had bolted, that he hasn't left a copper behind him, that ever so many families are ruined.'

Then, laying the unused receipt on the stone table: 'There—there's your paper!' she added, 'it's all over, we haven't a *sou* left, we shall die of hunger!'

Tears welled into her eyes, and she began weeping and sobbing loudly, with anguish wringing her miserly heart, distracted, as she was, by this loss of a fortune, trembling too at the threatening prospect of misery.

Clotilde sat there thunderstruck, speechless, with her eyes fixed on Pascal, whose face at the first moment was expressive more of incredulity than of anything else. He endeavoured to calm Martine. Come, come! a person ought not to give way to such ideas as those. If her knowledge of the affair was confined to what she had heard from the folks in the street, it was probable that her information was mere exaggerated tittle-tattle. M. Grandguillot absconding, M. Grandguillot a thief! it was a monstrous idea, an impossibility. Such a scrupulously honest man, an establishment which all Plassans had respected, revered, for more than a century past! Why, one's money was safer there, people said, than at the Bank of France itself!

'Think a little, Martine, such a catastrophe would not fall on us all at once, like a thunderbolt—there would be all sorts of rumours beforehand—come, come, honesty of ancient date does not crumble away in a single night!'

Thereupon the servant made a gesture of despair. 'Ah! monsieur, it's just that which grieves me so much, for it makes me somewhat responsible, you see. I've heard a good many stories noised about for some weeks past. You others, of course, hear nothing; you don't even know if you are alive.'

Pascal and Clotilde could not help smiling at this, for it was indeed true that their love carried them out of the world, so far away and to such a height that nothing of the stir and din of human existence reached their ears.

'Only as all these stories were very horrible ones,' resumed Martine, 'I did not care to worry you with them. I thought they were lies.' Then she went on to relate that whilst some folks simply accused M. Grandguillot of gambling on the Bourse, others asserted that he kept up a bachelor establishment at Marseilles, where he indulged in terrible debauchery. And once more she began to sob: ' O God, O God! what will become of us? we shall die of hunger!'

Pascal, whose incredulity was shaken by Martine's last statements, and whose heart, moreover, was moved by the tears which he now saw standing also in Clotilde's eyes, began trying to remember on what footing he stood with the notary. He had deposited the hundred and twenty thousand francs—the interest of which had sufficed for his needs during the last sixteen years—with M. Grandguillot in various instalments at the time when he was practising at Plassans; and on each occasion the notary had handed him a receipt for the amount deposited. These receipts would doubtless enable him to establish his claim as creditor. Then a vague recollection dawned from the depths of his memory; the date he could not recall, but at some time or other, after certain explanations furnished by the notary, he had handed him a power of attorney, authorising the investment of all or part of his money in mortgages; and he was almost certain that the name of the person in whose favour this power of attorney purported to be drawn had remained blank. But, on the other hand, he did not know whether the document had ever been put to any use; he had never troubled to find out how his funds were invested.

Again did the anguish rending Martine's avaricious heart prompt her to speak. ' Ah! monsieur,' she exclaimed, ' your sin has found you out, this is the punishment of your negligence! Who, I should like to know, lets his money go like that? For my part, why not a quarter goes by but I know how I stand to a centime. I have the amounts and the numbers of the bonds at my finger-tips!'

Amidst all her grief, a smile had risen to her face at the thought that she had satisfied the stubborn passion of her life—that, by spending only a trifle of the four hundred francs she earned each twelvemonth, saving up and investing all the rest for thirty years past, she now, at last, through compound interest, possessed some twenty thousand francs. And this treasure was intact, invested in the very best securities, deposited, too, in a safe place known to herself alone. She became radiant with pleasure at the thought; however, with the prudence she invariably displayed when her little hoard was in question, she refrained from speaking of it any further.

' But who says that our money is lost? ' suddenly exclaimed Pascal. 'Monsieur Grandguillot had a private fortune of his own. He hasn't carried off his house and his estates, I suppose. We shall see; matters will be investigated; I can't accustom myself to the thought of his being a vulgar thief— the only worry is that we shall have to wait.'

He spoke in this strain in view of tranquillising Clotilde, whose disquietude he could see was increasing. She looked at him, and looked at La Souleiade stretching out around them, with the one thought of his happiness, with the ardent longing that she might ever live there with him, and ever love him in that dear secluded spot. And he, on his side, seeking to calm her, recovered his gay unconcern, like a man who has never lived for money's sake, and who does not imagine that one may be without it, and for want of it suffer. ' Come, come ! ' he exclaimed at last, ' what does Martine mean by saying that we haven't a copper left and are going to die of hunger? Why, I have some money, plenty of it—I'll show you ! ' And thereupon he gaily rose to his feet and compelled them both to follow him. ' Come along, come along ! I'll show you some money ! And I'll give some to Martine so that she may cook us a good dinner for this evening ! '

Then, when they were all three upstairs in his room, he triumphantly opened his *secrétaire*. There it was, in one of the drawers, that for nearly sixteen years he had flung all the notes and gold which his patients brought him of their own accord, for he never applied to any of them for remuneration. And never had he exactly known the full amount of his little treasure, dipping his hands into it whenever he pleased for his pocket-money, his experiments, donations and presents. For a few months past he had been making frequent and costly visits to this *secrétaire*, but after long years of quiet, steady life, free from all extravagance, he had grown so accustomed to find whatever sum he might require in the drawer, that he had ended by deeming his savings inexhaustible. So, quite easy in mind, he laughed and said : ' You shall see ! You shall see ! Look ! '

But he was utterly confounded when, after a feverish search among a mass of invoices and receipts, he found himself only able to get together the sum of six hundred and fifteen francs—two notes of a hundred francs each, four hundred francs in gold, and the remainder in silver. In vain did he shake the other papers, and explore every corner of the drawer with his fingers, exclaiming the while : ' But it's impossible ! why there was always a quantity of money here, there was still quite a pile only a few days ago—I must have been deceived by all these old bills—and yet only the other week, I assure you, I saw and handled a large amount of money.'

So amusing, so childlike was his sincerity, that Clotilde could not help laughing. Ah ! poor master, what a wretched man of business he was ! Then, on perceiving Martine's expression of anguish, her absolute despair at sight of the little sum which now represented their common livelihood, she herself was seized with distressful emotion, and her eyes became moist as she murmured : ' *Mon Dieu !* it is on me that you spent it all, I am the cause of our ruin, it is my fault if we have nothing left.'

Pascal had so far quite forgotten the many sums that he had taken from the drawer to purchase all the jewellery which he had given to Clotilde. That undoubtedly was how the bulk of his savings had gone. Now that he understood what had become of the money, he recovered his serenity. And when Clotilde in her grief spoke of returning everything to the jewellers, he exclaimed : ' Return what I gave you ! Why, with each thing that you parted with, you would give up some of my heart ! No, no, I would rather die of hunger ; I wish you to remain as I desired you to be!' Then superbly confident, as though he beheld in his mind's eye a vision of unlimited future happiness, he added: 'Besides, we shan't die of hunger to-night, shall we, Martine? We can go on for a long time with this!'

Martine jogged her head up and down. She would undertake to make that money last two months, three months perhaps, providing they were very careful, but not longer. Formerly, whatever amounts were taken from the drawer were returned to it every now and then; money continued coming in, from time to time, in small sums; but now, since Monsieur seldom if ever visited his patients, there were virtually no receipts. Any help from outside was, therefore, not to be relied upon. 'Give me the two hundred-franc notes,' she said in conclusion, 'I will endeavour to make them last right through the month—after that we will see—but you must be very careful; don't touch the four hundred francs in gold, mind; lock the drawer up, and don't open it again!'

'Oh, as for that,' exclaimed the Doctor, 'you may be at your ease. I would rather cut my hand off.'

In this wise everything was settled. The remaining money was placed at Martine's free disposal, and her thrift was to be depended upon; she would undoubtedly carry parsimony to its furthest limits. Clotilde, never having had a private purse, was not likely to notice the lack of money. The only one to suffer would be Pascal, at no longer possessing an inexhaustible treasure so easy of access. However, he had now formally undertaken to allow Martine to pay for everything.

'Ouf! well, that's satisfactory!' he exclaimed, quite relieved, as happy in fact as though he had just settled some weighty matter which ensured them an income for life.

A week went by, and nothing seemed to have changed at La Souleiade. Transported by their love, neither Pascal nor Clotilde seemed to have a suspicion of the misery threatening them. One morning however, when the girl had gone out to market with Martine, the Doctor received a visit which at first filled him with a feeling akin to terror. This visit was paid

him by the woman who had formerly sold him that marvellous
corsage in *point d'Alençon*, his first gift. He felt so weak
against temptation that he trembled at sight of her, and before
she had even opened her lips he began defending himself.
No, no, he could not, would not buy anything; and with outstretched hands he tried to prevent her from even opening her
little leather bag. She, however, very fat and affable, smiled
composedly, confident as she was of ultimate success. Speaking without a pause, in an insinuating, caressing voice, she
went on talking, telling him quite a pretty story of a lady
whom she would not name, but who was, she said, one of the
most distinguished ladies of Plassans. Misfortune had overtaken her, poor woman, and she was reduced to part with
an article of jewellery which she greatly prized. It was a
wonderful bargain, continued the dealer, for it had cost
more than twelve hundred francs, and such was the lady's
need that she was content to accept five hundred for it.

Speaking in this fashion, and paying no heed to the
Doctor's growing anxiety and distraction, the woman had
quietly opened her bag, and she now drew from it a slender
gold necklet, simply ornamented in front with seven pearls;
but the roundness, glimmer, and limpidity of these pearls were
beyond all praise. It was a jewel of exquisite freshness, re-
finement and purity. Pascal at once pictured it resting on
Clotilde's delicate neck, as the natural adornment of her soft,
silky skin. Another jewel would have uselessly burdened her,
but these pearls would only proclaim her youth. He had
already taken the necklet between his quivering fingers, and
experienced mortal grief at the idea of having to return it.
However, he still defended himself, swearing that he had not
five hundred francs to dispose of, whilst the dealer, in a voice
which neither rose nor fell, continued expatiating on the
cheapness of the jewel, which was real. Then, when, after a
quarter of an hour's talk, she felt she had him, she suddenly
consented to part with the necklet for three hundred francs;
and he thereupon surrendered—mastered by his mania for
giving, by the need he felt of pleasing and adorning his idol.
Such was his optimism, that when he went to take the fifteen

twenty-franc pieces from the drawer of the *secrétaire* to count them out to the dealer, he was convinced that his affairs at the notary's would be settled satisfactorily, and that they would soon again have plenty of money at their disposal.

When Pascal found himself alone with the necklet in his pocket, he was seized with a childish delight, and prepared his little surprise, distracted with impatience for Clotilde's return. As soon as he perceived her, his heart began beating as though it would burst. The ardent sun of August was now setting the whole sky aglow, and she came in feeling very warm, yet well pleased with her walk. Laughing gaily, she loosened her dress-body about the neck, and began relating what a capital bargain Martine had made, in securing a couple of pigeons for eighteen *sous*. Pascal, however, though suffocating with emotion, pretended that he noticed something on her neck: ' Why, what's that there ? ' he said ; ' here, let me see.'

He had the necklet in his hand, and managed to slip it round her neck, whilst he was pretending to examine the latter. She, however, began struggling merrily. ' Do be quiet,' said she, ' I know there's nothing. Why, what are you up to? What is that tickling me ? '

Catching hold of her arm, he thereupon led her up to the large cheval glass in her room, in which she could see herself from head to foot. The slender chain glittered like a golden thread around her neck, and on perceiving the seven pearls which looked like so many milky stars, gleaming on her silky skin, she gave vent to a delighted laugh, like the coo-coo of a coquettish dove. ' O master, master, how kind of you ! ' she said at last. ' So you only think of me ! How happy you make me ! '

At sight of the joy that was sparkling in her eyes, the joy of the loving woman, enraptured with the adoration lavished on her beauty, he felt divinely rewarded for his folly.

Quite radiant, she bent her head, offering him her lips. They kissed. ' So you are pleased ? ' he asked.

' Yes, I am, master, more than pleased. Pearls are so sweet, so pure ! And these suit me so well.'

For another moment she continued admiring herself in the cheval glass, innocently vain of that soft white skin of hers, on which the nacreous pearl-drops gleamed. Then hearing the servant moving about in the work-room, she yielded to a desire to show herself, and ran in to her. 'Martine! Martine! see what master has just given me. Am I not beautiful with this?'

But the severe mien of the old maid, whose face suddenly assumed an ashy hue, quite spoilt her joy. Perhaps she was conscious of the heartrending jealousy, the sight of which her dazzling youth inspired in that poor creature, who, ever worshipping her master, had wasted away during long years of mute and humble resignation. If, however, Martine's first feeling was one of jealousy, she was herself unconscious of it, so fleetly did it disappear; whilst Clotilde on her side felt but a faint and transient suspicion. And all that was left was the thrifty servant's visible disapproval, the black glance with which she passed condemnation on the costly gift.

As Clotilde noticed that glance, a chill came over her. 'Only master has been rummaging in his *secrétaire* again,' she said. 'Pearls cost a lot of money, don't they?'

Thereupon, Pascal, in his turn embarrassed, began to protest with great volubility, explaining what a wonderful opportunity he had met with, telling them all about the dealer's visit, and the capital bargain he had made with her. The thing was so remarkably cheap, it was impossible not to buy it.

'How much?' asked Clotilde at last, with genuine anxiety.

'Three hundred francs.'

At this, Martine, who had not yet opened her lips, but had stood there grimly silent, could not restrain this cry: 'Good Lord! Enough money to keep us all for six weeks! And we have no bread.'

Big tears gushed from Clotilde's eyes. She would there and then have torn off the necklet, had Pascal not prevented her from doing so. She talked of returning it immediately, stammering, in a state of utter distraction: 'It's true, it's true: Martine is right, master is mad, and I myself am mad also, to have thought of keeping this even for a moment in our sad position. It would burn me to wear it. Let me take it back at once, at once, I beg of you.'

To this, however, he would not consent, though he ad-mitted and bewailed his error in presence of them both, ex-claiming that he was incorrigible, and that all the money ought to have been taken away from him. And, at last, he ran to the *secrétaire*, and bringing the remaining hundred francs to Martine, compelled her to take them : ' I tell you, I won't keep a copper. I should again be spending it ! Here, take this money, Martine, you are the only one of us with any sense. You'll make it last, I'm sure, until our affairs are ar-ranged. And you, my darling, keep that present, don't grieve me by taking it back.'

There was no further question of this catastrophe. Clo-tilde, as requested, kept the necklet, and wore it under her dress. And there was something very discreet and charming about it all—that pretty, chaste little jewel, hidden away from everyone, and felt by herself alone.

At times, when she and Pascal were by themselves, she would smile at him, quickly take the pearls out of her dress-body, and show them to him, without saying a word. Then with the same swift movement, she could replace them on her warm bosom, with a delicious feeling of emotion. In this wise would she remind him of their folly, with a confused feeling of gratitude, a joyful radiance which never diminished. And never did she take the necklet off.

A straitened and yet pleasant life now began for them. Martine had made a careful inventory of their resources, and the situation was desperate. The supply of potatoes alone promised to be a good one. Unluckily, the jar of oil would soon be empty,[1] and in the same way, there was little left in the last remaining cask of wine. Comprising no longer any vineyards or olive groves, La Souleiade nowadays only yielded some vegetables and a little fruit—some pears which were not

---

[1] Olive oil, it should be remembered, is largely used for culinary purposes in Provence, and each household lays in a supply of several gallons at a time.—*Trans.*

yet ripe, and some trellis-grown grapes now destined to be their only treat. Moreover, it was necessary to buy bread and meat day by day. At the very outset, therefore, the old ser-vant began rationing Pascal and Clotilde—doing away with the creams and pastry, all the dainties of former times, and reducing the dishes to what was strictly necessary. All her former authoritativeness had come back to her, and she treated them as though they were children, whose likes and dislikes are not taken into account. It was she who decided on the *menus*, since she knew better than they did what they required. Indeed, she treated them in quite a maternal way, miraculously contriving, out of the paltry sum of money at her disposal, to make their life a tolerably comfortable one, lavishing, more-over, all sorts of attentions on them, and only scolding and hustling them occasionally in their own interest as one does with children who turn up their noses at their dinners. And it seemed as though this exercise of maternal duties, this last immolation of self, this freely chosen task of enveloping their love in illusive quietude, brought the old maid herself some little personal contentment, roused her from the gloomy despair into which she had fallen. Since she had thus been watching over them, her little calm white face had returned to her—the face of a nun dedicated to celibacy—with her tran-quil ash-gray eyes which expressed the resignation born of thirty years of domestic service. When, following upon the ever-lasting potatoes, and the little twopenny cutlet, looking lost amid the mass of vegetables, she occasionally managed to serve them a few pancakes, without upsetting her budget, she became quite triumphant, and laughed as gaily as they did themselves.

Whatever she served them Pascal and Clotilde invariably declared themselves quite satisfied, though this did not prevent them from jeering at her in her absence. They indulged more heartily than ever in their old jests respecting her avarice, relating that she even counted out the grains of pepper, so many for each dish, by way of husbanding them. When the potatoes came to table with scarcely a trace of oil about them and the cutlets dwindled down to a mere mouthful, they exchanged quick glances, and as soon as she had left the room, stifled their gaiety in their napkins. Everything supplied them with amusement, they artlessly laughed at their very poverty.

At the end of the first month, however, Pascal bethought himself of Martine's wages. As a rule she helped herself to her forty francs out of the funds she had in hand. 'How will you manage for your wages, my poor girl, since there's no money?' Pascal said to her one evening.

She remained for a moment with her eyes fixed upon the floor, in seeming consternation. 'Well, monsieur,' she at last replied, 'all I can do is to wait.'

He guessed, however, that she was not saying all she had on her mind, that she had some idea of an arrangement which she did not know how to suggest to him. Accordingly he encouraged her to speak out.

'Well,' said she, 'if monsieur is disposed to consent to it, I should like monsieur to sign me a paper.'

'A paper? What do you mean?'

'Yes, a paper on which monsieur would write every month that he owes me forty francs.'

Pascal immediately wrote and signed such a paper as she desired, and taking it from him with great delight, she put it very carefully away, as though it had been sterling money. Evidently enough, it quite tranquillised her. To Pascal and Clotilde, however, it supplied fresh matter for astonishment and mirth. What was that extraordinary power that money exercised over certain minds? There was that old woman, who served them on her knees, who worshipped her master to such a point that she had given him her whole life, and who asked for that idiotic guarantee, that scrap of paper which would be valueless if he were unable to pay her!

So far neither Pascal nor Clotilde had evinced any great merit in retaining their serenity amid misfortune, for this misfortune had not made itself felt. They lived far away from it, far above it in the happy, plenteous land of passion. They were ignorant of what they ate at table, they could dream that they were dining off princely dishes, served upon silver plate. They remained altogether unconscious of the growing scarcity and want around them, of the hungry servant dining off the few scraps they left, and they roamed through the empty house as through a palace hung with silk and full of riches. This was certainly the happiest period of their love. The house was full of happy souvenirs, and they spent long idle days in the workroom, luxurious!y draped, as it were, in the joy which they felt at having lived so many years there together. Then out of doors, over and beyond La Souleiade, king summer had pitched his azure tent resplendent with golden sunshine. Strolling of a morning along the perfumed pathways of the pine grove, plunging at noon into the deep shade of the plane-trees, where the spring sang on refreshing them, lingering in the evening on the cooling terrace or the still warm threshing-floor, in the bluey twilight of the earlier stars—still and ever in ecstasy did they promenade their impecunious existence, having but one ambition, to live together always, and feeling absolute disdain for all beside. The earth was theirs, with its treasures, festivities, princedoms, powers, since they belonged to one another.

Towards the end of August, however, the situation became very bad. They occasionally had anxious awakenings amid that life without ties, duties or work, which they found so pleasant, but which it was impossible, which it would moreover be evil, to live for ever. One evening Martine declared to them that she only had fifty francs left, and that it would be a difficult matter to go on for another fortnight, supposing even that they gave up drinking wine. On the other hand, the news from without was very serious, it seemed certain that notary Grandguillot was insolvent, that none of his creditors would receive a copper. At first his house and a couple of farms which he had necessarily left behind him on taking flight, had been looked upon as tangible assets, but it was now certain that all his property stood in the name of his wife, who—whilst he, according to all accounts, was feasting his eyes on the beautiful mountain scenery of Switzerland—continued residing on one of the farms, quietly cultivating it, far away from all the worries attending her husband's failure. The people of Plassans, quite upset by it all, related moreover that the wife had winked at her husband's scandalous goings on, to the point of tolerating the presence of the two creatures with whom he was now sojourning among the Swiss lakes. As for Pascal, with his customary heedlessness, he did not even trouble to call upon the Procureur de la République [1] with reference to his case; but remained content with such information as was conveyed by all the stories he heard, asking himself what would be the good of stirring up this nasty affair, since no satisfactory result was likely to be obtained by doing so.

And now the future appeared very threatening at La Souleiade. Absolute want and misery seemed to be in store for them within a brief delay. Clotilde, in reality, a sensible woman, was the first to tremble. She retained her vivacious gaiety whilst Pascal was with her; but, endowed, thanks to her womanly affection, with more foresight than himself, she became positively terrified whenever he left her for a moment. What, she asked, would become of him at his age, with such a heavy burden as that house upon his shoulders? During several days she secretly occupied herself in concocting a plan for averting the catastrophe; she resolved that she would set to work and earn money, a lot of money, by means of her pastels. Her strange artistic talent, so personal in character, had been much admired: and taking Martine into her confidence, she at last commissioned her to go and offer several of her chimerical bouquets of flowers to the artist's colourman on the Cours Sauvaire, who kept up a connection, it was said, with a Parisian painter, his relative. It was to be an express condition that nothing should be exhibited at Plassans, that every pastel should be sent far away. But the scheme ended in disaster, the colourman was terror-stricken by the fantastic nature of the designs, by the impetuous, slashing character of the work, and declared that it would never do, never sell. Clotilde was quite in despair on learning this, and big tears came into her eyes. Of what use was she in the world? It

---

[1] Public prosecutor.—*Trans.*

grieved and shamed her to be good for nothing! It was necessary for the servant to console her, and explain that all women apparently are not born to work, that some spring up like flowers in gardens, simply in order that they may diffuse a pleasant perfume around; whilst others are like the wheat growing from the soil, the wheat that is ground and provides sustenance.

Martine, however, on her side was ruminating another plan. This was to prevail upon the Doctor to return to practice. She ended by speaking of the matter to Clotilde, but the latter at once pointed out the difficulties, the material impossibility almost of bringing such an attempt to a successful issue. It so happened that on the previous day she herself had conversed with Pascal on this very question. He also was growing anxious, reflecting that their only chance of salvation lay in work. The idea of again opening a consulting-room was bound to occur to him at once. But for so many years now he had been simply the doctor of the poor! How could he dare demand payment for his services when he had so long given them gratuitously? Besides, was it not too late to begin one's career afresh at such an age as he had reached? To say nothing of all the absurd stories which circulated concerning him, all that legend which had sprung up of his being a half-cracked genius. He would not find a single patient; it would be useless cruelty to compel him to make the attempt, for he would assuredly emerge from it with his heart bruised and his hands empty. Clotilde, who realised all this, did her utmost to turn him from such a course, and Martine, acknowledging that her reasons were good ones, on her side exclaimed that he must not be allowed to run the risk of reaping such bitter grief. Whilst conversing, however, a fresh idea had occurred to her, at the recollection of an old register which she had lately found in a cupboard, and in which she had formerly made entries of the Doctor's visits to his patients. A good many of the latter had never paid him, in fact the list of them covered two long pages of the register. Now that they were in want at La Souleiade, why should they not try to make these people pay their debts?

This might easily be done without any mention of the matter
to Monsieur, who had always refused to sue his defaulting
debtors. The suggestion met with Clotilde's approval. It
was quite a plot between her and the servant; she herself
went through the list in the register, and wrote out the bills
which Martine thereupon carried round. But she did not
obtain a *sou* anywhere; at every door she received the same
answer, the bill should be examined and the parties would
call at the Doctor's. Ten days, however, went by, and
nobody came; and then only six francs remained in the
house, barely enough to provide for another two or three
days.

On the morrow, when Martine returned home empty-
handed, after again calling on some former patient, she took
Clotilde aside, and told her that she had just had a chat with
Madame Félicité at the corner of the Rue de la Banne. No
doubt the old lady had been watching for her. She still
refrained from crossing the threshold of La Souleiade. Even
the misfortune that had fallen on her son, that sudden loss
of money which had set the whole town talking, had failed to
draw her nearer to him. She was waiting, however, in a
passionate tremble; merely retaining the demeanour of a
rigorous parent who feels unable to condone certain errors,
because she felt certain that she now had Pascal at her mercy,
and that he would soon be compelled to summon her to his
help. When he no longer had a copper left and came to
knock at her door, she would dictate her conditions—compel
him to marry Clotilde, or better still, require the latter to
take her departure. Time went by, however, and still he did
not come. It was for this reason that she had stopped
Martine in the street, assuming a sorrowfully compassionate
air as she asked for news, and evincing a pretended astonishment that no appeal had been made to her purse, whilst
letting it be understood that her sense of dignity prevented
her from taking the first step.

'You ought to talk to monsieur and persuade him,' concluded the servant. 'After all, why shouldn't he apply to his
mother? It would be only natural.'

Clotilde, however, began protesting. ' Oh ! I can never undertake such a task as that. Master would be very angry, and I shouldn't blame him. I think he would rather let himself die of hunger than eat grandmother's bread.'

A couple of days later, in the evening, at dinner-time, when Martine served them some remaining scraps of boiled beef, she warned them of the position. ' I have no money left, monsieur, and to-morrow there will only be some potatoes, without oil or butter. For three weeks past you have had to drink water. Now you will have to go without meat.'

Even in this crisis, however, they again became mirthful and jested. ' Have you any salt, my good girl ? ' asked Pascal.

' Oh, yes, monsieur, I have still a little.'

' Well then, potatoes and salt are very nice, when one's hungry.'

She took herself off into the kitchen, and in an undertone they again began jeering at her extraordinary avarice. Though she had her own little treasure stored away some-where, in a safe place which nobody knew, she would never have offered to advance them a ten-franc piece. Still they merely laughed at it, free from any feeling of resentment, for they were aware that such an idea was as little likely to occur to her, as that of serving them the stars for their dinner.

Later on in the evening, however, Clotilde ventured to tell Pascal of her anxiety for him, for herself, in fact for the whole household. What would become of them, penniless as they were ? For a moment she even felt inclined to speak to him of his mother. But her courage failed her in this respect, and she contented herself with confessing the steps which she and Martine had taken—the discovery of the old register, the writing of the bills, and the fruitless applications for payment. In other circumstances this confession would have thrown him into great grief and anger ; it would have wounded him to have learnt that they had acted in this way without his con-sent, contrary indeed to the rules of his whole professional career. Now, however, he remained for some moments silent,

looking deeply moved, and this suffced to indicate the secret
anguish which he every now and then experienced, beneath
his affected heedlessness. Then, pressing Clotilde to his
heart, he forgave her, and ended even by saying that she had
acted rightly, that it was impossible to continue living in that
fashion any longer. They ceased speaking, and she divined
that, like herself, he was endeavouring to devise some means
of procuring the money necessary for their daily wants. This
proved their first unhappy night, a night of common suffering,
which she spent in despair at the thought of how he must be
worrying, whilst he, on his side, could not accustom himself
to the idea of seeing her in want of even bread.

On the morrow they had nothing but fruit for breakfast.
The Doctor remained silent throughout the morning ; plainly
enough a combat was waging within him. And it was only
at about three o'clock that he at last came to a resolution.
' Come, we must bestir ourselves,' said he, ' I don't want you
to fast again this evening. Go and put on your hat, we will
go out together.'

She looked at him, waiting for an explanation.

' Yes,' he added, ' since some money is owing to us, and
people wouldn't give it to you, I'll see if they will refuse it to
me as well.'

His hands were trembling ; it must have cost him a
frightful effort to resolve upon seeking payment for his
services in this fashion, after the lapse of so many years.
Still he strove to smile, and affected a brave demeanour.
She, who by the tremor in his voice divined the depth of the
sacrifice he was making, felt the tears rush into her eyes.
' No, no, master,' she said, ' don't go if it grieves you—Martine
might go back again.'

But the servant who was present fully approved of
Monsieur's determination. ' And why shouldn't Monsieur
go ? ' said she. ' There's never any shame in asking for one's
due. . . For my part I think it only right and proper that
Monsieur should show that he's a man.'

Then, as formerly, in the days of their felicity, Pascal
went out leaning upon Clotilde's arm. Neither of them was

as yet in rags; he still wore his black frock coat, she her red
spotted linen gown; still the consciousness of their want
doubtless lessened them, made them regard themselves as two
paupers, taking up but little room on the footways, gliding
humbly past the house-fronts. The sunlit streets were almost
deserted. A few inquisitive glances filled them with embarrassment, still they did not hasten their steps, so overpowering was their anguish of heart.

Pascal had decided to begin with a retired magistrate
whom he had attended for a complaint of the kidneys, and he
entered the house leaving Clotilde seated on a bench on the
Cours Sauvaire. He felt very much relieved when the magistrate, forestalling his application, explained that he received
his pension in October and would then settle his account. At
another house, that of an old lady, a paralytic septuagenarian,
matters were different; she expressed herself so offended at
his having sent his bill by a servant who had behaved anything but politely, that he made all haste to apologise and
offered her whatever delay she might require. Next he
climbed the three flights of stairs leading to the lodging of an
employé of the tax-office, whom he found still ailing and as
poor as himself, so that he did not even dare to ask for any
money. Then he called in turn on a haberdasher, an advo-
cate's wife, an oil merchant, a baker, and other people in
prosperous circumstances; but some of them got rid of him
with excuses, others could not even see him, and one actually
pretended that he did not understand him. There remained
the Marchioness de Valqueyras, the wealthy and notoriously
avaricious representative of a very ancient family, who had been
left a widow with one child, a girl of ten years old. He had
kept her for the last, for she altogether terrified him. However, he finally mustered up courage to ring the bell at her old
house in the lower part of the Cours Sauvaire, a monumental
pile dating from the time of Mazarin. And so long did he
remain inside, that Clotilde, walking to and fro under the
trees, at last grew anxious.

She felt extremely relieved, when, after the lapse of a long half-hour, the door opened and he reappeared. 'What was the matter?' she asked jestingly, 'hadn't she any change?'

However, he had failed with the Marchioness as with the others. She had complained of her farm tenants who did not pay her. And by way of explaining his long absence, he added: 'I found, too, that her little girl was ill—I fear an attack of fever—she showed me the poor little thing and I examined her.'

A smile came irresistibly to Clotilde's lips: 'And you left a prescription?' she asked.

'Of course. Could I do otherwise?'

With a feeling of deep emotion, she again took hold of his arm, and he felt her press it to her heart. For a moment they walked on at haphazard. It was all over, there was nothing for them to do but to return home empty-handed. But he refused to do so, obstinately desirous of providing her with something beyond the potatoes and water which awaited them at La Souleiade. Having walked up the Cours Sauvaire, they turned to the left into the new town. 'Listen,' said Pascal, at last, 'I've an idea. Suppose I apply to Ramond; he would willingly lend us a thousand francs, which I could return to him when our affairs are settled.'

She did not at once reply. Ramond, her rejected suitor, was now married to the solicitor's daughter. He resided in a house of the new town, and was fast becoming a fashionable and wealthy practitioner. She knew that he had an upright mind and a good heart. If he had not returned to see them, it was solely through discretion. Whenever he met them he bowed to them with an admiring air, like one well pleased to see them happy. 'Does it embarrass you?' at last asked Pascal ingenuously, he who would at once have opened his house, purse, and heart to his young colleague.

Thereupon she hastily responded: 'No, no, there was never anything but frank affection between us. I think that I deeply grieved him, but he has forgiven me—you are quite right, we have no other friend, it is to Ramond that we must apply.'

Ill-luck, however, was pursuing them. Ramond was away, summoned to a consultation at Marseilles, and would

only return on the following evening. They were received
by his young wife, a former friend of Clotilde's, whose junior
she was by some three years. She seemed slightly embarrassed, but evinced great amiability. However, the Doctor
naturally refrained from making his request, and simply
explained his visit by saying that he wished to see Ramond
professionally.

When they again found themselves in the street, Pascal
and Clotilde felt altogether alone, lost amid the wide, wide
world. Whither could they now go? What attempt could
they make? Once more they had to resume their walk,
wandering on hither and thither.

'I did not dare to tell you, master,' muttered Clotilde all
at once; 'but it appears that Martine met grandmother the
other day—yes, grandmother was anxious about us, and asked
Martine why we did not apply to her, if we were in need—and
see, there's her door yonder.'

They were now in the Rue de la Banne, and could just
espy a corner of the Place de la Sous Préfecture. Pascal,
however, silenced Clotilde, whose words he had at first failed
to understand. 'Never,' said he, 'never, do you hear! And
you yourself must not go there. You tell me all this because
you are grieved at seeing me in the street like this. I also
feel my heart heavy at the thought that you are in the same
straits and suffer—only it is better to continue suffering than
to do a thing which would assuredly leave everlasting remorse
behind—I will not and I cannot.'

They turned out of the Rue de la Banne and entered the
old town. 'I would a thousand times prefer to apply to
strangers,' continued the Doctor. 'Perhaps we still have
some friends left, though only among the humble.'

And now it was with the one thought of soliciting alms
that Pascal walked along on the arm of his Abishag; the old
beggar king went from door to door leaning on the shoulder
of his loving handmaiden, whose youth was now his only prop.
It was nearly six o'clock, the great heat was subsiding, people
were streaming along the narrow streets; and here, in this
populous district where they were cherished, folks bowed to

them, and smiled at them. A little pity mingled with the
popular admiration, for one and all were aware that they were
ruined. Yet, albeit struck down by fate, they looked handsomer than ever, close pressed to one another, he quite white,
she all golden. It could be divined that trouble had united
them more closely, that they were still unashamed, proud
in fact of their radiant love, that misfortune alone weighed
upon them, that if he was shaken and bowed, she, with a
valiant heart, was striving to keep him erect. Workmen in
linen jackets passed by, whose pockets contained far more
money than theirs. Still no one dared to offer them the alms
which are not refused to the hungry. In the Rue Canquoin
they thought of calling on Guiraude; but they found that
she, in her turn, had died a week previously. Two other
attempts which they made failed. Their dream now was to
borrow a ten-franc piece somewhere. They had been scouring
the town for three long hours.

Thrice again, at a slower pace, in that limpid close of an
ardent August day, did they cross through that town of
Plassans, which the Cours Sauvaire, the Rue de Rome and
the Rue de la Banne divided into three distinct districts, that
town of Plassans whose windows were ever closed, that sun-
burnt, seemingly lifeless town, where in the daytime nothing
stirred, but whose clubs and cafés filled at nightfall with
gamblers and chatterers. Some old coaches which ran to the
mountain villages, stood waiting, their horses unharnessed,
on the Cours; and tipplers, seated outside the cafés, under the
dark shade of the plane-trees, glanced at the Doctor and his
companion and smiled. In the new town, where servants
stood on the thresholds of the stylish houses taking an airing,
they felt less sympathy encompassing them than in the
deserted streets of the St. Marc district, whose old mansions
preserved a friendly silence. They wended their way back
into the old town as far as St. Saturnin, the cathedral with its
apse shaded by the chapter garden, a nook of delightful
quietude whence they were driven by a beggar who
solicited alms of *them!* A great deal of building was going
on in the direction of the railway station, a new suburb was

springing up there, and thither they next betook themselves. Then for the last time they came back to the Place de la Sous Préfecture, the hope suddenly arising within them that they would end by meeting somebody, that some money would be offered them. But all they reaped was the smiling forgiveness which the town extended to them, at seeing them so handsome and so united. The pointed pebbles from the Viorne with which the streets were paved now hurt their feet and they were constrained at last to return empty handed to La Souleiade—the old beggar king and his submissive hand-maiden, Abishag, in the flower of her youth, bringing back David aged and penniless, weary with having fruitlessly scoured the high roads.

It was eight o'clock. Martine, who was waiting for them, understood that she could have no cooking to do that evening. She pretended that she had dined, and as she seemed unwell Pascal at once sent her to bed. 'We can do without you,' repeated Clotilde, 'since the potatoes are on the fire, we can help ourselves.'

The servant, out of temper, gave way, mumbling indistinctly : ' What is the use of sitting down to table when there is nothing to eat ? ' Then, before locking herself in her room, she exclaimed : 'There are no oats left for Bonhomme, monsieur. I found him looking very strange just now. Monsieur ought to go and see him.'

All anxiety, Pascal and Clotilde at once betook themselves to the stable. The old horse was lying drowsily on his straw. For six months past he had not once been out on account of the rheumatism in his legs ; and lately he had become quite blind. No one could understand why the doctor still kept the poor old animal. Even Martine said at times that he ought to be slaughtered out of sheer pity. But Pascal and Clotilde invariably protested, as moved as though it were suggested that they should finish off some old relation who did not die quickly enough. No, no, he had served them for more than a quarter of a century, and he should die a natural death in their stable, like the good fellow he had always been. That evening the Doctor carefully examined him, raising his legs,

looking at his jaws, and listening to the beating of his heart.
' There's nothing the matter with him,' he ended by saying,
' nothing but old age. Ah, my poor old fellow, we shall never
again travel the roads together.'

The idea that Bonhomme had no oats worried Clotilde,
but Pascal tranquillised her ; an animal of that age, who no
longer worked, needed such very little food ! She then took
a handful of grass from a heap which the servant had left
there, and they were both delighted when the horse, in a
spirit of grateful friendship as it were, consented to eat this
grass from her hand. ' But you've still got an appetite,' said
she, laughing, ' you mustn't alarm us like this. Good night,
sleep in peace.' And when they both had kissed him on
either side of his nostrils, as was their wont, they left him to
doze off.

Night was falling, and they decided to take their dinner
with them upstairs. Whilst Clotilde hastily carried up the
dish of potatoes, with some salt and a decanter full of fresh
clear water, Pascal took charge of a basket of early grapes,
the first gathered from a trellised vine below the terrace.
They set the potatoes on a little table between the salt cellar
and the decanter, and placed the grapes on a chair near at
hand. And it proved a wonderful feast, reminding them of
that delicious breakfast which they had partaken of on the
day when Martine had shut herself inside her room, and so
obstinately refused to answer them. They experienced the
same delight as then at finding themselves quite alone, helping
themselves and eating, side by side, out of the same plate.
That evening of dire want, which they had made such an
effort to avert, brought them some of the most delicious hours
of their lives. Since they had returned home, to that large
peaceful room where they could fancy themselves a hundred
leagues away from the town which they had so fruitlessly
scoured, sadness and fear had been fading away again, and
even all recollection of that wretched afternoon spent in futile
wandering had vanished. Heedlessness of everything un-
associated with their passion had come back to them ; they

no longer had any idea of their poverty, no longer asked themselves if it would be necessary for them to seek out a friend on the morrow in order that they might not starve. What was the use of dreading misery and taking so much trouble to avert it, when it sufficed for them to be together in order to feel perfectly happy?

Still the change in their feelings somewhat alarmed Pascal. '*Mon Dieu*!' said he, 'to think that we were so afraid of this evening. Is it reasonable on our part to feel so happy now? Who knows what to-morrow may have in store for us?'

She placed her little hand before his lips. 'No, no,' she rejoined. 'We will love one another to-morrow as we do to-day. Love me, love me well, as I love you.'

Never had they partaken of any meal more heartily. Like the strong, healthy young creature she was, Clotilde displayed a splendid appetite, ravenously devouring the potatoes, and declaring with a laugh that they were delicious, more tasty indeed than the most vaunted meats. And Pascal, on his side, now recovered the appetite of his early manhood. The long draughts of clear water seemed exquisite, while the grapes, which they ate by way of dessert, those fresh grapes, the blood of the earth gilded by the sun, sent them into raptures. They ate immoderately, became drunk, as it were, with water, fruit, and gaiety. They could not remember having ever had such a feast before ; even their first breakfast, with its wealth of cutlets, bread and wine, had not yielded such intoxication, such a delight in life, such all-sufficing joy in being together, a joy which transformed earthenware into gold plate, and the commonest into the most celestial fare, a fare which even the gods are not privileged to taste.

The night gathered in, still they lit no lamp, but lingered there with the windows wide open on the vast expanse of summer sky. The evening breeze streamed in, still sultry, and bringing a perfume of lavender from afar. Then, on the horizon, the moon uprose, so large and full that it cast a silvery light over all the room, in which they beheld themselves as in the soft yet radiant glow of dreamland. On the previous night they had felt the first quiver of anxiety, of instinctive dread at the threatening approach of misfortune, but now the whole world again seemed to be forgotten. Good mother Nature granted them once again supreme happiness and rapture, blinding them to everything on earth excepting their mutual love.

CHAPTER XI

On the following night, however, their distressful insomnia returned to them. They gave no expression to their anxiety in words, but remained for long hours reflecting on the position of affairs, which was growing worse and worse. Forgetting their own needs, they each trembled for the other. To obtain food it now became necessary to run into debt. Martine bought the bread and wine, and a little meat, on credit, full of shame at having to do so, compelled as she was to tell falsehoods, besides displaying great prudence, for no one was ignorant of their ruin. The idea of mortgaging La Souleiade had certainly occurred to the Doctor; only this was the supreme resource—he indeed had nothing left him excepting this house and its grounds, valued at some twenty thousand francs, but for which he would perhaps not secure fifteen thousand should he decide to sell it. And afterwards would come black misery, life on the pavement of the streets, with not even a stone of his own on which to rest his head. It was on this account that Clotilde begged of him to wait, to take no irrevocable step, so long as all other hope was not shut off.

Three or four days went by. They were entering the month of September, and the weather unfortunately became very bad. Some terrible storms devastated the country-side. A portion of one of the walls of La Souleiade was thrown down and could not be set erect again, but lay there all of a heap disclosing a gaping breach. The baker was already becoming impolite, and one morning when the old servant brought home some soup beef she began to cry, saying that the butcher now always gave her the inferior parts. In a few more days it would even be impossible to obtain any credit. It was, therefore, absolutely necessary to come to some decision, and find the wherewithal for the petty daily expenses.

One Monday, when another week of worries began, Clotilde displayed great agitation throughout the morning. She seemed to be a prey to some internal combat, and it was only after breakfast, when Pascal had refused his share of a little beef that remained, that she appeared to make up her mind. Then with a very calm and resolute air, she went out with Martine after quietly placing a little packet in the servant's basket—some trifling remnants which she wished to give away, she said.

When she came back a couple of hours later her face was very pale, but her large, clear, frank eyes beamed radiantly. She at once came up to the Doctor, and looking him in the face confessed herself: ‘I have to ask your forgiveness, master,’ she said, ‘for I have just disobeyed you, and it will certainly cause you great grief.’

Though he did not understand, he felt anxious: ‘What have you done, then?’ he asked.

Slowly and without taking her eyes from him, she pulled an envelope out of her pocket, and drew from it several bank-notes. He suddenly divined the truth and raised a cry: ‘O my God!—the jewels, the presents!’

Then he, as a rule so kind and gentle, was transported with a painful anger. He caught hold of her hands, and tightly, almost brutally, pressed the fingers which were holding the bank-notes. ‘Ah, you wretched woman, what have you done! You have sold my heart itself! Yes, our hearts were in those jewels, and you have parted with them for money! Jewels that I had given you, tokens of our happiest hours, and they were yours, yours alone—how could you think I would take them back in any form, and profit by them? Is it possible, can you have thought of the frightful grief this was sure to cause me?’

She gently answered : 'And you, master, do you think I could let us remain in such a sad situation, in want of bread, when I had those rings, bracelets, necklets, and earrings slumbering in a drawer? My whole being revolted at the thought ; I should have deemed myself a miser, an egotist, had I kept them any longer—and if it grieved me to part with them—as it did grieve me, I own it, to such a point I almost lacked the courage I needed—at all events I am certain that I have only done my duty as an obedient and a loving woman.'

He was still grasping her hands and tears came into her eyes, whilst she added in the same gentle voice and with a faint smile : 'Do not hold me so tight, you hurt me.'

He released her and also began to weep, distracted, a prey to deep emotion. 'I am a brute to let anger carry me away like this,' said he; 'you acted rightly, you could not act otherwise. But you must forgive me, it was so painful to me to see you despoil yourself like that. Give me your hands again, your poor hands which I have hurt, and I will heal them.'

Gently taking hold of them again, he covered them with kisses, and delicate, bare, ringless as they now were, he prized them more than ever. Then, relieved and joyful, she related what she had done, how she had taken Martine into her confidence, and how they had gone together to the dealer's, to that woman who had sold him the *corsage* in old *point d'Alençon*. And at last, after well nigh endless examination and bargaining, this woman had given six thousand francs for all the jewellery. Again did Pascal restrain a gesture of despair: six thousand francs ! when those jewels had cost him more than three times that amount, some twenty thousand francs at the very least.

'Listen,' he said at last, 'I will take this money since it comes from your good heart. But it is understood that it belongs to you. I swear to you that I, in my turn, will now be more avaricious even than Martine, that I will only give her what little money may be strictly necessary for our keep, and that you will find the remainder in the *secrétaire*, supposing that I am never able to replace what is spent, and to return the amount to you entire.'

He sat down and took her on his knees, clasping her waist with quivering emotion. And then, whispering in her ear, he asked : ' And you sold everything—absolutely everything ? '

Without replying, she freed herself and with her finger-tips felt under her dress-body. Then, blushing and smiling, she drew out the slender chain on which the seven pearls gleamed like milky stars. . . Almost at once, however, she again put the jewel back, hid it away from sight. He also was blushing now ; his heart had suddenly bounded with delight. ' Ah ! how good of you ! ' he exclaimed, kissing her rapturously, ' and how I love you ! '

Still, when the evening came, the memory of the jewels sold and gone weighed heavily upon his heart ; and he could not gaze upon the money in the *secrétaire* without a feeling of suffering. The idea of impending, inevitable poverty oppressed him ; and yet greater anguish of heart came to him at the thought of his age, his sixty years, which rendered him useless, powerless to earn sustenance and comfort for the woman he worshipped.

The lying dream that he had made of eternal love was over, he had suddenly awakened to disquieting reality. He sank all at once into misery, felt that he was old, and a chill came over him ; remorse, despairing anger with himself, filled his heart as though he were now conscious of an evil action.

Soon afterwards a frightful light flashed upon him. One morning, whilst he was alone, he received a letter posted at Plassans, as the postmark showed, the handwriting on the envelope of which he could not, to his surprise, recognise. It was an anonymous letter ; and he had read only a few lines of it, when he made a gesture of anger as though he were about to tear it up. However, he sat down trembling, and compelled himself to read it through. The style of this epistle was, it must be admitted, decorous ; propriety and circum-spection were observable in each of the long sentences which followed one upon another like the phrases of some diplomatic memorandum, indited with a view to persuading and convinc-

ing. Arguments upon arguments were adduced to show him
that the scandal of La Souleiade had lasted too long. If
passion, in a measure, might explain and excuse the error he
had been guilty of, it was nevertheless certain that by persevering in his present course at his age and in his position, he
was rendering himself altogether contemptible. Could he not
understand that it was impossible for his young relative to
love an old man like himself, that she could, at the utmost,
only feel pity and gratitude with regard to him? Was it not
high time, therefore, that he should release her from her
equivocal position? He could no longer provide for her, he
no longer had any prospect of being able to leave her a little
fortune, so it was hoped that he would conduct himself like
an honest man, and find sufficient strength to part from her,
in view of assuring her future happiness if this were yet
possible. And the letter ended by reminding him that bad
conduct was always punished.

At the very first words Pascal had understood that this
letter came from his mother. It must have been dictated by
old Madame Rougon; whilst he read it he could distinguish,
as it were, the very inflections of her voice. However, after
commencing the perusal in a transport of anger, he finished
it pale and shivering, again a prey to that shuddering fit
which now came over him every hour. The letter said the
truth, it enlightened him concerning his discomfort of mind,
showed him that if he felt remorseful it was because he was
old and poor, unfit, unable to keep Clotilde with him. He
rose up, stationed himself in front of a looking-glass, and for
a long time remained gazing at himself; his eyes gradually
bedimmed by his tears, in despair at the sight of his wrinkles
and his white beard. That mortal chill which was freezing
him came from the thought that separation would now prove
necessary, fatal, inevitable. He thrust the idea aside, unable
to imagine that he would ever be able to entertain it; yet he
knew that it would return, no matter what he might do, that
he would no longer spend a minute without being assailed by
it, without being lacerated by that battle between his love and
his reason, until the terrible evening should come when, his

nerves and his tears exhausted, he would at last resign
himself. In his present cowardice he shuddered at the mere
thought that he would ever have such courage. But it was
all over, the irreparable was beginning; he began to fear for
Clotilde, so young and so beautiful, and nought remained but
the duty of saving her from himself.

Haunted by the words, by the sentences of the anonymous
letter, he at first tortured his mind by trying to persuade
himself that she did not really love him, that her only feelings towards him were feelings of pity and gratitude. Had
he been able to acquire the conviction that she was sacrificing herself, that in keeping her near him he was simply
satisfying his own monstrous egotism, he would, he thought,
have found rupture an easier matter. But try her as he
might, she was ever as tender, ever as passionate. Then he
sought to prove to himself that their separation was necessary,
and studied the reasons for it. The life they had been leading
for months past, that life without ties or duties, or any kind
of work, was certainly a bad one. For his own part, he considered that he was good for nothing but to lie down and
sleep for ever in some nook under the ground; only was not
this present existence an evil one for her, an existence whence
she would emerge indolent, spoilt, incapable of will-power?
He was perverting her, transforming her into an idol, whilst
scandal-mongers jeered and jested. Then he all at once
pictured himself dead, leaving her all alone in the streets,
penniless, scorned and dying of hunger. None offered her a
shelter, she had to roam the roads, henceforth without home,
husband or children. No, no, it would be a crime; for the
sake of the few days left him in the world, he could not
bequeath to her such a legacy of shame and misery.

One morning, after going out alone on some errand in the
neighbourhood, Clotilde came back distracted, quite white
and shivering. And as soon as she was upstairs in the workroom, she almost fainted in Pascal's arms, stammering dis-
connected words: ' O my God!—my God—those women!'

In great alarm he plied her with questions. ' Come, answer
me, what has happened?' he asked.

A rush of blood suffused her cheeks, and, clinging to him
with her face pressed to his shoulder, she told him how she
had just been insulted in the street by a couple of women. . .
Then she began to sob, whilst he, livid, unable to think of
anything to say to her, distractedly kissed her and mingled
his tears with her own. 'It is my fault, it is all through me
if you suffer,' he at last stammered ; ' listen, we will go away,
far, far away, to some spot where no one knows us, where no
one will insult you, and where you will be happy.'

But on seeing him weep, she, with an effort, bravely set
herself erect and forced back her tears. 'Ah ! it was cowardly
of me to tell you. I had sworn to myself that I would not
do so. But when I found myself at home again, anguish so
rent my heart that everything poured forth from it—but now,
you see, it is over, don't grieve—I love you—'

She was smiling now, and gently passing her arms around
him, she in her turn kissed him as one kisses a sufferer in
despair, in the hope of assuaging his torment. 'I love you,'
she repeated, 'I love you so dearly that I am consoled for
everything. The whole world centres in you; what care I
for anyone else ? You are so good, so kind, and make me so
happy.'

However, he was still weeping, and she on her side again
began shedding tears; and there followed a long spell of
infinite sadness and distress, during which their tears and
kisses mingled.

When Pascal found himself alone again he judged his
conduct abominable. He could not, must not bring further
misfortune and unhappiness upon that child. That very
evening, as it happened, an incident took place which at last
brought him the *dénouement* that he had been seeking, with
terror at the thought of finding it. After dinner Martine
took him aside in a very mysterious manner. 'I have seen
Madame Félicité, monsieur, said she,' 'and she requested me
to communicate this letter to you. She desired me to tell
you that she would have brought it in person if the thought
of her reputation did not prevent her from returning here

again—and she begs you to send Monsieur Maxime's letter
back to her, with Mademoiselle's answer to it.'

It was indeed a letter from Maxime, which Félicité,
delighted at receiving, was now using as a weapon of attack,
after vainly waiting for poverty and want to hand her son
over to her. Since neither Pascal nor Clotilde came to ask
her for assistance, she had once again changed her plan, reverting to her old idea of separating them. And this time the
opportunity seemed to her a decisive one. Maxime's letter
was a pressing one ; he had addressed it to his grandmother
in order that she might plead his cause with his sister. His
complaint, ataxia, had at last declared itself, and he could now
only crawl about leaning on a servant's arm ; still he was
more particularly worried at having lately succumbed to the
fascinations of a pretty brunette, who, he was now certain of it,
had laid siege to him at the instigation of his father, the latter
being ever anxious to finish him off, in view of seizing upon
his fortune. Accordingly he had just bundled the wench out
of the house, and shut himself up quite alone, denying his
door to everyone, and particularly to his father, whom he feared,
however, he might one day see climbing in through the
windows. But, on the other hand, his solitude terrified him,
and he despairingly asked for his sister ; she would serve as a
rampart to shield him from his father's abominable enterprises ; she would nurse him like the gentle, sensible woman
she was. The letter insinuated that if she behaved well with
him, she would have no reason to repent it ; and it ended by
reminding her of the promise she had given him at the time
of his journey to Plassans—a promise to come and join him
should he ever really be in need of her.

Pascal felt icy cold as he read this missive. Nevertheless,
he again perused it from beginning to end. Here then was a
means of bringing about their separation, in a manner acceptable to himself and satisfactory for Clotilde, so easy, so natural
indeed that they ought to consent to it at once. Yet, despite
the call of reason, he as yet felt so little firmness and resolution that his legs trembled, and he was compelled for a
moment to sit down. However, he desired to show himself

heroic, and having recovered his calmness he called Clotilde:
' Here,' said he,' read that letter which grandmother has sent
me.'

Clotilde read it through attentively, without a word or a
gesture. Then she simply answered : · Well, you will send
the answer, I suppose—I refuse.'

He had to restrain himself in order not to give vent to a
cry of joy. The next moment, as though another being within
him were raising its voice, he heard himself saying in a
sensible way : ' You refuse—come, it isn't possible,—one
must think it over. Let us wait until to-morrow before sending an answer. And now let us have a chat.'

She, however, became amazed and excited : ' Leave one
another ! ' she exclaimed, ' and why, pray ? Would you really
consent to it ? What madness ! we love each other, and yet
you would have us separate, have me go away yonder, where
nobody cares for me ! How can you have imagined such a
thing ! it would be senseless.'

He would not enter into a discussion from that point
of view, however, but began talking of promises and duty.
' Remember how grieved you were, my dear, when I warned
you of the illness threatening Maxime. And now, see he is
struck down, infirm, all alone, and begs you to come to him !
You cannot leave him in that position—there is a duty for
you to fulfil.'

' A duty ! ' she retorted. · Have I any duties to perform
with regard to a brother who has never in any wise occupied
himself about me ? My duty lies where I have fixed my
heart.'

' But you promised—I promised for you, I said that you
were sensible. You surely don't want to make me pass for a
liar.'

' Sensible ! it's you that are not sensible. It would be
senseless to part, when by doing so we must, both of us, die
of grief.' And with a violent sweeping gesture, she broke off
the discussion : ' Besides, what is the use of arguing ? The
matter is simple enough. One word from you would settle it.
Do you wish to send me away ? '

'I send you away, good heaven!' he cried impulsively.

'Then if you don't order me away, I shall stop!'

She was laughing now, and hurrying to her desk she scribbled, with a red pencil, the two words 'I refuse' across her brother's appeal. Then she summoned Martine, and insisted that she should at once take the latter back to her grandmother in an envelope. Pascal also was laughing, flooded with such felicity that he suffered her to do as she wished. Delight at the thought of keeping her with him carried away his reason.

That same night, however, how bitter was his remorse for the cowardice he had shown! He had once again surrendered to his longing for happiness; he knew very well that at his age he could never love any other woman, and it was the thought that in parting from her he must bid good-bye to love for ever, that made him groan aloud. The sweat of agony broke out upon him when he pictured her gone and himself alone, without her, bereft of all those subtle caressing charms with which she impregnated the very atmosphere, her breath, her delicate mind, her brave uprightness, her dear physical and moral presence, now as necessary to his life as the light of day itself. Yet a voice within him for ever and ever repeated that she *must* leave him, and that he must find the strength to die of it all. And then he scorned himself for his lack of courage, judged the situation with fearful lucidity. It was all over: a new life, with respect and fortune, awaited her yonder; he could not allow his senile egotism to detain her any longer amid such misery as his, hooted and jeered at. And he swore that he would be strong, that he would not suffer her to sacrifice herself, that he would restore her, despite herself, to happiness and life.

From that moment the battle of abnegation began. A few days went by during which he so effectually made her realise the harshness of the refusal which she had scribbled across Maxime's letter, that she wrote at considerable length to her grandmother in order to explain and soften her words. However, she was still determined that she would not leave La Souleiade. As he was now displaying great parsimony,

in order to spend as little as possible of the money derived
from the sale of the jewels, she began striving to surpass him
in this respect, and ate her dry bread with unfailing gaiety.
One morning he even surprised her advising Martine in
matters of thrift. And meanwhile a dozen times a day she
would gaze at him fixedly, fling herself upon his neck, and
cover him with kisses, to combat and banish that idea of
separation which she could ever see gleaming in his eyes.
Then, too, she brought forward another argument. One
evening, after dinner, he was seized with palpitation of the
heart and almost fainted. It astonished him, for he had
never experienced anything of the kind before, and he fancied
that his nervous disorder must be attacking him again. He
had lately not been feeling so strong as usual; a strange sensation had come to him, as though something delicate, deep
in the recesses of his being, had given way. Clotilde showed
herself most anxious and attentive when she beheld these first
symptoms of heart trouble. Now that he was ill he surely
would not talk any more of her leaving him. When a person
loved anybody and he fell ill, duty required that one should
stay with him and nurse him.

Thus the battle became a ceaseless one, a battle in which,
on either side, affection and self-forgetfulness continually
exerted themselves, in a pressing desire to ensure the other's
happiness. But if the emotion that he felt at beholding her
so kind and loving rendered the idea of separation yet more
excruciating, he, nevertheless, realised that day by day it was
becoming more and more necessary that they *should* part.
On that point he was indeed resolved. If he still trembled
and hesitated, it was only because he was at a loss how
to prevail upon her to leave him. He tried to picture the
scene of despair and grief. What would he do? What would
he say to her? How would they manage to embrace for the
last time and part, never to behold each other again? The
days went by, and he could devise no plan. Not an evening
came but he reproached himself for his cowardice.

She, however, would often jest on the subject with a
touch of affectionate malice. 'You are too good and kind,

master,' she said, 'I am sure you will keep me with you.'

But this angered him, and he would answer, saddened and agitated : ' No, no, don't talk of my kindness. If I were really kind you would long since have been over yonder, in comfort, respected, with a future of quiet, happy life before you, instead of remaining here, insulted, poor, and hopeless, the companion of an old fool like me. No, I'm only a coward and a base-minded man.'

At this she hastily silenced him. It was, indeed, his kindliness of heart that was bleeding ; that kindliness—due to his love of life—with which he regarded things and beings, ever anxious for the happiness of all. To be kind to her, did not that mean to make her happy, even at the cost of his own happiness ? That was the kindness he must do her, and he felt that he would do it, decisively and heroically. However, like a wretch resolved on suicide, he waited for the opportunity, the moment, and the means.

One morning when he had risen at seven o'clock, she was quite surprised, on entering the work-room in her turn, to find him seated at his table. For long weeks past he had neither opened a book nor taken up a pen.

' What, you are working ? ' she exclaimed.

He did not raise his head, but replied with a busy air : ' Yes, I hadn't even kept the genealogical-tree up to date.'

For a few minutes she remained standing behind him, watching him write. He was completing the entries concerning Aunt Dide, Uncle Macquart, and little Charles, noting their deaths and specifying the dates. Then, seeing that he did not stir, but seemed to be ignorant that she was there awaiting her customary morning kiss and smile, she stepped up to the window and leisurely came back again.

' Is it serious, then—are we really going to work ? '

' Yes, no doubt ; you see that I ought to have made entries of those deaths a month ago. And I have a lot of other matters to attend to.'

She looked at him fixedly, peering into his eyes with a questioning expression as though to divine his thoughts.

'All right, then let us work,' she said; 'if there are any researches that you want made, any memoranda you wish to have copied, I will attend to them.'

From that day forward he affected to devote himself to work. Moreover, one of his theories was that absolute repose was not beneficial, and ought never to be prescribed even to those who had overtaxed themselves. A man's life is bound up in his surroundings; the sensations that he derives from them become transformed within him into various kinds of motion—thoughts and actions; in such wise that if his repose be absolute, if he continues absorbing sensations without rendering them up digested and transformed, congestion must set in, with a feeling of discomfort, an inevitable disturbance of his equilibrium. Pascal had always found that work was the best regulator of life. Even on days of ill-health, whenever he managed to get to work he found it acted as a restorative and set him erect again. Never did he enjoy better health than when he accomplished the task which he had traced out for himself beforehand—so many pages of writing during so many hours every morning. He compared this task to a balancing-pole which kept him upright in the midst of daily worries, weaknesses, and stumblings. And thus he now accused the idleness, the indolence in which he had been living for long weeks past, of being the one cause of the palpitations which made him feel at times as though he were stifling. If he wished to cure himself he need only take his great work in hand once more.

During several hours he developed, explained these theories of his to Clotilde with a feverish, exaggerated enthusiasm. That love of science, which prior to his passion for her had alone consumed his life, now seemed to have seized hold of him again. He repeated to her that he could not leave his work incomplete, that he yet had a very great deal to do if he wished to rear a lasting monument. He again became full of concern too with regard to those family documents of his; he would open the large oak press a score of times during the day, take the portfolios from the topmost shelf and add new memoranda to them. His ideas on heredity were already becoming transformed, he would have liked to examine and arrange everything afresh, to synthetise the natural and social history of his family, welding it as it were into a broadly outlined *résumé* applicable to the whole of humanity. At the same time he reverted to his system of puncturing, to extend it, with a confused intuition of the therapeutics of the future, a yet vague, far-off theory, suggested both by his convictions and his personal experience with regard to the salutary, dynamical influence of work.

And, now, he never sat down at his table without complaining : ' Ah ! I shall never have time enough, life is too short ! '

It might have been thought that he could no longer afford to lose an hour.

One morning, abruptly raising his head, he said to his companion, who sat beside him copying some MS. : ' Listen, Clotilde, if I should die——'

' What an idea ! ' she exclaimed, quite scared.

' Listen to me, if I should die you must lock up the doors at once. Keep the family documents for yourself, yourself alone, mind. As for my other manuscripts, as soon as you have got them together you must hand them to Ramond— you hear, that is my express desire——'

' No, no, don't talk so foolishly,' she interrupted, refusing to listen to him.

' Swear to me that you will keep the family documents, and hand my other papers to Ramond,' he repeated again and again.

At last, growing quite grave, with tears in her eyes, she swore as he desired. . . This calmed him, and he began talking of his fears—those old fears which seemed to have taken possession of him again, since he had once more been endeavouring to work. He now, as of yore, kept a watch upon the old press, asserting that he had seen Martine prowling around it. Might not an enemy act upon the old servant's blind devotion, impel her to commit a bad action, by persuading her that she would be saving her master ? Suspicion had already caused him so much suffering ! And now that he was

threatened by the approach of solitude, he sank again into a
state of torment, the torture of the *savant* who is threatened
and persecuted by those belonging to him, even in his own
house, in his very flesh, the labour, the fruit of his brain.

One evening, when he was again talking on this subject
to Clotilde, he let his thoughts escape him: 'You understand,' said he, 'when you are no longer here——'

These words made her turn quite white, and, seeing that
he stopped short, shuddering, she exclaimed: 'O master,
master! so you are still thinking of that abomination. I can
tell it by your eyes, you are hiding something from me, I no
longer share your thoughts. But if I were to go away and
you were to die, who would be left to defend your work?'

He fancied that she was growing accustomed to that idea
of departure, and mustered sufficient strength to answer gaily:
'Do you think that I should allow myself to die without seeing you again! I shall write to you of course! And you will
come back to close my eyes.'

She had sunk upon a chair, and was sobbing. 'Is it
possible? You would have us parted to-morrow, we who
never leave one another for a minute.' She longed for some
link, some bond that might have rendered separation impossible. Ah! if there had only been a child! Pascal's
thought had long been the same; but no, it was not to be.
He felt that he must resign himself.

He now seemed to bury himself more deeply than ever in
his work. He would sit at his table for four or five hours at
a stretch, through the whole morning, the entire afternoon,
without raising his head. He affected exaggerated zeal, declared that he must not be disturbed, must not even be spoken
to. But at times, when Clotilde left the room on tip-toe,
having some orders to give downstairs, or some errand to
execute in the neighbourhood, he would glance furtively
around him to make sure that she was no longer there, and
then let his head fall upon the table like one who is utterly
overwhelmed. Thus did his nerves painfully relax after the
extraordinary effort which he had to make, in order to remain
seated at his table when he felt her near him. Ah, work,

work, how ardently did he appeal to it to grant him a refuge
in which he might shake off, annihilate his thoughts! But
more often than otherwise he was unable to work, was constrained to feign attention, with his eyes fixed upon some book,
his sad eyes which grew dim with tears, whilst his mind, ever
full of the same image, and racked with anguish, became
confused and fled away from him. Would even work fail him
then—work which he deemed sovereign, the sole creator, the
regulator of the world? Must he fling away his books, renounce all exertion, content himself simply with living? Was
it the effect of senility that he could no longer write a page?
With his cheek resting on the table, strengthless and utterly
miserable, he would dream of becoming young and active
again. But it was not to be. Tears coursed down his white
beard; and then, if he heard her coming up the stairs again,
he would swiftly raise his head and take his pen in hand once
more, so that she might find him as she left him, absorbed
in seeming meditation—which in reality was only blank
distress.

It was now the middle of September; two long weeks had
gone by amidst all this discomfort without bringing any
solution, when, one morning, to her great surprise, Clotilde
saw her grandmother Félicité walk into the house. Pascal
had met the old lady in the Rue de la Banne on the day
before, and impatient for the sacrifice, feeling that he himself
lacked the necessary strength to bring about the rupture, he
had, despite his repugnance, confided in her and begged of
her to call on the morrow. It so happened that she had just
received a fresh letter from Maxime, a most urgent, supplicating, sorrowful appeal.

On reaching La Souleiade she began, of course, by explaining her presence there. ' Yes, it's I, my dear,' she said
to Clotilde, ' and if I set foot here again, it is, as you will
understand, because I have very serious reasons for doing so.
Truly now you are losing your senses, and I cannot let you
mar your life like this without trying for the last time to enlighten you.'

Thereupon, in a tearful voice, she read Maxime's letter.

He was now compelled to remain in an arm-chair, stricken, it seemed, with a very rapid and painful form of ataxia. And so he begged his sister to give him a definite answer, still hoping that she would come to him, and trembling at the idea of having to seek another nurse. This, however, he must do, if he were abandoned to his terrible position.

Having finished her perusal, Félicité let it be understood that she thought it most undesirable that Maxime's fortune should pass into a stranger's hands; but she spoke more especially of duty, of the help and succour which one owes to a sick relative, at the same time pretending that there had been a formal promise on Clotilde's part. 'Now just try to remember, my darling,' said she. 'You told him that you would go and join him if he should ever need you. I can hear you now—was it not so?' she added, addressing herself to Pascal, who, since her arrival, had let her act as she chose, remaining for his own part silent, with his face very pale, and his head bowed.

His only answer was a nod.

Thereupon Félicité, in her turn, marshalled forward all the reasons for separating which he himself had already laid before Clotilde—the frightful scandal which was turning into insulting scorn, the abject misery threatening them both, the impossibility of continuing to lead this wretched life in which he, already old, would lose what health and strength remained to him, and amid which she, so young, would end by marring her whole existence. What kind of future could they hope for, now that poverty had fallen on them? It was idiotic and cruel to remain so obstinate.

Erect, with an expressionless face, Clotilde remained silent, refusing even to discuss the situation. Pressed and harassed by her grandmother, however, she at last replied: 'Once more, I owe no duty to my brother. It is here that my duty lies. He can dispose of his fortune as he pleases, I have no desire for it. When we are too poor to keep Martine, master will send her away, and I will be his servant.' So saying she waved her hand expressively.

Yes, that was what she desired to do—to devote, sacrifice

herself to her prince, to give him her life, to beg alms, if need were, along the roads, leading him by the hand . . .

Old Madame Rougon jogged her head. 'Before being his servant,' said she, 'it would have been better if you had begun by being his wife—why did you not marry? It was by far the more simple and decorous course.' She remembered that she had one day called at La Souleiade to insist upon their marrying, in view of nipping the scandal in the bud; and the girl, though evincing great surprise at the suggestion, had then answered that if need were they would indeed marry, only later on.

'Marry! I am quite willing!' Clotilde now exclaimed. 'You are right, grandmother.' And, turning towards Pascal, she added: 'You have told me a hundred times that you would do whatever I asked of you—you hear, marry me. I will be your wife and stay here with you. A wife does not leave her husband.'

He answered her, however, merely with a gesture, as though he feared lest his voice might betray him, lest he might, with a cry of gratitude, accept the eternal bond which she proposed to him. His gesture might be taken as implying either hesitation or refusal. What would be the use of this marriage *in extremis* when all was crumbling away?

'Those are fine sentiments, no doubt,' resumed Félicité; 'you settle everything very well in your little head. But marriage won't give you an income, and meantime you cost him money, you are a heavy burden on him.'

These words produced an extraordinary effect on Clotilde, who rushed towards Pascal with purple cheeks and tearful eyes: 'Master, master, is it true what grandmother has just said? Do you regret the money that my keep costs?'

He turned yet paler but did not stir, still retaining the attitude of one who is overwhelmed. And, as though he were talking to himself, he murmured: 'I have so much work to do! I should so much like to take my documents, my manuscripts, my notes in hand again and finish the work of my life! If I were alone I might be able to arrange everything. I should sell La Souleiade, oh, for a mere trifle, for it's

not worth much, and settle myself with all my papers in a
little room. And then I could work from morning till
evening, and strive not to feel too unhappy.'

Whilst speaking he avoided looking at her; and in her
agitated state those painful mutterings could not possibly
satisfy her. Not a second elapsed but she grew more terrified,
for she fully realised that the fatal, inevitable words were now
soon to be spoken. 'Look at me, master,' she exclaimed,
'look me in the face. And I pray you, be brave, and choose
between your work and me, since you seem to say that you
would send me away so that you might be the better able to
work!'

The moment had come for him to tell the heroic lie. He
raised his head, bravely looked her in the face, and with the
smile of a dying man who welcomes death, in a tone of inef-
fable kindliness, he replied: 'How excited you get! Cannot
you do your duty, simply, like everyone else? I have a great
deal of work to do.—I need to be alone. And you, darling,
you ought to join your brother—so go to him—it is all
over.'

For a few seconds there reigned a terrible silence. She
still gazed at him, fixedly, in the hope that he would weaken.
Was he indeed speaking the truth? Was he not sacrificing
himself in order that she might be happy? For a moment
she experienced a subtle feeling that such was the case; it was
as though some quivering breath emanating from his heart
had warned her of the truth. 'And do you send me away for
ever?' she asked. 'Will you not let me come back soon?'

He remained brave, and answered, so it seemed to her,
with a fresh smile, that one did not part like that to meet
again so speedily. Then all intermingled in her mind, and
she had but a confused perception of the truth; it became
possible for her to believe that he had really made his choice
in all sincerity, like a man of science in whose mind work
triumphs over woman. She had again become extremely
pale, and for a moment remained waiting as it were, amid the
fearful silence. Then, with her wonted air of loving, absolute
submission, she slowly said: 'Very well, master, I will leave

whenever you please, and I will only return on the day when you may summon me.'

Thus fell the hatchet blow which severed them. The irrevocable was accomplished. Félicité, who was surprised that it had not been necessary for her to speak at greater length, at once wished to fix the date of the departure. She congratulated herself on her tenacity, imagined that the victory had been gained by her own prowess. It happened to be a Friday, and it was arranged that Clotilde should leave on the following Sunday. A telegram to that effect was sent to Maxime.

For three days past already, the mistral [1] had been sweeping the country-side. That evening it blew with increased violence, and Martine, in accordance with the popular belief, declared that it would last at least another three days. The winds which rush across the valley of the Viorne towards the close of September are terrible ones. Accordingly the servant carefully went from room to room to make sure that all the shutters were properly fastened. When the mistral blew it swept over the roofs of Plassans to the little plateau on which La Souleiade stood, rushing upon the house slantwise, buffeting it with unremitting fury, shaking it from cellar to garret for days and nights together, without a pause. The tiles flew away, the ironwork of the windows was torn off, the wind swept in through every aperture with a wild plaintive clamour; and the doors, whenever they were forgetfully left open, banged to with a loud noise like the report of a cannon shot. It was like standing a siege, amid ceaseless uproar and anguish.

And it was in this dreary house, shaken by the fierce blast, that Pascal, on the morrow, insisted upon helping Clotilde in her preparations for departure. Old Madame Rougon was only to return on the Sunday at the moment of parting. When Martine heard of the approaching separation she remained thunderstruck, speechless, her eyes lighting up for

[1] The name given in Provence to a violent north-west wind, in some respects peculiar to the region.—*Trans.*

a moment with a bright flame. Then, on being sent out of
the room and told that they did not need her help in packing,
she betook herself to the kitchen again, and returned to her
usual work as though ignorant of the catastrophe which was
rending the household. Whenever Pascal chanced to call
her, however, she hastened to him so promptly, with so light
a step, so bright a face, in her zeal to serve him, that she
seemed to have become a girl again. For his part he did not
leave Clotilde for a moment, intent as he was on helping her,
on making sure that she was taking with her everything that
she might require. Two large trunks stood open in the
middle of the room where all was in disorder ; packages,
clothing, lay about everywhere ; each drawer, each article of
furniture was ransacked a score of times. This work, this
anxiety to forget nothing, served to deaden the bitter anguish
which they both felt. For a moment they would shake off
their thoughts ; the Doctor carefully assured himself that no
room was lost, packed some small articles away in the bonnet-
box, slipped some little cardboard boxes between the handkerchiefs and chemises ; whilst she, taking her dresses from
the pegs on which they hung, folded them upon the bed with
the intention of packing them the last, on the top trays.
Then, whenever they felt a little tired, and rose from their
knees and again found themselves face to face, they would
smile at one another till all at once they had to restrain the
tears which rushed into their eyes as the memory of their
irreparable misfortune once more seized upon them. Still
they remained firm, although their hearts were bleeding. O
God ! was it true then that they were already parting ? And
as they paused in silence they heard the wind, the terrible
wind which threatened to rip the old house open.

How many times during that last day did they step up to
the window, attracted by the uproar of the tempest, longing
that it might sweep the whole world away ! Whilst the
mistral was raging in this wise, the sun did not cease shining ;
the sky still remained blue, but it was a livid blue, dimmed
by dust, and a quiver seemed to pale the yellow sun. They
gazed at the huge clouds of white dust which flew up from

the high roads far away ; at the bent, dishevelled trees, which
all seemed to be fleeing in the same direction and at the same
mad speed ; at the whole stretch of dry country laid bare by
the unabating violence of this blast, which ever and ever
swept by with a roar like that of thunder. Branches broke,
were carried off and vanished ; roofs were lifted off the houses
they covered and transported to such a distance that they
could never again be found. Ah ! thought Pascal and Clotilde,
why did not that mistral take them up together, bear them
away, and cast them on the shores of the unknown land where
happiness has its abode ? The trunks were almost packed
when the Doctor wished to reopen a shutter which the wind
had just blown to ; but when he set the window ajar the blast
swept in with such extreme violence that she had to hurry
to his help. They had to bear upon the shutter with all
their weight, and then at last managed to fasten it back.
Meantime, inside the room, the few little articles remaining
to be packed had been scattered here and there, and on picking up a small hand-glass, fallen from a chair, they found it
shivered to pieces. Was this an omen of approaching death,
as the women of the Faubourg were wont to say ?

In the evening, after their mournful dinner in the light-
panelled dining-room, decked with large pastels of flowers,
Pascal spoke of going to bed early. Clotilde was to leave on
the morrow by the train starting from Plassans at a quarter-
past ten ; and he was somewhat anxious on her account
owing to the length of the journey ; she would have to spend
quite twenty hours in the train. . . Then came their last
good-night, a bitter one indeed . . . How damp and dreary
did his own room, long since forsaken, now seem to him ;
how icy the couch on which he must henceforth for ever
sleep. It seemed to him that he was again falling into old
age, that it was closing in upon him like a leaden coffin. At
first he deemed the wind to be the cause of his sleeplessness.
Shrieks and howls seemed to fill the lifeless house ; angry
and imploring voices seemed to intermingle amidst continuous
sobs. Twice did he rise and listen outside Clotilde's door,
but he heard nothing. Then he went downstairs to secure a

door which was shaking with a hollow sound as though misfortune were knocking for admittance. Cold currents of air were sweeping through the black rooms, and he returned to bed frozen, shivering, haunted by lugubrious visions. . . Then he suddenly became conscious that the loud voice which he heard, which made him suffer so keenly, and robbed him of sleep was not the voice of the raging mistral. It was the call of love and despair. . . O God, to think that they were parting, and that he need but say one word to keep his loved one with him. At thirty a man may love again, but at his age parting meant severance from love for ever. . . His frightful attack of despair lasted until dawn, amid the rageful buffeting of the wind which made the old house tremble from top to bottom.

It was six o'clock when Martine, thinking that she heard her master knocking on the floor of his room to summon her, came up with the lively, excited air which she had worn for two days past. But she stopped short with anxiety and wonder when she beheld him lying half-clad across his bed, worn out with anguish, biting his pillow to stifle his sobs. He had wished to get up and dress himself, but a fresh attack had struck him down—giddy and stifled by palpitation of the heart.

He had scarcely recovered from a brief fainting fit when he again began to stammer forth his torturing sufferings: ' No, no, I cannot—I suffer too greatly—I would rather die—die now at once.'

However, he recognised Martine, and, his strength exhausted, drowned, carried away by grief, he relinquished struggling and confessed himself to her. ' My poor girl, I am suffering too much, my heart is bursting—she is carrying away my heart, my entire being—and I can no longer live without her—I almost died during the night, I wish I could die before she goes, that I may not feel the pang of seeing her leave me—O God ! she is going, I shall never see her more, and I shall be all alone, alone, alone——'

A waxy pallor, a stern, pain-fraught expression had now come over the face of the servant, who, a moment before, had climbed the stairs so gaily. For a moment she watched him as he tore at the sheets with his clenched hands, gasping forth his despair, with his mouth upon the counterpane. Then, with a sudden effort she seemed to make up her mind : ' But it's senseless to sorrow in this way, monsieur. It's ridiculous—since it's like that, and you can't do without Mademoiselle, I shall go and tell her in what a state you've put yourself.'

These words made him rise from the bed impulsively, violently, though still staggering, and needing to cling to a chair for support. 'I forbid you to do that, Martine!' he exclaimed.

' Why, do you think I would listen to you ? To find you here again, half dead, weeping all the tears in your body ! No, no, indeed, I shall go for Mademoiselle and tell her the truth, and compel her to stay with us ! '

He had caught hold of her arm, however, and, transported with anger, would not release her : ' I order you to keep quiet, do you hear ? Or else you shall go away with her. Why did you come in ? It was that wind that made me feel ill—it concerns nobody but myself.'

Then softening again, his wonted kindliness once more gaining the upper hand, he ended by saying with a smile : ' There, you've actually been making me angry, my poor girl ! Let me act as I ought to act, for the happiness of us all. And, mind, not a word, you would grieve me very much.'

Martine's eyes in their turn filled with tears. It was time they came to an understanding, for almost immediately afterwards Clotilde entered the room. She on her side had risen early, eager to see Pascal, hoping till the last moment, no doubt, that he would yet keep her with him. Her own eyes were heavy with sleeplessness, but she at once gazed at him fixedly, with that questioning expression of hers. He still looked so dejected that she became anxious.

' Oh, no ! there's nothing the matter with me, I assure you,' he protested ; ' I should even have slept very well had it not been for that wind—I was just telling you so, Martine, wasn't I ? '

The servant nodded by way of confirming his words. And Clotilde on her side submitted, and refrained from revealing what a night of struggling and suffering she herself had spent, whilst he lay in despairing anguish so near her. In all docility both women now confined themselves to obeying him and helping him in his work of abnegation.

'Wait a moment!' he resumed, opening his *secrétaire*, 'I have something here for you. Here! there are seven hundred francs in this envelope.'

Then, although she began protesting and refusing, he insisted upon going into accounts with her. Barely two hundred francs had been spent of the six thousand realised by the sale of the jewellery, and he was keeping one hundred to provide for himself till the end of the month, with that strict economy, that sordid avarice which he now displayed. Next month he would doubtless sell La Souleiade, set to work, find some means of extricating himself from his difficulties. On one point he was resolved : he would not touch the remaining five thousand francs, for they were her property, and whenever she might want them she would find them in the drawer.

'Master, master,' she exclaimed, 'you grieve me very much——'

'I insist on it,' he interrupted, 'and you would break my heart if you refused—come, it is half-past seven; I'll go and cord your boxes since they are locked.'

When Clotilde and Martine found themselves alone, face to face, they gazed at one another for a moment in silence. Since the advent of the new order of things they had been conscious of their covert antagonism, the bright triumph of the young mistress, the dim jealousy of the old servant, with regard to that master whom they both worshipped. And now, it seemed that victory rested with the servant. However, at that moment of farewell, their common emotion drew them nigh to one another.

'You must not let him starve himself like a beggar, Martine,' said Clotilde. 'Promise me that he shall have meat and wine every day.'

'Have no fear of that, mademoiselle.'

'And, you know, those five thousand francs lying there belong to him. You won't let yourselves starve, I hope, with that money lying there. I want you to spoil him.'

'I repeat to you, mademoiselle, that I will attend to it all, and that Monsieur shall not want for anything.'

There was a fresh pause. They were still looking at each other.

'Keep a watch on him, too, so that he may not work too much. I am going away feeling very anxious about him, for his health has not been so good for some time past. Take care of him, won't you?'

'I'll take care of him, you may be quite easy, mademoiselle.'

'Well, I confide him to you. He will only have you left him, but what tranquillises me a little is that you love him well. Love him with all your strength, love him for both of us.'

'Yes, mademoiselle, as well as I possibly can.'

Tears were rising to their eyes, and Clotilde again spoke: 'Will you kiss me, Martine?'

'Oh, yes, mademoiselle, willingly.'

They were in one another's arms when Pascal returned to the room. He pretended not to notice them, for fear, no doubt, lest he also might give way to emotion. In an unnaturally loud voice he began talking of the last preparations for departure, like a man in a hurry who is anxious not to miss the train. He had corded the trunks, old Durieu, the carman, had just taken them away, and they would be found waiting at the station. It was, however, as yet scarcely eight o'clock, and they still had two long hours before them. These proved two hours of blank, mortal anguish, spent painfully and restlessly in moving hither and thither, chewing as it were, again and again, the bitter cud of severance. The breakfast lasted scarcely a quarter of an hour. Then it was necessary to get up, walk about, and sit down again. They did not cease looking at the clock. The minutes seemed interminable.

'Ah! what a wind!' exclaimed Clotilde, as she heard

the mistral buffeting the house, and making the doors groan.

Pascal approached the window, and gazed at the trees bending, fleeing distractedly, beneath the onslaught of the tempest. 'It has become still more violent this morning,' said he, 'I shall have to see to the roof by-and-by, some tiles have already fallen.'

It seemed as if they were no longer together. They heard nothing now but that furious blast, sweeping everything off, carrying their life away.

At last, when half-past eight struck, Pascal quietly said: 'It is time, Clotilde.'

She rose from the chair on which she was seated. Every now and then she forgot that she was going away. But all at once the frightful certainty returned to her. For the last time she looked at him, yet he did not open his arms to detain her. It was all over. And then, as though stricken to death, her face became quite lifeless.

They simply exchanged some commonplace words at first.

'You will write to me, won't you?' said she.

'Certainly, and you must send me news of yourself as often as possible.'

'And mind, if you should fall ill you must send for me at once.'

'I promise you I will. But there is no danger, I am hale yet.'

Then, at the moment of leaving that house so fondly loved, Clotilde surveyed it all with a wavering glance. And suddenly she fell upon Pascal's bosom, and clasped him in her arms, stammering : 'I want to kiss you here, I want to thank you —It is you, master, that have made me what I am. As you have often told me, you have rectified my heredity. What would have become of me, yonder, amid the surroundings in which Maxime grew up ?—If I am worth anything I owe it to you alone, to you who transplanted me to this home of truth and kindliness, where you reared me, made me worthy of your love—and to-day, after taking me to your heart, loading me with your gifts, you send me away. Your will be done ;

you are my master, and I obey you. Despite everything I love
you, I shall love you evermore.'

He pressed her to his heart and answered : 'I only desire
your good, I am completing my work.'

Then, amid the last kiss, the last heart-rending kiss which
they exchanged, she sighed, in a faint, faint voice : 'Ah! had
there only been a bond between us, had there only been a
child.'

And in a fainter voice even than hers, in a tremulous sob,
she fancied she could hear him stammer indistinctly : 'Yes,
the other dream, the only dream that is good and true in life.
Forgive me, strive to be happy.'

Old Madame Rougon was at the station, very lively and
active in spite of her eighty years. She was triumphing, she
believed that she now held her son Pascal at her mercy.
When she saw how stupefied they both seemed, she took charge
of everything, obtained the ticket, registered the luggage, and
installed Clotilde in a compartment 'for ladies only.' Then
she spoke at length of Maxime, gave instructions, and requested that she might be kept informed of everything. Still
the train did not start, and five more terrible minutes went by,
during which they remained face to face, no longer exchanging
a word. But at last the end came, they embraced, and a noise
of revolving wheels was heard followed by a waving of white
handkerchiefs.

All at once Pascal perceived that he was standing on the
platform, whilst yonder the train had disappeared from view
round a bend in the line. Then, refusing to listen to his
mother, he rushed away with the furious energy of a young
man, ascended the slope, climbed the walls of dry stones, and
in three minutes found himself upon the terrace of La
Souleiade. The mistral was raging there, a mighty squall was
bending the centenarian cypresses as though they had been
mere bits of straw. High up in the pale sky was the sun,
looking very weary of that violent blast which, for six days
now, had been sweeping across his face. However, like the
dishevelled trees, Pascal bravely held out, whilst his coat-tails

flapped like flags, and his beard and hair, lashed by the tempest, streamed hither and thither. Short of breath, with both hands pressed to his heart to restrain its beating, he watched the train fleeing far away over the level plain, a tiny microscopical train, which the mistral seemed to be sweeping along like some little withered bough.

CHAPTER XII

DOOM

On the very next day Pascal shut himself up in the big empty house. He no longer stirred from it, but put a stop to the few professional visits which he had yet been making, and lived on there with doors and windows closed, in absolute solitude and silence. Strict orders had been given to Martine: she was not to admit anybody, on any pretext whatever.

'But your mother, monsieur, Madame Félicité?'

'My mother less than anyone else. I have my reasons. You can tell her that I am working, that I need to be alone to reflect, and that I beg her to excuse me.'

Three times, at brief intervals, did old Madame Rougon present herself. He could hear her storming down below, raising her voice, growing angry, trying to force her way in. Then the noise would cease, and only whispered words, suggestive of complaining and plotting, could be heard between her and the servant. And not once did Pascal give way, not once did he lean over the banisters to call to her to come upstairs.

'It's very harsh all the same, monsieur,' Martine ventured to say to him one day, 'to forbid the door to one's own mother. More especially as Madame Félicité comes here in a good spirit, for she knows what a straitened position Monsieur is in, and is only anxious to offer him assistance.'

'Money! I want no money!' he cried in exasperation. 'I'll work, I'll find a means of earning my living well enough.'

Nevertheless the pecuniary question was becoming a pressing one. He was obstinately determined that he would not touch a copper of the five thousand francs locked up in the *secrétaire.* Now that he was alone he became altogether heedless with regard to material life; bread and water would have contented him. Whenever the servant asked him for money to buy any wine, any meat, anything at all nice, he simply shrugged his shoulders. What was the good of it? There was a crust left from the day before, was not that sufficient? Then Martine, in her affection for this master of hers, whom she knew to be suffering, felt sorely worried by the avarice he displayed, an avarice harsher even than her own, a self-denial which made his position one of absolute destitution. The labourers in the Faubourg lived in less want than he did.

And thus, throughout an entire day, a terrible combat waged within her. Her love for her master—the love of a docile dog—battled with her love of money, the money which she had saved up copper by copper, and hidden away in some secret nook where it was fructifying. She would have preferred to have parted with some of her flesh rather than with any of that money. As long as her master had not been suffering in solitude, no idea of taking aught from her treasure had ever occurred to her. But now, one morning, unable to endure it any longer, seeing her kitchen still fireless and the sideboard empty, she displayed extraordinary heroism, took herself off for an hour or so, and came back again carrying a quantity of provisions with the change out of a hundred-franc note.

At that moment Pascal happened to come down stairs, and, astonished at the sight of this money, he asked her where it came from, already beside himself and ready to fling everything into the street at the thought that she had been to see his mother.

'Oh, no! monsieur, oh no!' she stammered, 'it is not that at all.' And she wound up by telling him a lie which she had previously concocted. 'The fact is that things are righting themselves at Monsieur Grandguillot's, or at least it looks very much like it. It occurred to me this morning to go and see how matters were going on there, and I was told that something would certainly come to you out of it all. They said I could take a hundred francs—yes, and even contented themselves with a receipt from me—you can set it right yourself later on.'

Pascal scarcely seemed surprised at these tidings. Martine certainly hoped that he would not go out to verify her statement, and was relieved to see with what easy unconcern he accepted it. 'Ah! so much the better,' he exclaimed. 'I said that one ought never to despair. This will give me time to arrange my affairs properly.'

These affairs of his were the steps that must be taken to sell La Souleiade, as he had vaguely thought of doing. But how frightful it would be to leave that house where Clotilde had grown up, where he had lived for eighteen years beside her! He had already resolved to allow himself two or three weeks to think the matter over. And on acquiring the hope of recovering a little of his lost money, he no longer thought of it at all. Again did he surrender himself, eating whatever was set before him by Martine, never noticing even the little comforts with which she was again surrounding him, worshipping him, as she did, on her knees, in anguish at having to touch her little treasure, but so happy at the thought she was now feeding him, whilst he had no suspicion that he owed his sustenance to her.

Pascal, it must be said, scarcely recompensed her for her zeal. He would often soften, and regret his angry outbursts. But, in the state of feverish despair in which he was now living, he could not refrain from beginning again, from flying into a perfect passion with her, whenever there was the slightest occasion for displeasure. One evening, when he had again heard his mother talking for a long time in the kitchen, he was seized with a fit of furious anger. 'You hear me, Martine, I won't have her enter La Souleiade again. If you once let her in downstairs, I will send you away!' he shouted.

She listened to him quite thunderstruck. Never before, during the two and thirty years that she had been in his service, had he threatened her with dismissal in this style. Tears rose to her eyes: 'O monsieur! how could you bring yourself to do that?' she exclaimed. 'But I wouldn't go away, I would rather lie down across the doorstep.'

He was already feeling ashamed of his outburst, and continued more gently: 'You see I know perfectly well what is going on. She comes here to school you, to influence you against me, is it not so ? Yes, she is lying in wait for my papers, she would like to steal and destroy everything which I have upstairs, in the press—I know her, when she sets her mind on anything she never rests till she gets it—Well, you can tell her from me that I'm on the watch, and that I will not even allow her to approach the press as long as I am alive. Moreover, I keep the key upon me, in my pocket.'

All the old terror of the haunted, persecuted *savant* had indeed returned to him. Since he had been living alone he had become conscious that he was again in danger, that an ambuscade prepared in the dark was ever threatening him. The circle was contracting, and if he so stoutly resisted all attempts at invasion, if he so promptly repulsed each of his mother's assaults, it was because he was well aware of her real plans, and feared lest he might grow weak. If he should once let her into the house, she would so entwine herself about him that he would be unable to shake her off ; little by little she would master and annihilate him. And thus his torments began afresh : he spent whole days on the watch ; locked the doors in the evening himself ; and often got up during the night to make sure that no attempt was being made to force the locks. His fear was that the servant, gained over and believing that she was ensuring his eternal salvation, might one night open the door to his mother. He could picture his batches of documents burning in the fireplace ; and he mounted guard over them, with a pain-fraught passion, a love full of anguish for all that icy mass of papers, all those cold folios of manuscript, for which he had sacrificed the love of woman and which he strove to love sufficiently well to banish from his mind all thought of the rest.

Since Clotilde had taken her departure Pascal had plunged into work, seeking to drown himself, lose himself in it. If he shut himself up in the workroom, if he no longer set foot in the garden, if one day, when Martine came up to tell him that Dr. Ramond was below wishing to see him, he found the strength to answer that he could receive no one—if he showed himself so fiercely bent on solitude, it was all because he

wished to annihilate himself, as it were, amid incessant toil.
That poor Ramond, how pleased he would have been to
embrace him ! He guessed what a generous, delicate feeling
had prompted him to call—he wished, doubtless, to console
his old master. But why lose an hour, why run the risk of
emotion and tears whence he was bound to emerge weakened ?
As soon as the daylight broke he sat himself at his table, spent
the whole morning, the whole afternoon at it, and often continued seated there by lamplight until very late. He wished
to put his old idea into execution, to re-arrange his entire
theory of heredity on a new plan, to employ the documents
with which the history of his family supplied him, so as to
set forth how life is distributed in a given group of human
creatures, how it leads from one man to another, according to
the influence of environment. His work was to be a huge Bible
so to say, the genesis of families, of society, of entire humanity. He hoped that a plan of such vast scope, the effort
which would be necessary to carry such a colossal idea into
execution, would so influence, so possess his entire being that
he would regain health, faith, and pride amid the refined enjoyment with which the accomplishment of work is fraught.
But in vain did he seek to impassion himself, in vain did he
devote himself, unreservedly, desperately ; he only succeeded
in overtaxing his body and his mind. Despite everything
he was unable to fix his attention ; his heart was not in his
work ; day by day his health grew worse, his despair more
intense. Was the power of work for ever failing him, forsak-
ing him for good ? Was he, whose existence had been consumed by work, who regarded work as the unique motor,
benefactor, and consoler, was he to be forced to the conclusion
that to love and to be loved surpasses all else in the world ?
At times he fell into prolonged meditation, sketching out his
theory of the equilibrium of forces, which consisted in demon-
strating that a man must restore, in some form of motion,
everything which he receives in the form of sensations. How
healthy, full and happy would life have been could one only
have lived it completely, with the action of a well-regulated
machine, which restores in power what it consumes in fuel,

maintaining itself in a state of vigour and beauty, by the simultaneous, logical play of all its component parts! He pictured life composed of as much physical as intellectual labour, as much sentiment as practical sense; gave a due share to the exercise of each physical and mental faculty, without any strain or excess, as these meant disequilibrium and illness. Yes, yes, to begin life afresh, and to know how to live it, to dig the ground, study the world, love woman, attain to human perfection, reach the future abode of universal happiness, by the proper employment of all one's faculties—what a fine testamentary prescription for a philosophical physician to leave behind him! But this far-away dream, this faintly discerned theory only made his own feelings more bitter, at the thought that he himself could never put it into practice, that he was henceforth but a wasted, a lost force.

In the depths of his grief, the sensation which dominated over all others was that he was finished. Regret for Clotilde, suffering at no longer having her beside him, the certainty that she would never be with him again, from hour to hour penetrated him with an anguish which swept everything else away. Work was vanquished, at times he would let his head sink on an unfinished page and weep for hours without the courage to take up his pen again. His desperate application to his work, his long days of voluntary self-annihilation, only led to terrible nights, nights of ardent sleeplessness, during which he bit his sheets that he might not shriek the name of Clotilde aloud. She was everywhere in that dreary house in which he had cloistered himself. He found her crossing every room, seated on every chair, standing behind every door. Down below, in the dining-room he could not seat himself at table but she was there facing him. In the workroom, up above, not a second elapsed but she was his companion; she herself had lived shut up there, so long, so much, that her image seemed to emanate from every object. At each moment a vision of her arose beside him, he could see her slender form standing at her desk, espy her delicate profile as she leant over some pastel drawing. And if he did not go out

of doors to flee the haunting presence of that dear and torturing memory, it was because he felt certain that he would also
find her everywhere about the garden, dreaming at the edge
of the terrace, slowly pacing the pathways of the pine grove,
seated under the plane-trees, refreshing herself with the eternal
song of the spring, stretched upon the threshing-floor in the
twilight, and waiting with dreamy eyes for the stars. But
there was one spot above all others which at once fascinated
and terrified him—her room, the key of which he carried
about him. He had left everything there as it had remained
on the sad morning of her departure, and a forgotten skirt
was still lying upon an armchair. In that room he inhaled
her very breath, the scent of her fresh youth which lingered
in the atmosphere like a perfume. Opening his arms
distractedly, he would press to his heart the phantom form
which he could picture in the soft half-light stealing in
through the closed shutters, a light to which the old, aurora-
tinted cotton hangings imparted a roseate tinge. And here
he would linger and sob, wearing himself out to such a point
that at last he almost feared to enter the room, preferring to
cloister himself in his own cold chamber, where the vision
which arose before him during his sleepless nights did not
seem so near, so full of life.

In the midst of his obstinate toil, Pascal derived a pain-
fraught joy from the letters which Clotilde sent him. Twice
a week regularly, she wrote him long letters, covering eight
and ten pages, in which she recounted well-nigh every incident
of her daily life. She did not seem to be happy in Paris.
Maxime, who no longer stirred from his armchair, tormented
her no doubt with the ceaseless demands which he made upon
her—the unreasonable demands of a spoilt sick child—for she
wrote as though she lived a life of strict seclusion, always on
duty beside him, unable even to approach the windows to
glance out at the avenue, along which streamed the crowd of
fashionable promenaders on their way to and from the
Bois de Boulogne. Moreover, some of her remarks enabled
one to divine that her brother, after so pressingly soliciting
her help, was already growing suspicious of her, beginning to

distrust and dislike her, as he disliked and distrusted all those who served him, in his incessant dread of being exploited and robbed. She had twice seen her father, who always seemed to be very gay, up to his neck in business, triumphing both politically and financially, now that he professed Republicanism. And he had taken her aside to explain to her that poor Maxime was altogether unbearable, that nobody could get on with him, and that she would need a rare dose of courage to stay there with him, for he would unfailingly victimise her. As she was unable to attend to everything, Saccard had obligingly sent her a helpmate—his hairdresser's niece, a little chit of eighteen, very fair and apparently very candid, whose name was Rose, and who now assisted her in waiting on her sick brother. Whilst relating these things Clotilde in no wise complained; on the contrary, like one who has resigned herself to taking life as she finds it, she affected a combination of indifference and satisfaction. Her letters were full of courage; no outburst of anger with regard to their cruel separation, no despairing appeal to Pascal's love, in order that he might summon her back to him, was to be found in them. Nevertheless, reading between the lines, he could divine that she was quivering with a feeling of rebellion, that her spirit ever rushed forth to meet him, that she was ready to perpetrate the madness of returning to him, at the first word of encouragement she received.

That was the word, however, which Pascal would not send her. Things would right themselves; Maxime would grow accustomed to his sister; the sacrifice must be carried out to the end now that it was accomplished. One line from his pen in a momentary fit of weakness, and the result of his effort would be lost, the wretched life would begin afresh. Never had Pascal required more courage than when he answered Clotilde's letters. Sometimes during the night, struggling with his heart, he would call for her in distraction, and spring up to write out a telegram to call her back. But on the morrow, after much weeping, his feverishness would subside, and he would simply send her a short and almost coldly-worded note. He kept a watch upon each sentence he penned, and would begin his letter over again whenever he fancied he had allowed his feelings to escape him. But what a torture it was to pen those frightful letters, so brief, so icy cold, in which he had to fight against his own heart for the purpose of detaching her from himself, of assuming all the odium of callousness, of making her believe that she might well forget him, since he had forgotten her! After writing one of those notes, he would find himself streaming with perspiration, utterly exhausted, as after the accomplishment of some mighty deed of heroism.

The last days of October had arrived, and Clotilde had been gone a month, when one morning Pascal was seized with a sudden feeling of suffocation. He had already on several occasions experienced a slight sensation of stifling, which he had attributed to excessive toil. But this time the symptoms were so precise that he could make no mistake. A sharp pain in the region of the heart, invading his entire chest, and darting down his left arm—a frightful sensation of prostration and agony, whilst a cold sweat broke out all over him— plainly this was an attack of *angina pectoris*. It scarcely lasted a minute, and he was at first more surprised than alarmed at it. Blind to the state of his own health, like many another medical man, he had never suspected that his heart was affected.

It so chanced that while he was recovering breath Martine came up to say that Dr. Ramond was below again, and insisted on seeing him.

Unconsciously giving way, perhaps, to a desire to know the truth concerning himself, Pascal hastily exclaimed : 'Well, well, since he's so obstinate let him come up. I shall be pleased to see him.'

The two men embraced, and the only allusion to the absent one, to her whose departure had rendered the house so desolate, was an energetic handshake instinct with grief.

' Do you know what brings me ? ' Ramond at once exclaimed. ' It's a question of money. Yes, my father-in-law, Monsieur Lévêque, the solicitor whom you are acquainted with, was speaking to me again only yesterday about the funds you deposited with Grandguillot the notary. He strongly advises you to bestir yourself, for some people, it appears, have succeeded in recovering some of their money.'

' Yes, I know that things are righting themselves,' replied Pascal, 'Martine has already received some money—two hundred francs, I think.'

Ramond looked very astonished : ' What, Martine ? And without you interfering ? Well, will you authorise my father-in-law to take your matter in hand ? At all events he will find out what the situation is, since you have neither the time nor the inclination to do so.'

' Certainly, I willingly authorise Monsieur Lévêque to do whatever he may think fit ; and pray give him my best thanks.'

This matter being settled, and the young man, who had observed his pallor, having questioned him with regard to his health, he answered with a smile : ' Do you know, my dear fellow, I have just this moment had an attack of *angina pectoris.*—Oh ! it's no fancy of mine, I detected all the symptoms —and, by the way, since you are here, you must just auscultate me.'

Ramond at first refused to do so, affecting to treat the matter as a joke. Was it for a conscript like him to pronounce an opinion on his general ? Nevertheless he examined him whilst speaking, noticed that his face was drawn, contracted as though by pain, and that there was a strange, wild gleam in his eyes. And he ended by auscultating him with extreme care, lingering for a long time with his ear close-pressed to his chest. Several minutes elapsed in deep silence.

' Well ? ' asked Pascal, when the young doctor rose up again.

Ramond did not immediately reply. He felt, however, that the master's eyes were plunging into his own, so he did not avert them, but rendering homage to the quiet bravery of Pascal's question, answered : ' Well, it's true there's some sclerosis, I fancy.'

' Ah ! it's kind of you not to try to deceive me,' resumed Pascal. ' I was afraid for a moment that you might tell an untruth, and the idea grieved me.'

Ramond had begun listening again, saying in an under-tone, ' Yes, the impulsion is energetic, the first sound is a dull one, but the second, on the contrary, is very loud. It seems as if the point had fallen and been carried towards the axilla. There's some sclerosis—at all events, it's extremely probable.' Then rising up again he added: 'A man may live for twenty years with a complaint like that.'

'At times, no doubt,' answered Pascal, 'unless he dies all at once, struck by lightning as it were.'

They went on talking, expressing their astonishment with regard to a strange case of sclerosis of the heart which they had both observed at the hospital of Plassans. Then the young doctor took his leave, saying that he would come back as soon as he had any tidings to communicate respecting Grandguillot's affairs.

When Pascal found himself alone he felt that he was lost. Everything was becoming quite clear to him now, the palpitations he had been experiencing for some weeks past, the fits of vertigo and stifling that had seized upon him; and he no longer had any doubt as to the feeling of utter weariness, of approaching dissolution which came over him at times—his poor heart, over-taxed with toil and passion, was worn out. However, he did not as yet feel afraid. His first thought was that in his turn he was paying the penalty of his heredity; that in this sclerosis, this species of degeneracy, lay his share of pathological misery; that this was the fatal bequest of his frightful ancestry. In others the original neurosis had turned into vice or virtue, into genius, drunkenness, holiness; others had died of phthisis, epilepsy, ataxia; whilst he had lived on passion and was to die of the heart. And he no longer trembled, no longer felt irritated with this manifest heredity, which was doubtless both fatal and necessary. On the contrary, he was penetrated with humility, with a conviction that any rebellion against the laws of nature is evil. Why, in other times, had he felt so triumphant, so joyful at the idea that he did not belong to his family, that he was quite different to his relatives and had nothing in common with them? It was fallacious to do so. Only monsters grow up apart from other creatures. And after all, *mon Dieu!* it seemed to him as good, as honourable to belong to his family as to belong to any other—for was not one like another, was not humanity everywhere identical, a commingling of good and evil? And so, in an humble, gentle spirit, with the threat of suffering and death suspended above his head, he brought himself to accept whatever life might have in store for him.

Henceforth he lingered on with the one thought that he might at any moment die. And this helped to raise and exalt him to a total forgetfulness of self. He did not cease working; but never before had he understood so well that effort should embody its own reward; work ever having a transitory character, and, despite all attempts, ever remaining incomplete. One evening at dinner Martine informed him that Sarteur the journeyman hatter, the ex-inmate of the Asylum at Les Tulettes, had just hanged himself! Throughout the evening he continued reflecting over this strange case, thinking of this man whom he fancied he had cured of homicidal mania by means of his hypodermic punctures, and who, evidently experiencing a fresh attack, had possessed sufficient lucidity of mind to kill himself in order to avoid seizing some passer-by by the throat. He saw him again, looking so perfectly sensible, whilst he advised him to return to a life of steady work. What was this destructive force, this longing to kill, which thus changed into a suicidal impulse, so that death after all obtained its victim? With this man vanished Pascal's last feeling of pride as a healer; and now of a morning, when he sat himself down to work, he realised that he was but a mere school-boy spelling over his lesson, and still and ever seeking truth whilst it incessantly expanded and receded.

There remained one worry amidst the serenity which had come to him, a feeling of anxiety as to what would become of Bonhomme, his old horse, should he, Pascal, be the first to die. The poor animal, now quite blind and paralysed in the legs, no longer rose from his litter of straw. Still he could hear, and whenever his master came to see him he would turn his head and show that he was conscious of the kisses which Pascal imprinted beside his nostrils. All the folks in

the neighbourhood shrugged their shoulders and jeered about
this 'old relation' whom the Doctor had refused to have
slaughtered. Would he himself be the first to die, with the
thought that the knacker would inevitably be summoned on
the morrow? One morning, however, when he entered the
stable Bonhomme did not hear him and did not raise his
head. He was dead, poor beast! and lay there with a tranquil
air as though it had been a relief, a comfort to him to die in
peace in his old home. His master fell upon his knees and
kissed him yet once more, bidding him farewell in a tremulous
voice, whilst tears coursed down his cheeks.

It was on that day, also, that Pascal for the last time
caught sight of his neighbour, M. Bellombre. He had
approached a window and perceived the old gentleman taking
his usual walk in his garden, in the pale sunlight of the early
days of November. The sight of that old professor living on
in such perfect happiness, at first filled him with astonishment. It seemed to him as if he had never previously thought
of this singular case—a man of seventy, with no wife, no
child, not a dog even, deriving an egotistical happiness from
the very circumstance that he lived entirely apart from life.
Then he remembered his outbursts of anger with regard to
this man, his ironical denunciation of his fear of life, the
disasters which he had called down upon him, the hope he
had felt that punishment would some day come in the form
of some servant-mistress, some unexpected relative personifying vengeance. But no, he found him still as hale as ever, and
he felt that he would long continue ageing like that, stern, avaricious, useless, but happy. However, he no longer execrated
the old fellow; he would willingly have pitied him, so ridiculous, so wretched did he deem him in not being loved. To
think that he himself was ever in agony because he was
alone! that his heart was about to burst because it was too
full of thoughts for others! Ah! rather suffering, suffering and naught besides, than such egotism—the death of all
that is alive and human within us!

During the following night Pascal experienced a fresh
suffocating pang. It lasted nearly five minutes, and he

thought that he would stifle without being able to call the
servant. Then, having recovered breath, he refrained from
disturbing her, preferring not to speak of this aggravation of
his complaints. However, it brought him the conviction that
he was done for, that he would perhaps not last another
month. His first thought then was for Clotilde. Why should
he not write to her and summon her? It happened ;that
he had received a letter from her the previous day, and
intended answering her that morning. Then, too, the thought
of his documents suddenly occurred to him. If he were to
die all at once his mother would remain the mistress and
would destroy them. Moreover, not merely were the family
documents in peril; there were also his manuscripts, his
papers of one kind and another, all the fruit of his intelligence
and toil during the last thirty years. Thus would the crime
which he had so feared be consummated; the crime, his
dread of which during his feverish nights sufficed to make
him spring out of bed quivering, listening eagerly in the
idea that the lock of the old press was being forced. A cold
sweat again broke out upon him, he beheld himself robbed,
outraged, the ashes of all his labour flung to the winds. And
then his thoughts reverted at once to Clotilde—he said to himself that he need simply summon her back to him; she would
then be there to close his eyes and defend his memory. The
idea had scarcely entered his mind when in all haste he sat
himself down at his table to write to her, so that his letter
might go off by the morning post.

However, when he found himself pen in hand, face to face
with the sheet of paper, a growing scruple, a feeling of dis-
content with himself took possession of him. Was not this
solicitude for his documents, this fine plan of giving them a
keeper and saving them from destruction, a suggestion born
of his weakness, a pretext invented for the sole purpose of
again having Clotilde beside him? There was egotism at the
bottom of it all. He was thinking of himself, not of her.
He pictured her returning to that poor house, condemned to
nurse a sick old man; he pictured her in a paroxysm of grief,
in fearful agony on the day when he terrified her by falling

dead at her feet. No, no, he must spare her that frightful
moment, those days of cruel farewell, so soon to be followed
by misery and want—that was a legacy he could not bequeath
to her without deeming himself a criminal. Her tranquillity,
her happiness alone were of any consequence ; what mattered
the rest ? He would die in his hole, happy in the belief that
she was happy. As for saving his manuscripts, he would try
and find strength to part with them by giving them to
Ramond. And even if all his papers were to perish, he would
consent to it ; he was willing that nothing of him should
subsist, no trace even of his mind, provided that henceforth
nothing disturbed the life of that dear loved one.

Accordingly he now began writing one of his usual answers,
which with great difficulty he contrived to render insignificant
and almost cold. Without complaining of Maxime, Clotilde
in her last letter allowed it to be seen that her brother was
beginning to treat her with indifference, deriving apparently
more amusement from Rose, that little fair-haired girl with
the candid look, who was niece to Saccard's hairdresser.
Pascal scented in all this one of the father's stratagems, a
cleverly combined scheme for unduly influencing the sick man,
who was becoming vicious again now that death was near at
hand. However, in spite of his anxiety, he gave Clotilde some
good advice, repeating that it was her duty to devote herself
to the end. Tears were dimming his eyes when he signed
his name. It was his death-warrant that he was signing, the
death of an old, solitary animal, death without a farewell kiss,
without even the pressure of a friendly hand. Then, too, a
doubt had come to him : was it right to leave her yonder, in
that pernicious atmosphere, surrounded, he divined it, by all
sorts of abominations ?

The postman reached La Souleiade with the letters and
newspapers every morning at about nine o'clock ; and Pascal
had got into the habit of watching for him whenever he wrote
to Clotilde, so as to hand him his letter in person. In this
wise he could be certain that his correspondence was not in-
tercepted. That morning, on going down to give him the
letter which he had just written, he was greatly surprised to

receive a fresh one from the young woman, for it was not the day when letters usually arrived from her. However, he let his own go off, and returning to the workroom, again took his seat at his table, tearing her envelope open.

On reading the very first lines he experienced a great shock, a feeling of stupefaction. Clotilde wrote him word that she was *enceinte*. . . Her letter was a short one, simply announcing these tidings, but in words fraught with extreme tenderness, with a pressing desire to return to him at once. Distracted, fearing that he might not understand her correctly, Pascal began reading the letter again. A child! ah, how the thought filled him with happiness and pride. His researches into heredity, his fears respecting his own descent—all had vanished. A child was to be born, what mattered its nature, provided it were the continuation, life bequeathed and perpetuated, one's other self? Pascal was profoundly stirred, his whole being quivered with emotion; he laughed, he spoke aloud, and madly covered the letter with his kisses!

The sound of footsteps, however, constrained him to calm himself. Turning round he perceived Martine at the door. ' Dr. Ramond is downstairs, monsieur,' said she.

' Ah!—let him come up, let him come up.'

More happiness was at hand; for as he reached the threshold, Ramond gaily cried : ' Victory ! I've brought you your money back, master; not all of it, but a good lump sum.'

Then he began explaining matters—a piece of rare good luck which his father-in-law M. Lévêque had brought to light. Grandguillot's receipts for the hundred and twenty thousand francs, which had been handed him by Pascal, were worthless since he was insolvent. The one document of value was that power-of-attorney which the Doctor had one day given him, in order that all or part of his money might be invested in mortgages. The name of the person in whose favour the power-of-attorney purported to be drawn had been left blank by Pascal, and the notary, as often happens, had filled in that of one of his clerks. And in this way eighty thousand francs of the Doctor's money had been found, well invested in mortgages, quite apart from the notary's business, through the medium of this clerk, a worthy fellow. If Pascal had bestirred himself, called on the public prosecutor, he might have unravelled all this long ago. At all events, here he was again in possession of a safe income of four thousand francs.

He had caught hold of Ramond's hands and pressed them, his eyes still moist with tears; 'Ah, my dear fellow! if you only knew how happy I am! This letter from Clotilde has just brought me great happiness. Yes, I was about to recall her, but the thought of my miserable position, of the privations which I must impose upon her, spoilt all the joy that the thought of her return would otherwise have brought me—And now fortune is coming back, or at least enough to enable me to make some provision for her.'

In his expansive emotion, he had handed Clotilde's letter to Ramond, forcing him to read it; then when the young man returned it to him smiling, moved to see him so upset, he gave way to his pressing need of affection, and clasped him with both arms like a comrade, a brother. They kissed one another vigorously on the cheeks.

'Since happiness has sent you here, I will ask you to do me another service,' resumed Pascal. 'You know that I distrust everyone about me, even my old servant. So I want you to take a telegram for me to the office.'

He had again seated himself at his table, and simply wrote these words, ' I await you, start this evening.'

'Come,' he resumed, 'to-day is the 6th of November, eh? It is nearly ten o'clock. She will receive my telegram about noon. That will give her all the time she requires to pack her trunks and take the eight o'clock express this evening, which will reach Marseilles to-morrow at breakfast-time. As there is no train on to Plassans, however, for some hours, she will only be able to get here to-morrow, the 7th, at about five o'clock.'

Having folded the telegram he rose up. ' *Mon Dieu!* at five o'clock to-morrow! How far off it still is! What shall I do with myself till then?'

Then his anxiety returning to him, becoming quite grave again, he said; 'Ramond, my good fellow, will you show yourself a true friend by being very frank with me?'

'In what way, master?'

'Oh, you understand me. You examined me the other day. Do you think I can live another year?'

Gazing fixedly at the young man he prevented him from averting his eyes. However, Ramond sought to escape the difficulty by jesting; was it possible that a doctor could ask such a question?

'Be serious, Ramond, I beg of you.'

Thereupon the young man in all sincerity gave it as his opinion that he might very well hope to live another year. He brought forward his reasons for these views—the fact that the sclerosis was as yet but little advanced, that the other organs were still in a healthy state. No doubt one must make allowance for unknown contingencies—no matter what the complaint, an accident was always possible. Thereupon they began discussing the case, with as much composure as though they had been summoned in consultation to some patient's bedside, examining the various *pros* and *cons*, each enunciating his views, and fixing the date of the fatal issue, in accordance with the most reliable clues that they possessed.

Pascal had fully recovered his sang-froid, his heroic self-forgetfulness, as though indeed there were no question of himself in this discussion. 'Yes,' he muttered at last, 'you are right, a year of life is still possible. But do you know, my friend, what I should like would be two years—it's a mad desire no doubt, an eternity of delight—' and yielding to this dream of the future he added: 'From what Clotilde writes, the child will be born towards the end of May. It would be so delightful to see it grow a bit, till it's eighteen or twenty months old, say, not longer! Just the time for it to get out of its swaddling clothes and take its first steps. It isn't so much that I ask, I should so just like to see the little one walk, and after that, *mon Dieu*, why, after that——'

He expressed his idea with a wave of the hand. Then, mastered by his illusions, he resumed: 'After all, two years

are not impossible. I recollect having had to deal with a
very curious case, a wheelwright in the Faubourg, who lived
for four years, belying all my anticipations. Two years, two
years, I shall live them! I *must* live them!'

Ramond had lowered his head and did not answer. He
was seized with embarrassment at the idea that he had possibly
evinced too much optimism; and indeed Pascal's delight made
him feel anxious, became painful to him. It was as though
the very excitement now transporting the master's mind, once
so strong, conveyed a warning of hidden but imminent danger.

'Didn't you wish to send this telegram off at once?' the
young man at last inquired.

'Yes, yes, leave me now and make haste, my dear Ramond.
I shall expect you on the day after to-morrow. She will be
here then, and I want you to come and embrace us.'

The day proved a very long and tedious one. And that
same night, or rather the next morning, at about four o'clock,
soon after Pascal had at last dozed off, after a long spell of
sleeplessness spent in happy, hopeful reverie, he was brutally
awakened by another frightful attack of his complaint. It
seemed to him this time that a fearful weight, the whole house
indeed, had fallen on his chest, pressing upon it with such
force that his flattened thorax touched his back; and he could no
longer breathe, the pain extended to his shoulders, his neck,
and paralysed his left arm. Still his consciousness remained
complete; he felt that his heart was ceasing to beat, that his
life was ebbing away, under this vice-like pressure which
stifled him. Before the attack had reached an acute stage,
he had fortunately had strength enough to rise and tap upon
the floor with a walking-stick with the view of summoning
Martine. And then he had fallen upon his bed again, no
longer able to stir or to speak, and covered with a cold sweat.

Happily Martine had heard him amid the profound silence
which reigned throughout the empty house. She dressed
herself, wrapped a shawl round her, and came up quickly,
carrying a lighted candle. It was still quite dark, though the
morning twilight was near at hand. And when she perceived
her master, whose eyes alone still seemed to be alive, and who

gazed at her with his jaws clenched, his tongue fast tied, his
face distorted by his terrible anguish, she was utterly scared
and terrified, and could only spring towards the bed, crying:
' *Mon Dieu, mon Dieu*, monsieur, what is the matter with you ?
—Answer me, monsieur, you frighten me ! '

During another long minute, Pascal continued stifling,
unable to recover his breath. Then, as the vice-like pressure
on his ribs slowly relaxed, he murmured in a very low voice :
' The five thousand francs in the *secrétaire* belong to Clotilde.
—You must tell her matters are settled at the notary's, and
that she will there find the wherewithal to live on——'

At this Martine, who had listened to him gaping, was seized
with a fit of despair, and ignorant as she was of the good
tidings brought by Dr. Ramond, she confessed that she had
lately lied.

' You must forgive me, monsieur, I lied to you. But it
would be wrong for me to lie any further—when I saw you all
alone and so unhappy I took some of my own money——'

' You did that, my poor girl ? '

' Oh ! I certainly did hope a little that monsieur would
some day pay it back to me ! '

The attack was passing off, and Pascal was now able to
turn his head and look at her. He was both stupefied and
stirred. What could have taken place in the heart of that
miserly old maid, who for thirty years had been sternly,
stubbornly getting a little treasure together, and, never before,
had taken a copper from it either for herself or for others ?
He did not yet understand everything, and was simply desirous
of showing himself grateful and kind. ' You are a good
woman, Martine,' said he, ' everything shall be refunded to you.
I am very much afraid that I am going to die——'

But she did not let him finish, rebelling with a quiver of
her whole being, and a loud emphatic cry of protest. ' Die—
you, monsieur ? Die before I do ! I won't have it, I will do
everything, I will prevent it, sure enough.' She had flung
herself upon her knees beside the bed, and had caught hold of
him with her distracted hands, feeling him in her desire to
know where he was suffering, clinging to him as if to say that

like that no one would dare to take him from her. 'You must tell me what is the matter with you,' said she, 'I will nurse you, I will save you. If it be necessary to give you any of my life I will give it you, monsieur. I can very well give you my days, my nights ; I am still strong, I will prove stronger than your suffering, you shall see. Die, die ! oh, no ! it isn't possible ! Surely our good God will never be so unjust. I've prayed to Him so often in my time, that assuredly He'll listen to me. Yes, He will hear my prayer, monsieur, and save you.'

Pascal looked at her, listened to her, and a sudden light flashed upon him. Why she loved him, that poor woman loved him, had always loved him. He remembered her thirty years of blind devotion ; her mute adoration of former times when she served him on her knees, when she was young ; then, later on, her covert jealousy of Clotilde, all that she must have unconsciously suffered at that period. And there she was, still on her knees, to-day, beside his death-bed, with grey hair, and ash-grey eyes glimmering forth from her pale nun-like face, wasted by celibacy. And he felt that she was ignorant of all ; that she knew not even with what love she had loved him ; that she loved him solely for the happiness of loving him, of being with him and serving him.

Tears had risen to Pascal's eyes. A pain-fraught compassion, a feeling of infinite affection was overflowing from his wretched, half-broken heart. 'My poor girl,' he murmured, 'you are the best of women. Come, kiss me as you love me, with your whole strength.'

She too was sobbing. She let her grey head, her face worn away by long years of service, fall upon her master's chest ; and she kissed him distractedly with a kiss instinct with all that was alive within her.

'Come,' said he, 'we must not give way, for no matter what we may do, the end is near. If you want me to love you well, you must obey me.'

The feeling which had now taken hold of him was an obstinate disinclination to remain in his own room. It seemed to him icy cold, too lofty, empty and black. A longing had come to him to die in Clotilde's room, that room fraught with

so many memories, which he never entered now, without a
shudder of awe. It was necessary that Martine should give
this last proof of abnegation, help him to get up, support him
and lead him, staggering, to that other room. He had taken
from under his pillow the key of the old press which he kept
there every night ; and when the servant had helped him to
get into bed, he replaced this key under Clotilde's pillow that he
might continue defending it as long as he was alive. The
morning twilight was as yet scarcely breaking; the servant
had placed the candle on the table.

'Now that I am in bed again and can breathe rather
better,' said Pascal, 'you must be kind enough, Martine, to
go to Dr. Ramond's—you must wake him up and bring him
back with you.'

She was already going off when a sudden fear came to
him. 'And mind,' he exclaimed, 'I forbid you to go to my
mother's.'

She turned round embarrassed, and stepped up to him
with a supplicating air : 'O monsieur! Madame Félicité
made me promise so truly.'

He was inflexible, however. Throughout his life he had
treated his mother with deference, and he considered that he
had acquired the right to defend himself from her at the
moment of his death. He refused to see her. The servant
was obliged to swear to him that she would remain silent ;
only then did a smile return to his face. 'Make haste,' said
he, 'oh ! you will find me alive when you return, it is not for
yet awhile.'

The dawn was at last breaking, the gloomy twilight of a
pale November morning. Pascal had made Martine open the
shutters, and when he found himself alone he watched the
growth of this light, the light, doubtless, of the last day that
he would live. It had rained the day before, the sun had
remained obscured by clouds, but it was still warm. He could
hear the awakening of the birds among the neighbouring
plane-trees, whilst far away in the depths of the sleeping
countryside, a railway-engine began whistling with a shrill,
continuous plaint. And he was alone, quite alone in the big

dreary house, to the deep silence of which he lent an attentive
air, and the utter emptiness of which he could divine. The
light increased but slowly, he continued watching its growing
reflection as it whitened the window-panes. Then at last the
candle-flame was altogether bedimmed, and everything in
the room became visible. He had expected some relief from
this, and was not disappointed; the sight of the aurora-tinted
hangings, of each familiar article of furniture, of the large bed
in which he had lain himself down to die, brought him some
consolation. Under the lofty ceiling, athwart the quivering
chamber, there was still wafted the pure scent of youth, the
infinite sweetness of love, enveloping him and comforting him
like a faithful caress.

And yet, though the acute stage of the attack was over,
Pascal still experienced frightful suffering. He felt a sharp
pain in the pit of the chest, and his left arm, quite numbed,
hung from his shoulder like an arm of lead. In the long
interval of waiting for the help which Martine was to bring
him, he ended by concentrating his thoughts on this suffering
which so sorely tried his flesh. Yet he resigned himself to
it; he no longer felt within him the rebellion which formerly
had filled his heart and mind at the mere sight of physical
pain. Suffering had exasperated him as being so much
monstrous and useless cruelty. Amidst the doubts that had
shaken his faith as a healer, he had ended by treating his
patients solely with the view of alleviating such pain as they
might feel. And if he ended by accepting suffering now that
it was torturing himself, was it that he was climbing yet
higher in his faith in life, attaining to that serene summit
whence life appears wholly good, even though it be fatally
fraught with suffering—suffering which is perhaps its main-
spring? Yes, to live life entirely, to live and suffer it wholly
without rebellion, without fancying that one might improve it
by rendering it painless, therein—his dying eyes perceived it
clearly—therein lay true courage and true wisdom. To be-
guile his waiting moments, to divert his mind from his pain,
he passed his last theories in review, and dreamt of a means
of utilising suffering, of transforming it into action, into work,

If man as he gradually rises in civilisation feels pain more acutely, it is also certain that in suffering he becomes stronger, better equipped, endowed with more resistive power. Providing that equilibrium be not disturbed, the organ which works —the brain—develops, acquires solidity between the sensations that it receives and the labour that it gives forth. Consequently, might one not dream of a humanity whose sum of work would be equivalent to its sum of sensations in such wise that even suffering would be utilised, employed, and, as it were, suppressed?

And now the sun was rising and these far-away hopes were revolving in Pascal's mind as he lay there in the semi-somnolence induced by his complaint, when in the depths of his bosom he felt another attack preparing. He experienced a moment of atrocious anxiety: *was this the end*? Was he about to die all alone? But at that very moment came the sound of hasty footsteps on the stairs, and Ramond hurried in followed by Martine. Before the suffocating pang had mastered him Pascal had time to say: 'Puncture me, puncture me at once with pure water!'

Unfortunately, the young doctor had to look for the little syringe and then prepare everything. This took him a few minutes, and the attack proved a frightful one. With keen anxiety he watched its progress, the distortion of the face, the bluish tinge which came over the lips. Then, having made the puncture, he noticed that the symptoms, after remaining stationary for a moment, slowly diminished in intensity. Once again was the catastrophe averted.

However, as soon as he was relieved of his stifling sensation Pascal, casting a glance at the clock, said in a weak, tranquil voice: 'It is seven o'clock, my friend. In twelve hours, at seven this evening, I shall be dead.' And as the young man evinced an inclination to protest and argue, he added, 'No, don't lie. You witnessed the attack, you are as well informed as myself. Henceforth everything will proceed mathematically, and I could describe to you the phases that will follow hour by hour——'

He paused to draw breath, which he did with difficulty.

Then he resumed : ' However all is well. Clotilde will be here at five o'clock ; I now ask nothing more than to see her and die in her arms.'

He soon experienced, however, a perceptible improvement. The effect of the puncture was really miraculous. He was able to sit up in bed, leaning against some pillows. He could speak too with greater ease, and never had his mind seemed to him so clear.

' I'm not going to leave you, master, you know,' said Ramond. ' I warned my wife ; we are going to spend the day together. And, no matter what you may say, I hope that it will in no wise be the last—you will kindly let me make myself at home, I trust.'

Pascal smiled and gave Martine some directions, desiring her to get breakfast ready for Ramond. If they should need her help, they would call her. The two men then remained alone together, in familiar converse ; the elder one, with his long white beard, lying in bed and discoursing like a sage, whilst the other sat near him, listening and displaying the deference of a disciple.

' Really now,' muttered the master, as though he were talking to himself, ' the effect of those punctures is marvellous.' And raising his voice he added almost gaily : ' It's not, perhaps, much of a gift, Ramond my friend, but I am going to leave you my manuscripts. Yes, Clotilde has instructions to hand them to you when I am gone—you can search through them, and in the mass you will find perhaps a few things which are not so bad. Should you some day derive any good from them, well, so much the better for everybody.'

Starting from this point he began sketching out his scientific testament. He was fully conscious that he had been nothing more than a solitary pioneer, a precursor, merely outlining theories, experimenting in practice, failing because his method was still a crude one. He recalled his enthusiasm at the time when he fancied that he had discovered the universal panacea in his injections of nervous matter ; then his disappointment and his despair, the brutally sudden death of Lafouasse, the fate of Valentine killed by phthisis despite all his efforts to prevent it, and the victory which madness had achieved in the case of Sarteur, whom it had impelled to hang himself. So he—Pascal—was now quitting the world full of doubt, no longer possessing the faith which is necessary to the healer ; but so enamoured of life that he had ended by putting his sole faith in it, in the conviction that it derived all needful health and strength from itself alone. Still he did not wish to shut off the future ; on the contrary, it pleased him to bequeath his theories to the young generations. Theories, he reflected, changed every twenty years ; only the acquired truths on which science continued building remained unshake-able. Even if he could claim no other merit than that of supplying the hypothesis of a moment, his work would not be lost ; for progress lay assuredly in effort, in intelligence ever marching on. Besides, who could tell ? Though he might die weary and disturbed in mind, having failed to realise the hopes which he had centred in his punctures, other workmen would come after him, young fellows ardent and convinced, who would take his idea in hand again, elucidate it, and expand it. And that perhaps would be the starting-point of a new century, a new epoch in the life of humanity.

'Ah ! my dear Ramond,' he continued, 'if we did live another life ! Yes, I would begin again, I would take my idea up once more, for I have been greatly struck lately at finding that my injections of pure water proved quite as effi-cacious as the others—so it is of no consequence what liquid may be used ; evidently enough the action is purely me-chanical. I wrote a good deal about all this last month. You will find some notes of mine, some curious observations among my papers. Briefly, I fancy I should have come to believe exclusively in work, to look upon health as the equi-librious play of all the organs of the system—I should have relied on what I will call dynamic therapeutics, if you will allow me to coin such an expression.'

He was gradually growing impassioned, to such a point, indeed, that he forgot death now so near at hand, and became altogether absorbed in his ardent curiosity with regard to life. In this wise he broadly outlined his last theory. Mankind was immersed, so to say, in an atmosphere—Nature—which, by contact, continually irritated the sensitive extremities of the nerves. Not merely the senses, but the entire surface of the body, both external and internal, was set at work. The sensations imparted to it, by reverberating in the brain, the marrow and the nervous centres, there became transformed into tonicity, motion and ideas; and he felt convinced that good health lay in the normal fulfilment of this work : the reception of sensations and their rejection in the form of motion and ideas, the nourishment, in fact, of the human machine by the regular play of its organs. Work thus became the great law, the regulator of the living universe. If equilibrium were disturbed, if the stimulation from without ceased to be sufficient, it was necessary that science should provide artificial stimulation in such a way as to restore tonicity which is the state of perfect health. Then he dreamt of a new system of treatment—suggestion, the physician exercising an all-powerful authority over the senses ; electricity, frictions, *massage* for the skin and the sinews ; a special alimentary regimen for the stomach ; air cures on the lofty tablelands for the lungs ; and finally transfusion and puncturing with distilled water for the circulatory system. It was the undeniable and purely mechanical action of his injections that had put him on the scent ; with his inclination to generalise he was now only extending the hypothesis, again picturing the world saved by the perfect equilibrium which he dreamt of—a sum of work thrown off equivalent to the sum of sensations received, the world's performance of its eternal toil once more fittingly regulated.

Then, with a frank laugh, he exclaimed : ' Why, here I am off again !—I who in the depths of my being believe that the only true wisdom lies in not intervening at all, but in letting nature act as she pleases. Ah ! what an incorrigible old madman I am ! '

Ramond, however, had caught hold of his hands, in a transport of affection and admiration : ' Master, master,' he exclaimed, ' it is of such passion, such madness as yours that genius is compounded. Have no fear, I have listened to you,

I will endeavour to prove myself worthy of the legacy you leave me; and I am of the same opinion as yourself—all the great to-morrow, perhaps, lies in what you say.'

Then Pascal's voice again sounded through the quiet, peaceful room. Once more he began talking with the grave tranquillity of a dying philosopher who is giving his last lesson. He now reverted to his personal observations, and explained that in former times he had often cured himself by work, settled, methodical work, free from all excess. When eleven o'clock struck he was anxious that Ramond should breakfast, and whilst Martine served the young man he continued talking in a lofty, far-away strain. The sun had ended by piercing through the grey morning clouds, but it was still somewhat shrouded, and beamed with a soft radiance which pleasantly warmed the large room. However, after drinking a little milk, Pascal abruptly became silent.

The young doctor was at that moment eating a pear. 'Are you in greater suffering, master?' he asked.

'No, no, finish your meal,' replied Pascal.

But all falsehoods were useless. A fresh attack, and a terrible one, was at hand. Suffocation came upon him like a lightning flash, and threw him back on the pillow with his face already blue. He had caught hold of the sheet with both hands, and clung to it as though seeking in it some point of support that would enable him to raise the fearful weight which he felt crushing his chest. Overwhelmed, livid, he lay there with his eyes wide open, fixed upon the clock, with a frightful expression of despair and grief. And thus he remained, during ten long minutes, apparently on the point of expiring.

Ramond had immediately punctured him. But relief was slow in coming, the remedy was already proving less efficacious.

Big tears stood in Pascal's eyes when life returned to him. He did not speak for some little time, but continued weeping. Then, still looking at the clock with his dim eyes, he said : ' I shall die at four o'clock, my friend I shall not see her.'

Ramond strove to divert his thoughts by asserting against all evidence that the end was not so near ; whereupon, again mastered by his passion for science, the dying man wished to give his young colleague a last lesson based upon personal observation. He had attended several cases similar to his own, and remembered having dissected at the hospital the heart of a poor old pauper who had died of sclerosis.

'I can see my heart,' said he, 'it is the colour of dead leaves; the fibres have become brittle; it looks as if it were shrunken, though in reality its size has slightly increased. Inflammation must have hardened it; you could only cut it with difficulty.'

He went on speaking in a lower tone. Just before that last attack, he had plainly felt the weakening of the action of his heart; had realised that it was contracting more slowly and gently. Instead of the usual flow of healthy blood, only a kind of red foam passed into the aorta. Behind, the veins were full of black blood; the sensation of stifling became greater, as the action of the lift and and force-pump, regulating the whole machine, slackened. Then, after he had been punctured, he had, in spite of all his suffering, followed the progressive awakening of the organ, the whip-stroke, as it were, that had set it on the march again, clearing the black blood out of the veins, and again infusing strength with the red blood of the arteries. But another attack would come as soon as the mechanical effect of the puncture had ceased. He could, within a few minutes, predict the time when it would seize hold of him. Thanks to the punctures, he would have yet three more attacks. The third would carry him off; he would die at four o'clock.

Then, in a voice which grew weaker and weaker, he for the last time vented a feeling of enthusiasm—enthusiasm for the bravery of the heart, that stubborn artisan of life which is ever at work, throughout each second of one's existence, even whilst one is asleep, when all the other organs lie idle and resting.

'Ah! brave heart,' he murmured, 'how gallantly you battle! What faith, what generous strength you display as though never wearied; but you have loved too much, you have beaten too much, and this why you are breaking, brave heart, intent though you be on not dying, and though you still rise to beat again ! '

But in due time came the first of the three attacks which he had predicted. From this he emerged panting, haggard, only able to articulate with difficulty in a hissing kind of voice. Hollow groans, too, escaped him in spite of his courage. Would that torture never cease ? And yet he had but one ardent desire, to prolong his agony, to live yet a little while even amid the most intense suffering, so that he might embrace Clotilde for the last time. If he were after all mistaken, as Ramond stubbornly repeated he was. If he could only live till five o'clock ! His eyes had again sought the clock ; they no longer stirred from its hands, each minute seemed fraught with the importance of an eternity. How often, in times gone by, had he and Clotilde jested about that clock, with its gilt bronze milestone, leaning upon which a smiling Cupid was gazing at sleeping Time. Its hands pointed to three o'clock. Then to half-past three. Only two hours, only two hours more life, that was what he longed for. The sun was sinking towards the horizon, deep peacefulness fell from the pale wintry sky ; but at intervals he could hear distant railway engines whistling across the level plain. That train was the one which passed Les Tulettes. But the other, the one coming from Marseilles, would it never, never arrive ?

At twenty minutes to four Pascal signed to Ramond to approach him. He could no longer speak loud enough to make himself heard at any distance. ' To enable me to live till six o'clock,' he murmured, ' my pulse ought not to be so weak. I still hoped, but feel, the second beat has almost ceased—' Then the name of Clotilde came to his lips, a stammered farewell, full of agony, full of the frightful grief he felt at not seeing her again. And afterwards anxiety for his manuscripts returned to him, a feverish alarm which moment-arily brought lustre back to his eyes. ' Don't leave me—the key is under my pillow,' he gasped. ' You must tell Clotilde to take it, she has my instructions.'

At ten minutes to four, a fresh puncture remained without effect. And four was on the point of striking when the second

attack took place. Then, all at once, having recovered from
the pang, he threw himself out of bed, bent upon getting up
and walking, in a sudden revival of his strength. A need of
space, of light and air urged him forward, yonder. Besides,
he heard the irresistible call of life, of his own life, summoning him into the adjoining work-room. And thither he
hastened, staggering, suffocating, his body inclined to the left
side, his hands clutching for support at the articles of furniture.

Ramond had hastily sprung forward to detain him :
'Master, master, come back, lie down, I beg of you,' he called.

But Pascal was obstinately intent on dying on his feet.
The passion of being yet alive, the heroic idea of work, these
were still paramount with him, and carried him along. 'No,
no, there, there ! ' he stammered, amid the rattling coming
from his throat.

His friend was obliged to sustain him, and thus, haggard
and stumbling, he made his way to the end of the room,
where he let himself sink into his chair, in front of his table,
on which, among books and papers in disorder, lay an unfinished page of manuscript. He remained for a moment
drawing breath, with his eyes closed. When he opened them
again, he began seeking his work with fumbling hands, which
at last lighted upon the genealogical-tree, lying there among
other scattered notes. Only a couple of days previously he
had rectified some of the dates on it. He recognised it, drew
it towards him, and spread it out.

'Master, master, you are killing yourself ! ' repeated
Ramond, quivering, quite overcome with pity and admiration.

But Pascal did not listen, did not hear. He had felt a
pencil rolling under his fingers. He grasped it and leant over
the genealogical-tree, as though his failing eyes could scarcely
distinguish what was written on it. And then, for the last
time, he passed the members of the family in review. At
Maxime's name he stopped and wrote 'Dies of ataxia in 1873,'
certain as he was that his nephew would not survive the year.
Then, close by, Clotilde's name arrested his attention, and he
completed the memoranda concerning her. 'Has a child by
Pascal in 1874,' he wrote. He was, however, looking for the

entry concerning himself, wearing himself out, losing himself
in his search for it. At last, when he had found the place,
his hand became firmer, and he completed the entry in a
brave, tall writing: 'Dies from disease of the heart, on November 7th, 1873.' This was the supreme effort, his rattle was
becoming more pronounced, he was almost stifling, when all at
once above Clotilde's name he beheld a blank leaf. His fingers
were scarce able to continue holding the pencil. Nevertheless,
in unsteady letters, fraught with all the tortured affection, the
distracted anguish rending his poor heart, he contrived to in-
scribe upon this leaf the words: 'The unknown child, to be
born in 1874. What will it be?' Then he fainted, Martine
and Ramond were scarcely able to carry him back to the bed.

The third attack took place at a quarter past four. In
this final access of suffocation, Pascal's face wore an expression of frightful suffering. To the very end he was
destined to endure martyrdom both as a man and as a *savant*.
His dim eyes still seemed to seek the clock to see what time
it was. And Ramond, seeing his lips move, leant forward,
placing his ear close to his mouth. He was, indeed, still murmuring some words, so faintly, however, that they seemed a
mere breath. 'Four o'clock, the heart is stopping, no more
red blood in the aorta—the valve is giving way and tearing.'

A frightful rattle began to shake him, the words he yet
faintly murmured seemed to come from far, far away. 'It is
progressing too quickly—Don't leave me—the key is under
the pillow—Clotilde, Clotilde——'

Choking with sobs, Martine had fallen on her knees at the
foot of the bedstead. She could well see that Monsieur was
dying. Despite her desire, she had not dared to go in search
of a priest; but she herself was repeating the prayers for the
dying, ardently praying to God to forgive Monsieur his transgressions, and to carry him straight to Paradise.

Pascal died. His face was quite blue. After a few
seconds of absolute immobility he tried to breathe, his lips
protruded, he opened his poor mouth, the beak as it were of a
little bird seeking to inhale a last draught of air. And then,
in all simplicity, came Death.

CHAPTER XIII

LIFE'S LABOUR LOST

It was only after the second breakfast, at about one o'clock, that Clotilde received Pascal's telegram. It so happened that her brother Maxime, who was now making her feel his whims and tantrums with increased harshness, was that day sulking with her. On the whole she had not been successful with him; he found her too simple, too serious to enliven him, and he would shut himself up with Rose, that little fair-haired girl with the candid air, whom he considered infinitely more amusing. Since his complaint had been confining him to his arm-chair, weakened and motionless, he had lost much of his whilom, prudent egotism, of his distrust of the women who prey upon men. And so, when his sister came to inform him that she was recalled to Plassans and was starting that same evening, he at once signified his approval. If he begged her to return as soon as possible, as soon as she had attended to whatever matters might require her presence at Pascal's, it was solely from a desire to behave politely. He did not insist on the subject.

Clotilde spent the afternoon in packing her boxes. In the fever, the bewilderment into which Pascal's sudden decision had thrown her, she did not pause to reflect, but gave herself up entirely to the joy of returning to La Souleiade. When she had scrambled through her dinner, however, taken leave of her brother, jolted in a cab through Paris, from the Avenue du Bois de Boulogne to the terminus of the Lyons line; when she found herself in a compartment for 'ladies only,' and, setting out at eight o'clock in the darkness of a rainy, shivery

November night, was already rolling away from the capital,
she calmed down, gradually yielded to the reflections assailing
her, and was at last disturbed by a dim anxiety. What was
the meaning of that curt, pressing telegram : 'I await you,
start this evening.' It was an answer, no doubt, to the letter
in which she had informed Pascal of her condition. Only
she knew how desirous he was that she should remain in
Paris, where he pictured her happy and contented, and she
now felt astonished at the haste he displayed in recalling her.
She had not expected a telegram, but a letter, followed by the
making of all necessary arrangements, and her return to
Plassans in a few weeks' time. So there must be something
apart from this matter of her own ; an indisposition perhaps,
a desire, a longing to see her again at once. Thereupon the
fear that there must be something wrong penetrated her with
the force of a presentiment, increasing to such a point that it
at last wholly possessed her.

All night long a diluvian rain lashed the window-panes of
the train as it rushed across the plains of Burgundy. The
downpour only ceased at Macon. After passing Lyons the dawn
broke. Clotilde had Pascal's letters in her pocket, and had
been impatiently awaiting the sunrise in order that she might
again read and study those short notes, the handwriting of
which seemed to her to have changed. And, indeed, she felt
a chill at the heart as she noticed the hesitating, straggling
manner in which many words were penned. He was ill, very
ill ; it was now becoming a certainty, conveyed to her by a
real power of divination, in which there was less reasoning
than prescience. The remainder of the journey seemed
terribly long to her, and she felt her anguish increase as she
gradually drew nearer to her destination. The worst was
that on alighting at Marseilles at half-past twelve she found
that there would be no train to Plassans till twenty minutes
past three. She had three long hours to wait. Having
breakfasted in the refreshment-room, eating with feverish
haste as though she were afraid of missing her train, she
dragged herself about the dusty garden adjoining the station,
wandering from one seat to another under the pale sun, amid

the crush of omnibuses and cabs. At last she again found herself on her way, but obliged to stop every quarter of an hour at some little station. She thrust her head out of the carriage window; it seemed to her as though her absence had lasted twenty years, as though everything must be greatly changed. The train was leaving Ste. Marthe when, craning her neck forward, she experienced keen emotion as she espied La Souleiade far off on the horizon, with the two centenarian cypresses of its terrace, which could be recognised three leagues away.

It was five o'clock, the twilight was already falling. The station was reached, and Clotilde sprang out of the train. But a keen pain shot through her heart when she saw that Pascal was not on the platform awaiting her. Ever since passing Lyons she had been repeating to herself: 'If I don't see him there on my arrival, it will be that he is ill.' Perhaps, however, he had remained in the waiting-room, or perhaps he was outside procuring a vehicle. She rushed out, but only found old Durieu, the carman whom the Doctor usually employed. She hastily questioned him. Like the taciturn Provençal he was, the old man evinced no haste to answer her. He had his cart there and asked her for her registration-ticket, wishing to attend to the luggage first of all. Thereupon in a trembling voice she repeated her question: 'Is everyone well, Père Durieu?'

'Why yes, mademoiselle.'

She was obliged to insist before she could elicit from him that it was Martine, who, on the previous evening at six o'clock, had given him instructions to be at the station with his cart to meet the train. Neither he nor anyone else had seen the Doctor for a couple of months past. Since he was not there, it might indeed be that he had been obliged to take to his bed; it was rumoured through the town that he was not in very good health.

'Wait till I get the luggage, mademoiselle,' added the old man, 'there's room for you on the seat.'

'No, it would take too long, Père Durieu—I shall go on foot.

Then with long, fast strides she began ascending the slope, her heart contracting to such a degree that she felt stifling. The sun had sunk behind the hills of Ste. Marthe. A fine dust fell from the grey sky with the first shiver of November, and as she was turning into the Chemin des Fenouillères, La Souleiade again rose up before her, chilling her from head to foot, so dreary was the aspect of its façade in the twilight, with every shutter closed, and suggesting the sadness of desertion and mourning.

But the most terrible blow of all fell upon her when she recognised Ramond standing on the threshold of the hall and apparently awaiting her. He had, indeed, been watching for her arrival, and had come down in a desire to try to soften the tidings of the fearful catastrophe. She was coming up out of breath, after passing through the quincunx of plane-trees near the spring by way of taking a short cut; and on beholding the young man there instead of Pascal, whom she had still hoped to meet at the door of the house, she was penetrated with a consciousness of irreparable misfortune, everything seemed to be crumbling away. Ramond was very pale, overcome in spite of his effort to be brave. He did not utter a word, but waited to be questioned.

She too was suffocating, and said nothing. Thus they went in, and he led her into the dining-room, where they again for a few seconds remained face to face, mute with anguish.

'He is ill, is he not?' she stammered, at last.

'Yes, ill,' he simply repeated.

'I understood it on seeing you,' she resumed; 'I realised that since he was not there he must be ill.' Then she began to press him: 'He is ill, very ill, is he not?'

He did not answer, he was becoming yet paler, and she gazed at him. And at that moment she beheld Death upon him, on his hands still quivering, which had ministered to the dying man, on his despair-fraught face, in his dim eyes which retained a reflection of the last agony, in all the disorder apparent in his person after the twelve hours that he had spent there, fighting but powerless to save.

'But he is dead!' she shrieked.

And staggering as though struck by a thunderbolt, she fell into the arms of Ramond, who like a brother pressed her to him, with a loud sob. And with their arms around one another's necks, they wept.

Then, when he had seated her on a chair and was able to speak, he said : ' The telegram which you received was sent off by me yesterday at about half-past ten. He was then so happy, so full of hope! He was forming plans for the future, hoping to live another year, another two years. And this morning at four o'clock he was seized with the first attack and sent for me. He at once realised that he was lost. But he hoped that he might linger on till six o'clock, last long enough to see you again. The advance of his illness was too rapid, however. He described its progress to me, minute by minute, to his very last breath, like a professor lecturing in an operating-room. He died with your name on his lips—calm—disconsolate only at not seeing you—like a hero.'

Clotilde would have liked to hasten from her chair, and with one bound reach the chamber of death ; but she remained there without strength to rise. She listened with her eyes swimming in tears, which flowed on without cessation. Each of Ramond's sentences, the whole narrative of that stoic death resounded in her heart, became deeply engraved in it. She pictured each successive hour of that awful day, which she herself was destined to live over and over again.

But especially did her despair brim over when Martine, who had entered the room a moment previously, exclaimed in a harsh voice : ' Ah, Mademoiselle has good reason to weep, for if Monsieur is dead, it is certainly on account of Mademoiselle.'

The old servant was standing there, apart from the others, near the door of her kitchen, swayed by such grievous anger at the thought that her master should have been taken from her and killed, that she made no attempt to address a word of welcome and comfort to that girl whom she had reared. And, careless as to the result which her indiscretion might have, the grief or pleasure that it might bring, she eased her mind, and spoke all that she knew : 'Yes, if Monsieur is dead, it is because Mademoiselle went away.'

From the depths of her despair Clotilde raised a cry of protest : ' But it was he who sought a quarrel, who compelled me to leave ! '

' Ah, well, if Mademoiselle didn't see through it all, it was perhaps because she didn't take much trouble to do so. Why, the very morning that Mademoiselle went away, I found Monsieur half stifled, so dreadful was his grief; and when I wanted to go and warn Mademoiselle, it was he who prevented me. And then, too, while Mademoiselle was away I saw well enough what was going on. Every night it began afresh ; he needed all his strength to refrain from writing and telling Mademoiselle to come back. And he died of it all, that is the plain truth.'

A flood of light was penetrating the mind of Clotilde, who felt both very happy and very distressed. *Mon Dieu !* so that which she had for a moment suspected was indeed true ! In presence of the violent obstinacy displayed by Pascal it had been possible for her to believe that he was not lying, that having to choose between herself and work, he had chosen the latter in all sincerity, like a man of science in whom the love of work surpasses the love of woman. Yet he *had* lied ; he had carried devotion, self-forgetfulness to the point of immolating himself for the sake of what he deemed to be her happiness. And as it unfortunately happened, he had been mistaken ; in thinking to make *her* happy he had wrought their common woe.

Again did Clotilde begin protesting and lamenting : 'But how was I to know ?—I obeyed, I centred all my affection in obedience.'

' Ah ! ' cried Martine, ' for my part I think I should have guessed the truth ! '

Ramond intervened, speaking gently. He had taken hold of his friend's hands again, and explained to her that, although sorrow might have hastened the fatal issue, Pascal had unhappily been beyond all cure for some time past. The disease of the heart from which he suffered must already have been of somewhat distant date ; he had largely overtaxed himself ; heredity, too, had had its share in the complaint ; then had come all his last passion, and in the end his poor overworked heart had broken.

' Let us go up,' said Clotilde. ' I wish to see him.'

The shutters had been closed, the melancholy twilight had not even entered the room upstairs. Two tapers standing in tall candlesticks were burning on a little table at the foot of the bed, and cast a pale yellow gleam over Pascal, who lay there stretched out, his legs close together, his arms bent, and his hands half-clasped upon his breast. His eyes had been reverently closed. He seemed to be asleep, a more tranquil expression had now come over his face, which still had a bluish hue however, amidst all the whiteness of his streaming hair and beard. He had been dead scarcely an hour and a half. Infinite serenity, eternal rest was beginning.

On beholding him like that, thinking that he could no longer hear her, that he no longer saw her, that she was now alone, that she would kiss him once more, for the last time, and then lose him for ever, Clotilde, in an impulse of violent grief, threw herself upon the bed, unable to stammer more than this loving call : ' O master, master, master ! '

She had pressed her lips upon the dead man's forehead ; and finding him as yet scarcely cold, still retaining some of the warmth of life, it was for a moment possible for her to deceive herself, to imagine that he was conscious of that last caress which he had so long awaited. Motionless though he was, had he not smiled, at last happy and contented, able to finish dying now that he felt them both near to him—she and the child she bore within her ? Then, breaking down in presence of the awful reality, she again began sobbing distractedly.

Martine came in with a lamp which she placed on a corner of the mantelpiece. And in doing so she heard Ramond, who was watching Clotilde, anxious at seeing her so distracted— say to the young woman :

' I shall take you away if you don't show more courage. Remember that you have not only yourself to think about ;

remember that dear little being whom he spoke of to me with so much joy and affection.'

The servant had already felt surprised at certain remarks which she had overheard during the day. She now suddenly understood them, and, instead of leaving the room, stopped short and continued listening.

Ramond had lowered his voice: 'The key of the press is under the pillow,' he said; 'he told me several times to warn you. You know what you have to do?'

Clotilde endeavoured to remember and answer him. 'What I have to do—for the papers, eh? Yes, yes, I recollect, I am to keep the family documents, and to give the other manuscripts to you. Don't be afraid, I have not lost my head, I will behave sensibly. But I won't leave him, I shall spend the night here, oh! very quietly, I assure you.'

She looked so grieved, and yet so resolved upon watching over him, remaining with him until he were removed to his last resting-place, that the young doctor let her take her own course. 'Well then,' said he, 'I will leave you. They must be waiting for me at home. Besides, there are all sorts of formalities—the declaration at the town hall, the funeral, the worry of which I want to spare you. Don't trouble about anything. To-morrow morning, when I come back, all will be settled.'

Having again embraced her, he went off. And then only did Martine in her turn disappear, locking the door downstairs and hurrying along in his wake through the night, which was now dense.

In the room upstairs Clotilde remained alone. Amidst the deep silence, she realised the emptiness of the house around and beneath her. Clotilde remained alone with Pascal's body. She had placed a chair near the head of the bed and sat there, motionless. On her arrival she had merely taken off her bonnet; then, noticing that she was still wearing her gloves, she had but a moment previously pulled them off her hands. However, she still retained her travelling dress, dusty and creased after a twenty hours' railway journey. Old Durieu, no doubt, had long since deposited her boxes downstairs. But she had no idea of washing herself and changing her clothes, no strength to do so, crushed, overwhelmed as she felt as she sat there on that chair. One thought, one fearful feeling—a feeling of remorse—filled her whole being. Ah! why had she obeyed him? Why had she resigned herself to leaving him? She experienced an ardent conviction that if she had remained beside him he would not now be dead. She would have loved him so fondly that she would have cured him! She would have lulled him to fortifying rest, have infused some of her own life into his veins with her kisses. When you wish to prevent death from taking any loved one from you, you stay with him to strengthen him with your blood if need be, and to put death to flight. It was her fault if she had lost him, her fault if she could now never more rouse him from his sleep. What a fool she had been not to understand the truth; how cowardly she had behaved in not devoting herself; her guilt was manifest, and she would ever be punished for having gone away, when common sense, let alone love, should have kept her there, fulfilling her task, watching like a submissive and affectionate subject over her aged king.

The silence was becoming so deep, so perfect, that for a moment Clotilde let her eyes stray from Pascal's face, and wander about the room. Everything she beheld seemed vague and shadowy; the lamplight fell obliquely on the large cheval glass which looked like a plate of dull silver; and the only bright spots under the lofty ceiling were the somewhat ruddy flames of the two tapers. At that moment Clotilde suddenly bethought herself of the letters Pascal had written her—such short cold letters—and she understood how tortured he must have felt in having to stifle his love. What strength he must have needed to carry into effect the sublime if disastrous plan of happiness which he had formed for her! He had stubbornly resolved to disappear, to save her from his old age and poverty; he had pictured her rich, free to enjoy her youth, far away from him, altogether forgetting himself, annihilating himself in his love for her. And, thinking of it all, a feeling of gratitude, sweet and deep, mingled with the bitter irritation which the harshness of fate had brought to her heart. Then, all at once, the happy years uprose before her, her childhood, her youth, spent by his side, and he ever so gay and kind. How completely, with a slowly increasing passion, he had won and conquered her; how fully, after the passing severance of rebellion, she had felt that she belonged to him; how joyfully she had thrown her arms around him and told him that she was his own for all in all! That room, where he was now lying, growing cold for evermore, seemed to her yet warm with all the rapture of love.

The clock struck seven o'clock, and the tinkling sound breaking upon the deep silence made Clotilde start. Who had spoken? Then she remembered, and looked at the clock, which in past times had recorded so many happy hours. It had the tremulous voice of an aged friend. Each object in the room, indeed, wore a friendly look, awoke some loving memory. Once more, from the pale, silvered depths of the cheval glass the reflections of both of them peered forth, drawing, nearer and nearer, vaguely outlined, almost intermingling with smiles straying over their faces, as on those days of rapture when he had led her thither to deck her with some jewel, some present which he had been hiding since the morning. Then, too, that table on which the tapers were burning, that little table was the one on which they had partaken of such a scanty yet delightful meal, on that well-remembered night of bitter want. Every object that she cast her eyes upon reminded her of some incident of their love; a whisper—the echo of loving prattle—came from the very hangings, from that discoloured cotton stuff now faintly pink like the first blush of dawn; whilst in its folds there lingered the perfume of her hair, a perfume as of violets, which had so enraptured him.

After long lingering in her heart, however, the vibration of the seven strokes of the clock at last died away, and then once more her eyes reverted to Pascal's motionless face, and once more, too, she yielded to her bitter grief.

A few minutes later, whilst she was in this state of growing prostration, the sound of sobbing suddenly reached her ears. Someone entered the room like a gust of wind, and on looking round she recognised her grandmother, Félicité. Still she did not stir, she did not speak, so benumbed was she with grief already. Anticipating the orders which would doubtless have been given her, Martine had hastened off to acquaint old Madame Rougon with the dreadful news ; and Pascal's mother, stupefied at first by the suddenness of the catastrophe, then thrown into profound agitation, had hastened to the house, brimming over with noisy grief. She sobbed before her son's body, and embraced Clotilde, who returned her kiss, as in a dream. From that moment, from the faint stir of coming and going which resounded here and there about the room, the young woman, without emerging from the prostration in which she isolated herself, became fully conscious that she was no longer alone. It was Félicité crying, coming in, going out on tip-toe, setting things to rights, prying, whispering, sinking on to a chair and rising up again to move about hither and thither. When it was almost nine o'clock she strove to persuade her grand-daughter to eat something. Twice already had she lectured her in a whisper ; and now she approached her to murmur in her ear : ' Clotilde, my darling, it is very wrong of you, I assure you. You must keep up your strength, you will never be able to go on to the end.'

With a shake of the head, however, the young woman stubbornly refused to take anything.

' Come,' resumed her grandmother, ' you had some breakfast at Marseilles, at the refreshment-room, didn't you ? And you have had nothing since then. Is it reasonable, I ask you ? I don't want you to fall ill in your turn—Martine has some *bouillon*. I have told her to make some light soup, and to cook a fowl. Go down and eat a mouthful, only a mouthful, and I'll take your place here while you are gone.'

With the same pain-fraught shake of the head, Clotilde continued refusing. At last she stammered : ' Oh, do leave me, grandmother, I beg you—I couldn't eat anything, it would choke me.'

She spoke no further. However, she did not sleep, her eyes were wide open, stubbornly fixed upon Pascal's face. For some hours she did not stir, but sat there erect, rigid, with her mind far, far away—there, whither the dead man himself had gone. At ten o'clock she heard a slight noise; it was Martine winding up the lamp. At the approach of eleven, Félicité, who sat watching in an armchair, appeared to grow anxious, and left the room, but soon returned to it. From that moment there was constant coming and going, unremitting, impatient prowling round about the young woman, who was still awake with her large eyes still fixed upon the corpse. Midnight struck, and now only one stubborn thought still remained in her otherwise empty head, preventing her, like some sharp pain, from falling asleep. Why had she obeyed him, why had she ever left him? If she had remained there she would have tended him, and he would not now be dead! And it was nearly one o'clock before she felt even this thought grow vague and dim within her and at last fade away in a nightmare. Exhausted with grief and physical weariness, she fell into a heavy sleep.

When Martine had gone to inform Madame Rougon of her son's unexpected death, the old lady, in the first moment of her stupefaction, had raised a cry of anger. What! Pascal had refused to see her even when he was dying; had made that servant swear that she would not warn her! This was the most bitter, most cruel cut of all; it was as though the life-long battle between him and her were to be prolonged even beyond the tomb. Then, when after hastily dressing she hurried off to La Souleiade, the thought of the terrible documents, the manuscripts filling the old oak press, threw her into quivering excitement. She no longer dreaded what she called the abomination of Les Tulettes now that Uncle Macquart and Aunt Dide were dead. Another of the most humiliating family sores, too, had been effaced by the death of poor little Charles. Only Pascal's documents remained, those abominable documents which threatened with destruction that legend of the Rougons, to the building up of which she had devoted her entire life—which had become indeed the one thought of her old age, the task to which she dedicated all the remaining energy of her active, artful mind. For long, long years she had been on the watch for those documents, never wearying of the struggle, beginning it anew when it was thought that she was defeated, ever lying in ambush, ever displaying the same tenacity. Ah! if she could at last get hold of them and destroy them! That would mean the annihilation of all the shameful past; and then the hard-won glory of her kith and kin, delivered from all that menaced it, would freely bloom and expand and impose its lie upon history. She could see herself wending her way through the three districts of Plassans, with the demeanour of a queen, right nobly wearing her mourning for the fallen *régime*, and bowed to, saluted by all. And so, when Martine told her that Clotilde had arrived, she hastened her steps toward La Souleiade, pursued by the fear that she might, after all, arrive too late.

As soon as she had installed herself in the house, however, she recovered her composure. There was no hurry, she had all the night before her. Still, she wished to make sure of Martine without delay; and she knew right well how to influence the mind of that simple creature, immured within the narrow limits of her religious creed. Accordingly, amidst all the disorder prevailing in the kitchen, whither she betook herself to watch the fowl roasting, her first care was to affect deep grief at the thought that her son had died without making his peace with the Church. She began questioning the servant on the subject, asking her for particulars. But Martine shook her head despairingly—no, no priest had come, Monsieur had not even made the sign of the cross. She alone had fallen on her knees to repeat the prayers for the dying, and this assuredly would not suffice to ensure the salvation of a soul. And yet how fervently she had prayed that Monsieur might be carried straight to Paradise!

With her eyes on the fowl which was turning before a large bright fire, Félicité resumed in a lower voice, with a thoughtful air: 'Ah! my poor girl, it is those abominable papers that the poor fellow has left upstairs in the press, which, more than anything else, prevent him from going to Paradise. I cannot understand how it is that the thunder of heaven has not yet fallen on those papers, and reduced them to ashes. If they are ever allowed to leave this house, it will mean pestilence, dishonour, hell for evermore ! '

Martine listened to her, looking very pale. ' So Madame thinks it would be good and right to destroy them ; that it would ensure the repose of Monsieur's soul ? '

' Believe it, indeed ! Why, if we had those frightful papers I would throw them into that fire there this minute. And you would not need to add any more vine-branches ; with those manuscripts upstairs there would be fuel enough to cook three fowls like that one.'

The servant had taken up a ladle to baste the bird. She also now seemed to be reflecting : ' Only we have not got them,' said she. ' And, by the way, I even heard something said about them which I may very well repeat to you, madame —it was when Mademoiselle Clotilde went into the bedroom —Dr. Ramond asked her if she remembered the orders she had received—before she went away to Paris, no doubt. And she said that she did remember them, that she was to keep the family documents and give him all the other manuscripts.'

Quivering with excitement, Félicité could not restrain an anxious gesture. She already beheld the papers escaping her ; and it was not merely the family documents that she wished to secure, but every page of writing—all that unknown, shady, suspicious work which, to the passionate, obtuse brain of a proud old woman of the middle class like herself, could only be productive of scandal.

' But one must act ! ' she cried ; ' act this very night. To-morrow it might be too late ! '

' I know where the key of the press is,' Martine resumed, in an undertone. ' Dr. Ramond told Mademoiselle.'

Félicité pricked up her ears at once : ' The key—where is it, then ? '

' Under the pillow, under Monsieur's head.'

In spite of the bright blaze of the fire of vine-branches, a faint, icy quiver swept through the kitchen ; and the two old women became silent. The only sound to be heard was the fizzle of the gravy as it fell into the dripping-pan.

However, after Madame Rougon had dined all alone and

as speedily as possible, she went upstairs again with Martine. Without any further exchange of words they had come to an understanding. It was decided between them that they would secure possession of the papers before daybreak, by any means that might be possible. The simplest plan would be to take the key from under the pillow. Clotilde would certainly end by falling asleep : she seemed so exhausted it was impossible she should not succumb to fatigue. So it was only necessary to wait.

They accordingly began spying and prowling about, flitting backwards and forwards between the workroom and the bedroom, on the watch to see if the young woman's fixed, dilated eyes were at last closing. One of them would go to have a look whilst the other waited impatiently in the workroom, where a lamp was burning low. This took place every quarter of an hour, and lasted until nearly midnight. Nevertheless, those deep eyes, full of shade and intense despair, did not close. A little before midnight Félicité again installed herself in an armchair at the foot of the bed, resolved not to leave the room so long as her granddaughter was not asleep. She no longer took her eyes from her, and waxed more and more irritated as she noticed that the young woman seldom even lowered her eyelids, but gazed and gazed at the corpse with a despairing fixity which defied the power of sleep. In the result it was Félicité herself who began to feel drowsy. Quite exasperated at this, she could stay there no longer, but went and joined Martine once more.

'It's useless, she won't sleep,' she muttered in a stifled, trembling voice. ' We must think of some other way.'

The idea of forcing the press open had already occurred to her. But the oak doors looked as though they could defy any onslaught ; the old iron hinges held on strongly. How could she manage to break the lock ? Even if she did so, it would make a terrible noise which would certainly be heard from the adjoining room. Nevertheless, she planted herself in front of the thick doors, feeling them and seeking for some weak spot. ' Ah ! if I only had a tool,' said she.

'Oh ! no, no, Madame,' interrupted Martine, who was less

impassioned, 'we should be heard. Wait a minute, perhaps mademoiselle has fallen asleep.'

Thereupon she again betook herself, on tip-toe, into the bedroom, whence she speedily came back, saying: 'Yes, she's asleep now! Her eyes are shut and she doesn't move.'

They at once went to see her, holding their breath and taking infinite care that the floor should not creak under their footsteps. Clotilde had indeed just fallen asleep, so soundly to all appearance that the two old women felt emboldened. Still, they feared that they might waken her, should they brush against her, as was possible, for her chair stood close beside the bed. Moreover, to slip one's hand under the dead man's pillow to rob him was a terrible, a sacrilegious act, which filled them with a fearful dread. Would they not disturb him in his rest ? Would they not jog him whilst fumbling for the key ; would not the shock make him move ? They turned pale at the mere thought.

Félicité, who had already stepped forward with her arm outstretched, recoiled in dread. ' My arm's not long enough,' she stammered ; 'you had better try, Martine.'

In her turn the servant approached the bedstead, but such a trembling came upon her that, to avoid falling, she had to step back. ' No, no, I can't,' she gasped. ' It seems to me as if Monsieur were about to open his eyes.'

Shuddering, distracted with fear and awe, they remained yet a moment longer in that room where reigned the deep silence and majesty of Death, in front of Pascal, now for ever motionless, of Clotilde prostrated beneath the crushing burden of her widowhood. Possibly, at sight of Pascal's silent head, defending with all its weight the key which would give access to his work, they became conscious of the nobility of a lofty life of labour. The tall tapers were burning with paling flames. A breath of religious terror swept through the room, and drove them from it.

Félicité, so brave as a rule, and who in all her life had never recoiled from anything, not even from blood, now fled as though she were being pursued. ' Come, come, Martine,' she gasped, 'we'll find some other means, we will go and fetch a tool.'

Reaching the workroom they paused to draw breath. And then the servant remembered that the key of the *secrétaire* must be lying on Monsieur's pedestal table, for she had noticed it there the day before, at the time of his first attack. They went to look, and finding it, the mother, without any scruples, opened the *secrétaire*. But she only found in it the five thousand francs which Pascal had so carefully treasured up and which she left in their place in the drawer—for money at that moment was of no importance to her. In vain did she search for the genealogical-tree which she knew was usually kept there. She would so gladly have begun her work of destruction with that hateful document! It had remained lying on the Doctor's table in the workroom, and she did not even notice it there, but in haphazard fashion went on ransacking every article of furniture that she could open, instead of conducting her search in a methodical manner. For that, however, she would have needed calm lucidity, whereas a feverish passion was consuming her.

At last her desire brought her back to the old oak press. She took her stand before it, measured it, gazed at it with ardent eyes glowing with the desire of conquest. Despite her fourscore years she drew her little figure erect and displayed wonderful activity and strength. 'Ah!' she repeated, 'if I only had a tool!'

Again did she seek some crevice, some crack, through which she might insert her fingers so as to pull the monster to pieces. She tried at first to devise some plan of assault, some violent means of destruction; and then she reverted to artfulness, endeavoured to think of some treacherous trick by which the doors would open of their own accord. All at once her eyes flashed; she had hit upon a plan. 'I say, Martine,' she exclaimed, 'the doors are held back on one side by a hook, are they not?'

'Yes, Madame, a hook which fastens in a screw-ring, just above the middle shelf. There! it's somewhere near that moulding.'

Félicité waved her arm as though certain of victory. 'You must surely have a gimlet, a large gimlet. Bring it me.'

In all haste Martine went down into the kitchen, whence she returned with the required tool.

'Like that, do you see, we shall not make any noise,' said the old lady as she set to work.

With remarkable strength, which none would have deemed her little hands, withered by age, to be capable of, she inserted the gimlet and bored a first hole at the spot pointed out by the servant. But it was rather too low; after perforating the door she felt that the point of the tool was penetrating the shelf. A second attempt brought her right against the hook. This was too direct. Thereupon she began multiplying her borings to right and left until, by means of the gimlet itself, she was at last able to raise the hook and drive it out of the screw-ring. Then the bolt of the lock slipped back and both doors opened.

'At last!' cried Félicité, quite beside herself.

Then she paused, motionless and anxious; listening to ascertain if any sound came from the adjoining room, fearing that her exclamation might have awakened Clotilde. But the whole house was slumbering in the deep black silence. The august peacefulness of death still reigned in the bedroom, and she only heard the clear tinkle of the clock striking one in the morning. And now the press stood wide open, gaping, displaying all the masses of papers piled upon its shelves. She rushed upon it and the work of destruction began amid the religious gloom, the infinite peacefulness of that funereal vigil.

'At last,' she repeated in a low voice. 'For thirty years I've been determined on it; for thirty years I've been waiting for it. We must make haste, Martine, we must make haste; come and help me.'

She had already brought the high chair which stood before the desk, and sprang upon it with a bound, so that she might first of all secure the papers on the top shelf, for she remembered that this was the place where the family documents

were kept. But she was surprised not to see the stout blue
wrappers there. Instead of them she perceived numerous
bulky manuscripts, the finished, but unpublished, works of the
Doctor; writings of great value, all his researches, all his discoveries; in fact, the monument of his future fame which he
had bequeathed to the keeping of Ramond. Some days before
his death, no doubt, thinking that the family documents alone
were threatened, and that nobody in the world would dare to
destroy his other works, he had removed the former and
placed them somewhere else so that they might be less easily
found.

'Ah! so much the worse,' muttered Félicité, 'there's
such a lot of them. We must begin at once, anywhere, if we
want to finish. Since I'm up here we'll clear out all these.
Here, catch, Martine!'

Thereupon she began clearing the shelf. One by one she
flung the manuscripts into the arms of the servant, who placed
them on the table, making as little noise as possible in doing so.
When the whole pile was there, Félicité sprang off the chair.
'To the fire! to the fire with them!' said she. 'We shall
end by laying our hands on the others, on the ones I want.
To the fire, to the fire with them! These first, even the
merest scraps of them, the smallest memoranda—we must
burn them all if we want to prevent the spread of evil!'

She herself, like the fanatic she was, fiercely hating truth,
passionately eager to annihilate the testimony of science, tore
off the first page of a manuscript, lighted it at the lamp and
threw it flaming into the large fireplace, where no fire had
been kindled perhaps for twenty years. And she went on
feeding the flame, flinging all the remainder of the manuscript
upon it in pieces. The servant, as resolute as herself, had
come to help her, bringing another large batch of writing,
the leaves of which she separated singly. From that moment
the fire did not cease burning and a blaze soon illumined
the lofty chimney-place—a bright sheaf of leaping flame,
which only fell for a moment to spring upward again with
increased intensity whenever fresh fuel came to revive it. A
brazier gradually expanded, a mass of fine ash ascended, a

thick layer of black leaves of paper, across which darted
millions of sparks. But it was a long, a seemingly endless
business; for when many leaves were thrown on at once, they
did not burn; it became necessary to stir them, to turn them
over with the tongs. The best course was to crumple them and
wait till they were well alight before adding others. In time
Félicité and Martine became more and more skilful, and at
last the work went on right briskly.

In her haste to fetch a fresh armful of papers Félicité
came into collision with an armchair.

'Oh, madame! be careful,' said Martine. 'If anyone were
to come!'

'Come? Who could come? Clotilde? She's sleeping
too soundly, poor girl! And besides, if she comes when it's
all over I sha'n't mind a bit! Oh! I sha'n't hide myself, I
shall leave the press empty and wide open, and I shall say
that I've purified the house. Provided that not a page of
writing is left, I care nothing for anything else.'

During nearly a couple of hours the fire continued flaring.
They had returned to the press; they had cleared the other
shelves; and now there only remained the bottom, which
seemed choke-full of unsorted memoranda. Intoxicated by
the heat of this bonfire, out of breath, covered with perspiration, they gave full rein to their savage fever of destructive-
ness. Crouching before the fireplace, they blackened their
hands in pushing back falling fragments of paper that were
but partially burnt, gesticulating the while so wildly, so
violently, that their grey hair became unfastened and fell
down upon their disordered garments. It was like a meeting
of sorceresses, accelerating the combustion of a diabolical
pyre, in order that some abomination might be carried into
effect; it was like the martyrdom of some saint, like the
public burning of man's Thought by the common hangman,
the destruction of a whole world of truth and hope. And the
bright glow—so bright that the lamplight paled—filled the
entire spacious room, projecting huge dancing shadows of
both of them upon the lofty ceiling.

However, when she had burnt all the loose memoranda

lying at the bottom of the press, and returned to clear out
what still remained there, Félicité, in a choking voice, gave
vent to a cry of triumph : ' Ah ! here they are ! To the fire,
to the fire with them ! '

She had at last come upon the family documents. The
Doctor had hidden the blue-paper portfolios at the very back,
behind that barricade of loose memoranda. And now Félicité
gave rein to all the madness of destruction, a rageful passion
carried her along, she caught up the portfolios by the handful, and flung them among the flames which were filling the
chimney-place with the roar of a conflagration.

' They are burning ! they are burning ! ' she exclaimed.
' Yes, at last, they are burning ! Here, this other, Martine ;
here, this other one ! Ah, what a fire, what a splendid fire ! '

The servant, however, was becoming anxious : ' Take
care, Madame, you will be setting the house on fire. Don't
you hear that roar ? '

' Oh ! what does it matter ? Everything may burn !
They are burning, they are burning, how beautiful they look !
Another three—another two—and, there, there's the last one
burning ! '

She was laughing with glee, beside herself, frightful in
her triumphant mirth, when all at once a quantity of burning
soot came down. The roar was becoming something terrific,
and the chimney never being swept, the soot in it had caught
alight. This, however, only appeared to excite her the more,
whilst the servant, losing her head, began shouting and
running about the room.

Amid the sovereign peacefulness of the bedchamber,
Clotilde was sleeping beside Pascal's body. Nothing had
sounded there but the clock striking three in the morning.
The tapers were burning with tall motionless flames ; not a
breath stirred the atmosphere. And yet, in the depth of her
dreamless sleep she heard something tumultuous, a growing
nightmare-like gallopade. Then, as she opened her eyes, she
at first failed to understand where she was, why she felt such
a heavy weight bearing upon her heart. The consciousness
of reality returned to her in a shudder of terror : she again

saw Pascal, and heard Martine's shouts near by. At once, in a state of anguish, she rushed into the workroom to ascertain what the matter was.

With one glance, on reaching the threshold, she took in the whole scene, in all its brutal clearness—the press wide open and completely empty, Martine distracted with fear of the fire, her grandmother Félicité radiant, pushing the last fragments of the documents into the flames with her boot. A horrid smoke, a quantity of flying soot was filling the room where the roar of the fire resounded like a rattle of murder. This was the devastating gallop which she had heard in the depths of her slumber.

And the cry which now burst from her lips was the cry which Pascal himself had raised on that stormy night when he had surprised her stealing his papers.

'Thieves ! Murderesses ! '

She at once darted towards the fireplace : and, in spite of the terrible roar, in spite of the red-hot soot which was falling, at the risk of setting her hair alight and burning her hands, she seized hold of the sheets of paper not yet consumed and bravely extinguished them by pressing them to her. But, after all, it was a mere trifle that she rescued,—only a few fragments, not a perfect page, not even the crumbs of that colossal toil, that patient, that vast labour of a lifetime which the fire had destroyed in a couple of hours. And Clotilde's anger grew within her, exploded in an outburst of furious indignation.

' You are thieves, murderesses ! You have perpetrated an abominable crime ; you have killed thought, killed genius ! '

Old Madame Rougon did not recoil. On the contrary, she had stepped forward, remorseless, her head erect, defending the sentence of destruction pronounced and executed by herself : 'Is it to me, your grandmother, that you are speaking ?—I have done what I had to do, what you yourself formerly wished to help me do.'

' Formerly, you turned my head. But I have loved since then—I have loved, I have come to understand. Moreover, it was a sacred inheritance entrusted to my courage, the last thought of a dying man, it was all that remained of a great brain, and I was to have imposed it on one and all.   Yes, you are my grandmother !   And it is just as though you had burnt your own son.'

'Burn Pascal because I have burnt his papers ! ' cried Félicité.   'Why, I would have burnt down the whole town to save the glory of our family ! '

She still stepped forward proudly, like a victorious combatant, and Clotilde, who had placed the charred fragments which she had rescued on the table, screened them with her body, for fear lest her grandmother should again throw them into the flames.   But Félicité disdained to touch them, she did not even show any concern respecting the fire in the chimney, which, fortunately, was dying out exhausted, whilst Martine pressed the shovel on the burning soot and the last flamelets rising from the ashes in the fireplace.

'You know very well,' continued Félicité, whose little figure seemed to grow tall with pride, ' you know very well that I have never had but one ambition, one passion—the fortune, the power of our family.   I have battled, I have watched all my life, I have only lived so long in order that I might sweep away all evil stories and leave nothing but a glorious legend of us all.   Yes, I have never despaired, never disarmed, I have always been ready to profit by the slightest opportunity—and all that I wished to do I have now done, by having known how to wait.'

With a sweep of the hand she pointed out the empty press, and the fireplace where the last sparks were fading away.

'Now it is all over,' she resumed, ' our honour is safe ; those abominable papers will never more accuse us, and I shall not leave a threat behind me.   The Rougons triumph ! '

Clotilde, distracted, raised her arm as though to drive her away.   But she walked out of the room of her own accord, and went down into the kitchen to wash her blackened hands and fasten up her hair.   The servant was on the point of following her, when, turning round, she caught sight of the gesture made by her young mistress.   Thereupon she stepped

back again : ' Oh ! as for me, mademoiselle,' she said, ' I
shall leave on the day after to-morrow, when Monsieur has
been taken to the cemetery.'

Silence fell for a moment.

' But I don't send you away, Martine,' said Clotilde. ' I
know very well that you are not the most culpable. You
have been living in this house for thirty years. Stay, stay
with me.'

The old maid raised her grey, pale, wasted head : ' No, I
served Monsieur, I will serve no one after him.'

' Not me ? '

Martine raised her eyes, her wavering eyes, and looked at
that young woman, that child, whom she had seen grow up.

' No, not you,' she said.

Then Clotilde experienced some embarrassment, wishing
to speak to her of the child that would soon be born, the
child of her master, whom she would, perhaps, consent to
serve. Martine, remembering the conversation she had heard,
divined her thoughts, and for a moment seemed to reflect.
Then plainly, frankly, she added : ' The child, eh ?—No ! '

That said, like a practical woman who knows the value of
money, she proceeded to settle affairs and went into accounts :
' Since I've got the means,' she said, ' I shall go and live
quietly somewhere on my income—I can very well leave you,
mademoiselle, for you are not poor. Monsieur Ramond will
explain to you to-morrow how four thousand francs a-year
have been recovered from the notary. Meantime here's the
key of the *secrétaire*, in which you will find the five thousand
francs that Monsieur left there. Oh ! I know very well that
we shall have no difficulties together. Monsieur hasn't paid
me any wages for three months past—I've got papers to prove
it. And besides that, I've recently advanced about two hundred francs out of my pocket, without Monsieur knowing
where the money came from. It's all written down ; I'm
quite easy in my mind ; mademoiselle won't wrong me of a
centime, I'm sure. The day after to-morrow, when Monsieur
is no longer here, I will go away.'

In her turn she went down into the kitchen, and although

this woman had in her blind piety helped to commit a crime, Clotilde nevertheless felt very sad at being abandoned by her. However, as she was gathering the fragments of the documents together before returning to her room, her feeling suddenly turned to one of delight, for spread out on the table before her she beheld the genealogical-tree which neither of the old women had perceived. It was the only entire document of them all—a holy relic. She took it, and locked it, with the charred remnants she had rescued, in the chest of drawers in her room.

And now, on again finding herself in that chamber rendered august by death, a deep feeling of emotion penetrated her. What sovereign quietude, what immortal peace was here, close to the destructive savagery which had filled the adjoining room with smoke and ashes. A sacred serenity fell from the shades around and above her, the tapers burned with pure, motionless, unflickering flames. And she saw that Pascal's face had become very white, amid all the streaming of his white hair and beard. He seemed to slumber amid a radiant light, crowned with an aureole, majestically handsome. She stooped and kissed him yet again, and her lips could feel how cold had become that marble visage with closed eyes, now dreaming the eternal dream. Her grief was so great at not having been able to save the work which he had entrusted to her keeping that she fell upon both knees sobbing. The temple of genius had been violated, it seemed to her as though the whole world must be destroyed through this savage annihilation of the work of an entire life.

CHAPTER XIV

MOTHER AND CHILD

SEATED in the workroom, with her child—to whom she had just given the breast—still upon her knees, Clotilde buttoned up her dress-body. It was about three o'clock on the afternoon of a bright Sunday at the end of August. The sky was glowing with heat, and the shutters, carefully closed, only allowed some slender sunbeams to penetrate, arrow-like, through the slits in the woodwork, into the warm, drowsy shade that prevailed in the spacious apartment. The deep idle peacefulness of Sunday seemed to spread through the room from without, with a distant pealing of bells ringing the last call to vespers. Not a sound ascended from the empty house where mother and little one were to remain alone till dinner-time, the servant having asked permission to go and see a cousin in the Faubourg.

For a moment Clotilde looked at her child, a big boy already three months old. He had been born towards the end of May. During well nigh ten months now she had been wearing mourning for Pascal, a long, simple black dress in which she looked divinely beautiful, so delicate and slender, with so sad an expression on her young face which her lovely fair hair decked as with a nimbus. She was unable to smile; still she took pleasure in gazing at that fine, fat, rosy child of hers, whose lips were still moist with milk, and whose eyes were fixed on one of the sunbeams in which myriads of specks of dust were dancing. He seemed greatly surprised at the sight and could not take his eyes away from that golden sheen, that dazzling light. But sleepiness came over him at last, and then he let his little bare round head, on which some light-coloured hairs already strayed hither and thither, fall upon his mother's arm.

Clotilde gently rose and laid him in his cradle, which was near the table. For a moment she lingered, leaning over him, to make quite sure that he was asleep, and then lowered the muslin curtain, shrouding him, as it were, in a deep twilight. Noiselessly, with extreme suppleness of motion, stepping so lightly indeed that she scarcely touched the floor, she now began busying herself, putting away some linen which lay upon the table, and twice crossing the room in search of a little sock which had been mislaid. She was very silent, very gentle, very active ; and as she thus went about in the silent deserted house she began thinking, recalling in turn all the events that had happened during the past year.

First, after the frightful shock of the funeral, had come the departure of Martine, obstinately intent on going away at once, and bringing to take her place the young cousin of a neighbouring baker, a plump, dark-complexioned girl, who fortunately had proved fairly clean and devoted. The old servant was now living in an out-of-the-way nook at Ste. Marthe, in so penurious a fashion that doubtless she was even saving up a part of the income derived from her little treasure. She was not known to have any relatives, any heirs, so who would benefit by her rageful avarice ? During the whole ten months she had not once crossed the threshold of La Souleiade. Monsieur was no longer there, and she did not even give way to a desire to see Monsieur's son.

Then the image of Grandmother Félicité rose up in Clotilde's mind. In the condescending spirit of a powerful relative, broad-minded enough to forgive all transgressions when they have been cruelly expiated, the old lady came to visit her from time to time. She would make her appearance unexpectedly, kiss the child, preach morality, and give advice ; and the young woman greeted her with the same passive deference that Pascal himself had been wont to display. Félicité, it should be said, was now quite absorbed in her triumph. She was at last about to carry into execution an idea which she had long been thinking of, long hugging to her heart, an idea which was to establish the family's pure glory for all time to come. She intended to devote her fortune, which had grown into a considerable one, to the erection and endowment of an asylum for the aged, which was to be called the Asile Rougon. She had already purchased the necessary ground, a part of the old Mall, outside the town, near the railway station ; and that Sunday precisely at five o'clock, when the heat should have somewhat subsided, she was to lay the foundation-stone of this asylum—a real solemn function honoured by the presence of the authorities, at which she would figure as a queen amid the plaudits of a vast concourse of the inhabitants.

In spite of all that had happened Clotilde could not help feeling some gratitude towards her grandmother, who, when Pascal's will was opened and read, had displayed wonderful disinterestedness. Pascal had named Clotilde his residuary legatee ; and his mother, although legally entitled to a fourth part of his belongings, had renounced her right to it, expressing the desire that her son's last wishes should be fully carried out. She was quite prepared to disinherit all her children, to leave them nothing but glory, by devoting her large fortune to the building of that asylum which was to transmit the respected, revered name of Rougon through all the future ages ; but after showing herself for half a century so eager to amass money, she now treated it with disdain, purified, as it were, by a loftier ambition. Thanks to this liberality of hers, Clotilde had no anxiety for the future : the 4,000 francs a year left by Pascal would suffice for herself and her child. She would bring up the little fellow —make a man of him. She had invested the 5,000 francs formerly kept in the *secrétaire* in his name ; and she further possessed La Souleiade, which everybody advised her to sell. Doubtless the place did not cost much to keep up, but how solitary, how dreary life would be in that large, deserted house, far too spacious for her wants, and in which she seemed, as it were, lost ! So far, however, she had not

been able to make up her mind to leave it. Perhaps she
would never do so.

Ah! that Souleiade; all her love was there, all her life, all
her remembrances. It seemed to her at times as though
Pascal were still living there, for she had changed nothing
that might recall the life of former times. The articles of
furniture stood in the same places; the clock in striking seemed
to summon her to the same wonted occupations. All she had
done was to lock up Pascal's room, into which she alone now
entered as into a sanctuary, to weep there whenever she felt her
heart too heavy. She still occupied her own room, sleeping in
the bed on which he had died, and placing baby's cradle beside
it every evening. It was still the same pleasant room as of
yore, with the same familiar old furniture and hangings toned
by age to a pinky hue, like the blush of Aurora; the same old
room, indeed, which the presence of the child, however, now
seemed to rejuvenate. Then, down below, although conscious
that she was altogether alone in the gay, bright dining-room,
she could nevertheless hear there an echo of the old-time
laughter, the keen appetite of youth, when she and he had sat
there eating and drinking so gaily, pledging life in each
draught of wine. And the garden, too, the entire place
seemed closely bound up with her existence; she could not
take a step anywhere but she beheld him there beside her.
How often, on the terrace, standing in the slender shadow
cast by one or another of the centenarian cypresses, had they
gazed upon the valley of the Viorne, limited by the bar-like
rocks of La Seille and the scorched heights of Ste. Marthe!
How often, competing together like truant school-children,
had they tried their agility in climbing up the giant steps of
dry stones between the meagre olive and almond trees! And
there was the pine grove, too—that warm, balmy, shadowy
spot where the cones crackled under one's feet; and the vast
threshing-floor, carpeted with soft grass, whence one discerned
the whole sky when the stars began to peer forth in the
evening! And, moreover, there were the giant plane-trees,
whose delightful shade they had so often sought on summer
days, where they had listened enraptured to the refreshing

song of the spring—the pure crystalline refrain which the clear
water had been sounding and sounding for centuries past.
There was not one of the old stones of the house, not a scrap
of the ground, not an atom of all La Souleiade, indeed, in
which she could not feel the warm throbbing of some little
of their blood, some little of their past life together.

She preferred, however, to spend her days in the workroom,
for it was there that she lived once more her happiest hours.
Only one additional article of furniture met her eyes there—
her infant's cradle. The Doctor's writing-table stood in the
same old place, before the left-hand window. He could have
come in and sat down at it, for his chair had not even been
moved. Upon the old pile of books and pamphlets on
the long table in the middle of the room the only new things
visible were some of baby's little garments, which she was
inspecting. There were the same rows of books in the bookcases; and it might have been thought that the old oak press,
securely closed, still contained in its depths the same collection
of precious papers. Under the smoky ceiling the pleasant
scent of work still floated on the atmosphere, the chairs stood
about here and there in their old-time confusion; all the familiar
disorder of yore still reigned in the room, once their joint
atelier, and for so many long years the scene of the girl's
whims and of the *savant's* researches. But that which now
touched Clotilde more than all else was to gaze upon her old
pastel-drawings nailed to the walls—the minute copies of real
living flowers, and then the imaginative flights into the land
of chimeras, those flowers of the dreamland whither her wild
fancies had at times transported her.

She had just finished setting baby's little garments in
order on the table, when on raising her eyes she saw in front
of her the pastel-drawing of old King David resting his hand
upon the bare shoulder of Abishag, the young Shunammite.
She, who no longer laughed, thereupon felt a sudden joy
ascending to her face, so gladsome was the emotion she
experienced. How fondly they had loved one another; how
fondly they had dreamt of eternity on the day when she had
amused herself in making that design, symbolical of pride

and love ! . . . And now he was gone; he lay slumbering in the ground ; and she, clad in black, was all alone with her child, who typified how fully, how entirely she had loved him, careless of what a canting and hypocritical world might say or think of it.

She ended by sitting down beside the cradle. The slender, arrow-like sunbeams shot across the room from one end to the other; and in the sleepy shade due to the closed shutters the heat of that ardent day was growing heavy and oppressive ; the silence of the house also seemed to have deepened. She had put some little garments on one side, and was slowly sewing some tapes on to them, sinking the while into a reverie amid the great warm peacefulness that encompassed her, whilst out-of-doors the sun was scorching everything. Her thoughts at first strayed back to her pastels, both the precise and the fanciful ones ; and she reflected that all the duality of her nature lay in that passion for truth which at times had kept her for hours at work upon a single flower, striving to copy it with absolute exactness, and in that longing for what was beyond life which at other times had transported her out of reality, carried her off into wild dreams to the paradise of an increate flora. She had always been thus ; she felt that in the depths of her being she to-day remained what she had been yesterday, and this despite the flood of new life which was incessantly transforming her. Then her thoughts leapt away to the deep gratitude which she felt towards Pascal for having made her what she was. Doubtless he had given way to the inclinations of his good heart when long, long ago, in her childhood, he had removed her from the abominable sphere of life in which she found herself, and taken her to live with him. But doubtless he had also been desirous of experimenting with her, of watching to see how she would grow up in another sphere, full of truth and affection. That had been a constant preoccupation of his, an old theory with which he would have liked to experiment on a large scale—culture by means of environment, the human being suffering from some hereditary taint absolutely cured and saved both physically and morally. She was certainly indebted to him for the best part of her being; she could divine what a fantastic, violent creature she might have become, whereas through him she had simply been endowed with passion and courage. . . .

Looking backward in this wise, there came to her a clear perception of the long work of transformation which had gone on within her. Pascal had rectified her heredity, she again lived through all the slow evolution, through all the battle that had waged within her between the real and the chimerical. It had originated at the time of her fits of anger as a child. She remembered the ferment of revolt within her, the disequilibrium which had plunged her into unhealthy reverie. Then had come her great fits of devotion, her longing for illusions and immediate happiness, in the thought that due compensation for the inequalities and injustice of this wicked world must be found in the everlasting joy of a future paradise. That had been the period of her battles with Pascal; it was then that, scheming to annihilate his genius, she had plunged him into such bitter torment. And afterwards had come the bend in the road : she found him her master once more, conquering her by the terrible lesson of life which he had given her on that stormy night so well remembered. After that, environment had exerted its influence ; the evolution had been precipitated till at last she had recovered mental balance and common-sense, willing to live life as it should be lived, in the hope that the sum of human labour would some day free the world of evil and of pain. She had loved ; she was now a mother, and she understood.

All at once she remembered that other night—that night which they had spent on the threshing-floor. She again heard her own cry of lamentation rising to the starry vault : nature atrocious, humanity abominable, science bankrupt, and the necessity of seeking a refuge in the Mysterious. Apart from the annihilation of one's human nature there could be no durable happiness. Then she heard him, on his side, reciting his *credo*—the progress of human reason through science ; benefit to be derived solely from the truths, so slowly but for ever acquired ; the belief that the sum of these truths, ever increasing, would end by endowing man with incalculable power and serenity if not happiness. All was summed up in an ardent faith in life. As he had said to her, one must march on with life, which was ever on the march. No halt was to be hoped for, no peace would again be possible in the immobility of ignorance, no relief was to be gained by turning back. It was necessary that one should have a firm mind and the modesty to admit that life's only reward lies in living bravely, in accomplishing the task which existence imposes. And looking at things in this wise, evil became merely an accident, as yet unexplained ; whilst from that lofty point of view humanity appeared to be a vast piece of mechanism, ever in motion and working ceaseless change. Why should the workman who disappeared when his day was ended—why should he curse the work because he was unable either to see or to judge its finish ? And even if there were never to be any finish, why refrain from tasting the joy of action, inhaling the keen air of the forward march, enjoying the sweetness of repose after long fatigue ? To the children belongs the duty of continuing the work of the fathers ; it is solely for this that they are born and loved, solely that they may in their turn transmit the life which is transmitted to them. And therefore the only course is to bravely resign oneself to assisting in the great common labour, and to silence the revolt of egotism, which demands a special, absolute happiness for self.

When Clotilde questioned her heart and mind she no longer felt the distress which in former times had plunged her into such anguish whenever she thought of *the day after death*. She was no longer preoccupied with the haunting, torturing thought of what there might be on the other side of life. Formerly she had longed to snatch from the heavens the secret of human destiny. Formerly the fact of *being*, without knowing *why she was*, had filled her with infinite sadness. Why was mankind placed upon the earth ? she had often asked herself. What was the meaning of this execrable human existence, in which there was no real equality or justice, and which seemed to her like the evil dream of a delirious night ? But now her shudder had left her, and she

could reflect upon all these things courageously. Perhaps it
was her babe, that continuation of herself, who now in some
wise masked the horror of the inevitable end. But her composure was also largely due to the equilibrium in which she
at present lived, to the thought that one must live for the
effort of living, and that the only peacefulness possible in the
world lies in the joy that attends the accomplished effort.
She recalled a remark which had often fallen from the
Doctor when he chanced to see some peasant peacefully
returning home after his day's toil : ' There goes one whom
the controversy of what there may be beyond life won't prevent from sleeping soundly.' He meant by this that the
point at issue only carried away and perverted the feverish
brains of the idle. If all were to perform their duties, all
would sleep in peace. She herself had felt the beneficial
almightiness of work amidst her sufferings and bereavement.
Since, thanks to him, she had learnt how to employ every
hour, and especially since she had become a mother, always
occupied with her child, she had no longer felt that shudder
with regard to the Unknown passing like an icy breath across
the nape of her neck. Without a struggle she was now able
to brush all disturbing reveries aside ; and if any fear still
came to trouble her, if any of the bitternesses of daily life
filled her heart with nausea, she found invincible comfort and
strength of resistance in the thought that her child had
numbered another day that morning, and that on the morrow
he would number yet another one ; that day by day, indeed,
page by page, his life-work would go on till its accomplishment. This proved a delightful salve for every worry. She
had a function, an object in life ; she could tell it well by her
happy serenity ; she was assuredly performing the task which
she had come into the world to perform.

And yet, at this very moment, she realised that the
creature prone to chimeras was not altogether dead within
her. A slight sound had sped by through the deep silence,
and she had raised her head, listening. What divine media-
tor was passing ? Perhaps the dear one whom she mourned,
whom she fancied she could divine around her. Thus she

was ever to remain, in a slight degree, the believing child of yore, so inquisitive as to the Mysterious, instinctively longing for the Unknown. She made allowance for that longing; she even explained it scientifically. However far science may extend the limits of human knowledge, there is a point, no doubt, that it will not cross; and it was in this that Pascal centred the one interest there was in living—the incessant desire to know yet more and more. She, then, admitted the existence of the unknown forces amid which the world is plunged—a vast, dim domain, ten times as great as that already conquered; an unexplored Infinite, through which the humanity of the future would ever and ever climb. There, surely, was a region vast enough for imagination to roam and lose itself. There in her dreamy moments she slaked the imperious thirst which human beings feel for the Unknown, the need that is experienced of escaping from the visible world, of satisfying one's illusive belief in absolute justice and future happiness. There was pacified whatever remained of her old-time torments, since suffering humanity cannot live without some lie or other to console it. But all intermingled felicitously within her. At the turning-point of an epoch overtaxed with science—an epoch alarmed at the ruin it has wrought, seized with fear in presence of the dawning twentieth century, and wildly desirous of going no further but of rushing backward—she personified perfect equilibrium, a passion for the True broadened by concern for the Unknown. Sectarian *savants* might limit the horizon, strictly confine themselves to phenomena; but it was allowable for a good, simple creature like herself to take into account all that she did not and would never know. And if Pascal's *credo* were the logical conclusion to be drawn from the labour of humanity, on the other hand the eternal question which, despite everything, she continued asking of the heavens—the question of what might lie beyond life—again set the portals of the Infinite wide open to mankind, for ever marching on. Since we must always continue learning, resigning ourselves to the thought that we shall never know everything, is there not an incentive to motion, to life itself, in the reservation of the Mysterious—an everlasting doubt and an everlasting hope ?

A fresh sound like the flutter of a passing wing, a light touch like that of a kiss upon her hair, made her smile. Assuredly he was there. A feeling of deep affection pervaded her entire being. How kind and gay he was; with what love for others had his passion for life imbued him ! He himself, perhaps, had only been a dreamer ; certainly he had indulged in the most splendid of dreams—that belief in the advent of a superior world when science should have invested man with incalculable power, when humanity would accept everything, employ everything for the attainment of happiness, know everything and foresee everything, reduce nature to the position of a servant, and live in the tranquillity which contentment of the mind affords. Meanwhile, determined, regulated work sufficed for the good health of all. Some day, perhaps, even suffering would be put to use. And surveying the huge labour, surveying the whole mass of mankind, the wicked and the good, so admirably courageous and laborious despite everything, she now beheld but a fraternal humanity, experienced a feeling of unlimited indulgence, infinite pity, and ardent charity. Love, like the sun, pervades the world, and kindliness is the great river from which all hearts drink.

For a couple of hours, with the same regular movements, Clotilde had been plying her needle whilst her thoughts thus strayed away. The tapes were now sewn on to the little garments, and she had further marked some diapers which she had purchased the day before. Her sewing ended, she rose up to put all these things away. The sun was sinking out-of-doors ; at present its golden darts were very slender, and only penetrated obliquely through the slits in the shutters, one of which she had to go and open, for she could scarcely see. Then for a moment she lingered at the window, gazing out upon the long line of the horizon suddenly spread before her. The great heat was subsiding, a light breeze was sweeping across the unspotted azure of the lovely sky. On the left she could plainly distinguish the smallest tufts of pines among the fallen, blood-red rocks of La Seille ; whilst on the right, beyond the heights of Ste. Marthe, the valley of the Viorne spread far away, amid the golden haze of the sunset. She gazed, too, for a moment at the tower of St. Saturnin, which also shone out quite golden above the pinky town, and then she was on the point of retiring when a spectacle which she suddenly beheld detained her, kept her leaning for a long time yet upon the window-sill.

A swarming crowd was hurrying across the old Mall beyond the railway line. She at once remembered the ceremony, and realised that her grandmother Félicité was now about to lay the first stone of the Asile Rougon, that monument of victory destined to transmit the family glory to all the future ages. Vast preparations had been made during the past week, and there was a talk of a silver hod and trowel which the old lady was to use herself; for despite her two-and-eighty years she was bent on taking part in the ceremony, on triumphing in presence of all the townsfolk. She experienced a feeling of regal pride at the thought that she was on this occasion completing the conquest of Plassans for the third time; for she had compelled the entire town, each of its three districts, to gather round her, escort her, and acclaim her as a benefactress. There were to be a number of lady patronesses, selected from among the noblest dames of the St. Marc district; a deputation of the friendly societies of the old town; and finally, the best-known inhabitants of the new town, advocates, notaries, and doctors, not to mention all the petty townsfolk— a stream of people clad in their Sunday best, and hurrying to the Mall as to some popular festivity. And amidst this crowning triumph, she, one of the queens of the Second Empire, the widow who so nobly wore mourning for the fallen *régime*, grew yet prouder at the thought that she had conquered the young Republic by compelling it, in the person of the Sub-Prefect, to come and bow to her and thank her. It had originally been announced that the only speech to be delivered on the occasion would be one by the mayor; but on the previous day it had become known for certain that the Sub-Prefect also would address the gathering. From that distance Clotilde could only distinguish a kaleidoscopic tumult

of black frock-coats and light-coloured dresses flitting hither
and thither under the dazzling sun. Then came a vague sound
of music—the local amateurs' band was there, and from time
to time the sonorous notes of the brass instruments were
wafted to her by the breeze.

Leaving the window, she opened the large oak press in
order to put away her work, which had remained lying on the
table. In this press, once so full of the Doctor's manuscripts
and now so empty, she kept her baby's layette. Open, yawning widely, the press looked immense, of extraordinary depth;
and on its large bare shelves there now only lay some soft
swaddling clothes, little braces, little caps, little socks, piles
of diapers, all the fine linen, the light down of the fledgling
yet in the nest. There, where so many ideas had slept in
heaps, where a man's stubborn labour had for thirty years
piled up an overflowing accumulation of papers, there were
now only a little being's flaxen coverings, scarcely garments,
his first wraps, shielding him merely for an hour, and soon to
prove too small for him. And all these little things seemed
to brighten and revivify the roomy depths of the antique
press.

When Clotilde had set the cloths and garments on one of
the shelves, she noticed there a large envelope in which she
had placed the fragments of the documents that she had
saved from the fire. And she thereupon remembered a
request which Dr. Ramond had again addressed to her on
calling at La Souleiade the day before—he wished her to look
and see if among these remnants there remained anything of
importance or interest from a scientific point of view. He
was in despair at the loss of the priceless manuscripts which
the master had bequeathed to him. Immediately after
Pascal's death he had endeavoured to draw up some record of
that supreme conversation when the dying man, with such
heroic serenity, had expounded so many vast theories to him;
but in all this Ramond only found short *résumés*, and what
he desired were the complete studies, the record of the
master's daily observations, the results obtained and the principles which these results established. The loss of those

manuscripts was an irreparable one; all Pascal's labour must be performed afresh, and Ramond lamented that he only possessed the merest clues. The march of science, said he, would be delayed for at least twenty years—a quarter of a century would in all probability go by before the ideas of the solitary pioneer, the fruit of whose toil had been so savagely and foolishly destroyed, were taken in hand once more and utilised.

The genealogical-tree, the only document that remained complete, lay there with the envelope, and Clotilde brought everything to the table, near which the cradle stood. When she had taken the fragments one by one out of the envelope, she found, as she had fully expected, that there was not one perfect page of writing, not one complete memorandum having any sense, among them all. Merely fragments remained: scraps of paper, charred, half-burnt, without beginning or end. Still, as she went on examining them, those imperfect sentences, those words half-consumed by the flames, which another person would have failed to understand, became for her invested with interest. She remembered the stormy night; she could guess the finish of the imperfect sentences; and now and again some mutilated word sufficed to conjure up before her a vision of one or another of her relatives and his or her career. Thus her eyes fell upon the name of Maxime, and she pictured the life of that brother who had remained a stranger to her, and the news of whose death, a couple of months previously, had been received by her almost with indifference. Then a mutilated line in which she noticed her father's name brought her a feeling of discomfort, for she had reason to believe that Saccard had pocketed his son's house and fortune, thanks to the help of his hairdresser's niece, Rose, that candid little chit whom he had remunerated for her pains with a liberal percentage of the pelf. Continuing her inspection, Clotilde came upon other names—that of her uncle Eugène, the Vice-Emperor of former days, now sinking asleep; and that of her cousin Serge, the priest of St. Eutrope, who, she had been told, was consumptive, and, from what she had heard the day before, was now fast dying. In this wise each fragment of paper that she examined became animated, all her hateful yet fraternal family sprang into being from those scraps, those black ashes in which only incoherent syllables could now be deciphered.

At last the idea came to Clotilde to unfold the genealogical-tree and spread it out on the table. Deep emotion had come over her, the contemplation of all those relics had quite stirred her heart, and when she read the memoranda which Pascal had added in pencil to the tree a few minutes before expiring tears came into her eyes. How bravely he had written in the date of his death! And how well one could realise his despairing regret for life in the tremulously traced words announcing the birth of the child! The tree was ascending, stretching out its branches, shooting forth its leaves, and for a long while she remained absorbed in contemplating it, reflecting that all the master's work was there, in that classified, annotated vegetation. She could again hear the words in which he had commented on each hereditary variation in the family; she well remembered his lessons. It was, however, in the children that she took most interest. The practitioner at Noumea to whom the Doctor had written for information concerning the child of Étienne Lantier, who had married out there, had lately made up his mind to send an answer; only he had contented himself with stating that the child was a girl and appeared to be healthy. Clotilde was further aware that quite recently Octave Mouret had narrowly missed losing his daughter, who was very delicate; whereas his little boy continued thriving. The finest health and vigour in the whole family, however, were still to be found at Valqueyras, in the household of Jean Macquart, whose wife had in three years given birth to two children and was now again *enceinte*. In the full sunlight, amid the fruitful fields, the little brood was growing up in sprightly fashion, whilst the father was ever at work tilling the soil, and the mother courageously discharged her household duties, prepared the *soupe*, and wiped the youngsters. There was assuredly enough sap in that nook at Valqueyras, enough love of work to pro-vide for the creation of another world. Reflecting in this wise, Clotilde again seemed to hear Pascal's cry: 'Ah! our family, what will become of it, what being will spring from it at last?' And she herself began pondering on it all, gazing the while at the genealogical-tree which was stretching its last boughs into the future. Who could tell whence the healthy branch would spring? Perhaps it was there that the sensible, strong-minded being would germinate.

A faint cry roused her from her reflections. The muslin curtain of the cradle began to move as though suddenly animated; baby had woke up, was calling and stirring. She at once took him in her arms and gaily held him up in the air so that he might bathe in the golden light of the sunset. But the infant evinced no interest in that serene close of a lovely day; his vague little eyes turned away from the vast expanse of heaven, and he widely opened his little pink beak, like a fledgling ever hungry. And he began crying so loudly, he had awoke with so gluttonous an appetite that she decided to give him the breast again. Besides, it was time to do so; he had not sucked for three hours.

The mother retraced her steps, and once more sat down near the table. She had placed baby on her knees, and he was anything but well behaved, for he cried yet louder and louder, impatient for his repast. Still, she looked at him smiling whilst she unfastened her dress. And scarcely was this done than the child scented the breast, tried to raise himself, and moved his lips as though seeking the nipple. When she had placed his mouth to it he gave a little grunt of satisfaction, and rushed upon it, as it were, with the fine voracious appetite of a little gentleman who is determined to live. And, holding the nipple tightly between his lips, he began sucking with avidity. At first, with the little hand which he was free to use, he had caught hold of the breast as though to assert his possession of it, as though to defend it, retain it for himself alone. Then in his delight as the warm milk coursed down his throat, he raised his little arm erect in the air like a flagstaff. And Clotilde still retained her unconscious smile as she gazed at him, so sturdy already, deriving all his sustenance from herself. During the earlier weeks a chap had caused her much suffering, and even now her breast was very sensitive; nevertheless, she smiled with that tranquil expression peculiar to mothers, who are as happy to give their milk as they would be to give their blood.

When she had unfastened her dress-body, displaying her maternal bosom, another mystery, one of her best hidden, most delightful secrets had been disclosed—that delicate necklet adorned with seven pearls, seven milky stars, which the master, in his passionate mania for giving, had fastened around her neck one day of dire want. Since it had been reposing there no one save him and herself had ever seen it. The simple jewel had become, as it were, a part of her flesh, a thing to be modestly hidden away. And whilst the child was sucking she alone beheld it, deeply moved, recalling all the kisses whose warm scent it even now seemed to retain.

However, a burst of music in the distance suddenly startled her. She turned her head, looking towards the country-side, which the oblique sun-rays were gilding. Ah, yes! that ceremony, that foundation-stone which was being laid over yonder. Then she again let her eyes fall on the child, again became absorbed in the pleasure which she took at seeing him possessed of such a fine appetite. She had drawn a stool near her so as to raise one of her knees, and rested one elbow on the table beside the genealogical-tree and the blackened fragments of the documents. Her mind soared, attained to a state of infinite rapture, as she felt the best part of herself, that pure milk, flow forth with a faint sound, making that dear little one whom she had brought into the world yet more and more her own. The child had come, a redeemer possibly. The bells had pealed, the wise men had set out, followed by the nations, by all nature in festive array smiling at the babe in his swaddling clothes. And whilst he imbibed some of her life, she, the mother, already began to dream of the future. What would he become when by giving herself wholly to him she had made him tall and strong? A *savant* who would teach the world some of the eternal truths? A captain who would bring glory to his country? Or, better still, one of those pastors of the nations who quiet passions and ensure the reign of justice? She pictured him very handsome, very good, and very powerful. It was the dream in which all mothers indulge, the conviction of having brought some saviour into the world; and in this hope, in this stubborn belief in the certain triumph of her child which possesses every mother, there indeed lies the very hope which makes life, the belief which endows humanity with the ever-renewed strength that it requires to continue living.

What would the child become? She looked at him, sought to determine whom he resembled. He had the eyes and the brow of his father, certainly; something lofty, something solid in the shape of the head. And she also recognised herself in him—in his refined mouth and delicate chin. Then, covertly anxious, she sought for traces of the others, the terrible forerunners, all those whose names were there on the hereditary leaves shooting forth from the genealogical-tree. Would he resemble that one, or that one, or that other? Nevertheless, she grew calm again. The eternal hope so swelled her heart that she could not do otherwise than hope. The faith in life which the master had planted within her maintained her erect, courageous, unshakable. What mattered the woes, the sufferings, the abominations of life! Health lay in universal toil, in the power which fructifies and brings forth. The work was good when love yielded life. And in that case, no matter what sores might be displayed around, no matter what might be the blackness of human shame and misery, the portals of hope were thrown open once more. For then life was perpetuated, tried yet again—life which mankind is never weary of believing to be good, since it is lived with such keen eagerness even in the midst of injustice and suffering.

Clotilde had involuntarily glanced at the genealogical-tree spread out near her. Yes; the threat was there—so many crimes, so much mire, among so many tears and so much grieved kindliness! Such an extraordinary mixture of the excellent and the vile, an epitome of humanity, as it were, with all its taints and all its struggles! It was a question whether it would not have been better to destroy that wretched, diseased swarm with a thunderbolt. However, after so many terrible Rougons, after so many abominable Macquarts, yet another one was born. Life, with the brave defiance of its eternity, was not afraid to create yet another. Yes; life pursued its work, diffused itself according to its laws, indifferent to theories, ever marching on for the accomplishment of its infinite labour. And, indeed, at the risk of forming monsters, it was needful that it should continue to create; we can all see that, despite the sickly and the mad whom it brings into the world, it never wearies of creating, in the hope, no doubt, that the healthy and the wise will some day appear. Life! life which flows in torrents, which continues and begins afresh, ever tending towards the unknown goal! Life in whose midst we are immersed, life with its infinite, its adverse currents, life ever in motion and immense, like a sea that has no limits!

A transport of maternal fervour ascended from the heart of Clotilde, happy at feeling that voracious little mouth imbibe sustenance from herself without a pause. It was a prayer, an invocation—to the unknown child, as to the unknown God! To the child who is to be, to the genius who is possibly being born, to the new redeeming leader whom the coming century awaits, and who will extricate the peoples of the earth from their doubts and their sufferings! And since the nation of mankind had to be reconstituted, had not that one, that child of hers, come to help in the mighty task? He would take the experiment in hand once more, raise the fallen walls, restore certainty to men now groping in the dark, build up the city of justice, where the one law of work for all would ensure happiness. It is, indeed, in times of trouble that prophets should be expected. Unless, however, he should prove to be Antichrist, the devastating demon, the Beast whose advent was predicted, and who is to purge the world of its impurity. But even then life would subsist, continue; it would only be needful to remain patient for a few more thousand years, until the other unknown child, the benefactor, should appear.

Whilst Clotilde was thus pondering, her infant had

imbibed all the milk in her right breast, and as he now showed signs of displeasure she turned him round and gave him the left one. Then she again began smiling as he caressed her with his gluttonous little lips. Despite everything, she remained hopeful. A mother suckling her child—does not this symbolise the world continued and saved? Leaning forward she met the glance of her baby's limpid eyes, which were opening enraptured, longing for the light. What was he saying, the dear little one, that she felt her heart beating with delight beneath the breast whose milk he was exhausting? What glad tidings was he announcing with the gentle suction of his lips? To what cause would he give his blood when he should be a man, strong from having imbibed so much of that milk? Possibly he said nothing, possibly he was already lying; yet she was so supremely happy, so full of absolute confidence in him!

Once more did the sound of distant music, the triumphant flourish of brass instruments, burst upon her ears. It must have been the moment of the apotheosis, the moment when Grandmother Félicité with her silver trowel laid the foundation-stone of the monument to be reared to the glory of the Rougons. As though enlivened by the gaiety of Sunday, the vast blue sky wore a festive aspect. And in the warm silence, the lonely peacefulness of the workroom, Clotilde smiled at her babe, who was still sucking, with his left arm raised erect in the air, like the rallying standard of Life.

THE END